ACCLAIM FOR MA
TIME F...

"McArthur has arrived on the SF scene . . . [with] a rich
prose a... ...man
nature."

"Rich in detail . . . *Time Future* shows that Maxine
McArthur has an astute mind, a ferocious sense of detail, and the capacity to become one of the world's most
distinguished SF writers."

Also by Maxine McArthur

Time Past

Time Future

LESS THAN HUMAN

MAXINE McARTHUR

ASPECT®

NEW YORK   BOSTON

Copyright © 2004 by Maxine McArthur

Cover design by Don Puckey
Cover illustration by Shasti O'Leary Soudant
Book design by Giorgetta Bell McRee

The Aspect name and logo are registered trademarks of Warner Books.

Warner Books

Time Warner Book Group
1271 Avenue of the Americas
New York, NY 10020
Visit our Web site at www.twbookmark.com

Printed in the United States of America

First Paperback Printing: October 2004

10 9 8 7 6 5 4 3 2 1

For Toshihiro and Junko

ACKNOWLEDGMENTS

Writing is a solitary task, but research and rewriting are not. Without the help and generosity of the following people, this book could not have been written.

Thanks first to my agents Tara Wynne and Russ Galen, and editors Jaime Levine and Devi Pillai. Also to Arts ACT and Arts Council Australia, which funded my 2002 Asialink Literature Residency in Asia, during which the last third of the book was written. The Research School of Pacific and Asian Studies at the Australian National University gave me a General Staff Development Award to go to Japan on that residency. Dr. David Austin of the Robotics Systems Lab, Australian National University, patiently answered my clumsy questions and gave us a tour of his lab. The WRiters On the Road group—Rowena Cory Lindquist, Marianne de Pierres, Margo Lanagan, Tansy Rayner Roberts, Michael Barry, and Trent Jamieson—offered invaluable critical advice. Mitsuhiro Hayashi gave me his opinion about small businesses in Japan, Ben Dorman suggested useful sources of information about Japan's New Religions, and Robert McArthur and Tristan Norman offered technical advice. I am, of course, solely responsible for any errors that remain in the story.

Last but never least, many thanks to my family, both in Australia and in Japan.

PROLOGUE

The white building towered over the surrounding jumble of shops and dwellings like the prow of a huge ship. It was a Betta, the multistoried residential complexes that were transforming the cityscapes of Japan. The size and cleanness of the Betta set it apart from the corrosion black concrete, sagging wires and ad-lib extensions of the old town. Here, it declared, is the future.

As if the sight of the Betta were not advertisement enough, vid panels on every street corner extolled the advantages of living there. No more tiny apartment crowded with junk, burbled the vid, as cinematographically superb shots of the Betta interior rolled past on the screens. Get rid of all those appliances. In the Betta, the world's first totally integrated living environment, everything is built-in. Streamlined rooms with robotic helpers and digitally controlled shopping, cooking, and cleaning will simplify your day. You can relax in one of the rooftop gardens or browse through the internal shopping mall if you get sick of ordering your groceries online. Buy your piece of comfort and security now, before interest rates rise!

The late-afternoon sun beat down on four teenagers hurrying past the now-unused train station and through the deserted streets in the old town. The teenagers were students, by the look of their bright clothes and the phone implants glinting in their hair. They carried bulging supermarket plasbags. They bustled past the grimy doorways, along the neat concrete paths and landscaped gardens surrounding the Betta, and entered the main building.

They must have been residents at the Betta, because the elevator doors in the main lobby read their microchips, opened for them immediately, and took them up to the sixth floor. They whispered as they walked down the corridors, nudging one another uneasily past the closed doors that contained families eating meals, children doing homework, mothers scolding babies, dying grandmothers, and who knew what else, for Betta walls were soundproof; past a couple of cleanbots, like automated vacuum cleaners humming along the corridor walls; past the wall holos showing peaceful summer scenery, until they reached their apartment door. They tumbled in, and the door swished shut behind them.

"I'm worried." The shorter of the two girls lifted her plasbag onto the kitchen bench and looked anxiously at the others. "Niniel-sama asked me why I had to visit home today. I felt so bad lying to him." She wore a short, sleeveless dress made out of squares of different pink fabric. As she was round and tiny, the effect was of an animated patchwork cushion.

"He asked all of us," said the boy with a line of nose studs and bronze circles of tattoos on his cheeks. He was all knees and ankles, as some boys were. "That's why this weekend was such good timing. Bon holidays give us the perfect excuse."

"What if they find out?" the short girl persisted.

The other girl, tall and narrow-hipped, began to unpack groceries. Her green-checked trousers and white shirt were wrinkled and stained as though she didn't worry about appearances. "Tomoko, if you don't want to do it, go back." She called out to the other boy who was in the living room. "I didn't think we'd be able to get in here. How did you float the ID so the system listened to us, Dai?"

"Easy," the boy named Dai called back. "I just told Iroel-sama . . ."

"But he'll tell Niniel!" wailed the short girl, Tomoko.

"No, he won't. I said I wanted to take some things I'd left at my uncle's place, but my uncle doesn't approve of the Children, so I had to get in while he's away."

"This isn't really your uncle's place, is it?" said the slim girl uneasily.

"No, of course not." Dai chuckled. He was small and sturdy, with a round face that looked too large for his body. "The owner's on our movie chat group, and he told us he was going away. Used his e-mail addy as an alias, would you believe? I traced him from that."

The boy with the tattoos raised his hand solemnly. "Hey. Before we start—no matter what happens, we keep this secret, right?" The girls nodded, and Dai said, "Right."

"And it's not like we're doing anything wrong," added the tall girl. "We're just practicing early so that when we get to be novices, we'll be really good. Right, Tsuneo?"

The boy with the tattoos nodded, although his expression was uneasy.

They ate the noodles with absentminded haste, then gathered in front of the wide computer/vid screen in the living room. The short girl passed around blue capsules, which they all swallowed.

The gawky boy with the studs and tattoos, Tsuneo, rummaged in a stylish backpack.

"Who's going first?" He held up two spray cans.

"Do we have to do the paint?" the tall girl complained. She tugged at the neck of her T-shirt as though it was too tight, then reached up and pulled off her hair, tossing the wig onto the sofa with a flourish. Her head was shaved smooth, except for a gleaming phone implant.

"I thought we agreed," said Dai. He was squatting in front of the computer panel in the living room wall, attaching wires to its external ports. "To get into the spirit of the thing."

Tomoko giggled and snatched one of the paint cans. "I'll go first. But you have to promise to go next, Dai."

Dai shrugged. "Whatever."

"Are you sure it's safe?" The slim girl watched Tomoko disappear into the bathroom.

"Lissa, it's the stuff they use in the theater."

Lissa pouted. "I want to have incense, too."

"We didn't bring any."

"Why not?"

"Why do you always argue when you're high?"

They grumbled at each other until Tomoko came out of the bathroom, carrying her pink dress and hiding her silver-painted body behind a towel. Dai went next, then Tsuneo, then the tall girl Lissa. By that time they had abandoned the towels and were all giggling at each other's silver nakedness.

"Tomoko and I go first, like we decided." The boy Dai, gleaming like a stocky gnome, knelt in front of the monitor and fitted biometal attachments onto his fingertips.

"Is that what the novices use?" Wide-eyed, Lissa watched Tomoko do the same.

"They get permanent ones," said Tsuneo.

Wires ran from the fingertip attachments to the wall computer and also to some hand computers they'd brought with them.

"Are you ready?" Tsuneo said, his hand on the start switch of one of the handcoms.

Little Tomoko coughed. "Can you turn the aircon colder, Tsuneo? I'm really hot."

Lissa nodded. "Yeah, it's making me breathless . . ." She pushed herself back on her heels, one hand to her throat.

Tsuneo clicked the air conditioner right down.

"Come on, you guys, let's get going . . ." Dai clutched his chest midsentence. "What's . . . wrong?"

"I haven't started the program yet . . ." Tsuneo's voice dissolved in paroxysms of coughing. He started to crawl to the kitchen for water, but his breath ran out and he couldn't find more. The last thing he heard was Lissa's choking cry as she fell. The last thing he thought was, *What did we do wrong?*

ELEANOR エレナ

To: E. McGuire, Mechatronics Research,
Tomita Electronics Co.
   Sender: A
   Subject: Re: catching up
   Eleanor-san
   I am glad that you found my notes on
artificial synapses interesting. I have
been engaged in some private research
on the matter and believe that my
"angle" is one that will provide scope
for further development. I would like
to discuss this personally with you in
the near future. You tell me that your
current integrated systems project will
be reviewed soon. Perhaps after that? I
can take leave and come to Osaka, so
tell me when I should book the train.

Eleanor blanked her personal com screen with a frown.
Akita's requests for a meeting were getting hard to ignore.

She hadn't seen him since he left the company, twelve years earlier, and that was how it should stay. He'd given her a couple of ideas to use on her robot, but he'd always struck her as being a little too on edge, even in those days. The last thing she needed now was to be distracted by personal relationships. Not now that she was close to results with the Sam project.

The robot Sam had four gangly metallic limbs, an almost nonexistent trunk, and an oversized, upside-down triangular head with huge camera eyes. Multicolored wires twisted in and out of the limbs, and its battery pack gave it a hunch. But it stood by itself and was learning to navigate. She wanted it to walk across the room and pick up a beaker from the bench. It should recognize the bench on the far side of the lab from the perceptual map she'd helped it build over the past two years.

One foot rose slowly, moved forward, and descended again. Then that pendulum became the fixed point, and the other leg swung forward. The robot took three more steps. It stood next to the bench.

Pick up the beaker.

She imagined the order as a liquid, flowing through the silicon synapses and pushing the robot irresistibly toward its goal.

Its eyes found the beaker on the bench top.

Pick up the beaker.

In her chair on the other side of the lab, Eleanor wiped sweaty palms on her trousers. The robot had to work out how to do it by itself.

Its arm extended. The three-fingered hand opened, reached out.

The fingers would curl around the beaker, and data from its surface would pass through the haptic sensors, through the synapses into the tapestry of artificial neural networks that determined reaction, all in an infinitesimal amount of real time. I feel, therefore I am. I act, therefore I think . . .

The phone buzzed.

Eleanor spun her chair and glared at the source, the wall unit near the lab door. Not more interruptions . . . it was a holiday. Why couldn't they let her work?

It was Saturday of the Bon holiday week in mid-August, the slowest day of the year. Most Tomita Electronics staff were either at home or visiting relatives in the country. But the blasted building sensors knew her employee microchip was in the lab.

Eleanor pushed her chair back, slowly, so as not to distract the robot, and tapped the RECEIVE button. The readout of the dialer's number below the screen showed an internal line, Public Affairs.

"McGuire here." She didn't bother trying to sound civil.

"This is Degawa." The screen showed a swarthy man of about thirty-five wearing, a long-sleeved white shirt in spite of the heat. His voice sounded vaguely familiar. "Public Affairs Department," he added unnecessarily.

She remembered Degawa. A year ago he had helped her conduct a press conference when her department failed to win a government grant. His job was to act as a buffer between R&D departments and the rest of the world.

"We have a situation," he said, now using formal speech. "I've called the division chief and the managing director, but they won't be able to get back to town until this evening."

"What's the problem?"

"There's been a fatal accident. With one of our robots."

Her cheeks went cold, and all she could think to say was, "Where?"

"A factory in Minato Ward. Kawanishi Metalworks. It seems advisable that you attend." There was a sheen of sweat on Degawa's otherwise impassive face.

Eleanor knew how he felt. The room felt suddenly hot, despite the air-conditioning. She wiped her palms on her trousers. "But I don't do industrial robots now. You want Number Four Lab."

"There's nobody at Number Four." Degawa's formal verb endings had dissolved, and his voice held a hint of panic. "You worked on this robot. Your personnel data is linked to the relevant research records."

Degawa didn't want responsibility for this. He expected her to waste time going out to a factory in one of the hottest parts of the city because some idiot had ignored safety warnings . . . Then she felt ashamed at the thought.

"You're the most senior staff here right now," he said, as if that decided the matter.

There was a clunk behind her. She turned and saw the robot sweep its hand along the bench top in search of the beaker that was rolling at its feet.

"Damn," she said in English.

"I beg your pardon?"

"Nothing." She'd have to take the robot back to the beginning of the sequence. "When did it happen?"

"They think it must have been early this morning," said Degawa. "A security robot found the body on the factory floor. It raised the alarm; the company called an ambulance and the shop manager. The manager called his superiors, and they notified us."

"What about the police?"

"The manager said the police response team called an engineer. The engineer said it was clearly human error, and they logged it as an accident. There's still one constable there until the local station clears the scene."

Degawa sounded smugly sure of his facts. Good that the police had finished—Eleanor didn't want detectives staring at her while she checked the robot.

"Was the dead man . . ." She would have liked to use more than the bare phrase, but couldn't remember an alternative. It wasn't a word one used every day. "Was he operating the machine or trying to fix it?"

"I don't know the details. But protocol demands that we recall the robot and issue an official message of condolence."

The first part of that job was hers, and the second Degawa's. She hoped she could take one look at the scene and approve the recall; otherwise, she'd be contradicting the police report, and goodness knew what kind of protocol *that* would offend.

Degawa's eyes met hers briefly, then glanced politely away again. "Supervisor, I realize you are probably aware of the rules, but you will forgive me reminding you that you should not speak to the press about this accident. The company will make a statement tomorrow."

Eleanor tried not to let her annoyance show. "I know the rules. How soon should I go?"

"I have just ordered a taxi for you. Please send a copy of your report to this office as well as to the director's office." He inclined his head at exactly the correct angle and the screen went blank.

Eleanor sighed. Degawa was right, she'd worked on industrial robots when she first came to Osaka and joined Tomita. Worked on them with Akita, in fact. But that was fifteen years ago. And how could there have been a fatal accident if the factory followed safety regulations? If they hadn't, it wasn't her company's problem.

She'd never seen a factory accident that wasn't due to human error. Someone had ignored barriers and warning signs. Or a maintenance technician tried to do too much.

She picked up the beaker and paused the robot. It didn't seem to be processing its sensory input efficiently. They had to do something about the reactions, and quickly. On the wall above the bench, an old-fashioned paper calendar showed a red circle drawn around next Tuesday. Her project was due to come before a budget committee that was looking for projects to ax.

The hints she got from Akita offered some prospect of

development in this area, but they didn't have enough time to go back and redesign sensors. It was Saturday afternoon now, which didn't even leave enough time to polish a different sequence. They'd have to stick with the walk-and–pick up, but maybe try something easier to grasp, like a soft toy.

She patted the robot on its unwieldy head. It was just the right height to pat, about that of a five-year-old child.

"It's not your fault."

As Eleanor got out of the taxi a wall of heat hit her in the face. Gasping and squinting against the late-afternoon glare, she looked around. The taxi pulled away from a gate set in a two-meter wire fence. A metal plate set in the post beside the gate said KAWANISHI METALWORKS INC. EST. 1954. The whole area was full of large blocks of sprawling factories, and the air smelled thick and metallic. It smoked gold as the sun lowered.

She rarely went outside these days, and certainly not in the heat of the day. Tomita Corporation was linked by rail to the Amagasaki Betta, where Eleanor and most of the researchers lived. Everyone used either subway or skyway connections. She hated being driven. It made her sweat with nervousness, even if the car was in autodrive.

The taxi honked farewell at the end of the street. The driver, released by autodrive from the irksome task of actually watching the road, had talked to her constantly, demanding the usual personal information—where she came from, why she worked in Japan, whether she was married, how she learned Japanese, was her red hair a natural color, why was she carrying a tool kit and hard hat . . . Eleanor had exhausted her store of stock answers and was reduced to brusqueness.

In a side street opposite the factory some of Osaka's huge homeless population camped in lines of blue vineel tents. Nobody moved near the tents, which stood in the shade of the buildings. Everything else was gray concrete, baking in the heat. Osaka even looked gray from a distance—gray angles stretched from horizon to horizon, fading into a gray haze broken only by the immense, squat silhouettes of Bettas.

The town always looked gray outside the Bettas. Eleanor could remember when nearly every street in Osaka was like this—dirty, colorless, treeless. The Great Tokyo Quake of 2006 had been a terrible thing, but life for ordinary Japanese had certainly improved afterward. Who wouldn't prefer to live in a temperature- and humidity-controlled environment with autocleaning facilities? Not to mention the smart appliances. Total Interactive Environment, they called the Bettas.

Eleanor wiped sweat clumsily from her upper lip with the hand that held her hard hat and wished she was home in her Betta. She could feel her fair skin frying.

After the Quake, the government and big business had teamed up to initiate the Building for Life Plan, or "Seikai," as it was commonly abbreviated, for the Japanese archipelago. No more unplanned, disaster-prone development. All Japanese would live in safe, self-contained minitowns connected to fast transport networks. Bettas, they called the huge complexes. A Betta Life for All. Which was fine in Tokyo, which had to be rebuilt from the sewers up anyway; but in Osaka, the Seikai plans had not progressed as far or as comprehensively. Bettas and the new train networks co-existed uneasily with remnants of the old city.

The Kawanishi factory gate was latched, but not locked. There was an intercom unit set on one of the gateposts, but it remained silent when she announced herself. Inside the courtyard she could see a blue-and-white police car parked against a single-story building, and a uniformed policeman waited at the entry. He stared at her with official impassivity but his eyes registered every detail of her face, hair, and body.

Sometimes she thought she didn't care, but just then it fed her frustration. People never used to stare so much. Since the U.S. closed its borders and the European Union began to regulate foreign travel, white foreigners were as rare as when she'd first lived in Japan as a child.

Eleanor inclined her head as much as she could be bothered in the heat. "I'm from Tomita Electronics Corporation," she said. "The makers of the robot involved in the accident."

The constable's round, red face dripped sweat as he nodded. That dark blue uniform must be stifling. "They're expecting you." He opened the steel door of the building.

It was even hotter inside. Lights blazed along the ceiling, and the place stank of metal. A large poster on the wall next to the door showed a rotund blue cartoon cat brandishing a hard hat. *Safety First Don't Forget Your Helmet* said the speech balloon. Eleanor settled hers onto her plait obediently.

The ovenlike air was ridiculously nostalgic. Life had seemed simpler when she worked on industrial robots. It was easier to believe such robots made a difference to people's lives. Eleanor had worked on an assembly line when she was a student, and, as far as she was concerned, the robots were welcome to it.

The rows of machines were silent and still. Voices echoed at the other end of the floor. That glassed-in cubicle on the wall at the other end of the factory would be the control room. Banks of computer monitors were visible through the glass, and two men stood talking in front of it.

One was portly and in his midforties, polo shirt and golf slacks incongruous with his hard-hat. The other was a younger man, midtwenties, wearing stained and crumpled overalls. They watched suspiciously as she approached.

Eleanor bowed properly and proffered a business card. "My name is McGuire, of Tomita Electronics Corporation."

Gotoba started visibly. "Eh, you can speak Japanese."

One of these days, Eleanor thought, I'll scream. And nobody will understand why.

"I'm the supervisor of our robotics department in the research division. The department that developed your robot." How useful formality could be.

The portly man took her card and bowed grudgingly. "I'm Gotoba, floor manager here. This is Sakaki, one of our maintenance technicians." Gotoba inclined his head at the young man in overalls. "He knew Mito. That's the deceased," he added, dropping his voice.

Eleanor bowed again. "Manager, please accept our sincerest apologies." Not that I think we did anything wrong, she was tempted to add. "We will, of course, remove the offending machine as soon as I have examined it for our records."

She glanced meaningfully at the tall, angular shape of the Tomita welder on the far side of the factory floor. Orange tape stretched around its workstation.

"You're going to examine it?" Gotoba said. He exchanged a glance with Sakaki, who looked down.

"The machine is under extended warranty," she said. In other words, if a design flaw caused the accident, Tomita was obliged to fix or replace it.

"If you'll excuse me." Eleanor indicated her tool kit, bowed again, and walked with relief toward the robot. Behind her she heard a flurry of whispers, then Sakaki caught up with her.

"Did you handle this robot?"

Sakaki nodded. "I'm responsible for routine maintenance."

His tilted eyes squinted tighter, as if holding in some emotion. Maybe he'd been close to the dead man. Eleanor knew she should make a show of being more sympathetic, but she hadn't known the dead man, and all she really wanted to do was get the initial examination over so she could go back and finish her own work. And, dammit, she'd forgotten to phone Masao and would have to wait till they got outside. The phone link would never work inside, with the electronic interference from the machines plus the shield for the factory network.

"What sort of modifications have you made?" All companies would revise any specifications that didn't exactly meet their needs, but few of them consulted the manufacturer. "Have you adjusted the safety sensors in any way?"

Sakaki shook his head. "We gradually widened the job parameters, but the safeties haven't been touched."

Eleanor ducked under the orange tape, which was merely looped over peripherals. The welder stood beside the long bench that was its workstation, arm outstretched at the point the emergency stop function cut in, end-effector dangling forlornly. As far as she could see from a safe distance, the force of the blow had knocked the manipulator half-off, leaving some connective wiring exposed.

Judging from the height of the arm at its stop position, the dead man had been standing when he was hit. There were chalk marks on the floor, just like in televid police dramas. The marks didn't tell her much—unlike in the dramas, they didn't form a neat outline, just a squiggle. The white chalk had mixed with dust to become orange.

"Anyway, I don't adjust the controller." Sakaki stopped outside the tape. "I only do routine stuff. Check batteries and connections, keep an eye on accuracy ratings. You know."

There was no other sign of disturbance at the workstation. The peripherals—the positioners that fed the pieces onto the line and held them for the robot to weld—and the pieces themselves, waited for work to resume.

"Your Japanese is really good," he added shyly. "Better than mine."

Eleanor gritted her teeth and smiled through them.

If nothing was wrong, why did Mito come inside the robot's work envelope? The control panel was here on the perimeter if he wanted to adjust anything. The teach pendant with its portable stop button was in its place. Factories like this couldn't afford the latest instruction software—they still relied on sims followed by teaching, like they'd done since the late nineties.

But sensor-based safety measures had progressed since then, and why didn't they function last night? Eleanor didn't design robots in which you could turn every safety off. The operator was always protected.

"Were there any tools nearby when they found him?" She glanced back at Sakaki.

He met her eyes briefly then looked down. "No. But the controller was unlocked."

So Mito intended either to pause or adjust the robot's program. Maybe so he could move into the work envelope. It should have stayed paused. Her robots didn't have minds of their own.

At least, she smiled to herself, thinking of Sam back at the lab, these ones don't.

Maybe Mito made a mistake, thought he'd disabled the robot properly, went to physically check something and got hit.

Why didn't he have his tool kit, then?

"Was he a cautious kind of fellow?"

Sakaki was staring at the blurred chalk marks, and she had to repeat herself before he heard properly.

Sakaki paused and bit his lip. It wasn't a fair question—for him to admit Mito was careless might be interpreted as admitting Mito was to blame for what happened.

"He was very careful. He was a very serious fellow," said Sakaki eventually.

Eleanor sighed and turned back to the only real witness. The robot's controller opened easily.

"Uh-oh." She frowned at the screen inside, where neat rows of code displayed the robot's status. They bore out the hypothesis that Mito had adjusted the robot's program, as normally the screen would be set at operator interface, in ordinary Japanese.

The robot should have gone to emergency stop as soon as Mito breached the security devices. But it stood at halt. The police would have switched off the power as soon as the body was discovered, so the robot must have gone to halt after striking Mito.

That, Eleanor told herself crossly, is impossible.

As the police and their engineer were satisfied Mito's death was an accident, all she had to do was add her stamp to the papers, and the whole thing would be over. The robot would be recalled and because it was an old model—nearly eight years out of date—it would either be scrapped or resold on the secondhand market.

And she could get back to her budget committee preparations, never knowing why the robot went to halt instead of emergency stop.

Sakaki caught her eye. "Excuse me, but I need to go and log in. I'll be back soon."

"You're on duty tonight?"

He nodded. "Normally there are two of us, but everyone's gone away for Bon." They both averted their eyes awkwardly until Sakaki sidled away.

She walked around the robot enclosure again, slowly, with half-closed eyes, plotting its arcs of possible movement from what she remembered of the program. Even the most experienced technicians can make mistakes, become too familiar with their charges. An industrial robot could be unpredictable. Signals from surrounding machinery and its own sensors could get scrambled; it might get confused by electronic noise from other robots, peripherals, neons, trains, and phones. All the new factories were noise-proofed, but you couldn't expect that in a place this old.

The problem was probably a glitch in the display. She unscrewed the casing and checked its wiring. Perfect. Not a glitch in the display, then.

Nothing wrong with the physical safeties. All on a different power source to the robot, as specified. All active, as specified.

She'd give herself one hour to find the answer. If she couldn't find it, she'd get a train back to the office and forget about the whole thing.

ISHIHARA　　　　　石原

Assistant Inspector Ishihara of Osaka Municipal Police slammed the car door. The automatic closing mechanism *booped* in outrage and he grinned. He preferred to shut his own doors, thank you.

Saturday of the Bon weekend, and he had to go out in the heat. Why did he have to be on call during Bon? When he was a young constable, he'd been the one on call all holidays because the older men thought they'd earned the rest. Now they let the young ones with a family have the time off because otherwise they might quit the police force for a better civilian job. A niggling internal voice pointed out that if he'd had more time with his family when he was younger, he might still have a family, but he ignored it.

Anyway, in three months it wouldn't be his problem. Retirement loomed, an endless vista of formless days, and he was finding an obscure pleasure in the discomforts of duty that he would undoubtedly miss once he'd left.

Dock loading zones and small factories covered most of the old harbor town. One skylink ran from the center of the city to the nearby harbor complex where big companies kept showrooms; around it clustered high-rise blocks of casual labor apartments, cheap diners and tiny bars, family factories-cum-homes, trodden dirt parks with dusty trees and outdated concrete play equipment. Not enough money around to attract big investors in entertainment like the gangster clans. A sense of community still clung here, unlike in the wretched Bettas.

Damn, but it was hot.

This factory was like those he remembered from his childhood in an industrial area of Fukuoka City. A big iron barn. Piles of scrap towered over a side fence. In a flower bed below a side window sunflowers grew tall against a neatly tied lattice of bamboo.

Someone had been found dead in there, hit by an industrial robot. The medical report said dead between one to four hours. Security scans showed that nobody went in or came out. The man must have thought he'd turned the robot off but didn't do it properly. At least someone else had been working over Bon. Ishihara just had to check the local police report and stamp it.

The constable at the door of the factory stiffened to attention at the sight of Ishihara's ID. He swiped it carefully in his phone to confirm and gave it back to Ishihara with a bow. His face was shiny with sweat, and an empty water bottle stood against the wall.

Ishihara nodded by way of greeting. "Hot job out here."

The constable relaxed at Ishihara's informal tone. "It's the humidity that gets you. The manager's gone to arrange the funeral," he added. "There's one technician overseeing the floor. One of the maker's engineers is still looking at the robot. She's been in there over an hour."

"She?" Ishihara paused in straightening a cigarette from the half-crushed packet in his shirt pocket.

The constable started to say something, changed his mind. "Yessir."

The engineer would want to make sure the manufacturer

doesn't get blamed, thought Ishihara. He'd check the scene. Never met a female robot engineer.

He couldn't see her at first. She must be over the other side, past that row of minicranes and ridged tabletops. All the machines silent and waiting. Enough to give anyone the creeps. He had to move right down one lane and back up another—there were no shortcuts across the floor. Sweat trickled down the middle of his back and into his underwear.

The single figure near the robot didn't notice him approach. She had her back to him and was looking from a flat box in her hand to an upright panel next to the robot. One hand tapped keys on the panel. Chalk marks inside the robot's enclosure were nearly obliterated. It didn't matter— the response team would have taken a video scan of the scene anyway.

Quite an attractive figure. He'd been expecting plainness. Why? He expected women working in an all-male field to be there for a reason—they couldn't compete with other women. *Idiot*, he heard his ex-wife's voice in his head. *You're an ignorant dinosaur.*

Anyway, this figure was a pleasure to ogle. Reasonably tall, slim. Long legs in cotton trousers. Short-sleeved white blouse. It was the legs that gave her away. As he coughed, he knew even before she turned that Japanese women didn't have legs that long. She wasn't tall, then, not for a gaijin.

She started in surprise and fumbled the box.

Red hair, too. Long strands escaping from under the helmet. The skin under its sheen of sweat and smudges of grime was really white. Ishihara made a note to keep an eye on the constable, who'd refrained from blurting out the obvious. Tactful constables were rare.

"This is . . ." the woman started to say in Japanese, then stopped and blinked at Ishihara in surprise. "Who are you?"

"Assistant Inspector Ishihara, West Station Police, Religious Affairs. Who are you?"

She brought her thoughts back from wherever they were.

"My name is McGuire. I work for Tomita. We designed this robot." She reached for a dilapidated brown handbag on the floor near the robot, rummaged in it for a moment, then proffered a card to him.

The only accent in her Japanese was that of Osaka. Ishihara noticed she gave him only midlevel politeness. He hadn't even used ordinary level for her.

He knew enough foreigners—third- and fourth-generation Koreans, Brazilians and Filipinos on work visas—not to be surprised that she spoke reasonable Japanese. A relief, though, not to have to dust off his high school English. Or Russian—they saw a lot of Russians since the Sakhalin Treaty, but not many of them worked in big companies.

She had gray eyes, a color he found less alien than blue. To see if it would faze her, he dropped his gaze slowly down to her boots and up again.

It didn't. She merely stopped her hand before it could begin to brush strands of hair out of her eyes.

"Well. Nice to meet you." She started to turn back to the robot.

"What are you looking for here?" said Ishihara. "I thought it was an accident, human error."

"I'm just making certain." She didn't look directly at him this time. "Before we move it."

Ishihara looked at the robot properly. A big, ungainly cranelike thing. "This is it?"

"You were expecting Gundam?" she said.

He had to stop himself grinning. He'd been thinking of Mighty Atom and Sam Number Five, in fact. "What were you about to say?"

"When?"

"When I came in."

McGuire hesitated, then pointed to the robot. "This is at the wrong position."

" 'Wrong'?"

"It's at halt, not emergency stop." She stepped closer to

the robot and ran her hand along the arm and the pointy bit at the end. He noted how her long, grimy fingers gripped the box and the familiar way she moved among the tangle of wires and leads.

"This part hit Mito," she went on. "It's programmed to come to a complete emergency stop as soon as something interrupts its arc of movement. So unless someone has tampered with the controls, it should still be in that position. But it's at halt."

"What's halt?" Ishihara could guess from the pronunciation of the characters used for the word, but he wanted to be sure.

"Halt is when the robot pauses in its job. It doesn't go back to the beginning of the sequence. None of the peripherals"—she pointed at the machines around the robot—"should be affected."

"So were they affected this time?"

She nodded, her long, bony features exaggerating the serious expression. "They were all off-line. Which is what I'd expect in emergency stop."

"So someone turned it from stop to halt?"

"It's not a matter of turning the switch back," she retorted. "Once it's at emergency stop, the robot's got to be completely restarted. That leaves a record in the programming file. But there's nothing."

"The only entry card used last night belonged to the person on duty," said Ishihara. The factory's security system report was clear. Unless the dead man had let someone in, he'd been there alone.

"Another thing." McGuire stepped back from the robot again, keeping her eye on it as if the thing might still move unexpectedly. "The safeties must have been tampered with."

"Safeties?"

She pointed to the wire barrier, a post with a cameralike box on the top, some wire netting mats inside the gate, and the warning signs posted all around the enclosure and the line itself. "Measures designed to prevent this happening."

"Don't work very well, do they?"

"This is the real world, Assistant Inspector." She stepped right back from the wire and slotted the box into a stand outside the cage. "An industrial robot is a complex computer, but its hardware has to interact with the real world, with the possibility of infinite errors."

"Like us humans." In spite of the heat, Ishihara was interested.

"Exactly." She smiled, pleased that he'd understood, and slipped into what Ishihara mentally labeled "lecture mode."

"The robot is programmed to do one thing very accurately and continuously, for years and years. It needs to be stable—we don't want it shifting out of alignment, or your car window, for example, mightn't be fixed on straight. It has very sensitive sensors, but only for its own job, not for what's around it. Unlike your Helpbots in the Betta, it gets no feedback from the environment. It's taught to go from A to B to C through certain coordinates. It doesn't know or care if there's air along the coordinates or someone's head." She winced at her own words and was silent.

Ishihara fished his cigarette packet from his shirt pocket and extracted one. "Could Mito have altered the program to keep the robot active while he did something?"

"I would be able to see a change like that. There isn't anything. In fact . . ." She stared at the controller, then at Ishihara, raising her chin as if facing an unpleasant fact. "The controller log shows nothing after 4:30 A.M., and the program files are unreadable. I won't know why until I've had a chance to investigate further."

"The security office wasn't called until 5:20, and the body wasn't discovered until 5:30." Ishihara twirled the cigarette between his fingers. "Would Mito have noticed a malfunction and come close to the robot to investigate?"

"If there's a m . . . minor malfunction"—she frowned at

the stammer—"a signal to check it is sent to the control
booth. The whole line wouldn't stop, or a signal would have
been sent to the security company as well. That didn't happen until . . . 5:20, did you say?"

"Yeah. So this robot only had some problem and halted.
Or could it have kept running without leaving a record in the
log?"

"That's impossible." There was almost enough authority
in her voice to make him cancel that possibility. "All I can
suggest is that Mito went to investigate whatever wiped the
welder's log, but he was hit, and the line actually stopped at
5:20."

"Maybe the safety precautions developed a problem."

"In that case he definitely wouldn't enter the work envelope."

"So you're saying somebody else altered the safeties?"

She shook her head. "I don't know. Normally I'd say no,
not without leaving traces that I'd find."

"Have you got any concrete proof it wasn't an accident?"
Ishihara scrunched the empty cigarette packet and dropped
it on the floor.

McGuire glared at him and bent to pick it up. She
scrunched the packet harder than he had. "I'll know m . . .
more when I've had a chance to go through the program.
You can't smoke in here," she added, looking pointedly at
the closest NO SMOKING sign.

"I'll go outside then." He stared her straight in the eye—
wasn't that what foreigners expected? "Nice meeting you,
McGuire-san."

"I can't say the pleasure is mutual."

He got a real kick out of how she changed the usual polite expression.

He didn't go outside immediately. As he spoke to
McGuire he'd seen a man in overalls enter the factory from
a side door and go to the glassed-in booth in the back.

The technician was sitting in front of a computer and jumped nervously when Ishihara tapped on the glass.

"Yes?" He opened the door about three centimeters.

"Assistant Inspector Ishihara, West Station." Ishihara flashed his ID perfunctorily. "You on duty tonight?"

"Y . . . yes." The man brushed a long fringe out of his eyes. He was young, probably in his mid-twenties, with slanted fox-eyes and a dissatisfied expression.

Ishihara pushed the door open farther with his foot. "Nasty business, this." He jerked his head back in the direction of the accident scene. "Just wanted to ask you a couple of questions about the deceased."

"I wasn't here," the man said quickly. He had a high, petulant voice.

"What's your name?"

"Sakaki. Tomihiro Sakaki. Look, detective-san, I have lots of work to do because we're behind schedule . . ."

Funny how people think bluster will hide the tremor in their voices. "Was Mito a friend of yours?"

"No."

Pause. Sakaki looked pointedly at his computer.

"Did he have any personal problems?"

"Not that I know of."

"Just wondering if he had anything on his mind, that's all. He might have made a mistake and turned off the safety devices." Ishihara wasn't going to mention McGuire's opinion.

"That's probably right." Sakaki was sweating.

Mind you, Ishihara was sweating, too. The factory was damn hot. "Could be the power cut off for a second."

"Could be."

Ishihara considered shaking Sakaki up a bit. One of his coworkers just had his head smashed in, and this bastard wouldn't even be honest about basics. He was probably worried about some petty misdemeanor—had some Betta-specific hardware tucked away in his apartment or something.

No, leave Sakaki for now and come back and question him if necessary. First, see what McGuire finds in the robot's program. And run a background check on the factory, the company that owned it, personnel, and suppliers. Including Tomita's gaijin robot expert. And especially close-mouthed Sakaki here.

"If you remember anything, give me a call." Ishihara shoved his card into the breast pocket of Sakaki's overall. "Anything at all."

"Yeah." Sakaki leaned away from the contact and shut the door.

He could be ex-gang, mused Ishihara. Got the right attitude. Or even still affiliated, maybe doing petty theft or dealing.

In the loading bay, McGuire stood outside the robot's cage. She looked very small in the middle of all that machinery. He decided to keep the constable outside until she finished.

The evening hadn't even begun to cool off, but it still felt better outside than in the ovenlike factory. Ishihara's sweat-soaked shirt clung to his back and chest. He lit his cigarette and blew out the first lungful of smoke with a sigh.

Outside the gate a loudspeaker blared a rhythmic chant. It was the recorded voice of one of Osaka's last mobile tofu salesman. In a tiny utility truck loaded with tanks, the pale ranks of tofu would be swaying like rectangular corpses in a watery morgue.

Tofu! Get your fresh to-ofu! The voice called up the ghosts of a more leisurely age, when children played outside until dusk and men returned from work in time to practice golf shots on the sidewalk.

On top of the building opposite, a huge billboard flashed captioned images of the latest Betta. *Beat the heat.* A shaded dome full of neat rows of leafy plants. An indoor swimming pool with kids splashing happily and adults seated in lounges by the poolside, reading newspapers or talking on phones. *Housework made easy.* An immaculate lounge room, housewife smiling as a cleanbot whiffled over the carpet at her feet. *This lifestyle can be yours at Kusatsu Betta.* The Betta itself, a jumble of immense gleaming white domes and towers, loomed over the shabby remains of an older town.

Yeah right, thought Ishihara sourly. For those who can afford to mortgage the rest of their lives.

"Was everything satisfactory inside?" The constable at his post stared straight ahead at the sunflowers. In the fading light they looked like a row of drooping heads.

"Not bad." Ishihara didn't elaborate. "I'll keep the report tonight. Got to finalize a couple of things."

He felt inclined to dismiss McGuire's discoveries as expert babble, except that she and her company had nothing to gain by finding a problem with the robot. And Sakaki was hiding something. Probably nothing relevant to Mito's death, but you never knew.

エレナ

Eleanor yawned as the monorail carriage rocked soothingly and invisible underground walls whooshed past. Bright white lights, multicolored glare of advertisements. Yodogawa station. She felt grimy and crumpled, in spite of the chilly air-conditioning. Someone got in at the other end of the carriage. The pillars of the station and the reflection of the wall holos got mixed up in the window opposite. Her reflection stared back in familiar surprise—she looked so alien, with her angular gawkiness instead of compact Japanese elegance; undignified obviousness instead of tasteful reticence; bright flame of hair like a signal flare to warn of the heresy of difference.

She'd had to work later than she intended on Sam's presentation for the budget committee after getting back from the Minato Ward factory. None of her team would be at work the next day—all of them had gone to their hometowns for Bon. She couldn't possibly go in tomorrow either—she hadn't spent an evening with Masao for a month.

But the problem that kept jerking her mind out of drowsiness was not her own project. The Kawanishi Metalworks welder must have been radically reprogrammed to allow it to move without activating the safeties. The dead man, Mito, couldn't have done it. He was a C-grade maintenance officer. He could have resolved most lower-level programming and teaching problems, but certainly not perform the surgery involved here. The robot must have been off-line during a reprogramming of that magnitude. Sakaki said he didn't think it had been off-line for months. She'd have to call again on Monday and look at the maintenance schedule.

The train whooshed smoothly into Amagasaki station; the doors swished open and shut. She was the only person left in the carriage. Then the muffled roar of the tunnel ceased as the carriage emerged into open air. Rattle-click, rattle-click, as it crossed the bridge. Behind her reflection in the window, lights spread in great swaths across the pale backdrop of the Osaka night sky, each of the Bettas a constellation in itself.

The robot hit Mito, which meant it should have gone to emergency stop. She didn't like the way her thoughts were heading, but possibly Mito had surprised someone who was trying to interfere with the robot. That person then wiped the control log after Mito died. If so, it was police business, not the company's, and she could file her report.

The trouble was, she'd found a different clue that might indicate Tomita was responsible—an unknown signature in the robot's recognition file. All commercially manufactured robots, whether mobile home helpers or fixed factory manipulators, had their own identity codes, which were theoretically impossible to copy. They consisted of the maker's electronic signature, the type of robot, the series, the date of manufacture, and the number of the individual machine. In the Kawanishi robot, the robot's individual number didn't match the number on record at Kawanishi and Tomita. Until she checked it with the Industrial Lab at Tomita on Monday, she wouldn't know if it was deliberate or a mistake in registering the ID code. She didn't see how it could affect the

robot's behavior with Mito, but it was a discrepancy that
must be cleared up.

The train stopped at Tachibana station. Home. No climb-
ing down stairs and into the sticky night air, into the dark
streets echoing with her own footfalls, like in the old days.
All she had to do was walk along the brightly lit corridor to
her own Betta.

The corridors were always bright. No dark corners, no
ambiguities. This particular corridor was rounded and tunnel-
like, with walls sloping outward up to a domed ceiling.
Smaller corridors branched off at regular intervals. Along
the ceiling, holos advertised products made by the business
conglomerates that sponsored the Bettas. Their jingles were
muted at that time of night. Along the walls notices to residents shimmered between text and graphic directions for
newcomers or those who lost their way easily. Eleanor never
lost her way. It was the same sense that woke her when the
train reached her station.

The corridors were safe, one of the great selling points of
the Bettas. Security cameras watched all corridors and were
programmed to alert human security guards at any sign of
trouble. She remembered without regret the days when she
had to take a taxi home if she worked late, or had to call
Masao from the station to come and meet her because he
didn't like her to walk home alone through ill-lit streets. She
didn't like it, either. The accident so many years ago that left
her with her stammer had happened on a dark street. A car
hit her bicycle, they said.

The damn stammer. That long string bean of a man, the
detective, Ishihara, noticed although he didn't say anything.
All it meant was that she was overtired, but he wasn't to
know that. It made her sound like such a fool. And she didn't
want to appear a fool before that man, who obviously didn't
believe a woman could do her job. He didn't look like her
image of a detective, which was based on the young, dash-
ing actors of popular vid shows. Ishihara's stoop, his crum-

pled short-sleeved shirt and shiny-kneed trousers, and lined, dour face could have been that of many aging engineers she knew, passed over for promotion and relegated to administrative tasks. He'd looked at home in the dingy factory.

She shrugged off the memory. The Kawanishi incident was closed as far as the police were concerned, and it was unlikely she'd meet Assistant Inspector Ishihara again.

Cleanbots scuttled out of her way on wheels and jointed legs as their infrared and movement sensors told them she was approaching. Then they returned to their tasks, skimming the corridor for rubbish like the insects they were modeled upon. Anticockroaches, she thought sleepily, admiring their clustering behavior. Tomita produced a smaller, down-market version of Spick and Scram, as the cleanbots were properly known, although she hadn't been directly involved in its development.

She turned right where the corridor branched, then stopped. One of those cleanbots seemed out of synch. She peered back around the corner and saw it approaching purposefully, away from the herd. Immediately it sensed her, it swung around and zoomed back to the others. Almost as if it had been . . . following her?

She laughed at herself and kept walking. It would be a glitch in the recognition function. The bot probably thought she was one of its herd.

As she entered her elevator, she thought she saw a movement down the corridor. She'd better mention the wayward bot to management tomorrow. If it kept leaving the herd, it could disrupt the entire sequence for the others as well.

The elevator doors shut as soon as she entered. Its sensors would have read her chip signal, accessed her resident information, and noted that she had placed a high priority on privacy in her preferences section. She hated standing in crowded elevators while people stared at her, then pretended nonchalance when she caught their eyes.

She and Masao lived on the outer third floor in a four-room unit. Not high enough to have a view, but they were lucky to live in a Betta at all. Even if the Sam project was axed—horrible thought—she couldn't afford to leave the company. It would mean leaving the Betta.

She kicked her sandals off in the entry to their apartment and left her bag propped against the wall. Masao was asleep in the inner room, curled happily in their futon with the air conditioner set to autumn chill. Eleanor turned it up five degrees, peeled off her clothes, and crawled in beside him.

"I'm home," she said.

He muttered and rolled over automatically, curling the other way so she could snuggle.

She was dimly conscious that her last waking thoughts were about that damn welder.

Eleanor and Masao reached the station closest to the Tanaka family house shortly before midday. The temperature had reached thirty-eight degrees again, according to the environment monitor outside the station, and there was no shade between the station and the house except for the overhang of blocks of flats and two trees drooping brownish leaves over a temple wall. Eleanor carried a parasol.

"You know how in the movies you can hear cicadas in summer?" said Masao. "When I was a child, we couldn't find any insects to study in our summer holiday projects. People suddenly realized that the reason they didn't hear cicadas anymore was that the larvae were stuck under concrete."

"What did they do?" asked Eleanor.

"There was a bit of a fuss, some people made gardens in their backyards, but the developers kept coming." He pushed his glasses straight—they tended to slide off crookedly when he spoke about something that affected him.

After the Quake came the Seikai reforms and the Bettas, with their self-contained roof gardens. But by that time the cicadas were gone from the city. Now, enterprising tourist agencies ran summer tours for people to go to the countryside to experience the sound.

Masao gestured at the bitumen and concrete around them. The only living things were pot plants arranged carefully in some doorways. "When my father was a boy it was still a suburb. There was a creek and rice paddies. It was a lot cooler then. You could see to the mountains."

Now vistas of tall buildings stretched into the thick air. The streams were either buried beneath the concrete or had degenerated into smelly storm water outlets, and the closest mountains had been leveled to build a Betta.

It won't be like this when they set up a Betta here, thought Eleanor. We can stay cool all the way from our place. It's not that I don't like visiting, she told herself, but getting here is so exhausting.

But she said nothing to Masao, who tramped stolidly along the road that was too narrow to allow a footpath, his round face running with sweat. He regarded the visits as a necessary duty and would never dream of shirking. The outline of his undershirt showed through his shirt, pasted with sweat to his back, and Eleanor felt a surge of affection for the familiar broad curves.

"Hot, isn't it," she said.

"It's the humidity. Phew."

She hadn't mentioned how she'd stammered in front of Inspector Ishihara. Masao worried too much, which both annoyed her and made her feel safe. Sometimes, when the annoyance grew overwhelming, she would remember how he came to her after she had the accident. It was at the end of her Ph.D. program in Boston. She stayed in the hospital for six months, then returned to her uncle's motor repair business in small-town Iowa to spend another year trying to finish rehabilitation and thesis at the same time. A year and a half of her life gone, eaten up by hospital beds and chunks of vanished memory.

She'd only talked to Masao a couple of times before the accident, and he said he visited her once in the hospital, although she didn't remember. One of many memories that the accident had taken away. Then he arrived one day in the town and asked her to go back to Japan with him. She'd never forgotten the feeling of the world opening up for her again. Masao had rescued her. Rescued her from more years in a town of wide, dusty streets full of abandoned shops, heat, the stink of oil and metal in the workshop, and a house permeated with sour toilet smells.

She grimaced and touched his shoulder again like a talisman.

They panted past the brick building of Masao's old primary school, through the dusty dirt of the tiny local "park," past the car repair workshop closed for the day, picked their way through potted plants Grandma insisted on placing on both sides of the narrow footpath, and finally turned in the gate next to the Tanaka workshop entrance. The shop's metal shutters were closed for the holiday. Tanaka Manufacturing, the sign above the shutters said, in old-fashioned cursive characters carved into a wooden board. The small two-story house was attached to the workshop by a walkway. Before the house was built after the war, the entire family, ten people at that time, had lived in two rooms at the back of the factory.

The stone path from the gate ended in three concrete steps up to an entrance hall. Masao pushed open the sliding door.

"We're home," he announced, sitting on the step to unlace his sneakers. Eleanor folded the parasol and eased off her sandals. The air inside the dark hall was cooler. It smelled of herbal disinfectant overlaid with omelet. Here we go, she thought.

Masao's sister Yoshiko, plump, round-faced, and perpetually worried, emerged from the kitchen at the far end of the hall. She had the same dark olive skin as Masao, without his wide, humorous mouth. She wore a skirt and T-shirt and was wiping her hands on a dishcloth.

"You're late," she said to Masao.

"We got held up," he said blandly. "Buying cakes."

Eleanor remembered she was carrying the present and held out the bag of sweet rice cakes. "Hello, Yoshiko-san."

Yoshiko didn't like Eleanor calling her the traditional "Elder Sister." Eleanor suspected it was because although Masao was three years younger than Yoshiko, she and Eleanor were the same age. Or maybe Yoshiko didn't want the level of intimacy that "Elder Sister" implied. So they called each other "Eleanor-san" and "Yoshiko-san," and kept their distance.

Yoshiko tucked the towel into her apron pocket and took the rice cakes. Back in the kitchen, she placed them on a table carrying plates of food in various stages of preparation.

"It's hot, isn't it? Not so much the heat, as the humidity. I'm in the middle of the sushi mix." She paused long enough for Eleanor to offer to help.

Eleanor did so, with a mental scowl at Masao, who had disappeared into the air-conditioned living room. He was happy to do more than his share of housework in their own home, but when he came back here, he regressed into a spoiled Japanese boy. It infuriated her.

"Have a glass of tea first. We don't stand on ceremony here." Yoshiko laughed without humor and began slicing beans.

Eleanor drank some cold barley tea and still felt hot. An old electric fan purred in the corner. The usual kitchen table mess had been pushed to one side to make way for the food. Yoshiko always complained about the table, saying she couldn't keep it tidy because everyone else dumped their things on it. Just then it held a saltshaker, two pickle containers, rubber bands, chopsticks standing in a cup, a rolled-up newspaper, Grandma's medicine cup, a piece of carrot on some wet cotton wool, many small plastic packs of mustard

that came with ready-made dumplings, and a jar of red,
squishy-looking ovals. In her more whimsical moods,
Eleanor visualized the table as a symbol of the dingy chaos
she'd moved to the Betta to get away from.

"There's an apron in the second drawer down," said
Yoshiko, neatly lifting the sliced beans with the flat of the
cleaver to a different location.

"No, thank you." Eleanor shuddered at the thought of
more layers of cloth between herself and the fan. In the
Betta and the train she'd been cold in her thin blouse; now
it felt like a blanket.

"Grandma and Papa," said Yoshiko, referring to her
mother and own husband, Kazu, "have gone to do the
graves. They'll be back soon."

During the two weeks of Bon most Japanese families
cleaned up their family gravestones and presented fresh
flowers and offerings to the departed, whose souls would
visit at that time. Many city dwellers returned to their hometowns, or their family's hometowns, for the festival. The
post-Quake Seikai reforms tried to get each part of the country to do so at different times, to avoid traffic congestion and
confusion, but it never caught on, not even at the urging of
the Buddhist clergy. Some customs were too old to change.

"Can you slice this carrot? Small, please." Yoshiko
passed Eleanor pieces of cooked vegetable and peered criti-
cally over her shoulder. "You know, for someone who's
good at repairing things, you're not very dexterous, are
you?"

Eleanor half-smiled automatically. "No, not very." Five
or six years earlier she might have made a lighthearted comment about not criticizing a person holding a cleaver, or perhaps tried a joke about it being hard to repair robots with a
knife. But Yoshiko never smiled.

Eleanor scraped her clumsy carrots into another bowl.

Yoshiko emptied the contents of all the little bowls one
by one onto the mound of sushi rice and mixed it together.

She seemed more flustered than usual—she dropped a couple of peas and didn't notice.

"Mari-chan's here for the day," she said, with a quick glance at Eleanor's face.

So that was the problem. Yoshiko had never liked the way her daughter enjoyed Eleanor's company.

"She can't stay, she's got summer classes next week."

I bet she's working, and doesn't want Mum and Dad to know, thought Eleanor. Mari was smart enough to pass all her courses without the need for extra classes.

Yoshiko mounded the sushi rice with unnecessary vigor. "While she's here, Eleanor-san, I've got some important things to discuss with her." She kept her eyes on the rice.

So don't butt in, you mean, Eleanor thought. "Yoshiko-san, I haven't seen Mari-chan since last New Year. We don't have much to talk about anymore."

She had a swift, vivid memory of an overweight ten-year-old lying on her stomach on the fluffy pink carpet of her room, pages of her latest effort at drawing manga strewn around her. Face glowing with achievement, she read the pages aloud to Eleanor, who had been glad to listen and escape the minefield of family relationships that at holiday times extended to dozens of people. Eleanor had also solved problems with computer games for her niece, and played them with her over the years.

But Mari was now eighteen and had probably grown out of both manga and games.

The back door opened and Masao's father came in, placing his sandals neatly facing outward on the lower step. He was a heavy man with rounded shoulders beginning to shrink with age, his face dragged down by worry and sobriety.

"Welcome, Eleanor-san," he said with his usual careful decorum. "It's hot, isn't it? Grandma not back yet?" he asked Yoshiko, who brought him a glass of iced tea.

"Not yet."

Grandpa grunted in reply and went into the living room.

Eleanor picked up the plates Yoshiko indicated and followed him. On holidays they always ate at the low table in the living room.

Grandpa Tanaka folded himself, carefully because of arthritis, into his usual seat at the head of the table under the family altar. The doors of the altar stood open, and incense burned on either side, framing Grandpa's sagging cheeks and tufted eyebrows like some strange Buddhist deity. He held out his hand to Masao, who passed him part of the newspaper without comment. The little statue of Kannon, goddess of mercy, seemed to wink at Eleanor from deep in the altar as the light caught its peeling gold leaf.

As she arranged the plates on the table she thought how uncomfortable Grandpa's uprightness would have made her own father, whom she had seldom seen sober. Her early memories were fragmented—she suspected because of the accident—but she could clearly remember long Sunday afternoons in Nagasaki, her mother taking Bible classes and her younger sister sleeping. Eleanor would sit outside with her father while he explained some mechanism to her—a clock, a pump, an engine. He was always patient, always willing to go over it again, a tiny tea bowl almost invisible in his thick, freckled fingers, his malty breath mingling with hers as they bent over the mechanism. In exchange for not telling mother where he kept his "stash," Eleanor was allowed to disassemble something in the house or yard and try to put it together again. She knew the parts of an auto engine before she could write her own name. All that ended when her sister graduated from naps, for Marion could never learn to be quiet about the wee bottles dotted around the yard, and her father eventually retreated to the local Go parlor, where he could nip in peace. But by then Eleanor had taken everything in the house apart at least once anyway.

She looked up as a tall girl carried more bowls into the

living room. She had the Tanaka skin and round face, but long, careless limbs.

"Aunt Eleanor. Uncle Masao. Welcome," she said happily, and knelt at the table beside Eleanor.

Eleanor smiled broadly at Mari, something she only did in front of children or other foreigners. It just didn't seem to fit in to normal Japanese conversation.

"Nice to see you, Mari-chan."

Masao peered over his glasses. "You're looking very grown-up."

It wasn't her clothes, which were long shorts and a tank top, or her hair cut in an unfashionable bob; she held herself very straight as she arranged the bowls. She seemed more poised, more contained within herself.

"You're looking fatter," retorted Mari.

Eleanor chuckled. Masao had indeed put on a couple of kilos since New Year. The university had moved his office closer to a new subway station, so he wasn't getting as much exercise.

"It's all muscle," Masao managed, before retreating behind the paper.

Grandpa Tanaka was engrossed in the Politics section and gave no sign he knew they were there.

"So," said Eleanor awkwardly. "How's university?"

"It's okay." Mari crossed her legs, boy-style.

"Do you still draw comics?" said Eleanor.

Mari shook her head. "That's kids' stuff."

"You think so? I named my current research project after a robot in a manga. Can you guess which one?"

Mari smoothed her hand over her hair and didn't answer for a moment, and Eleanor wondered if she'd dismissed the question as kids' stuff. Then she looked up and said slyly,

"Toramon?"

"Hah." Toramon was a fat, badger-shaped robot sent from the future to help a clumsy boy get through school. It used a variety of magic tricks, thinly disguised as future technology. "No, *not* Toramon," Eleanor said haughtily. "More dignified."

Mari chuckled. "Arai-chan?"

Eleanor chortled, too. Arai was a tiny girl robot who didn't know her own superhuman strength. The stories and characters were bizarre.

"No, definitely not."

Mari glanced at her again. "It has to be Sam Number Five, from *Journey to Life*."

Out of the thousands of robots in Japanese manga lore . . . "How did you know?" The main character of *Journey to Life* who wants desperately to become mortal had always seemed a particularly apt namesake.

"You never gave me back my copy of Volume One," said Mari. "I lent it to you years ago. I must have been in junior high. Don't you remember? I said it was freaky, and you said you liked it when you were little but couldn't remember the details."

"Now that you mention it . . ." Eleanor did recall borrowing a book from her niece, but she'd been too busy at work to read anything. It must have got pushed into one of the bookcases at home and forgotten.

"I'll have a look for it," she said. "It's probably at home."

"Don't worry. I've got textbooks to read." Mari didn't sound particularly interested. "So what does your Sam Number Five look like?"

"It's about eighty centimeters tall . . ."

"Mari-chan!" Yoshiko called from the kitchen. "Give me a hand in here."

Mari sighed and unraveled her legs. "She's having one of those days."

Eleanor remembered Yoshiko's injunction in the kitchen and nodded, although she could see why Yoshiko felt put out. When Mari was smaller, she'd ogled Eleanor in wide-eyed adoration and brought a succession of fascinated small girls to do the same whenever Eleanor and Masao visited.

The Amazing Gaijin Aunt, Masao used to tease Eleanor. And when Mari grew older Eleanor had often unwittingly supported her in defying her parents, whether over reading manga or about buying a private phone.

So Yoshiko was probably justified. But it didn't make their visits any more comfortable. And Eleanor was damned if she'd diminish her relationship with Mari to please Yoshiko.

石原

Ishihara sat at his desk in West Station and read through the incident report again. He was the only detective in the big room, as the duty officer was in Homicide upstairs. Everyone wants Sunday off these days. We're like bloody salarymen now, he thought disgustedly.

He hadn't yet signed off on the robot accident at Kawanishi Metalworks. He'd gone over the reports at least three times, letting his eyes skim the words again and again, while his intuition prodded memory into spewing up whatever was making him uneasy.

Man gets hit by industrial robot. Man dies. Nobody else there to see what happened. No forensic evidence to indicate that anyone else was near the man when he died or that the body was touched. Security records show nobody went in after the previous shift ended.

Logical conclusion: Man made a mistake and paid the price. Dangerous things, these big machines.

Except that he had one smart-aleck expert who said there was a problem with the robot. Why trust her—because she's a long-legged foreigner with skin like milk?

He tipped his chair back until its wheels creaked, considering this.

No, he trusted her opinion because she designed the robot, and her company made it, so it was in her interest not to find any problems. Yet she did. *The robot should have gone to emergency stop but instead it went to halt. Therefore, someone must have tampered with it.*

Ishihara sat down, stared into the computer's recognition sensor until the machine started up, and searched for the relevant file. If he took McGuire's opinion seriously, he'd have to arrange another expert opinion to confirm it; he'd be knee deep in reports for weeks.

McGuire hadn't been sure, though. And it was a long way from a technical problem in how a robot stopped to suspecting something suspicious about the death. So why did he find himself unable to close the case?

He found the transcripts of the interviews with the security company, the manager, and the technician, Sakaki.

The dead man, Mito, was described by them all as "quiet." The manager had added, "modest, thorough, always careful." Ishihara hoped that when he died, he'd have made enough enemies to deserve a more colorful obituary.

What was it one of Mito's coworkers had said? "He was a by-the-book man. Started on the dot, checked out right on time." In answer to a question about socializing, he added, "Mito hardly ever came out for a drink with us. Always had to get home. I mean, sure, it's a good thing people have their own lives outside work . . . but you never really got to know Mito."

He flicked back one screen. Mito was a registered member of Happy Universe, one of the largest New Millennium Religions. This meant that the group would take all Mito's assets, whatever they were. Anybody who knew him would realize that, so if he was killed, it wasn't for money. It also explained his preference for a quiet home life—Happy U members spent most of their spare time praying.

Mito had arrived at work just in time for the late shift at 10:30 P.M., as usual. Normally, the manager had added, Mito would spend most of his shift in the control booth. He'd go out and visually check the lines twice, probably at about midnight and again at 5:00 A.M. before the morning watch arrived.

The factory itself was in the middle of Minato Ward gang territory, so none of the local thieves would break in for fear of offending the gang. And the security system, while not up-to-date, was sufficient to keep out casual intruders. One guard robot patrolled continuously, and a human security guard would check it at the beginning of each shift. Cameras kept a record of the exterior of the building, but not of the factory floor.

Financially, Kawanishi Metalworks was barely hanging on. The company assembled auto and machine parts for two large manufacturers, and also did some work for a third. The owner was middle-aged, had a heart condition, and was gradually losing his urge to succeed. According to one of Mito's workmates, the owner now left more and more to the managers. He hardly ever came to the factory, and rumor had it that he was playing the market in the hope of bailing the company out. Not a situation to promote confidence in the future.

Mito seemed to have been content enough. Sakaki said he was "dependable" and "careful" but seemed to have a lot on his mind lately. When pressed as to whether Mito might have been tired and, therefore, have made a mistake, Sakaki stammered a bit and said he didn't know.

Ishihara frowned and turned back a couple of pages. What was Sakaki doing at the company on Saturday morning to be interviewed? His shift had finished at 10:30 the previous night, and his next shift wasn't until Saturday night.

He found the incident report recording and ran it on his

desk screen. Here was Sakaki, looking distraught as he told Detective Yamaguchi what time he left the factory.

> "About 10:45, I think. I didn't get changed because I always do my laundry on Saturdays."
>
> Detective Yamaguchi: "Did you talk to Mito?"
>
> Sakaki: "I handed him the day report as usual. There wasn't anything special on it."
>
> Yamaguchi: "Why'd you have to work this weekend anyway?"
>
> Sakaki: "The manager told you. We had to finish a big contract."
>
> Yamaguchi: "And you're so keen that you came back to work a day early?"
>
> Sakaki: "I told you, I forgot it was Saturday. You get into a rhythm, you know? I came as far as the station before I realized. Then I thought, what the hell, I'll go and pick up the magazine I left in my locker. When I get here, there are cops all over the place."

Not the most persuasive explanation Ishihara ever heard. Sergeant Yamaguchi, too, had noted in the Investigating Officer's Notes that Sakaki "seems to be hiding something but there is no evidence to link this with Mito's death, which would appear to be an accident."

McGuire didn't think it was an accident. Blast the woman. He wondered if any of his usual informants had information about Kawanishi that might help.

And speaking of McGuire . . . He checked his phone for

new messages. Aha. Bon holiday or not, newspapers were working. His usual contact at *Yominichi News* had sent him the requested information.

A few scanned newspaper cuttings, short biographic note. Too many damn roman letters.

Eleanor McGuire, born Naha 1978, father U.S. serviceman, Navy. One younger sister. Father recalled to U.S. in 1992, discharged for health reasons (someone had noted "alcoholic" in the margin). Died 1995. McGuire entered Tokyo Industrial University, Mechanical Engineering faculty on a scholarship in '96. The scholarship was revoked because of involvement in the student movement, but she still finished her degree in '99. Returned to U.S., entered Ph.D. course at MIT but didn't complete it due to illness, returned to Japan in 2002 to take up position as researcher at Tomita. Note in margin: "recruiting officer, N. Izumi."

The newspaper cuttings were arranged in chronological order. They ranged from a short piece about engineering students and the university, in which McGuire's name was mentioned as the first female foreign student in a new department, to an article from a year ago in the SciTech section of a big daily. It was an actual interview with McGuire. She gave predictable answers to predictable questions, which disappointed Ishihara—he expected more from a foreigner. She was supposed to be part of the "Seikai creative boost," whatever that meant, but all she said was things like, "It's our goal to use mechatronics to assist the transition from a postindustrial society to an IT-integrated one."

He hadn't found a mention of her in police records, at least in the computerized ones. He wasn't going to rummage through paper archives, although if she'd been involved with the student movement, there might be a mention. It did mean that Tomita must have made a special effort to get her visa put through.

She was married when she returned from the U.S. Masao Tanaka, student. Sounds like there's a story there. Why wasn't she calling herself Eleanor Tanaka? He flipped back several screens to a scan of a handwritten note about Tanaka. Born 1981 Hirano Ward, Osaka, father owned small business. No outstanding vices or distinguishing characteristics. Now lecturer in modern history at the Buddhist University. Hardly the husband you'd expect.

A note on the bottom of Tanaka's bio said "out of favor with admin for criticizing NMRs." A lot of old-style Buddhists criticized New Millennial Religions, and they often ended up like Tanaka, in a dead-end job. One of the reasons the NMRs succeeded was that they were better at making money than the old religions, and could buy political influence.

He ran a search for Tanaka in police records, no result as expected. The man was totally mediocre. Except, of course, that he married a gaijin.

He'd call McGuire the following day and ask if she'd found any more technical evidence that Mito's death wasn't an accident. If not, the case was closed as far as he was concerned.

"Oy, Ishihara." The duty officer from upstairs beckoned him from the doorway. "We got some buddhas in a flat. I've called a team to meet us there. Let's go."

Dead bodies on Sunday. Ishihara closed the McGuire file and flicked off the accident report. Criminals don't take holidays.

エレナ

After the meal, Grandpa Tanaka disappeared upstairs for a nap, the signal that lunch was over. Grandma went to water the azaleas. Yoshiko very obviously asked Mari to help her in the kitchen without looking at Eleanor.

Masao and Kazu, Mari's father, were stretched out on the tatami mats with their eyes shut. Eleanor reached over to turn off the television, which had been annoying her with its inane chatter throughout the meal.

"Eleanor-san?" Kazu sat up and regarded her with his serious stare. He was a short man with bulging eyes like a worried blowfish. "Can I get your opinion on something in the factory?"

She blinked at him in surprise. "I suppose so."

Normally an unspoken rule kept Eleanor away from the Tanaka business. No one ever explained why. Perhaps it was because the machine tools they used were made by one of her firm's rivals, and Grandpa Tanaka felt it would be uncomfortable for both of them. Or perhaps he didn't want her snooping around. Or, more likely, he'd had enough of being the object of local gossip when his younger son married not only a foreigner, but also an older woman who worked as a mechanical engineer. Then again, maybe he just didn't approve of women on the factory floor.

Kazu had always followed Grandpa Tanaka's wishes in his precise, undemanding way. Eleanor found it impossible to imagine why he might be disobeying now. She followed his bandy legs through the walkway and into the workshop.

Kazu had been "adopted" by the Tanaka family upon his marriage to Yoshiko, and he now managed the business. Tanaka Manufacturing was a tiny supplier for one of the many subcontractors of a construction machinery manufacturer. Although the post-Quake Seikai reforms were fueling a construction boom, small suppliers seemed no better off. The only small businesses with any prospects were those with the technical savvy to keep up with the big companies, or at least to be useful to them. And, while Kazu knew how to operate the factory machinery and maintain the status quo, he certainly didn't have the capacity to improve it.

In the workshop Kazu switched on the lights and the overhead fans and led her between two rows of workbenches to the desk at the end of the room. There was a single hard drive and monitor on the desk, a common brand, slow but reliable. On one side stood the set of wooden pigeonholes dating from the Meiji period that Masao's great-great-grandfather had used in his bicycle repair shop.

Like every small Japanese machine shop Eleanor had ever seen, everything was spotless; floors neatly swept, all tools put away neatly, clean overalls and caps folded and placed ready on each worker's locker. No film of dust was allowed to collect on the top of shelves or in corners under benches. Uplifting slogans and posters of peaceful scenery decorated all available wall space—a distinctly Grandpa Tanaka touch.

"Sorry it's so hot." Kazu offered her the chair in front of the computer.

"What's the problem?"

"The spot welder has been inaccurate several times this month and we can't find out why."

"How long has it been working?" Eleanor typed up details of the robot's programming. I haven't looked at a welder for ten years, she thought, and this is the second one I'm examining in as many days.

"Nearly two years now." Kazu watched her fingers on the keys.

"It's rented, isn't it?"

"Yes."

"Well, don't they give you a free service every year?" She knew about the industrial robot rental scheme, aimed at small businesses that could not afford to buy one outright, but not the details.

Kazu shifted uncomfortably. "It's a long story . . . basically we can't afford to get it repaired at the moment, but we can't leave it idle. We're in the middle of a big order."

"All right, then. Let's look at the software . . ." It didn't take long. "There's no problem here." She swung the swivel chair around and stared at the rest of the factory. "How is it malfunctioning?"

He showed her some imperfect welds.

"Looks like an alignment problem," she said, moving over to study the robot itself. It stood between two benches for easy access—a cylindrical base, stocky body, and one long arm bent like an inverted L.

"That's what we thought, but we really don't want to take it apart ourselves," he said. "At least"—with a glimpse of sincerity—"I want to, but the boss doesn't like the idea." The word he used for Grandpa Tanaka was old-fashioned, meaning "master" rather than "employer," the same word many women still used when referring to their husbands.

Eleanor shifted so she could look him in the face. "Shall I try to fix it?" She didn't mind trying a new family dynamic, but would Kazu?

Kazu turned away from the eye contact, fidgeted, then met her gaze again. "I think that may be for the best. Thank you."

He sounded relieved and apprehensive at once.

A sweaty hour or so later, they'd found the problem and jury-rigged a temporary solution.

"If you take care when you're feeding in the pieces," Eleanor said to him as they drank tins of cold coffee from the vending machine that stood outside the shop, "you'll have a couple of months' grace. Then I really suggest you get a complete overhaul."

Kazu nodded, more cheerful than she had ever seen him, and she felt as relaxed with him as she'd ever been. This was the first time in fifteen years they had talked about anything that interested either of them. They shouldn't have waited so long.

"Eleanor-san?" Kazu paused in passing a rag over the table. "Have you ever thought of moving to small business? Wouldn't you get more scope to do the research you want?"

She kept replacing screwdrivers in their case. "Not really. My work needs considerable infrastructure. Besides, small businesses are so unstable that it wouldn't be worth trying. Imagine completing all your basic research, then going bust before you could develop it."

Kazu started wiping again. "I see what you mean. But in small . . ."

He was interrupted by Grandpa Tanaka flinging aside the sliding door with a bang.

"Kazunori, what is the meaning of this?"

Kazu opened his mouth and shut it again, looking more like a blowfish than ever.

"Kazu asked me to take a look at some machinery that's malfunctioning." Eleanor wiped greasy hands on another rag. "It's no big deal."

Grandpa ignored her. "You know I don't like outsiders poking around in here."

Outsiders? For a moment Eleanor was speechless. For fifteen years this man had preached to her about the enlightened way Japanese families welcome their sons' wives.

"Well, Eleanor is family, you know," Kazu mumbled, "And as she's a better mechanic than I . . ."

"That's not what I mean, and you know it." The two of them seemed to be operating on a separate wavelength of shared secrets, at which she could only guess.

Kazu flung his rag on the workbench. Both Grandpa and Eleanor jumped.

"If you'd start moving with the times, we might be able to afford to get it fixed properly," he said bitterly.

Eleanor had never heard Kazu talk this directly. All his polite nuances had gone.

Grandpa bristled. "If by 'moving with the times' you mean accepting jobs outside our area of expertise, you're setting us up for failure."

"How can you know when you've never tried?" Kazu's voice rose in frustration. "You only deal with the same old companies, and half of them are going out of business anyway."

"I've seen you fail." Grandpa seemed to think this was his trump card. "Didn't you learn anything?"

Eleanor was suddenly embarrassed for Kazu, for herself. Even embarrassed for Grandpa, who was always so careful not to be emotional about anything, but was now red with rage. She backed out of the workshop into the relative coolness of the garden.

Mari was sitting on the big rock under the twisted pine tree with her back to Eleanor, talking to someone on her phone. Eleanor caught a glimpse of the face in the phone— young and male.

" . . . terrible. But are you sure? . . . okay, I'll see you in an hour."

She got up and turned around. Her expression, soft and

inward-looking, tightened when she saw Eleanor. She slipped the phone into her shorts pocket and ran her hand over her bob.

"I have to go," she said. "A friend just called. We, um, have an assignment due."

"You know, if you ever need to talk about anything . . ." Eleanor began.

"Mari-chan!" Yoshiko opened the door. "We haven't finished soaking the plums."

"I'm sorry, Mother. I just got an urgent call and I have to go back now."

"Is this because of the implants? Mari-chan, you know your father and I . . ."

"No, Mother. I have to meet someone." She pushed past Yoshiko. "I'll get my bag."

Yoshiko looked at Eleanor as if it was her fault. "Did she say anything to you?"

"She said she has an assignment due."

Yoshiko frowned disbelievingly. "Why didn't she say that earlier? Where's Kazu-san?"

"In the workshop." Eleanor didn't mention the fight with Grandpa. Yoshiko would blame her for that, too.

Yoshiko clicked her tongue in annoyance and went into the workshop.

Mari rushed out the door, cramming her feet into sandals. "Mother, I'll phone," she yelled at the workshop door. "Nice seeing you, Aunt Eleanor," she added, then clattered down the path and out the gate.

Eleanor waved, but Mari didn't look back.

That night, back in the Betta, Eleanor couldn't sleep. For once it wasn't because of robots.

"Masao?" She poked him gently in the ribs.

He gave a barely awake grunt.

"Doesn't it bother you that Grandpa won't let me help out in the workshop?"

Masao turned toward her with a groan. "I never let Grandpa bother me. He'd drive me mad."

"Today he said something strange. He practically accused Kazu of making some mistake."

Masao was silent. She waited with growing impatience. Masao was always slow with his opinions.

"Grandpa's probably thinking of Kazu's failed venture," he said finally.

"Kazu? You're kidding."

"No, really." Masao shifted to face her. "A couple of years after the Quake, we were away that summer because you had a conference in Amsterdam."

She did remember. They took the obligatory souvenirs to Masao's parents after they got back to Japan, but the atmosphere was tense there. She never asked why.

"Kazu got together with some of his mates and rented part of the old milk factory building. You know, in the next block from ours. They were going to make robot toys you could program yourself, taking advantage of the slump after the Quake. They spent a lot of credit livelining the whole building for their equipment. It was the latest thing, but terribly expensive."

Liveline cabling had been invented before the Quake of 2006 but had not come into widespread use until afterward, when the rebuilding of Japan began. Liveline was the most secure of cabling, but even nine years later was still prohibitively expensive.

Masao stroked her hip reflectively. "Kazu said the factory was a mess. They had to move a lot of big equipment abandoned by the milk company down into the basement. And then some other company . . ."

"Mipendo," interrupted Eleanor. "Brought out their personal robot line. Which ruined the market for small companies in that field." Tomita had developed a similar, minor line, based on the Mipendo template.

"That's right." Masao rolled onto his back again. "And

Kazu went bust, along with the money he'd borrowed from Grandpa. Ever since then, Grandpa hasn't let him do anything creative. And he never lets Kazu forget it. Not deliberately, of course."

Eleanor winced at the casual way she'd dismissed Kazu's veiled invitation and her careless comment about small companies going bankrupt.

"You could have told me about this before," she said.

"You never asked. Besides, I didn't think it was fair to Kazu."

"I never saw Kazu as angry as he was today. He said Grandpa wasn't moving with the times."

Masao slid his arm under her shoulders and pulled her close to his side. His warmth dissolved some of her tension. "Grandpa is a stubborn old man. He doesn't want to change the way he's always done things."

"I suppose if I changed my name or produced a batch of grandchildren, he'd be friendlier."

Masao stayed cautiously silent. She didn't want to do the former and couldn't do the latter, after a miscarriage, before she met him, which left her unable to conceive. They had talked this over years ago.

After a moment she relaxed into him. "Do you know what Kazu asked me today?"

"To look at the machine, yes."

"Not just that." She twisted her head back so she could see Masao's face in the filtered moonlight. "He asked me if I'd ever thought about leaving Tomita."

Masao's face didn't change.

"Don't you think that's strange? He practically asked me if I'd work with them."

"Bet Grandpa doesn't know."

"Do you think Kazu was sounding me out before approaching Grandpa?"

"Dunno." Pause. "Yoshiko would be upset. You know about her and the shop, don't you?

She's got a bit of an inferiority complex because she wasn't much help to Kazu. Most of the wives of small business owners do the books. Yoshiko isn't any good at that. She messed up a couple of orders, and Grandpa decided she'd better stay out of it."

Not only did Yoshiko worry about Eleanor's influence on Mari, she probably also worried about Eleanor's taking what was Yoshiko's rightful place in the family business.

"You wouldn't leave Tomita, would you?" His disbelief was palpable.

Of course she wouldn't leave the challenges of research in a top company like Tomita for the claustrophobic drudge of a family workshop. They'd have to leave the Betta. Imagine trying to sleep beside that busy road. And she'd never find the infrastructure her research needed outside a large company or a university. Look at poor Akita, who had joined Tomita when Eleanor did. He worked for nearly four years on neurosilicon interfaces for prosthetic hands, then when the Seikai Lifestyle Reconstruction Plan was announced, the company put most of their funds into construction-related projects. Akita never accepted that. He raised a hell of a stink and left them for another company, although he didn't mention any of this in his recent e-mails.

"I'm worried about our project," she said. "Izumi thinks the budget committee isn't sympathetic."

"What's the worst they can do?"

"Cancel it."

Masao murmured something suitably appalled.

"It's so shortsighted!" she burst out. "Just because we can't give them immediate results . . ."

Masao turned on his side to face her. "It sounds like they're being practical, as management has to be. If there's no demand for humanoid robots, why build them?"

She resisted the urge to swat him. He was merely playing

devil's advocate. "But we have the technology. They're not willing to invest enough to develop it properly."

"That reminds me of the old human clone debates. Just because you can do something doesn't mean you should."

"It's not like that at all," she said crossly.

Silence for a few minutes. She wondered if he'd gone to sleep.

"How's Mari?" he said. "I didn't get a chance to talk to her."

"She got a phone call and had to leave before I had a chance to talk much."

"Probably a boyfriend."

"I hope so." Eleanor tried to think what was different about Mari. "It's like she's decided to keep her real life away from the family."

Masao grunted. "Sounds sensible to me."

She snuggled into him again. She had always envied his ability to drop off in moments. Soon she drifted into a dream in which Yoshiko tried to invite the technician Sakaki, of Kawanishi Metalworks, to tea, but he kept saying, "Ask the robot."

石原

"Here?" Ishihara's voice rose in disbelief.

"Yup." Assistant Inspector Beppu, Ishihara's usual partner, took his scene-of-crime kit from the back of the car and blipped his key twice at the doors to make sure the locks were active. Beppu, who had been on the driving range when Ishihara called him, was still wearing golf slacks and a regrettable Hawaiian shirt that strained over his paunch. The duty officer from Homicide had gone on ahead with the Forensics team.

Two marked police cars and the squat white morgue van were parked right up against the main entrance of the twenty-story, four-block Betta. It was one of the newest Bettas—Ishihara could see a pile of construction rubble to the side of one building, surrounded by a line of orange tape that flapped in the hot breeze, and the curved concrete walls shone blindingly white.

"We should have come by subway," added Beppu. "Too damn hot outside." He wiped the beads of sweat that had jumped out all over his face. Beppu needed to lose about twenty kilos. "That retirement village by the seaside looks better every day."

Ishihara scratched his head. "I thought they said a cult-related group suicide?"

"Yeah, either they got it wrong, or it's a weird one. Come on." Beppu jerked his head at the entrance.

Ishihara shook himself mentally. Don't doubt an incident because it doesn't fit the pattern. Cult-related group suicides had, as far as he knew, all occurred either at country retreats or in run-down midcity communes, often underground. It didn't feel right, this one happening at a Betta. As though he'd found a cockroach in his guaranteed fumigated and insect-free, shiny stainless-steel bathtub.

The lobby was cool inside and crowded with tall plants in blue pots. Natural-seeming light from hidden ceiling panels created the impression of a skylight and made the room look larger than it was. He couldn't tell if the plants were real or not—the flat leaves looked shiny and perfect enough to be artificial. On the other side of the room several men in casual clothes huddled together and stared at the police.

Three uniformed policeman stood talking to a portly man in a gray suit. The man kept raising a hand nervously to his mouth. His words floated through the fronds.

". . . called an emergency meeting of the Residents' Association. This is most irregular."

You bet it is, thought Ishihara.

Beppu chuckled. "I'll take the whiner, you take the stiffs. Right?"

Ishihara nodded. He preferred the company of the dead. They didn't talk. And Beppu had a knack of getting information from witnesses.

One of the uniformed policemen went up with Ishihara in the elevator. The elevator wouldn't move without some fancy button-pushing on the door panel and flashing of a card at ceiling sensors.

"He unlocked this elevator for us," said the constable, with a jerk of his thumb toward the manager. "You go direct to the sixth floor, and nobody will disturb us."

"That's where it happened?" said Ishihara.

"Yes. The owner of the apartment went away on a work trip and got a shock when he came back. Doc reckons the bodies have been there two, maybe three days." He grinned at Ishihara's expression. "The air-conditioning was set to about ten degrees, so it's not as bad as it could've been."

Ishihara chided himself mentally for showing any expression and said nothing more until the elevator doors opened. They followed a beige-walled, brown-tiled corridor.

In the apartment blocks Ishihara had lived in when he first married, the corridors were balconies open to the outside air, cluttered with children's toys, bicycles, and pot plants. In summer, doors were always propped open to let the breeze through. The air was heavy with cooking smells, and noisy with voices and television jingles.

Here, nobody spoke in the cool, aseptic tunnel of the corridor, and only one door stood open. A black-and-yellow crime-scene barrier blocked it off.

Ishihara sighed and pulled gloves and surgical mask out of his pocket. The only good thing about suicides was that he wouldn't be spending the next however many shifts chasing the culprit.

The entrance hall was full of solid, sensible, police shoes. The dead people's shoes would have been packed away as exhibits. The door and lock didn't seem to have been damaged. They must have broken in to use the apartment, but why didn't the alarms sound?

The smell, as the constable had said, wasn't too bad through the gauze mask, merely a sourness at the back of his throat.

"Assistant Inspector." One of the station's forensic pathologists, Dr. Matobe, beckoned him from the inner room.

The apartment was set out very much like his own. A short hall led on from the entry, with a study on one side and a tiny bedroom and bathroom on the other. Then the kitchen/dining room on the left, a living room beyond, and the main tatami room to the right of kitchen and living room. A small verandah completed the whole, which must have been about sixty meters square.

As Ishihara walked through the kitchen he noticed that the dining table was cluttered with cups and unwashed bowls. Just like at his own place. The familiarity made the scene in the room even more grotesque.

The living area was full of bodies. One lay stretched at his feet, as though fallen on the way to the door. Two curled in fetal crouches in front of the vidscreen and one sprawled half-in, half-out of the tatami mat room beyond. No sign of a weapon, no obvious wounds.

They were all naked and all silver.

Ishihara stepped carefully around the body near the door and squatted by the two in front of the screen. One male, one female. Beside them lay two hand computers. Wires were taped to their hands and shaven heads, leading to the hand-coms and the computer drive panel on the living room wall. Both had metal tips on their fingers where the wires were attached.

Can't be electrocution, thought Ishihara. We'd smell the singeing.

"Shock?" he said, raising his voice to be heard clearly through the mask.

"Always a safe guess, Detective." Slim little Dr. Matobe rubbed his hands together. His Playtex gloves squeaked. "From an initial examination that's all I can tell."

He squeezed easily past Ishihara and squatted beside the female body that faced them. "They've had some kind of anaphylactic reaction. You can't see the cyanosis because of the paint. It's a spray-on body paint." He pointed at the bathroom. "The tin's in there."

"You can see their airways have swollen and basically choked them." He raised the chin of one of the girls slightly to show Ishihara her blackened, protruding tongue. Ishihara put up with the sight, but looked away as soon as he could.

"Of course," Matobe hastened to add, "this is off the record. I can give no opinion until we've done an autopsy."

"Right, sure," Ishihara confirmed mechanically. He turned to the other bodies. The one near the living room door was male, the other female. He shivered involuntarily. The silver paint flattened the children's features, made them seem inhuman. Even the pert little breasts and flaccid penises seemed mechanical.

They'd have to interview the other residents—somebody might have noticed something unusual. They'd have to check the movements of the dead kids before they came here.

As he ran through the list of things to do in his mind, he could feel a knot of tension in his chest dissolve. Whenever he bent over a body, he was always afraid it would be his son.

"Assistant Inspector Ishihara." A cheerful voice called him from the entrance hall, and young Kusatsu from Forensics came in, bringing an atmosphere of healthy bustle and a handcom. Kusatsu was fresh and smart and knew his computers backward; for some reason Ishihara became irritated after five minutes in his company.

"I've ID'd them all." He grinned triumphantly.

Ishihara nodded acknowledgment. The Emergency Access Act could be helpful. Kusatsu could quote the case number, then input any information about an individual—in this case, probably photographs—and the National Data Network would find all other information on that individual. It could include everything from birth certificate to credit card status.

"All four were students, the two girls at Ohara Women's College, the boys at Osaka Engineering University."

Both elite universities, and expensive. Kusatsu offered the handcom, but Ishihara shook his head. "I'll look at the details later," he said. "How did they know each other?"

"Apparently they're all members of a local geography

club. They go for walks around Osaka, find neat places no-body's noticed before, that kind of thing."

"Uh-huh. We'll talk to some of the other members of this club, I think. Did any of the kids know the owner of this apartment?"

"Not according to him." Beppu appeared in the kitchen doorway, filling it almost completely. "I ran the photos past him. He's never seen any of them."

"So how did they know when he was going away?" said Ishihara.

"The manager?" Kusatsu looked at Beppu.

Beppu shook his head. "Don't think so, although we'll have to do a proper background check."

"We'll have to do that with all of them," said Ishihara.

"I've got a constable going through the camera logs," said Beppu.

"Good." Ishihara looked at Kusatsu. "What's in those computers?"

Kusatsu shook his head. "We're waiting for the doc to finish. My boys don't want to turn anything on until they've got the whole lot back to our labs. Don't want to risk wiping anything by mistake."

"I can guess what's in the computers," said a female voice behind Beppu.

Beppu stepped hurriedly into the kitchen, and a youngish woman wearing a trouser suit entered from the hall. She held up an ID that flashed more gold than a gangster's watch. Her heart-shaped face was youthful, but her eyes were hard and calculating. She looked surprisingly like that stock character of police manga, the young and attractive fe-male officer who shows up the older male characters.

"Inspector Funo, Prefectural Office Religious Affairs."

Ishihara knew most of the prefecturals in his area, and fe-male inspectors were too rare to forget. She must be a recent arrival from the National Police Authority in Tokyo.

"We've been watching some of these young people," said Funo. She shifted her handbag on her shoulder.

"Not close enough," muttered Beppu.

Funo ignored him. "They may have been involved with a particularly difficult group called the Silver Angels."

Ishihara thought of the paint can.

"Which of the kids did you follow, and how did you know they were involved with the group?" said Ishihara.

"Let's say one of the boys was indiscreet with his e-mail," said Funo. "I can't say more."

The kitchen felt uncomfortably warm and crowded. His imagination suggested that the smell from the bodies was getting stronger, and he was conscious of Dr. Matobe shifting from one foot to the other beside him.

"Let's go outside," he said. "The morgue boys are waiting. We've all seen enough here, I think." He'd have liked to look around a bit more, but he could check the videos later.

The career detective opened her mouth, shut it again, and filed out with the others. Ishihara had no illusions as to who was now in charge of the investigation—any "interest" shown by Prefectural Office meant they took over—but at least he'd kept control of the scene.

"The Silver Angels," began Inspector Funo, as they all finished shuffling into their shoes and flattened themselves against the wall to let the morgue stretcher-bearers past, "are a group of well-off, mostly talented young people. The oldest we know is twenty-five, although we think the leader is older."

"Who's the leader?" said Beppu. "And why haven't we heard of them?"

Inspector Funo raised a neatly plucked eyebrow at the rudeness. She looked like someone had puked on her shiny black shoes.

"The leader," she said slowly and precisely, "calls himself Adam."

Oh great, thought Ishihara. The Christian groups are the most confusing. "I never heard of him," he said. "What does he preach?"

Funo tightened her lips, then relented. "We don't have a lot of information. The group's very close-knit. What we do have is inferred, mainly from Net chat rooms. Our experts sift through material, and they've found postings that fit the group's profile. But we can't be sure the people who post messages are group members."

"And?" prompted Ishihara.

"It's a typical New Millennium group—predict the end of the world through cataclysmic event, personal cleansing through meditation, value of natural healing, rejection of consumerism . . ." She made them all sound like exotic diseases. "They want to use technology to achieve some posthuman state. The group is atypical because they don't have a legal existence and they don't solicit funds. We don't know where they get their money."

"So they haven't made any actual threats," said Ishihara, "But you're worried because if they do, they may have some capability of carrying them out?"

Funo hesitated. "That's right. And today's deaths indicate that whatever they're doing isn't safe. Our priority at the moment is to find Adam's real identity. You have not yet been informed of the group's details because we haven't decided whether they are to be treated as a cult and therefore fall within the jurisdiction of Religious Affairs, or whether they are a terrorist group and, therefore, will be handled by Home Defense."

"Terrorist?" said Ishihara. He knew he looked as dumbfounded as Beppu and Kusatsu. How could those flimsy, gaudy bodies be terrorists?

Inspector Funo paused as the stretcher-bearers maneuvered out the door and past them. Two bodies to a stretcher.

"Unfortunately the details may only be released on a need-to-know basis." She sounded cheerful for the first time. "Therefore, Prefectural Office will be taking over this investigation. We will, as usual, require liaison officers to be appointed from the local station and will require an incident room to be set aside there. My men will arrive shortly."

She bobbed her head. "I'm sure we'll work well together."

Ishihara wasn't sure at all. He consoled himself with the thought that in police manga, the young female detective is almost always rescued at the end by her more experienced male colleague.

エレナ

Eleanor left her apartment on Monday morning puffy-eyed and irritable. In the old days she'd have blamed her disturbed night on the heat, but the Betta nights were cool and comfortable. Must be the unfinished business with that welder and the prospect of a long day's work ahead, getting Sam ready for the budget committee display.

There weren't many people in the corridors at six-thirty. Masao hadn't even grunted in his sleep when she said she was leaving early. Simulated morning light streamed through the corridors, and cheerful music played just at the level of hearing. The ubiquitous cleanbots were still gathered in herds about their recharge stations, out of the way of passersby in small bays at certain intersections.

As she waited for the elevator she noticed one cleanbot marooned by itself near the wall, like a discarded ball with wheels. Perhaps it was the same one that had malfunctioned the other night. She crouched down to check its charge light. Green, which meant fully charged. Strange. She nudged it with her foot, but it didn't move, nor did any of its flaps open so it could raise arms or sensors. Definitely malfunctioning. She rummaged in the bottom of her handbag and found a sweet wrapper, which she dropped right in front of the bat's base sensors. After a ten-second delay, it sucked up the wrapper belatedly, then kept going, following the line of the wall until the corridor curved out of sight.

The elevator pinged at her. *Do you wish to descend?* it inquired in a polite female voice. Eleanor got in hurriedly. As the doors closed she thought she saw the cleanbot reappear. I must remember to tell management about it tonight.

In the lower, main commuting corridor the music was louder, and advertising jingles dopplered in and out of hearing as she passed.

Buy your new Generation S phone implant today and receive a free tattoo!

Where will your *next holiday be? Make it the blue waves of Tottori.*

Be the first girl in your office with the Miss Elegance look.

Two girls in blue high school sailor suits stood in front of this last wall advertisement, giggling and ordering with their phones at the interface. Eleanor wondered whether the makeup would be delivered to their school or to their homes, and what their parents thought about it. She couldn't see Yoshiko letting Mari order goods from a public ad.

The corridor bots here were busy, zooming neatly in and out of people's way if they needed to cross from one side of the corridor to the other. She found herself checking their herd behavior, then stopped, shaking her head at the idiocy. As if a cleaning robot would follow her. You have other things to worry about, she told herself.

In the train a man in a pink short-sleeved shirt and green string tie was sitting in her favorite seat, and all the other seats were occupied. She leaned against the doors and watched the roofs and crossings rattle past. Everything outside baked in the heat, while the fan blew a draft of icy cold air down her neck.

Many of the faces in the carriage were familiar, all residents of her Betta who took the same train every day. Sleepy faces, faces with a sheen of sweat, a keen face bent over a textbook. One or two people were completely asleep, hunched over bags on their laps or drooping to one side.

What would it be like to work in your own business next to home, like Grandpa and Kazu? She knew it wasn't a matter of pleasing oneself—more like being a Ping-Pong ball bounced continuously between contractors, customers, and suppliers. But at least they didn't have piles of senseless administrative work. Like the report she had to write on the Kawanishi Metalworks incident. She swore she'd finish that business with the welder by nine; otherwise, she'd be unable to concentrate on Sam.

The train doors swooshed open, and she retreated farther into the carriage to avoid being squashed by people entering at Amagasaki. In summer everyone left home early to avoid the heat.

A schoolgirl dodged through the crowd as she walked up the carriage, her bare legs in white socks and loafers balancing effortlessly against the train's motion. She didn't even stop reading her comic.

How do we do it so easily? Eleanor would have traded five years of her life to be able to make a robot that walked like that.

It's not done easily, she conceded. It takes years of continual practice for a child to learn to walk. Yet they want us to produce a robot that can walk in six months, a year. As well as integrate all the other systems. We don't give it enough time to practice. After my accident . . . she fingered the scar hidden under her long hair . . . I practiced like hell.

Practice had been the only thing that got her through. She'd done nothing for months but practice simple tasks. In retrospect, it seemed ridiculous, but at the time it was exhausting, and the victories were so very small. Nobody understood how long it took. People tried to conceal expressions of pity, frustration, or disgust as she spent minutes passing change to a shop assistant or stammering her destination to a bus driver.

Caged in the slowness of her own tongue and reflexes, she watched her peers get offered the interesting jobs and knew that by the time she recovered it would be too late; more brilliant young minds would roll along. Maybe that was when it started, the desire to build a robot body that wouldn't break down. She didn't want to return to those dreary days of pulling speech, limbs, thought together, but if it would help her coordinate Sam . . .

There was another message from Akita waiting for her. Tempted simply to delete, she ran her eyes over it, then stopped and read it from the beginning.

```
Sender: A
Subject: A query
Eleanor-san
     I am still awaiting your reply to my
previous message, subject 'catching
up.' I would very much like to see you,
as I have some more information about
my new synaptic converter, which you
will find fascinating.
     Until we meet, I have a question for
you to consider about your research. I
am interested in how you have pursued
the idea of a humanoid robot, and a
little disappointed also. There are
many avenues more worth pursuit. What
is the final goal of your research?
What will your humanoid robots be used
for—slaves to human beings? Companions?
     I look forward to discussing the mat-
ter with you in person.
```

Eleanor deleted the message with a savage jab at the keyboard. Far more satisfying than voice command.

How dare Akita question her research goals, sitting in his country university where they probably didn't even know the meaning of R&D . . .

"Recall deleted e-mail."

She typed her reply, not wanting to be overheard.

```
Akita-san
Before you question other people's
research goals, you should declare your
own. What are you working on now? You
sent me some interesting snippets of
information, but as far as I know, they
could be years old. Where do you stand
that you question my goals?
McGuire
```

That should make him think. If he wanted to insult her, why didn't he call? Vanity, perhaps. He'd always worried how he looked. He probably didn't want her to see his middle-aged paunch or balding head.

She sent the message and tried to put him out of her head. She had enough to do already.

"Industrial Lab Four? This is McGuire, of Systems Two."

The screen activated. "Nishino here. You're early." Her colleague in charge of large industrial robots was as stolid and inflexible as his machines.

Eleanor nodded acknowledgment of the pleasantry. "I've got a T56 welder here . . ."

"The Kawanishi welder?" Nishino interrupted. "Why is it in your lab?"

"As there was nobody here in your lab on Saturday, I responded to the call," said Eleanor stiffly. "The transport people probably had my name when they picked it up."

"I'll send somebody around to take a look." Nishino leaned forward, and the viewer was filled with his broad, red face. He seemed to think she couldn't see him otherwise. "The checkup is only a formality, isn't it? Human error, I was told."

"In a way," Eleanor said. "I wanted to ask you about the welder's ID. Why doesn't it match the one on record?"

He stared at her. "Of course it matches the record."

Eleanor sighed. "When I compare the two, the ID tail is different."

Sweat shone off Nishino's forehead. This was potentially a major problem—how could manufacturers keep track of their products if mistakes like this happened?

"I'll get someone on it."

Eleanor nodded. "I'm sure the number was just entered incorrectly in the first place." And should have been picked up a dozen times since then, she didn't add.

Nishino wiped his upper lip with a blue handkerchief. "How about we look into that while you finish the accident report?"

"Deal," said Eleanor. "I'll send you my notes." She cut the link and sent Nishino the file. She could finish the report as soon as he'd finished. She hoped there wasn't a problem with any other robot's ID processing. The industry would be in a real mess if robots weren't "themselves."

On the other hand, if the robot wasn't itself, maybe that explained why it didn't act like itself. Was she looking at a virus—or a person—that could change a robot's identity? Theoretically, it was impossible. Any attempt to do so would destroy the base programs first, then initiate barriers to prevent rewriting. No one at Kawanishi had the expertise, as far as she knew. So it must have been someone from outside. They could have placed a time-lag device in the robot sometime before the incident.

Kawanishi's maintenance logs should show who accessed the robot recently. She called Kawanishi's number. The day shift manager answered, on audio only.

He wasn't sure when the last maintenance was done. He'd ask the technician to check. Now? Well, if she wanted to waste phone time . . . she just wanted to check the access logs, right? He thought the police already did that. Eleanor repeated she wasn't from the police, she was with Tomita.

The floor manager's verb endings rose a level in politeness. They'd never had a problem with a Tomita robot before. He hoped she could find out what happened. They didn't want to have to get rid of their other Tomita machines.

Eleanor assured him that wouldn't be necessary. She merely wanted to know who serviced the robot last and when it was done.

The floor manager would let her talk to the technician in charge of maintenance. The manager would appreciate it if Eleanor didn't use up too much of the technician's time.

The technician had a young voice with nasal Osaka intonation. He told her that nobody on the floor was allowed access to the welder's controller except the floor managers.

"The last time the controller was checked . . ." He paused, and Eleanor could hear him tapping keys.

"Opened?" she said.

"No, just checked visually. We make sure it's secure. The last time was August 2. Security checks are always done at the beginning of the month. Makes it easy for everyone to remember."

"You haven't had a visit from our tech?"

"Not since, oh, early July. Our other welder is a Zecom machine. It was properly checked on the twelfth. Maybe you guys should be as thorough as Zecom."

Zecom was the biggest manufacturer in the field. They could afford to send their technicians out more frequently.

"What sort of checkup?"

"The usual, I suppose. He was here most of the day. Nice bloke."

"Thank you." She closed the connection and sat staring at the speakers for a while. Nobody at the factory had checked the Tomita welder's controller since the beginning of August. And nobody had opened it since the Tomita technician last visited in July. But the blank in the log showed that the robot was tampered with at least an hour before Mito's death. Which should have been impossible. She groaned inwardly.

Why didn't Mito notice sooner that the robot had stopped?

All controllers were linked on the factory network, so the foreman could see how each job progressed and which machines were at which workstation. The floor manager hadn't mentioned any other machines being off-line. But she hadn't asked, either.

She called Kawanishi again and spoke to the same duty technician. He said they had no other machines with problems.

"How about the other welder, the Zecom one—is it working normally?" she said.

"I can't tell you that." The technician sounded almost cheerful.

"Look, all I'm doing is trying to make sure a similar accident doesn't happen again."

"No, I mean I can't check the other welder because Zecom recalled it."

"When?"

"Yesterday afternoon. They brought a replacement along, too." This last was a dig at Tomita, which hadn't yet organized a replacement—because Eleanor hadn't finished the report.

"This is the number they said to call." He gave her a number with a long-distance prefix.

"Thanks." She closed the connection. Zecom might just be playing the public relations game, demonstrating that they put safety first and were prepared to take a loss if it was necessary to protect lives. But a company as large as Zecom wouldn't bother about a customer as minor as Kawanishi, especially not in these times of stringent budgets. Since the Seikai boom began to slow, everyone feared a return to the depression of the early 2000s. Zecom would be no exception.

Zecom might have recalled their welder because they thought it had been affected by whatever happened to the Tomita welder. The two companies were rivals in a number of fields, including industrial robotics. Zecom was where Akita had gone after he left Tomita. He hadn't stayed there long, obviously. Too much of a prima donna, she thought waspishly.

After a moment's hesitation, she tapped Zecom's number. It was nearly nine o'clock; somebody should be there.

"Robotics lab. What's the problem?" The whining voice sounded unpleasantly familiar. The other person to leave Tomita for Zecom. The one she didn't want to have to ask for favors.

"Hello, Nakamura-san. This is McGuire, from Tomita."

"My goodness. McGuire-san." Nakamura sounded less surprised than she expected. "It's been a long time."

"Yes, it has. How's everything there?"

"Wonderful. I've got a very fulfilling job here."

And you were totally neglected and downtrodden here, Eleanor said to herself. "Excellent. Um, the reason I'm calling is that we recalled one of our robots, a T56 welder, because of an accident. You might have seen it in the papers. We're sure it was human error, but I have found a couple of m . . . minor discrepancies in the controller log . . ." She inwardly cursed her stumbling tongue.

"Why are you calling here, then?" Nakamura interrupted.

"Because you . . . I mean, Zecom, recalled one of your 316 Series welders that was also at the factory.

"I don't know anything about that." Nakamura's tone

grew more pompous. "I've moved on from simple industrial stuff. This is our main research lab, you know."

Eleanor gritted her teeth. "Yes, I know. But the floor manager at Kawanishi—that's the factory where the accident happened—he said the Zecom people gave him this number to call if he had any queries."

Short silence. She wished she could see his face. "Can you activate your video?"

"Sorry, we can't show outsiders our lab." He cleared his throat with a self-conscious eh-hem, another of his little habits.

"So, is your 316 from Kawanishi there or not?"

"I'll go and check. As a personal favor to you."

He'd think it funny to put her in his debt.

"Possibly the carriers gave this number by mistake," he added.

A synthesizer rendition of an old Japanese folk tune replaced Nakamura's voice. The simplistic melody reminded Eleanor of the nationalist trucks that had patrolled the streets of Osaka in preform days, blaring lullabies and military songs so loudly that you couldn't talk as they drove by.

After a couple more bars the song faded, and a high female voice began telling Eleanor about Zecom's many achievements in the robotics industry.

. . . first machine tool factory in the world to use completely automated . . . international links formed in the 1990s have . . .

She wondered if you could put the latest cranial phone implants on hold. Most of the implants were simple vibrators that stimulated nerves in the skin to let users know when they had a call, as well as being fashion accessories. You still had to use a physical phone to listen from and speak into.

. . . Seikai reconstruction plan for Inner Tokyo and Yokohama. Zecom's central role was recognized in an address by the mayor . . .

She'd seen more sophisticated implants that combined ocular and neural navigation aids with tiny embedded microphones that let you listen to calls directly.

Zecom, a symbol of the New Japan. Synthesizer music again.

Nakamura was taking his time. Maybe it was a mistake. Certainly, a 316 welder shouldn't go to the main lab for a routine checkup.

"McGuire-san? Sorry to keep you waiting." Nakamura didn't sound sorry. "The robot is here, but only as a safety precaution. We wanted to reassure the factory owner that *our* machines are safe."

"Fine. So it hasn't been checked yet?"

"Not as far as I know."

"Well, please call me if you find anything that might affect other machines."

Nakamura eh-hemmed again. "I won't be handling such a minor chore, but I'll pass on your request. Good-bye."

"Good-bye," said Eleanor shortly. And good riddance. She wriggled her shoulders, which had stiffened with tension. Tomita had lost one good researcher to Zecom when Akita left, but they were welcome to Nakamura.

Should she tell the police about Zecom recalling their robot? It didn't seem important. She decided to attach a comment to her report and leave it at that. And then she could get back to her own project. At last.

Or so she thought.

"See, there, near the port? When we unscrewed the panel to check the wiring, we found that." Nishino's loud breathing rasped in her ear as she bent over the bottom of the welder's control panel.

A small disc, no bigger than an old one-yen coin, was seemingly welded to the circuitry. Presumably Nishino hadn't levered it off for fear of damaging it before they knew what it was.

"You said you found an interruption to this robot's connection to the factory network?"

She straightened up and stepped discreetly away. Nishino's size and sweatiness made her feel hot.

"Yes, but that's no a reason to go off-line, or to disrupt its program. Neither the port nor the network cable showed any sign of damage."

"I know, but maybe there's some connection with the accident."

She squinted at the faintly luminescent disc. It looked like some kind of biometal.

"We ran a level-two circuit analysis of the way the disc is attached." Nishino put his hand on her elbow and almost dragged her over to a seat before a computer on the lab bench. He was the most "touchy" Japanese Eleanor had ever met. Or he just liked pawing her.

The analysis indicated that the little disc seemed to be designed to carry impulses from the robot's circuitry and convert them (she was guessing here) into data to be transmitted. A transmitter as well as a receiver. It clung to the circuitry of the welder like a minute lamprey to a shark.

"Weird, huh?" Nishino beamed at her.

"Sure is." It was also a neat piece of work. If she could use a similar system to feed sensory input from their Sam robot onto its own neural networks, they might solve its reaction problems. Without having to work with Akita and his pompous e-mails, she added to herself.

"It didn't come from here," she said. "So it looks like Kawanishi did modify the robot, or somebody did. Which voids its warranty."

"That's what I thought. And by the way, the ID tag checked out fine when it left here. We've got visual records."

"Good. I'd like to take a closer look at how this thing works," Eleanor added, as casually as she could. "Can you keep the robot here for a while?"

Nishino leaned on the bench so that his thigh touched her shoulder. "It takes up too much space. Can't you just take the controller?"

And risk damaging it? Eleanor smiled up at him. "You could put it in storage for me. Only for a week or so."

He made a show of nodding reluctantly. "Okay by me."

The intercom buzzed. They could see one of the young women who worked in main administration through the clear upper half of the lab door. Nishino heaved himself off the bench with a grunt and opened the door.

"Good morning, Nishino-san." The girl inclined her head. "Chief Matsuki would like to see McGuire-san in his office."

Eleanor smoothed her hair uneasily. Matsuki only sent someone to fetch you, instead of using his high-resolution intercom, if he was in a bad mood. Nishino managed to pat her on the back as she left and shot her a look of commiseration.

She followed the girl's slim, blue-uniformed back in silence down the hall, up in the elevator, and across the covered walkway from the research labs to the main building. She wished she could have changed out of her ancient indoor sneakers and into outdoor shoes.

When had this kind of peremptory order ceased to annoy her? She remembered, long ago, feeling upset that Japanese bosses never said "please." Now, it was simply part of the job.

Chief Matsuki's office was on the second floor of the main wing of the central building. It occupied the entire width of the wing and looked out on the main gate and the trees and shrubs between the wings. This was the office to which guests were always shown first. It had deep carpet, a couple of Japanese landscapes on the walls, and solid oak furniture. Matsuki firmly believed in the weight of tradition, and that was not found in aluminum fittings.

He sat behind his desk, a round-faced man with round

glasses, all designed to give an impression of smoothness that he didn't deserve. The Mechatronics Division manager, Izumi, stood in front of the desk. Izumi, the closest she had to a mentor at the company, inclined his gray head fractionally and glanced a warning over his wire-rimmed bifocals.

Eleanor knew that look. It meant trouble. She straightened and applied the layers of protective blandness she'd acquired over the years.

"Did you wish to see me?" Her bow added "sir."

Matsuki deliberately ignored her while he finished adding papers to a file.

"McGuire. Where's your report on the robot that was involved in the accident?" Matsuki finally looked at her.

"I'm working on it now," was the best she could do.

"Stop dawdling and finish it." Matsuki wasn't yelling at her, something she'd seen him do to other people, but his language was rough. "The accident was on Saturday."

He stood up and walked to one of the side windows. He looked out, clasped his hands behind his back, and walked ponderously back to his desk again.

"On Saturday," Matsuki repeated. "We've already had three articles in the papers about it. Unfavorable publicity. In these competitive times, the company can't afford unfavorable publicity."

Someone at Head Office had complained to him, and he was passing it on.

"Until we get your report to Head Office, we can't close the case. It looks bad. Do you understand, McGuire?"

"Yes."

"There's nothing wrong with the robot, of course."

"Nothing that we . . . nothing that could have caused the accident."

"That's to be expected. It was human error, as usual." Matsuki sat down again behind his desk, a sign that the interview was over. "I told Head Office that your report was on its way. So make sure it is."

"I will." Eleanor bowed to Matsuki, then Izumi, and excused herself with the humblest phrase she knew.

Her knees were trembling as she stood waiting for the elevator, which annoyed her. Why don't you act more like a foreigner, she sneered at herself. Stand up to Matsuki. Because it wouldn't help—they would find a display of emotion embarrassing for her, and she'd be regarded as someone with no self-control and, therefore, unreliable.

She'd been going to submit the report today anyway. The only question was whether she should send a copy to the police as well. The tiny transmitter might conceivably have had something to do with Mito's death. How, she didn't know. Which meant the police wouldn't know, either. They'd be left with the same conclusion as now—that someone with specialist knowledge from outside Kawanishi tampered with the robot. But at least they'd have the information.

Matsuki wanted to hear nothing more about the whole incident. If she told the police about the transmitter and they started an investigation, it might mean more publicity for the company. Matsuki would be upset.

She had no illusions about her value to the company. They needed her skills, they needed her creativity, and in pre-Quake, pre–Seikai reform days, when international appearances still meant something, they'd needed her visibility as part of their global image. But only while she stayed a team player. As soon as she began to make what they perceived as trouble, that would be the end.

Perhaps not the end of employment, like Akita, but certainly the end of promotion and responsibility; she'd be shuttled back to the U.S. to languish as a regional manager, subordinate to the local Japanese manager and Head Office.

"Shit," she said in English, and slapped the corridor wall. Sometimes she wished she did work in a small workshop like the Tanakas. By herself.

"McGuire-san."

Izumi caught up with her.

"Another hot day we've had." He looked at her carefully. Izumi, stooped and grizzled, reminded Eleanor of an underweight badger, that creature of low cunning and sly sense of humor in Japanese folklore.

Eleanor nodded. The elevator doors opened and they both got in.

"You're off to the lab?" said Izumi.

"To finalize the report, yes." She tried to keep her tone neutral, but some bitterness must have crept in.

"McGuire-san, about that report." Izumi looked sideways at her. "It is important to the whole division that it gets done properly. The budget proposals are evaluated on Thursday, and I wouldn't want the evaluators to be distracted by minor matters." He didn't need to say more. If she upset Matsuki, it could inconvenience everyone in the division.

The doors began to open. Eleanor reached out and hit the shut pad again. Izumi looked at her in mild surprise.

"Chief Izumi, the robot seems to have been m . . . modified after it left here. That voids its warranty, of course, and it isn't our responsibility. But the police should know."

"Indeed." Izumi took off his glasses and polished them on the end of his tie, taking his time. "I think they will receive a copy of your report anyway."

"Will they? I assumed it was an internal matter."

"I should say, I believe they can acquire a copy should they desire one."

"Oh. If they realize they should have a copy, they can ask for one."

"Exactly." Izumi replaced his glasses and looked at her sharply over them. "The detective in charge of the case merely needs to ask."

Eleanor thought of Assistant Inspector Ishihara. He would not be shy about asking for a copy of the report. All she had to do was tell him it was available.

"Thank you for your advice." She bowed with as much sincerity as she knew how.

"One more word of advice, McGuire-san." Izumi half smiled. "You excel at following your instincts, but you are still learning to put the company first. Remember that there is always a way to do both."

He tapped the open pad and left the elevator.

Eleanor sighed and followed him. Life wasn't long enough to learn how to do that.

石原

Prefectural Office's idea of taking over the investigation into the four Silver Angel deaths was to let Ishihara and West Station do the slog work like interviews, while they sat in air-conditioned offices and fiddled with computers.

Ishihara wiped the sweat off his face with his third handkerchief of the day. Monday midday already. He'd like to see career officers like Inspector Funo get out into the hot streets. It would give them an idea what the real police force did for a living. The young network specialist, Kusatsu, had been incensed at the way Prefectural Office treated West Station, especially when he hadn't been allowed to observe the data that was downloaded from the handcoms found in the apartment.

Ishihara had long ago stopped complaining at how the elite of the police force treated the rest. You swallowed the condescension and did the best you could with whatever part of the job they left to you. Kusatsu should get used to it, too; otherwise he'd find himself doing traffic duty on Tsushima, or somewhere equally bucolic.

He tried to match the map in his phone against the street he stood in. If "street" was the right word. "Alley" might be better. It was one of the side streets that ran off the old station area. The new station was underground, several hundred meters away, near the new Betta where the four silver-painted children had died.

He rotated the map in a vain attempt to get his bearings. A tiny S indicated a supermarket somewhere near the old station, but he'd been walking for nearly half an hour now without finding it. Probably closed down, he thought gloomily. Like most of these other shops.

Deprived of their main source of customers, commuters walking to and from the station, most of the small boutiques, bookshops, hairdressers, restaurants, and cafes in the area were boarded up or simply abandoned. Some had been taken over by homeless people. Or perhaps they were the original owners. In the midday heat few people moved, and the place seemed abandoned. Above the tangle of electricity lines and tiled roofs loomed the angular white prow of the new Betta.

Soon this lot will be cleared away for a shopping mall or something connected to the Betta. Will it really be an improvement? He wiped his face again and kept walking.

The Betta where the deaths occurred was not yet fully occupied. The residents hadn't got used to their neighbors, and nobody had noticed anything strange on the sixth floor. Nobody had yet moved into the apartment on one side, and the family on the other side hadn't heard anything through the soundproof walls.

The autopsy report had just come through that morning, and showed that all four victims died of anaphylactic shock, possibly from a reaction to electric current, although this was unlikely. Other analyses were being done, but the results weren't ready yet. All the victims had phone implants augmented so that they could receive aural input directly. It looked like an accident, except that nobody knew what the victims had been trying to do. Prefectural Office's report, which might hold information about the Silver Angels that could give them a clue, wasn't available yet.

The Betta security cameras showed the kids going into the elevator and up to the apartment on Friday night. None of them ever came out again. They didn't appear to have any trouble getting in, which made Ishihara suspicious of the manager again.

One important item of information came from the interviews. The food in the kitchen didn't belong to the owner of the apartment. He said he'd only just moved in when he was called away on business, and hadn't had time to stock the pantry. There should have been only a couple of cans of beer and some mayonnaise in the fridge. Instead, several packaged meals and bottles of soft drink crowded the shelves, and wrappers from seven packets of instant noodles had been squished under the sink. Good job the kids were untidy and didn't put the rubbish in the automatic garbage dispenser. They'd obviously intended to stay a couple of days, indicating they knew when the owner was getting back.

None of the employees of the shops within the Betta recognized photos of the four children. And so far none of the employees of shops near the Betta recognized them either. The kids had probably brought the food with them from wherever they lived. But it was worth checking.

He saw a 24 HOURS sign above a grimy glass door that said QUICK MART in peeling letters. The door jangled a tune in the rear of the shop. Nobody was at the till, although an archaic electric fan wafted air that was barely cooler than outside. Four short lines of shelves filled the narrow space. He nearly turned away—it didn't seem likely that these shelves held the kind of meal that would appeal to four teenagers. At the back of the room refrigerator cabinets groaned with the effort of cooling ice cream, pickles, and cold meats. A door stood open beside the cabinets, but it was covered with dangling plastic strips, so Ishihara couldn't see where it led.

"Hello?" Ishihara called loud enough to be heard by someone in the back room.

Nobody answered, but he could hear the sounds of a television. He edged between the shelves and stood beside the door. "Is anybody there?"

After a long moment he heard shuffling footsteps, then the strips, their original colors faded to a uniform dirty pink, were pushed aside to reveal a wrinkled face topped with wispy gray hair.

Ishihara groaned inwardly. Grandma was minding the store. He'd have to come back later. "Good morning, Grandmother. Is the owner here?"

The old woman, a bent question mark of a person, cricked her neck up to look at him.

"Good morning," she returned equably. "He's just stepped out. And you are . . ."

"Assistant Inspector Ishihara of West Station police." He held up his ID. She squinted at it.

"Wait a minute. I need my glasses."

"There's no need . . ." he began, but she was already shuffling through the plastic strips. She shoved her feet into ancient sandals and hobbled over to the till. Ishihara followed, stepping over boxes of curry stacked beside the shelves.

"I'd just like the owner to look at a photo for me," he said loudly.

"There's no need to yell." She found her glasses next to the till and hooked them on her ears. "I'm nearly blind, but not deaf." She held out her hand for his ID and studied it in silence.

"What kind of photo?" she said finally, handing back the ID.

"It's a photo of some young people who might have come shopping here these last couple of days. We're trying to trace where they went."

"This isn't to do with the gangs, is it?" She clambered onto a high stool set behind the till so she could stare straight at him.

"No, nothing to do with gangs."

"Good. I don't hold with gangs. You'd better show me the photo, young man, because I'm the only one who works here."

Ishihara wondered uneasily if her memory, or eyesight, would be reliable. He magnified the images as large as he could and passed her his phone.

She studied the photographs of the four dead children.

Ishihara knew them all by now. Lissa Takada, nineteen, female, studied English at Ohara Women's College. Tsuneo Obayashi, twenty-one, male, mechanical engineering, Osaka Engineering University. Daichi Ikuta, twenty-one, male, same major as Obayashi. Tomoko Uesugi, nineteen, female, journalism major.

He added in his head, as he always did, *Junta Ishihara, nineteen, male. Economics major, missing since 2008.*

Junta was still alive, he knew it. Somewhere in Japan, maybe in another country if the gang of thugs that abducted him was still exporting its lies to a gullible world. He knew Junta wasn't dead because he'd looked at files of every unidentified body the police had found in Japan over the past seven years. Junta was alive; he just didn't want to talk to his parents.

"I've seen this girl," said the old woman, jerking him back to the present. She showed him Tomoko Uesugi's plump, smiling face, taken from her university ID card. "She came in last Thursday."

"Are you sure?" said Ishihara. The owner of the apartment hadn't gone away until Friday morning.

She gave him an insulted look and lifted a large ledger onto the table by the till with a groan and a thump. "The girl bought . . . let me see . . ." She leafed through pages covered densely with handwriting. "Here we are. Thursday, August 13. Fine weather." She ran her finger slowly down the page.

Ishihara could see there were only four or five entries, but said nothing.

"She bought ten packets of instant noodles, four large

Cokes, and four Cook Home meals." The old woman nodded, as if reflecting it had been a good day for the shop.

"Thank you very much," said Ishihara. "Your cooperation is most appreciated." He bowed, then felt obliged to pick one of the sweet bars stacked in front of the till. "I'll take this, please."

The old woman beamed at him. "Thank you very much." She clanged the till on his five-hundred-yen coin with a flourish. As he left she bent over the ledger, recording the transaction.

He called Beppu, who was still interviewing residents of the Betta.

"This is interesting. The kids bought the food the day before the owner of the apartment left."

Beppu's sweating face nodded at him, distorted in the cheap phone screen. "They knew the fellow was going away. I just talked to a ten-year-old who lives on the same floor. She recognized Daichi Ikuta because Ikuta had some kind of disc player implant, and the kid thought it was cool. She remembers it was Thursday because she'd just passed a difficult test at cram school. She wanted to ask her father to get her a player like that as a reward."

"The owner of the apartment swore he didn't tell anyone he was going, except a couple of people at his company."

"That's what he said." Beppu's voice was skeptical. "Mind you, so far there's no connection between him, the people at his company who knew he was going away, and the four kids."

"We'll find one," said Ishihara with more confidence than he felt. "See you in a few minutes. I'll do one final check of this area to see if I missed any other stores." He put the phone back in his pocket.

There would be some connection; they merely had to find it. Maybe in the kids' families, although he doubted it. None of the parents had any suspicion their child had joined a quasi-religious group. All of the children lived away from home, either at a student dorm or, in the case of Takada, in an apartment rented for her by her parents.

No evidence suggested any of them were close to the others before they joined the geography club, although the two girls might have taken the same classes. Obayashi and Ikuta were in the same prac group in their mechanical engineering class, so they must at least have known each other.

How did they know the man would be away so they could use his apartment? Normally, the only people with access to personal details in the Betta records would be the general manager and the systems manager, who organized the self-cleaning functions of the block. If a resident was away, they might ask the systems manager for extra security on their apartment, or perhaps that it be fumigated while they were away.

Beppu had investigated the manager's background as well and found no connection with any of the dead children. Nor any personal connection with the apartment owner, for that matter.

They were left with the unproved probability that the owner had let slip he would be away, and the children took advantage of that.

How? For that was the other problem. Bettas were supposed to be secure. The apartment door showed no signs of forced entry. Indeed, to take the elevator to the sixth floor, the children needed security chips for that particular block of that particular Betta. Or temporary visitor chips. Which had not been issued, according to office records.

Then, to get into the apartment, they would need the owner's eyes or fingers. Most of the Bettas used retina or fingerprint scans in the security systems. To get around that, they'd have to have an accomplice within Betta system management. There must be a link, somewhere.

The Residents Association had convened an extraordinary meeting yesterday and demanded an explanation from the company that ran Betta security. Beppu went along with one of the Prefectural Office detectives and reported back that the discussion had been "heated."

Ishihara grinned to himself. I bet it was heated. All those people thinking they're secure from the outside world, then some kids just waltz into an empty apartment.

He stood in the shade of a doorway—Polar Bear Dry Cleaning—and lit a cigarette. Nicotine always helped him to think.

At West Station they'd seen no mention of the terrorist suspicion that Inspector Funo had let slip at their first meeting in the Betta. Ishihara's superintendent had received a file that morning from Prefectural Office about the Silver Angels. He passed it on with a grunt to Ishihara and Beppu, commenting merely that they would do well to leave this one to the Prefs.

Ishihara could see why the Prefs were having trouble deciding whose jurisdiction the Silver Angels should fall under.

The group was merely a number of self-declared devotees who followed the instruction of a guru who called himself Adam, real identity unknown. They had not declared themselves a religious organization for tax purposes, nor did they seem interested in recruiting from the general public. Most of the known members were students. The rest were young professionals. There might be many more undeclared members. They didn't have a Web site or a known mailing list at any of the major servers, so it was difficult to eavesdrop on their communications. All the police could do was link the personal information of all of the known members on the National Data Network and hope to make some connections.

It might work. The NDN was the world's most advanced collection of personal data on a national scale. Since the introduction of Citizen Cards in 2005, every significant database in the country had gradually linked up, from government departments to banks, the stock exchange, medical records, everything including your local server usage records.

Most of the information held by the police in the Silver Angels file had come from student informants. The group didn't actually call itself Silver Angels, but participants in several chat rooms had used the phrase, so the police took it as a handy label. Ishihara didn't think this was a good idea—he'd prefer to know what they called themselves. Informants said the Silver Angels people were very close to each other, and close-mouthed. The only thing they let outsiders know was that computers were the key. And rebirth, connected in some way with computers. Literally connected, thought Ishihara.

One student informant said the Angels were up with the latest technology, including implant equipment. That meant money, either stolen or from parents, for none of them worked. None of them were interested in the usual student things—clothes, games, movies, or sex. They all had reasonable, but not good grades.

Ishihara ground his cigarette stub under his shoe and started walking again.

Why did Osaka Prefectural Police regard the Silver Angels as more than a few crackpots? They must have information they weren't sharing. Or they wanted the group classified as a "terrorist threat" so they could use the Defense Access Act to allow police to observe the known members.

A white dog wandered along the opposite side of the street, winding between parked cars and rubbish bins to keep pace with a shambling drunk. As a car backed out of an alley the drunk got in the way, then abused the driver with much shaking of fists and slurred curses. The dog waited patiently.

You and me both, mate, thought Ishihara. Waiting for someone to make the next move.

エレナ

The phone buzzed and somebody called, "It's for you, Chief."

Eleanor stepped over to the wall, chafing at the interruption. She and her team were finalizing adjustments to Sam for their project demonstration the next day. It was after seven-thirty in the evening. She'd called Masao earlier to say she'd be late—who could it be?

It was her ex-colleague Nakamura, calling from Zecom. He was on visual, although the space around him was blurred.

"Nakamura-san."

"It's hot, isn't it?" Nakamura looked exactly as she remembered him. Short, round, with an air of grimy pathos in his badly ironed shirts and ill-cut hair.

"Yes, and it's damn humid as well. Why are you calling?"

He eh-hemmed several times. "I thought you'd like to know, I've got the report from our industrial maintenance department. There is nothing wrong with our welder from Kawanishi."

Eleanor sighed inwardly. Probably the best thing, since she'd handed in her report that afternoon. "Thanks anyway."

"I called back because I realized there's something I forgot to talk to you about before."

"About the welder?" Her attention sharpened.

"Yes, and other things." Nakamura's language was polite enough, but his face was tight with tension, and his voice held a note of something she couldn't quite place.

"But you said there was nothing wrong with it."

"Not technically wrong . . ." He let the sentence hang mysteriously.

Eleanor rerouted the call to the empty lab next door. "I'll be back in a minute," she said to the other members of her team.

They nodded, all intent on their tasks.

Nakamura's image had a vertical tremor. She fiddled with the adjustment pads, then realized it was because he was jiggling his foot, as he used to do in meetings.

"Did you find anything wrong with the welder's ID code?" she said. "Or perhaps an unusual attachment near the network port?"

Silence. Had she given away important information?

"McGuire-san, this is not something we should discuss over the phone."

"This is a secure line. I presume your end is okay, too."

He shifted uneasily, one hand smoothing his shirtfront. "Can't you come here?"

Eleanor snorted. "You're joking. Do you know what time it is?"

"It only takes thirty minutes on the fast train," Nakamura whined. "You could be here before nine. I'm going to be here until about eleven."

"I'm incredibly busy right now. And why should I go all that way?"

"You won't regret it." He said this with such conviction that she almost wavered. "And I could give you a guided tour of the lab . . ."

That would be worth the trip. Rumor had it that the

Intelligent Systems Research Laboratory at Zecom wasn't open to anyone except authorized research staff, not even to Zecom's board of directors.

"McGuire-san, I, um, need your advice. It is to do with the welder, but I can't tell you how. I need to show you." Nakamura actually bobbed his head in clumsy appeal.

"I really can't get away tonight. Why don't I go later in the week?"

"Too late." That strange tone had crept back into his voice. "Please reconsider. I'll be here until late."

"I'll call you back tomorrow," said Eleanor shortly, and cut the connection. Typical Nakamura, creating an arbitrary deadline to manipulate people into doing what he wanted. Well, she wasn't falling for it this time.

The security guard on the main gate at the Zecom complex seemed surprised to see her. She was a bit surprised to be there, herself. But the Sam project was as ready as it would ever be, and something in Nakamura's face or voice had touched her intuition. She'd learned to trust that feeling.

"To see Nakamura-san, did you say?" The guard, paunchy and graying, scrolled down the screen, one thick brown finger pressed against it.

A list, she presumed, of employees, or maybe of approved guests. "That's right. In the Intelligent Systems Lab."

On a television on the side wall a popular host tried to embarrass the guest of the week.

"Don't have your name here." He stared openly at her, then flicked to a new screen. "But Nakamura-san is working late tonight." He slid on the chair to the far end of the desk and pressed a phone switch. They waited, but nobody answered at the other end.

Damn Nakamura. He brought her all this way and didn't have the courtesy to register her as a guest.

"Must've gone to the toilet," grunted the guard. He

glanced regretfully at the TV, then heaved himself out of the chair. He took his cap from a peg on the other side of the booth and disappeared out a door.

Eleanor wondered if he'd gone to look for Nakamura or had simply given up on the whole thing, when he appeared again inside the gates. "Go round the side," he called.

A door opened beside the large double gates, and the guard let her through, grumbling under his breath the whole time. He rolled as he walked, like a sailor.

Their feet scrunched on tiny pale gravel. Eleanor thought it was the overbright lights that made the gravel look pink, but when they entered the main lobby, she realized the gravel probably was pink. To match everything else.

The walls were pale pink. Photographs adorning the walls showed model employees in jackets of a darker pink. The interior of the lift they took down was a tasteful apricot; even the visitor's card the guard gave Eleanor was pink. It all clashed horribly with her hair.

Aside from the color, it was standard Big Company style, Aseptic mode; no friendly notices about QC circles or volleyball practice on the walls, no tea-making niches with unhygienic clutter, or sickly potted plants huddled around ashtrays in little bays. Zecom obviously kept up with non-smoking trends. She was reminded of the detective, Ishihara, wanting to smoke in the factory and the look of disgust he gave her when she objected.

The vinyl floors were squeaky clean and the overhead lights clear. Whichever series of cleaner robot they used, it did a good job.

To get in and out of the elevator the guard had to use his card key. He used it again at the entrance to the research lab, where two sets of doors formed a kind of air lock.

Their footsteps echoed. "Doesn't anyone work late here?" Eleanor wondered aloud.

"Not unless they get permission," said the guard. "Zecom is committed to ensuring its employees have private lives as well as company lives." This last was said in a rush, as if he didn't want to forget it halfway through.

Outside the elevator and at the start of the main corridor, a time clock and neatly labeled cards placed prominently on a table indicated that Zecom's research staff were expected to maintain the same work hours as the factory. Nobody had yet invented a computerized system as tamperproof as the time clock.

They walked through a large office space with desks arranged in neat rows. Each row had a larger desk at the end. Every desktop was clean and uncluttered, all the pale gray monitors and keyboards aligned at the same angle. There were no memos stuck carelessly to screens, no reference books left open at a particular page, no teacups or photographs or sweet wrappers or slippers under chairs, or any sign that human beings ever worked there at all.

The only wall decoration was a single heavily framed message in square calligraphy exhorting Care, Quality Control, and Cost Efficiency.

Was Nakamura happier here, in this atmosphere of rigid control? He'd always disapproved of the relaxed attitude at Tomita, especially in her department. But one of her section chiefs disapproved, too, and worked around it. Perhaps Nakamura needed the structure. Or perhaps he found himself stuck here with no way out. She could see why Akita hadn't lasted long, though. He'd been far less of a team player than Nakamura.

The guard led her through the office, down another corridor past rooms marked DEPARTMENT SUPERVISOR—he gets his own room here, thought Eleanor enviously—and DIVISION CHIEF, then used the card key to open another door marked NO ADMITTANCE AUTHORIZED PERSONNEL ONLY.

The lab was a large room, divided into an open central area with small bays down both sides. Each bay contained a desk, computer stations, and chairs. The open central area held several assembly line mock-ups and a number of robots and machine tools.

Most of the bays were dark, but strong lights illuminated the central area in the second half of the room. Only one of the bays was lit.

"Nakamura-san," called the guard. "You have a guest. I need you to stamp the forms, please." His voice echoed in the stillness.

No answer.

"This is strange," muttered the guard. He strode down the line of machines in the middle, keeping carefully to the outside of the striped safety tape on the floor.

Eleanor followed, trying not to peer too obviously at the robots and equipment.

The guard stopped so suddenly she ran into his back.

"Sorry," she said, flustered, "but you . . ."

Then she saw why he'd stopped.

A figure in a pink lab coat lay on the floor beside a medium-sized industrial robot. The robot's arm was outstretched above the man, and blood pooled under his head.

"Oh, no." The guard stepped forward, reaching for a pulse, and Eleanor woke from her shock in time to shout at him,

"Stop! Wait a second."

The guard, surprised, did stop.

She knelt, found the robot's power cable leading to a switch around the other side of the workbench, and shut it off. It should have been at total shutdown anyway, but she wasn't going to take chances.

"Now."

The guard felt the figure's pulse and shook his head. It was Nakamura. She stared at the crepe-soled loafers he always used to wear in the lab. The squeak had annoyed everyone. She kept her eyes away from his head.

"Are you okay?" the guard asked, his thumb tapping a

number on an old-fashioned hand phone. His own face was pale under its tan.

"Yes." She'd thought the guard shifty-eyed and unpleasantly presumptuous in how close he got to her in the elevator. But in the face of the shocking thing on the floor, he was a haven of normalcy.

He was calling 110. Ambulance? He looked at Nakamura, then quickly away again. No, they didn't need an ambulance. They needed the police.

Then he was talking to someone else, probably a senior manager from the way he bowed at nothing as he talked and the polite register of his language.

She must concentrate on something, or she'd be sick.

She backed into the bay and flicked the computer's touch pad, intending to check what Nakamura had been doing with the welder. But instead of humming alive, the drive stayed silent, and the screen remained gray. She held her hand right in front of the heat sensor. Nothing. She tapped the restart pad. Still nothing. Checked the wall connection—livelined here, of course, and plugged in.

Why would he shut down the computer in the middle of an investigation?

She looked back at the robot. It was the same 316 series welder as Zecom had at Kawanishi Metalworks. Possibly the same one. But Nakamura said Zecom's maintenance department found nothing wrong with the welder. Why did he bring it in here—had he found a disc like the one on the Tomita robot, after all?

The welder showed none of the stresses that should have been apparent from hitting an unprogrammed object in the middle of a movement. The end-effector was twisted under a dark and sticky coating, but the arm itself was right where it should be. None of the joints or leads showed impact fissures.

She walked around to the controller, which sat on a bench on the other side of the robot.

"Better not touch anything," said the guard. He'd finished his call and was checking each of the bays.

She nodded. The controller lights were off, as she'd cut the power at the wall. She couldn't remember if the lights had been on when they came in.

What's wrong with this picture? She let her eyes lose focus so she could look at the whole scene—the white lights illuminated the tableau as if on a stage. Man Sprawled Lifeless under Avenging Mechanical Arm of Death.

That's what bothered her—it was so obvious.

If Nakamura had been hit, then fallen where he now lay, the pressure-activated safety mat would have sounded an alarm. Nakamura might have disabled the mat, true. But Nakamura had never, in all the years Eleanor knew him, turned off a safety feature. If anything, he was obsessive about turning them all on.

Not only the safety mat. In fact . . . she walked around the robot to stare at it from the other side. In fact, Nakamura couldn't have been hit by this robot and fallen where he had. This time it wasn't a question of the robot arm moving outside its programmed arc, as when Mito was killed. This time it was physically impossible for the robot to make that arc.

The robot had been set up.

Her hands itched to examine it, but she didn't dare. She crouched down and tried to see its network port, but the corner of the table hid it.

Voices boomed in the corridor, then the door at the far end banged open.

Two uniformed policemen followed another security guard into the lab. All the overhead lights came on.

Eleanor straightened hastily.

"What happened here, then?" said the first policeman loudly and jovially, as though to idiots. He had a broad, red expanse of face out of which small eyes peered.

The other security guard disappeared back up the corridor.

The policemen advanced into the lab, and the speaker's tone changed when he saw Nakamura's body.

"Trouble all right. You did right to call us." He turned his back on them and spoke briefly into his phone.

"Was he like this when you found him?" asked the second policeman. He was small and colorless, like a bleached imp.

"Of course. We haven't touched anything." The security guard sounded cross, as though his professional reputation had been impugned.

"I always said these things were dangerous," said the small policeman.

But they shouldn't be dangerous, Eleanor thought, not if you take the proper precautions. And Nakamura always did.

The first policeman, the one with the piggy eyes, started toward Nakamura, then hesitated. He pointed at the robot.

"Is that thing turned off?"

"Yes," said Eleanor.

The constable knelt beside Nakamura and checked vital signs, ignoring the security guard's pointed comment that he'd done it already.

"Who are you?" said the small policeman to Eleanor.

"She's a visitor." The guard looked up from where he hovered over Nakamura and Piggy. "I brought her down here to see him." He jerked his chin at Nakamura.

Eleanor chuckled mentally. As a visitor, she'd been an outsider to the guard when she arrived. But now, in the face of police questioning, as a visitor to the company she was token "family," and therefore needed protection.

"At this time of night?" said the small policeman.

"He called me in Osaka," she said. "He wanted me to come and discuss some research."

"Research?" The policeman frowned in disbelief. Or perhaps it was his natural sour expression. "You'd better tell all this to the detectives when they arrive."

"He's definitely gone." Piggy stood up. "You two had better go upstairs and wait for the 'tecs."

He shepherded them toward the door. The guard muttered something about know-it-alls. Eleanor was glad to get out of there. Nakamura dead was horrible, but worse was the obvious falsity of it all. Someone had killed him, and it wasn't the robot.

石原

"Oy, Ishihara!" One of the other detectives held his hand over the pickup of the vidphone as he yelled across the room. "Line three."

Ishihara waved his hand wearily in reply and punched 3 on his desk monitor. It was after ten on Monday night and he didn't want to talk to anyone.

Only the audio came on. The voice at the other end of the phone said, "Hello, Ishihara. This is Mikuni, at Okayama Prefectural. It's been a while."

Ishihara shook himself awake mentally. "Mikuni, you old devil. It's been five years. How are things out in the sticks?" Mikuni was probably the only detective at Okayama whom Ishihara hadn't offended during his term there, or maybe he was just thick-skinned.

"We have our little problems," Mikuni's voice was still calm and mellow. "Like now. I thought you might be interested, seeing as how you had a similar case recently."

Not more Silver Angels, surely. Ishihara reached for a pen. "I'm listening."

"Bloke got hit by a robot. One of those industrial things, not a proper robot."

Ishihara opened his mouth and shut it again while his brain caught up.

Mikuni went on. "Fortunately, it's in a robot factory . . ." Someone spoke in the background. "I mean, a research institute. Zecom. Big machine tool company, high profile, international connections."

Okayama Head Office had probably put together a response team immediately.

"There's no shortage of experts," Mikuni said. "In fact, we've got one of yours as well."

"What do you mean, one of ours?"

"I mean that foreigner you quoted in your report on your factory case. I noticed it in the bulletin this morning."

"McGuire?"

Mikuni said something off to one side, then came back on again. "That's the one. She discovered the body. Don't quite know what to make of her evidence."

Ishihara opened his mouth to say that McGuire wasn't "his" foreigner, then shut it again.

"What do you mean?"

"She says it wasn't an accident."

"Give me an hour," said Ishihara.

"Good." Mikuni sounded relieved. "Go to the Zecom Industrial Engineering complex. If you're driving, come off the highway at Kusakabe interchange. Or change from the fast train at Zecom Hayakawa and go to the last stop on the Zecom monorail."

"No worries." Leave it to Mikuni, a dry, observing part of him said. It's not likely the two incidents are connected. McGuire can take care of herself. But his instinct screamed, "go," and he knew better than to ignore it.

"Forensics are still crawling around here," said Mikuni. "By the time you come we should have some results."

"Right." Ishihara signed off quickly and left.

*   *   *

Mikuni met him in the lobby at Zecom. A good thing, too, as he'd never have found his way in the huge complex. Mikuni hadn't changed much—the horn-rimmed glasses still gave him the deceptive look of a mild-mannered academic. His solid frame was a bit thicker around the waist, and his short hair was still dark, but had receded to a fringe around his ears. Ishihara stopped himself from touching his own gray thatch of hair just in time.

"You were quick." Mikuni pointed to a door at the back of the lobby. "We've got a temporary incident room set up in there."

"What happened?" said Ishihara as they walked.

"One of the researchers, Shigeo Nakamura, got hit with a robot arm. Looks like an accident, but we're not sure yet."

"What aren't you sure about?"

"Local constables found a window in a ground-floor toilet open. But the main building security system showed no intruders. Nobody on camera." He ushered Ishihara into a small room, set up as an interview room with comfortable chairs and a small desk. It was also now crammed full of laptops and handcoms, uniform jackets on the back of chairs, briefcases and incident cases on the floor, and disposable coffee cups everywhere, many of them used as ashtrays.

"This is Assistant Inspector Ishihara from Osaka, West Station," Mikuni announced to the two men and a woman who were arguing over something on a computer screen. They all said hello cheerfully and turned back to the screen.

Ishihara didn't catch their names and didn't worry about it.

"And?" he said to Mikuni.

"And your specialist says the robot was set up." Mikuni picked up a coffee cup and swirled the dregs in the bottom. "How reliable is she?"

Ishihara raised a hand in protest. "I only talked to her briefly about that Osaka case. It seemed like she was pretty clued in about the industry."

"I guess we should listen, then. We confirmed Nakamura did call her at seven-thirty. I've got one of our engineers standing by to examine the scene, but I wanted to let her explain first. We can always get our man to confirm what she says." Mikuni took off his glasses and polished them on his shirt. "You want to see the lab first, or the gaijin?"

"Is seeing the lab going to tell me anything?"

"Didn't tell me much."

Mikuni said that McGuire had been waiting in another meeting room for two hours. Ishihara hoped she wasn't too pissed off—he didn't want to waste time calming her down.

He needn't have worried. She was curled up asleep in one of the low chairs, shoes on the floor beside her. She was wearing a cream suit, and looked small and pale against the dark pink cushions.

He hesitated, then coughed loudly.

She jumped and half sat, smoothing down her rumpled jacket in an automatic movement. Her face relaxed a bit as she recognized him. "What are you doing here?"

Ishihara inclined his head. "That's my line."

She squished her feet into her shoes and stood up, smoothing her hair. "If you've come to get me out of here, you can have any line you like."

"Why are you here? Does it have anything to do with the death at Kawanishi Metalworks?"

She sighed. "I don't know if it's anything to do with the death. It's certainly something to do with the robot. The welder, you remember?"

Ishihara nodded.

"Which reminds me." She smacked her hand on her thigh in a flamboyantly foreign gesture. "My report on the Kawanishi robot is available. I suggest you request a copy."

"Okay, but when did Nakamura . . ."

"I called Kawanishi this morning . . ." She glanced up at the wall clock. "Yesterday morning, to ask if they'd had any problems with their other welder, the Zecom one. They said no, but it had been recalled. So I called Zecom, who said they basically only recalled it as a PR exercise."

She paused as if she didn't want to go on.

"And?"

She avoided his eyes this time and spoke to the pink carpet. "I spoke to Nakamura in the morning. He called me back last night and said he wanted to tell me something about the welder. Or something connected with it. When I got here, he was dead." She said the last quite flatly.

"Do you know what he wanted to tell you?" said Ishihara.

She shook her head.

"Why call you and not the police?" he wondered out loud.

McGuire shifted from one foot to the other, then looked up to meet his eyes directly. "He used to work at Tomita, in my department. Maybe he felt he could confide in me. Or maybe it wasn't a matter for the police."

Ishihara, momentarily distracted by the gray of her eyes, took out a cigarette and lit it. "Why did he leave your company?"

"He didn't like the way we did things," she said shortly.

Ishihara decided to leave it at that for the moment. "What did you tell Inspector Mikuni?"

She stared at the floor for what seemed a long time before replying, as though trying to decide something.

"It's not what it seems."

"What isn't?"

"Nakimura's . . . death."

"Were you good friends?"

She snorted and looked up. "I couldn't stand him."

"Then don't feel guilty if you're not upset."

"I'm not . . . this isn't a matter of how I feel. The evidence points to murder." She threw her hands up helplessly. "It sounds like a TV melodrama."

"Show me."

"He clocked in at seven-thirty last night," said Mikuni. They were in an elevator on the way to the lab. "We've got witnesses who saw him eating dinner in the canteen after six-thirty, but he didn't talk to anybody."

"These researchers work all bloody hours." Ishihara glanced at McGuire, but she stared blankly at the elevator doors.

"He wasn't supposed to." Mikuni let both Eleanor and Ishihara leave the elevator, then followed them out into the corridor. "They're fussy here. He had to get written permission from his supervisor."

"Who's that?"

"Director of research. Fellow called Yui."

"Weird name. Was he here when the body was discovered?"

"No, we called him at his apartment. He's been overseas, only got back this afternoon."

They went past the constable at the door of the lab and down to an area in the middle, cordoned off with familiar orange tape. McGuire looked a bit pale, but not like she was going to puke or anything.

A robot as tall as a man stood on a stand in the middle of the room, surrounded by equipment on a table and benches. He called it a "robot" in his mind, but it still only looked like an arm on a base, like a crane. Beside the robot was a chalked outline on the floor. Uniform branch liked their traditional chalked outlines.

"So what's the problem?" said Mikuni. "What's she going to show us?"

He looked at Ishihara as he spoke, as if expecting him to translate. Ishihara passed McGuire a pair of platex gloves and pulled on some himself.

She fiddled with controls at the bottom of the robot stand.

"I'm turning off the alarms," she said, without looking up. "Please stand where Nakamura would have been standing when he fell."

Ishihara looked at the chalk lines and positioned himself facing the table. 'This right?"

"Yes," said Mikuni and McGuire together.

Ishihara shifted one foot onto the rubber mat next to the robot and an alarm squawked, making everyone jump.

McGuire flicked a switch hurriedly. "Sorry."

Ishihara waited, keeping an eye on the long robot arm.

"I've disengaged the grasping part of the program. And I've got my finger on the stop button." She pointed to a large, red button on the other side of the robot's control box.

With a shudder, the robot started up. Ishihara stood quite still. For an insane second he wondered if McGuire was behind both deaths and he'd just given her the chance to dispose of himself.

The robot's arm moved quickly, but not too fast to follow. Back, forward, turn, dip swivel. And repeat.

"This is at one-eighth speed," said McGuire, loudly to be heard over the rumble of the engine.

Sweat dripped off Mikuni's forehead.

"Normally, it wouldn't use a continuous series of movements. It waits until a piece is placed on the table and the signal is sent to perform the next task."

The table on Ishihara's left ground around 180 degrees and fixed itself with a thunk directly in front of him.

"I'm skipping the next part because it doesn't move around."

The robot arm swept up to rest for thirty seconds before swinging back to its original position. At no time had the arm come near Ishihara's head or the upper half of his body, and he was a lot taller than Nakamura.

"Thank you, Assistant Inspector. That's the entire sequence." McGuire turned the robot off and faced them. "You see? It couldn't have hit Nakamura, even if he disabled the safeties for some reason. Which he wouldn't. And if something happened in the middle of its routine, I wouldn't have been able to start it up and put it smoothly through the program."

Ishihara stepped away from the work cell.

"So what are you saying?" Ishihara pulled his cigarettes from his pocket, then twisted the empty packet with a scowl.

"He was either assaulted here by someone and left to be found. Or he must have been hit somewhere else and brought here."

"But it's Nakamura's blood on the end there all right," said Mikuni. "And Forensics confirmed the wound fits the machine."

McGuire tapped at the controls again, then walked around to the front of the robot. She reached up, grasped the bloody end-part with her gloved left hand and unclipped some leads with her right. Two good twists, and she held the welding tool as a separate piece of machinery. Ishihara could see her wrist droop, and when he took it from her it was so heavy he could barely hold it in one hand himself.

"Will that do as a weapon?" she said.

Ishihara put the chunk of steel on the table. "We'll need to print this," he said to Mikuni. "Who could get in?"

Mikuni shook his head, his eyes on the robot hand. "It's a card-key entry. Only employees, and only those with permission can get their cards enabled after hours. The day shift finishes at six, and the factories are clear by half past. Senior duty staff and security services make sure the rooms are clear before locking up."

"There's no night shift?"

"Not people. The robots keep working all night. There's one person on duty in the central monitoring station of each factory."

The fingerprints and other residues would have to be checked against those of people with access authority and, possibly, with the rest of the company. Shit of a job, and sometimes the results took so long it was easier to try and break a suspect's alibi. Especially as organic residues weren't admissible as sole evidence.

"Nobody came in the front?"

Mikuni shook his head. "Only McGuire-san." He turned to McGuire. "Who would know how to do this?"

"Someone with a basic grasp of industrial robot maintenance who has access to the controller."

Ishihara raised an eyebrow. Half the company had a basic grasp of industrial robot maintenance.

McGuire saw his expression and shrugged crossly. "I don't know. This lab's supposed to be top secret."

"So you don't think it was someone from outside the company?" Mikuni seemed to be thinking aloud, and Ishihara enjoyed seeing McGuire look down her long gaijin nose at him.

"I don't think that's likely. How would they know about the robot, and how could they get in?"

"Nakamura might have let them in," said Mikuni.

There were no names on the visitor's list last night, not even McGuire's. If Nakamura forgot to list her, he might have forgotten to list someone else. Or the murderer might have entered through the downstairs toilet window, and Nakamura let them into the lab. And watched while they

disconnected a weapon? Ishihara frowned. Unless Nakamura had already disconnected the hand and the murderer
picked it up because it was the handiest weapon.

"Whatsisname . . . the director of research, Yui, said he
heard Nakamura has gambling debts in town."

In other words, it might be a gang killing. But someone
from the gangs would carry his own weapon. And Nakamura
surely wouldn't have stood placidly by while some gangster
wandered around the lab and hefted heavy objects. He'd
raise the alarm. Or try to leave. Or at least try to defend himself. And a gangster wouldn't know how to set up the death
to make it look like an accident.

"If you don't need me anymore, I should get back to
Osaka," said McGuire. She peeled off the gloves and
dropped them on the table. "When you start up that computer again, I'd appreciate it if you could pass on to me any
information about this welder or about Kawanishi Metalworks
that you find. It might help me determine what happened
there."

Mikuni gave Ishihara a look that meant trouble. "We
looked in that computer. There's nothing in it."

McGuire raised her eyebrows. "But that's the workstation Nakamura would have been using."

Mikuni rubbed his forehead tiredly. "Someone's wiped it,
then."

"That's all right. Nakamura always made backup files,"
said McGuire.

"What do you mean by backup files?" Mikuni gave
Ishihara another troubled glance.

"Computer files saved on discs, paper files, files saved on
another hard drive—probably one of the networked computers in this room." McGuire explained as if to a child.

"These discs and things would be in his desk?" said
Mikuni.

McGuire looked at him, her brows drawing her face together in one of those exaggerated foreign expressions. "You mean you haven't found any backups?"

Mikuni cleared his throat. "Not as such. We might have overlooked some."

"I hope so," said McGuire. "Because if you can't find any backups, that means whoever killed Nakamura took them. And the reason he was killed is probably in those files."

"How can you be sure . . . ?" Mikuni began, but Ishihara interrupted.

"We need to talk. McGuire-san, I'll give you a lift back to Osaka. Would you mind waiting in the lobby?"

She looked at him doubtfully. "I can take the fast train."

"It's easier by car," he said.

"Thank you," she said stiffly. She nodded at Mikuni.

"Thank you for your help," Mikuni said hurriedly. "The constable will see you to the lobby."

She left.

"Maybe Nakamura just forgot to make backups today," said Mikuni. He took off his glasses and massaged the bridge of his nose. "I can't build a case around that."

"No, but you can take it as another suspicious circumstance," said Ishihara. "McGuire worked with Nakamura for several years. She must know something about him."

"We'll check with his coworkers here," said Mikuni grudgingly.

Ishihara left it at that. "Can you check whose card was used on the door?"

Mikuni nodded. "We did that. Only Nakamura's card was used last night in the lab. Once at 7:00, then again at 7:50, then again at 8:05."

"Was Nakamura's card still on him?"

Mikuni shook his head. "No. He must have let the murderer in. The murderer took the card when he left. We're searching for it now."

"It's a damn small thing to search for."

Mikuni nodded glumly.

Ishihara straightened up and glanced at the time: 3:45. He'd better get McGuire back to Osaka.

"Good luck. Call me if I can help."

Mikuni raised his hand. "Thanks for coming down."

When Ishihara reached the lobby, a tall man in a striped suit with pointy lapels was talking to McGuire.

She turned to Ishihara, relief on her face. "This is Director Yui," she said. "He's the head of research here."

"Developmental research," corrected the man. He eyeballed Ishihara from behind thick-rimmed glasses, the latest fashion.

He must be in his early fifties to be in that job, but his tanned, smooth skin didn't show it. Rejuv therapy, maybe. Ishihara summed him up as *educated and still smart*. And obviously trying to pump McGuire.

"S'a pleasure," Ishihara grunted. "You're in charge of the lab, then?"

"In a sense, yes." Yui smirked at McGuire as though referring to a shared secret.

McGuire managed a small, expressionless smile.

"I am ultimately responsible for the research and personnel here, yes," Yui went on. "But I don't interfere in the, er, housekeeping, so to speak."

Yeah, yeah, we know you're too senior for all that. Ishihara sighed mentally.

"So you knew the corpse well?"

McGuire winced at the flat, unadorned phrase, but Yui ignored it.

"Young Nakamura was with us for, let's see, nearly four years. I didn't know him socially." Yui managed to imply the impropriety of such an idea. "But I took an interest in his work, naturally. And it concerned me if he wasn't happy at the company."

"In what way wasn't he happy?"

"I said, 'if,' Inspector. As far as I know, young Nakamura liked his job. Such a sad accident," he added belatedly.

"You didn't notice anything unusual about his behavior recently?" Ishihara didn't expect much of an answer.

"What are you implying, Inspector?" Yui drew himself straighter.

Ishihara sighed again. Nobody ever just answered the questions. "Nothing. I'm trying to find out what happened."

"Actually . . ." Yui paused.

McGuire watched him warily.

Ishihara waited a moment before prompting. He felt Yui was waiting for the prompt. "What?"

"Nakamura did seem a little preoccupied these past months. His work wasn't as thorough as usual."

McGuire made an ungenteel sound like a snort. "What was Nakamura working on? When he contacted me, he said he had some information about a welder from a factory in Osaka where there'd been an accident."

"I'm sure he was just being cautious," said Yui smoothly. "He was a cautious young man."

"Why was he preoccupied, do you think?" said Ishihara.

"I don't know." Yui spread one hand in denial. "But someone mentioned they'd seen him betting at an establishment in the town."

"Betting, huh?" Ishihara pretended to think aloud.

"It doesn't sound like him," said McGuire shortly. She met Ishihara's eye, then looked obviously at the door.

"He must have made cautious bets," said Ishihara. "You've been overseas this week, Director?"

"A short trip to Shanghai, Inspector. Zecom has a factory there."

"It's good of you to come in at this hour. You must be jet-lagged."

McGuire sighed and looked at the door again.

"I went home earlier," said Yui. "At about eight o'clock."

"Ah," said Ishihara. "Nice meeting you." He wished Inspector Mikuni luck with Yui. The man would be a bastard to interview.

Yui inclined his head in farewell, a little less than politeness demanded.

Out in the corridor, McGuire's shoulders drooped and her feet dragged.

"What did he want to talk about?" said Ishihara.

She concentrated with obvious effort. "He said he's upset about Nakamura, offered to call me a car back to Osaka. He didn't say so outright, but m . . . mainly he wanted to know why Nakamura invited me out here tonight."

"Why did Nakamura call you?"

"I told you, he said he had information about the Kawanishi welder."

"What information?"

"I don't know." She pronounced each syllable carefully. "He didn't have a chance to tell me."

Ishihara fished in his shirt pocket for his cigarettes, remembered the packet was empty. "I wonder why Yui was so concerned about that?"

"He's probably worried Nakamura was spilling info about their latest wonder robot, whatever it is," she said.

"Industrial espionage?" Ishihara considered the idea. As motivation for murder, he found it pretty thin, but he was aware that company men took this kind of thing seriously. "Was Nakamura's research important enough to make that a possibility?"

"I doubt it."

"Maybe he fell victim to professional jealousy?"

She half smiled. "If anything, he'd be jealous of others. But in a place like this, the content of research isn't the only cause for bad feeling. People get upset because someone takes a sunnier desk, or gets a newer computer, or takes an unscheduled half day of leave."

"Was he difficult? Made enemies easily?"

"He m . . . may have changed after he came here." Her eyes met Ishihara's, then slipped away.

He wondered if she stammered in English, too. It upset her, he could see her wince each time she did it.

"I thought foreigners got to the point," he said. "Why worry about being fair? The man's dead, it can't hurt him."

Her face went a little paler, if that were possible. When she spoke, he realized it was from anger.

"When he worked with us, he was devious, small-minded, and prying," she said tightly. "He had all sorts of annoying habits."

"Like?"

"Like he used to clock in early and go home early, but all he ever did for the first hour of the day was read the newspaper."

She ticked them off on strong, knobby-jointed fingers. "He always claimed more than his fair share of credit in a project, he criticized m . . . members of his team in front of senior staff, he argued with decisions that had been reached by fair process, and he used to lurk around the junior female locker room on Friday afternoons. That last is hearsay," she added reluctantly.

"Sounds charming. What kind of worker was he?"

She thought for a moment. "He would never explore an option that was unlikely or unorthodox," she said finally. "He never seemed to trust his intuition."

"Methodical, you mean?"

"Yes, he was good at setting up experiments once someone else had decided the parameters."

This cautious, methodical bloke would have hidden his backups in predictable places. If you knew his habits, that is. And as McGuire said, the murderer probably did.

"Why do you ask?" she interrupted his train of thought.

"I was wondering if he would have done something like hide the files in full view."

"The purloined letter method?" She used an English phrase but he thought he understood.

"Yeah, somewhere so obvious we looked right past it."

"Like sending e-mail to himself? Whoever killed him probably saw it first," she said gloomily. "Don't forget to check his extra locker."

He stared at her.

"Once when we were out drinking Nakamura told me that he always kept an extra locker in one of the other change rooms, possibly the women's," she explained. "Under another name. He swore me to secrecy."

Ishihara stared incredulously at her, and she shrugged crossly. "He said he felt safer."

"Safer, right. I'll pass it on," he said.

"And he m . . . might have rented a storage facility somewhere else," she added. "You know, one of those you can open with a password."

Ishihara groaned inwardly at the thought of the tens of thousands of rental lockers, rooms, and cupboards scattered throughout the Greater Osaka area. Even with increased apartment space in the Bettas, people seemed to need places to put things.

They left the building and walked to Ishihara's car, parked in the guest parking lot in front of the main lobby. The sky glowed blue-cream on the eastern horizon, although it was still too dark to see the time on his phone. The fluorescent dial in the car said 4:20. By the time they got back to Osaka it would be six-ish.

"You'd better drop me at Tomita," said McGuire faintly as they got in. The angles of her face looked sharper.

"You sure you want to go back to work?" he said, as they drove out the Zecom security gates and past the windowless first-floor walls of the Zecom Betta, built like a fortress.

"I'm sure. I've got a m . . . major demonstration today." She untwisted the seat belt and rebuckled it. Her movements were jerky and uncoordinated. "If it's inconvenient, put me down at the fast train station."

"You should go home. Tell me, McGuire-san, you ever heard of *karoshi?*"

"Death from overwork?" She focused on the dashboard. "You think Nakamura might have stayed one night too many and got careless? He never showed that much enthusiasm when he worked for us."

Ishihara tapped his fingers on the wheel, half-frustrated, half-amused. "I wasn't talking about Nakamura."

He drove up the ramp to the freeway entrance, only to find it blocked by several large trucks.

McGuire groaned. "I should have taken the train."

The car advanced a couple of meters. Didn't look promising. The auto navigator blipped a belated warning across its screen. *Use alternate route.* Ishihara unhooked the two-way radio below the dashboard and called Traffic Control.

"There's an accident being cleared away near Himeji," he passed on to McGuire, who hadn't followed the radio conversation. "It'll be an hour or so before the traffic starts flowing properly."

He rummaged under his seat, then in the door pocket, and with a grunt of satisfaction found a half-full packet of cigarettes. He opened the window and lit one.

When he looked over at McGuire again, she was asleep, her head tilted precariously on the seat belt sash. He looked out his own window, embarrassed to stare. Below the freeway and fast train overpass, the Zecom Betta spread in a protective square fence around the factory. Only a few lights flickered from its many windows. Too early for most people to rise.

Beyond the Betta he could see glimpses of fields against the dark backdrop of the mountains. Two or three lights gleamed faintly out there like stars through smog. He supposed many of the local families had moved into the Betta,

too. As the old people disappear, so do the customs and be-
liefs that hold families to places. Like himself, with no
hometown to return to. What was he going to do with retirement? Buy a tiny flat in some country town that accepted
the old people unwanted by the cities?

The car behind him tooted. The line inched forward. He
chucked the cigarette, started the engine, and drove off.

エレナ

The next thing Eleanor knew was the car shuddering to a halt. She peered out, trying to rub what felt like hot sand from her eyes.

"This isn't the lab." They were parked near an overhead railway line. As if in confirmation, a train with an orange stripe rattled past, drowning out Ishihara's answer. That was the Loop line, which ran through many of the last undeveloped areas in Osaka.

Ishihara was getting out of the car. "I'm hungry, aren't you?" He slammed the door. The automatic closing mechanism booped in protest.

She got out of the car to face him over the hood. "I told you, I need to get back to Tomita. If you won't drive me, I'll call a taxi."

"It's half-six," he said firmly. "I'm knackered. You're knackered. Let's have a decent meal, and I'll get you to your lab by eight."

Damn the man, he was right. She could feel fatigue dragging her down like a lead cape. If she didn't eat before she got to the lab, she'd be too busy later. The budget committee meeting wasn't until 2:00 P.M. She'd still have time for last-minute details.

A cool breeze stirred the still air. At this time of the day it was almost pleasant. Some of the little shops under the rails were already open. Shoe shops, dress material shops, knife-sharpeners and key-turners, pawnshops, secondhand bookshops, family-owned noodle stands; all tolerating the constant vibration and noise of the trains for the sake of the cheap rent. On the other side of the street a man in shorts and undershirt swept dust from the entrance to his blue tent.

Ishihara crossed the narrow street and pushed aside a hanging cloth that said BAR HEY! He had to bend to avoid banging his head on the lintel.

"Irrasshei!" called a deep, sleepy voice. The man behind the counter was shorter than Eleanor, but made up for it in width, like a deeply tanned wall. He tossed Ishihara a hot towel and wiped his own face with another.

"I'm not open for another twelve hours, you know. Next time you drop in unexpectedly, do it at night." Then his eyes widened as he caught sight of Eleanor.

"This is unexpected, Detective. Never seen you with a beautiful woman before." He gave a gap-toothed grin. "Never seen you with a woman before."

Eleanor bobbed her head to cover her embarrassment and squeezed in beside Ishihara at a tiny table beside the counter stools. The shop contained only the counter, five stools, and the one table. Plus working space for one behind the counter. Every centimeter of space from low ceiling to floor was used, with racks of bottles and utensils lining the wall behind the counter.

The owner placed a hot towel in front of Eleanor. She buried her face in it with a barely suppressed groan of pleasure and rubbed away the memories of the night before.

"What've you got for breakfast?" said Ishihara.

The owner disappeared behind the counter for a moment.

"Rice." He popped up again. "Soup. I can fry you an egg, do you some pickles and a seaweed salad." He looked at Eleanor uncertainly, as though she might order French champagne.

"That's fine," she said, and he relaxed.

Along the walls vertical wooden slats carried menu items in neat calligraphy. She hadn't been in a small bar like this since her student days. Most of the downtown bars nowadays were automated. You pushed the buttons and let it scan your cash card, then picked the food up from the appropriate slot.

"Your Japanese is good." The owner placed cups of steaming green tea and bowls of pickles and salad for each of them on the table. His observation didn't carry the typical undertones of surprise and faint censure, so she was disappointed when he added, "Better than mine, in fact."

She hated that phrase, first for its patent impossibility and second because there was no polite response except a deprecating negative.

"I'm Motoki, by the way," he added. "Taira Motoki. That's why the bar's named Hey." He looked at her slyly to see if she'd get the pun. She did, after a minute or two. The character for Taira could also be pronounced "hei."

Ishihara drank his tea in surly silence. That suited her. When the rice, soup, and eggs came, they both ate in silence, too. The soup was thick and salty, the eggs rich, and the seaweed—sweet, salty, and vinegary at the same time—slid down her throat easily. Wonderful, wonderful food. The world began to slide back into perspective.

Ishihara pushed his chair back all the ten centimeters it could move and lit a cigarette. The only sound was the low hum of a wall fan and the muted babble of voices from the television above the counter. And the regular roar of trains nearly overhead. Eleanor couldn't stop herself from yawning hugely. God, she was tired.

"So, why robots?" Ishihara tilted his head back and blew smoke at the ceiling.

She turned the soy container round and round as she tried to remember one of her formula answers.

"I can see why you'd want to make something like that welder," he went on. "The one at the factory. It's useful. Does the dirty and dangerous work for us. But you make those walking robots, don't you. The ones that are supposed to look like humans. What use are they?"

First Akita, now Ishihara. Why couldn't they leave her alone?

"I started in industrial robotics. That's why they called me out to Kawanishi. I started researching humanoid robots because . . . because they're like us, I guess. They learn."

"Learn what? What's your robot going to do when it grows up?"

Eleanor had a brief vision of a taller Sam in a business suit, its camera eyes bulging as it sat at a desk. She smiled. Ishihara stared at her.

"What's so funny?"

She caught Motoki grinning as he sloshed dishes around in the sink behind the counter.

"Nothing. Just the way you said 'grow up.'"

Ishihara waited for an answer. His questions surprised her—she'd been prepared for the usual curiosity about her personal life, but not philosophy.

"I suppose once a humanoid robot is developed," she said slowly, "its role will be companion for humans beings."

"Or slaves?"

"That's very cynical."

"Comes with my job." He stubbed out his cigarette and slurped the remainder of his tea.

"But development of humanoid robots on a commercial scale is still decades ahead." And may never happen at all, she thought gloomily, if companies like Tomita decide it's not worthwhile. "I do it . . . because I enjoy the process of research, rather than anticipate the result."

He cocked his head at her. "Like the physicists who developed the theory of the atomic bomb. They were only enjoying the research, I bet."

Motoki stopped washing dishes.

Eleanor's cheeks went cold with anger. "That's an unfair comparison. My robots aren't destructive. And if you follow that line of thought, we'd have no scientific progress at all."

Ishihara leaned back in his chair again, seemingly amused. "I'm just interested in why you do your job. What does your husband think about all this?" He waved his hand at the bar. "Working all night."

"He knows it's my job." Eleanor apologized internally to Masao. He hated her staying late at work. "What does your wife think about you staying late?"

"I'm divorced," he said shortly.

That answered her question. "Children?" she inquired, as people always did in Japan.

"No." His flat tone didn't change, but some emotion tightened his cheeks briefly. He stood up abruptly and squeezed past the table.

"Don't step on my futon," Motoki called after him as he disappeared through a bamboo curtain at the back of the shop. Motoki began to clear their empty plates from the table.

"It was very nice," said Eleanor inadequately.

"Don't mind Ishihara-san, you know." He paused in loading their teacups onto a tray. "He's an okay bloke under all that grouchiness. He'll stand by you if he thinks you're all right. He did by me."

"In what way?"

He paused before continuing. She got the impression it was a painful memory.

"Years ago I got into trouble with some moneylenders

and Ishihara helped me out. First time I realized there are such things as straight cops."

Eleanor hadn't considered the alternative to "straight cops."

Ishihara returned, wiping his hands on a crumpled handkerchief. "Let's go. I've got another case to get back to."

She was struck by the way his expression tightened and his stoop straightened as he said that. It struck her that for all Ishihara's criticism of her overwork, they were very much alike.

Masao called her that evening as she and her team tidied up the lab after the demonstration. He seldom called her at work, and she stared at the screen in surprise.

"Are you nearly done?" A vertical line of worry scored between his brows. He was calling from their kitchen. She could see dirty dishes stacked on the bench top, something he'd normally never tolerate.

"I'm about to leave. I left a message earlier this afternoon . . ."

"That's okay." He waved his hand to dismiss that problem, and she realized it wasn't worry about her. "I got a call from Kazu. Something's come up. Can you meet me at their place?"

"Tonight?" Her head spun at the thought. All she wanted to do was crawl into her futon in her nice, cool Betta.

"It's urgent." His normally ruddy face looked quite sallow. "I'll see you there." The screen went blank before she had a chance to say good-bye. Completely unlike Masao. What could be wrong at the Tanakas'?

"McGuire-san."

She spun her chair. Division Manager Izumi stood beside her desk. He glanced around at the now-deserted lab. The clutter on the benches had been ordered somewhat, and Sam and the service bot stood recharging side by side, an unmatched pair.

"The committee did not sound positive," he said.

"No." They'd sat in her lab in their dark suits like a row of carrion crows waiting to peck the project apart.

Izumi looked at her over his glasses with his deceptively gentle gaze. "I do not think they will recommend that funding for this project be renewed."

"No." Even though Sam had performed perfectly, as if it knew what was at stake. "What am I supposed to do now?" she said bitterly. "Design smart toilet seats for Bettas?"

Izumi didn't even blink, and she felt guilty for venting her frustration on him. He'd invested as much in the project as anyone. She leaned forward. "Tell me, Chief. Do you personally believe we should cut basic research to fund immediately profitable applications?"

She didn't really expect him to answer. But she hoped he would. If she couldn't get honesty from Izumi, whom she'd known for fifteen years . . .

Izumi aligned the bottom edge of a wayward file with the edge of the desk.

"What I believe doesn't matter. McGuire-san, you must understand that this company can no longer afford the luxury of research that brings no results for decades. We will be lucky if we survive with any research facilities intact at all."

"Survive what?"

He looked at her directly this time. "Everything is changing. First it was the end of lifetime employment, then the rise of contractors, then the offshore outsourcing of products. Now the Seikai reforms are pushing us all back inside. Soon we'll be as isolated as we were in the Edo period. Or as the U.S. is today."

He smiled at Eleanor's expression. She looked down, embarrassed at being caught staring at him with her mouth open. She'd rarely heard him talk so forcefully about anything.

"My apologies, McGuire-san. I speak metaphorically. You have heard of the Merger Scheme?"

"Ye-es." Something to do with encouraging intrafield co-operation among large companies, for the sake of Betta construction. *Build a better Betta* rang the appalling jingle. *A Betta life for all.*

"I predict that Tomita, as we know it, will cease to exist in about five years." He sighed. "You did not hear me say this, by the way."

She nodded. He might be wrong, of course. And if he wasn't, where did that leave her? She'd almost prefer making parts in the Tanaka family business to designing Betta (ha-ha) toilet seats.

"A restructure plan is under way." He said the words too precisely, which meant that he disapproved. "I suggest we develop some aspect of this project into a new proposal that takes advantage of the change. Perhaps we could concentrate on the perambulatory balance mechanism. Or perhaps the sensory processing. I believe we have a unique record in this area."

That was a good idea. They could use as much as possible from the Sam project to start a new one. Possibilities for a new proposal crowded her mind. And . . . she sat frozen in excitement. The sensory processing could be greatly enhanced if what Akita had hinted in his e-mails was true. He had found a reliable way to transfer sensory feedback into the neural net. She'd have to meet him and find out more.

"McGuire-san?"

"I beg your pardon. I was thinking."

"The lab is tidy," he said kindly. "I suggest you go home and get some rest. We'll discuss it in the morning."

"I'll do that. Good night."

"Good night." Izumi's gray head disappeared down the corridor.

Eleanor opened her e-mail. Better to contact Akita immediately, before the tension of the past few days caught up with her. He hadn't replied to her previous e-mail.

```
Sender: E. McGuire
Subject: Discussion
Akita-san
    Please excuse my previous e-mail. I
have been under some pressure lately
and perhaps did not consider your query
in the spirit in which it was offered.
```

That should smooth any ruffled feelings.

```
    I would very much like to discuss
with you your research on sensory input
for synthetic neural networks with a
possible prospect of collaboration in
this field. Can you call me please? My
private number is 993654110 if you need
to reach me out of business hours.
    Looking forward to hearing from you.
    Eleanor McGuire
```

To get to the Tanaka house she had to catch three trains, one of which was the Loop line she'd seen that morning with Ishihara. It seemed such a long time ago. Every time her eyes drooped shut on the train, an image of Nakamura's crumpled body flashed in front of her, and she jerked awake.

The rattling train, the grimy stations, the heat outside, the crowded alleys and neon-encrusted buildings around the stations transported her back in time to her early days at the company, before they moved to the Betta. Without the energy to feel uncomfortable, she drifted blankly through the crowds, ignoring the stares and comments.

"Ellie, over here." Masao was waiting for her at the exit. He peered at her face in concern mixed with exasperation. "You haven't slept, have you." He took her arm and steered her past waiting taxis and the blaring music and lights of a pachinko parlor, away from the station and through the ill-lit streets. The heat sink of concrete and asphalt swallowed them.

"What's wrong?" she said, as soon as the pachinko music was behind them.

"It's Mari-chan. They can't find her."

"Has she gone off somewhere with her friends?"

"Not with any of the friends we can find."

Eleanor forced her aching head to think back to Sunday. "She got a phone call on Sunday afternoon. I had the impression it was from a boyfriend. Could she have gone away with him?"

"It's not that simple." Masao stopped in the white street-light near the old milk factory, where Kazu had failed in his bid to escape Grandpa's control.

"The police called. They think she might be part of a religious group."

"What kind of a religious group?"

"Some postmillennial cult called the Silver Angels. I looked it up in the university database while I was waiting for you. All the database says is 'possibly apocryphal group classified in the neo-Buddhist area.'"

"Surely Mari's not that stupid."

He shook his head. "Kazu said two girls from Mari's school have been killed. The police think it might be something to do with the group."

"Killed? How?" Sharp pangs of worry began to penetrate the fatigue-sodden sponge of her mind. Over the past couple of decades, ever since the Soum cases of the nineties and early twenty-first century and the Happy Universe disaster of 2004, everyone in Japan knew what happened to people who ran afoul of the cults.

"The police won't tell exactly, although they did say it was probably an accident. I'll look up more information on these people," he continued. "It's possible they're not a real cult. Sometimes the police get the wrong idea. Or they want the group to be a cult so they can quote the Religious Protection laws against them."

"What does that mean?"

"If the courts recognize the group as a cult, the police can use a much wider range of search and interrogation powers than if it was, say, a group of kids getting together to play weird games."

Eleanor hoped it was the latter. "Let's go. Mari might be home already."

They hurried on through the hot streets.

Mari was not home.

"Her phone is disconnected, she's not answering mail." Yoshiko twisted her plump hands around a wiping cloth. Her eyes were red and swollen. "Kazu went to her apartment. The landlady told him Mari moved out months ago. Why didn't she *tell* us if she was in trouble?"

"Yoshiko-san, calm down." Grandpa folded his arms magisterially on the other side of the kitchen table. "I'm sure it's all a mistake."

He didn't explain how it could be a mistake, not if Mari had moved out long ago. Eleanor hoped Mari had merely moved into a boyfriend's flat and wanted some time free of her family.

"Eleanor-san, Kazu-san. Your tea." Grandma somehow found places to put two full cups in the mess on the kitchen table. Kazu and Masao stood by the doorway to the living room, muttering together.

Eleanor sipped the bitter green brew and hoped it would clear her head. There didn't seem to be anything she could do at the moment, which made it harder to stay awake.

"Mari is a good girl. She wouldn't do anything stupid," declared Grandpa, as though that made it so. But his stubborn mouth was unsteady, and his tufted eyebrows twitched as he blinked.

"Did you say anything to her about those implants?" Yoshiko suddenly turned to Eleanor.

"What implants?"

"On Saturday, she said she wanted to get one of those phone implants. You know, the ones you put under your skin."

Grandma looked puzzled. "How would you get a phone under your skin?"

Hastily, Eleanor explained. "It's a tiny receiver that a doctor attaches to your aural nerve. So you can hear messages without having to hold up a phone to your ear."

"They cost millions of yen," went on Yoshiko. "So of course I said we couldn't afford it. She didn't make a fuss. But maybe she was upset."

"She didn't say anything to me," said Eleanor. "I don't think that's why she left." She was remembering how urgently Mari had responded to the phone call on Sunday. Something important.

"How would you know?" said Yoshiko. "You hadn't seen her for six months."

"Yoshiko," said Grandma reprovingly.

"Well, it's true." Yoshiko set her jaw stubbornly, looking exactly like Grandpa. "She always pokes her long nose in things."

"She's part of the family, so that's all right," said Grandma soothingly.

Eleanor decided she didn't want to argue with Yoshiko at the moment. "When did the . . . accident with the other girls happen?" she asked Kazu.

"The policeman said last Friday." Kazu sat down at the table with a sigh. He was still wearing his grimy factory overalls. "We should have insisted Mari stay on Sunday night."

"I don't see that matters," said Grandma. She began to fold little boxes using junk mail from the local supermarkets, patiently pressing each fold and making sure all edges were even. "The child would have gone anyway."

"The policeman . . ." began Yoshiko.

"Detective. From the Religious Affairs Department," interrupted Grandpa.

"He said we should tell him if we hear anything from Mari, or if any of her friends call her," said Yoshiko.

Religious Affairs. Eleanor had a faint memory of a grating voice saying, *Assistant Inspector Ishihara, West Station Police, Religious Affairs.*

"That detective—he wasn't a tall, skinny man with a sour expression, was he?"

Yoshiko shook her head. "He was very nice. A solid man, mature."

Still, she would call Ishihara the next morning and ask him what they should do. She'd helped the police with Nakamura's murder, now they could help her.

"Mother, will you stop doing that!" Yoshiko snatched the junk mail pages away from Grandma. "It gets on my nerves."

"It steadies my nerves." Grandma stood up with dignity and went into the bathroom. "I'm having my bath." Her voice sounded muffled from behind the sliding door.

Eleanor stood up a little unsteadily and beckoned Masao into the living room. Threads of incense smoke curled white against the dark wood of the family altar. Three boxes of cakes and a basket of enormous, perfectly shaped strawberries crowded the offerings ledge. Any gifts received by the household were automatically left on the altar first.

Eleanor kept her voice low. "Are we staying all night?"

"They're worried," said Masao. "They need my support."

"I know. But I'm really tired."

"If you didn't work such ridiculous hours, you might be more use when you're home," he snapped.

"Last night wasn't my fault. There was an accident . . ."

"Can't you ask them to call someone else? I never see

you." He took a deep breath, then swallowed whatever he had been going to say. His hand traced the outline of her face, around her jaw, across her cheekbone. "I don't like to see you wearing yourself out for a job. That's all it is, you know. It's not the most important thing in the world."

"I know, but . . ." She had no idea how to finish the sentence. But it's important to me? But it's all I've got? The calm face of the little Kannon statue in the altar offered no help.

"I wouldn't mind, you know." He dropped his voice further. "If you decided to leave Tomita. We'd manage somehow."

She blinked at him, astonished. "I never knew . . ." I never knew you felt like that. How could she know? They rarely talked about Important Things, as opposed to the comfortable minutiae of daily living. You were supposed to understand how your spouse felt by emotional osmosis, or something.

"We'd have to move out of the Betta." The idea horrified her.

He shrugged. "People live outside the Bettas still."

"I couldn't leave Tomita," she said firmly. "It would be madness."

He sighed and hugged her to him. She relaxed into the hot, sweaty circle of his arms. She didn't want to think about the future right now. All she wanted was a nice sleep.

"Just take it easy," he mumbled, his breath warm in her hair.

石原

Ishihara took the outside route from the subway entrance to West Station on Wednesday morning. There was an underground connection, but he preferred the heat.

Living in the Betta, commuting in the train, working in the station—sometimes it seemed unreal. Too clean and two-dimensional.

Like one of those manga that Junta had always been watching when Ishihara got home from work. His mother thought he was studying, but as far as Ishihara could tell, all he did was watch discs, the VR mask covering his eyes and ears so that the only Junta-like part of his face was the small, half-open mouth.

The manga all featured superhuman heroes, often cyber-enhanced with ninjalike powers, who battled shadowy forces with lasers. The setting was usually a futuristic Tokyo, metal towers and streamlined traffic systems. Very similar, in fact, to post-Quake Tokyo. But the manga artists hadn't thought about what it might be like down in the streets.

Last time he went to Tokyo, he'd felt lost. It wasn't the high-rise canyons that disoriented him—Osaka had those, too—but the archaic, angular kanji on shop fronts and awnings. He felt like he was on the set of an old Hong Kong movie. And down in the sludge and among the street stalls, he heard more Chinese than Japanese. After the Quake it seemed Japan was less interested in the world than ever. And yet more people from all over came there, to get their piece of the Seikai boom.

In any case, sometimes he needed to make sure that the real world still existed, outside the Betta and the underground. He needed to confirm that the strange new ideas of reality could not invade his own and change what he knew to be true. The gritty asphalt under his shoes, the stink of exhaust fumes and urine in the airless canyons between tall buildings, the pinched faces of people living in cardboard boxes; these things were real and comforting in their solidity.

Not like the manga. Or cyberspace. Or cultish metaphysics. That's what you get from a generation who grew up with plenty of everything. Everything material, he reminded himself. They certainly didn't get enough of the things he and his parents had taken for granted—time to talk to friends, a family to come home to, parents who might be overbearing but who were always there when needed.

Like he'd been there for Junta?

The memory of his son jumped at him, catching him unawares as it always did. He hadn't been there for Junta. At least, that's what his wife said. She was right; no policeman could ever give enough time to both job and family. And Junta looked elsewhere for what he needed.

He blew a drop of sweat off the end of his nose. Bloody ironic, wasn't it. He was still chasing cult masters, and his own son's disappearance proved the job's futility.

The dilapidated front of West Station was sandwiched between a business hotel and a banking office block. Its cracked, stained concrete oozed in the humid air, and the air-conditioning in the lobby was always at half strength. The young female constable on front desk tried not to wrinkle her nose as Ishihara walked past in his sweat-gray shirt.

Beppu was waiting at Ishihara's desk to go over the Silver Angels case, the fluorescent light reflecting off his bald patch.

He pointed at the screen. "Here's what came in last night. Basically what we heard at the briefing yesterday afternoon."

Interviews with the parents of the dead, interviews with other students. Their own evidence that the dead Angels had known the apartment would be empty before the owner left. No evidence as to how they got past Betta security. No further information about the group as a whole.

"Don't take this the wrong way . . ." began Beppu, cutting into his thoughts.

"That means you're going to insult me."

Beppu nodded. "What's new? No, seriously, Ishihara, if you feel this case is not . . . I mean, if you think you might find it hard to stay objective with this one . . ."

It hit Ishihara that Beppu was talking about Junta. His immediate reaction was to say mind your own business. But he had been thinking about Junta more than usual. It might be a good excuse to get out of this case, which looked like going nowhere fast.

Yeah, and how many times in your life have you ducked out of a case because you didn't like it?

"I'm fine," he said gruffly.

"Okay. I gotta ask, you know."

"Yeah, once is enough." Ishihara looked back at the screen.

Beppu leaned back in his chair, giving Ishihara some space. "Have you thought about the house?"

"House?"

"By the sea. There's only one more in the complex. If you don't put down a deposit, someone else will." After years of poring over catalogues and attending information sessions, Beppu had finally decided where he was going to retire. Now he considered it his duty to make sure Ishihara did the same.

"I don't think I can stand being neighbors with you for the rest of my life." Ishihara tried to make it a joke. "Get off my back. I've got to report on the Okayama case."

Beppu slid his chair away, grumbling.

Ishihara was glad the Zecom case wasn't his. He could see the pressure put on Mikuni and the Okayama police by Zecom, and probably by the Tokyo police authorities, but he didn't think Mikuni was handling it very well. They needed to get their information in order.

The business with the robot, for example. Nakamura must have let his killer into the lab, and the killer knew how to get out without attracting attention. And McGuire said there should be backups—which argued, to his mind, that it was an inside job. Or an outsider who knew their way around the company and around a computer. A disgruntled ex-employee, maybe.

But Mikuni was spending more resources on chasing Nakamura's personal contacts outside the lab than in interviewing people in the company. Because that fellow Yui, the one with the authoritative PR manner, told them Nakamura had debts in the town.

How did Yui know all this? He was Nakamura's boss, sure, but not his mate. Mikuni hadn't taken into account McGuire's comments that Nakamura was a complete wimp. Would that kind of man make friends in a tough crowd to start with? And none of the other researchers in the unit had said anything about Nakamura's after-hours activity.

Yui himself stank of deception. It might be merely the desire to keep Zecom out of trouble. Yui had been with the company since he left university. He was Zecom's best, and also the type Ishihara trusted least. They were university-educated, so they thought they were cleverer than everyone else; they'd spent time abroad, so they thought they knew how to do things better; they had high-paying jobs with connections to government and business bigwigs, so they assumed they had protection.

The description might apply almost equally well to McGuire . . . no, not really. Her husband's family were ordinary people. And by "ordinary," he didn't mean white-collar Betta-dwellers.

So what was he to write in the report? *Dear Boss, I think Okayama Prefectural are pissing in Zecom's pockets and we're never going to find the killer because he's in the company.*

He groaned and started tapping his thoughts into something more tactful. Maybe he should get voice activation on his machine.

A quick glance across the room showed three detectives seated at their desks in earnest conversation with their screens. It looked so stupid. He really didn't want to start talking to machines. It reminded him of the Silver Angels kids, trying to wire themselves to computers.

"Enjoy your field trip?" Assistant Inspector Ube paused on his way past.

Ishihara grunted assent.

"Message from young Bato, too." Ube scratched his head. "He wants you to call. He won't be in today, but he's online."

After the Kawanishi incident, Ishihara had asked Constable Bato from Fraud to keep an eye open for the dead man's name in connection with loans, in case he'd been in trouble somewhere.

"Thanks." Ishihara reached for his normal, solid, unimplanted telephone.

Bato's voice faded in and out. ". . . nothing on Mito . . ."

One lead gone nowhere, thought Ishihara.

". . . the other man."

"Who?"

"You don't need to yell . . . hear you. From Kawanishi, technician called Sakaki . . . sent you a note. He's black-balled at every legal level. For over a year now."

And another lead entirely. "Thanks, mate."

"Happy to oblige."

Ishihara ruffled through the papers in his in-tray. There it was, a fax sent to him yesterday.

It looked like Sakaki had been sinking further and further into debt now for months. To get himself on the list of un-acceptable risks for legal loan houses, he would have had to miss several payments completely and at more than one place.

He laid Bato's fax about Sakaki on the left of his desk, the incident reports from Kawanishi in the middle, and his own notes, including what he thought McGuire said, on the right. About time he cleared this up. Was Mito's death an accident or not? If not, was it murder and who was responsible?

The evidence of the factory said accident—nobody was on the floor except Mito and the body was undisturbed.

The evidence of the robot was unclear, according to McGuire. Something caused it to move outside its pro-grammed sequence and to go to halt instead of emergency stop after hitting Mito. But she still didn't know for sure if that "something" was accidental electronic interference or deliberate sabotage. It wasn't mechanical failure.

Sakaki's turning up at work on the afternoon after dis-covery of the death was suspicious, also that he was deep in debt. But unless McGuire's examination of the robot showed how Sakaki could have done it, he wasn't a sus-pect.

A copy of McGuire's report to her bosses at Tomita had been sent to him, as requested. He skimmed through most of the technical details to the summing-up. She didn't speculate how the accident might have happened—all she said was "it is likely the robot was modified in some way that allowed it to move outside its program. This is supported by the erasure of the control logs at the time of the incident and the unidentified hardware attached to the controller."

The police specialist in industrial machinery said much the same thing, although he hadn't seen the "hardware" McGuire referred to. Some kind of transmitter.

A number of possibilities presented themselves: Mito and Sakaki might have gone gambling together, then quarreled over who should pay back the loan—except Mito was a Happy Universe member and didn't gamble; Mito might have found out about Sakaki's habit and threatened to tell the company, or even tried to get money from Sakaki in exchange . . .

Some of these possibilities assumed Sakaki had stayed on at the company after his shift ended. He could have clocked out, then hidden until everyone else had left. All the possibilities assumed Sakaki could have reprogrammed the robot or caused it to move. Could he have taken off the arm like Nakamura's murderer? The only person who could tell him that was McGuire.

He called her number from her business card, but she wasn't there. A young male voice that identified itself as Kato said McGuire-san hadn't come in yet.

Ishihara said he'd call back later and dropped the phone back in its slot in annoyance. No rush, really. If Sakaki did happen to be a particularly clever murderer, he wasn't likely to do anything else—he'd be happy for McGuire to discover nothing and the accident to remain an accident. Surely she'd have called Ishihara by now if she'd found evidence that it wasn't.

But why wasn't McGuire at work yet? He'd got her classified in his mind as "ambitious workaholic," one of those foreigners who delighted in beating the Japanese at their own game. Workaholics should go to work.

His desk phone buzzed, an outside line, voice only. Bato again?

"Religious Affairs, Ishihara."

"Um, this is McGuire. From Tomita . . ."

Ishihara sat up straight, the coincidence prickling the back of his neck. "McGuire-san. What can I do for you?"

"Can I ask you about a Religious Affairs problem?" Her Japanese was damn good. He'd never have guessed a foreigner was on the other end of the line.

"Yeah, sure. That's my job."

He could hear her take a deep breath.

"My niece seems to be involved with a weird group. The police think it's a cult of some kind. They talked to my brother-in-law, but he can't contact her."

"What's the group's name?"

"The police called them the Silver Angels."

Ishihara cursed inwardly and re-called the Silver Angels report onto his screen. Interviews . . . interviews . . . list of geography club members . . .

"Assistant Inspector?"

"Yeah, I'm here. What's your niece's name?"

"Mari Kitami."

There she was. In the list of geography club members who couldn't be found. The home address looked familiar—he'd seen it when he looked up the information on McGuire's husband.

"How should we go about looking for her?" Her voice was strained. "The police don't seem very worried, but we are."

"You can report her as a missing person."

"Will that help find her?"

No, it will do fuck-all, he wanted to say. If the kid wants to disappear, you can't do anything. Even if it tears you and your family apart.

"It means the police will be able to keep an eye out for her all over the country, in case she's left Osaka."

More silence. She's not stupid, he thought. She knows if the girl's left Osaka they've got less chance of finding her. He pushed his notes on the Kawanishi Metalworks accident to one side. It seemed less urgent.

"What can you tell me about these Silver Angels?" said McGuire finally. "I can't find anything on your police information boards, and there's not much online."

"I don't know much, myself," Ishihara heard himself say. "But I know someone who does. I'm going to see him. Would you like to come?"

"Where?"

"Be waiting at the taxi rank outside the Umeda subway east two exit. I'll pick you up in half an hour."

"All right." She closed the link.

He cursed himself for a fool. Yes, he felt sorry for her and her family if the niece had got involved with a cult. But he shouldn't involve McGuire. Mind you, the bastard priest would be more likely to talk with an attractive female present. An attractive *foreign* female . . . Ishihara almost looked forward to it.

McGuire looked washed-out, her bright hair and dark-ringed eyes standing out against pale skin. She always seemed to wear the same kind of outfit—white shirt and comfortable-looking slacks, flat shoes, no jewelry. Today's slacks were dull green.

"Where are we going?" she said.

"Northwest," replied Ishihara shortly, all his attention concentrated on getting them out of the scrum of taxis and trucks around the station. The Seikai traffic reforms were supposed to solve congestion, not make it worse.

When they reached the expressway he relaxed and put the car into autodrive.

"I called you this morning," said Ishihara. "About the Kawanishi Metalworks case."

She had to think for a moment. "The welder, you mean?"

"Yeah. We received some information that could have a bearing on the case. Tell me, and think about this carefully, could that technician, Sakaki, have reprogrammed the robot to do what you saw?"

"No." Her answer was immediate and definite. "To access the robot's basic programming, the programmer must input their own registration number and password. Sakaki wouldn't have that information."

"You're certain of that?"

"Unless Sakaki has skills nobody is aware of, yes."

"Could he have taken off the hand piece to hit Mito, like Nakamura's murderer at Zecom?"

She snorted. "Not at all. At Kawanishi the entire arm showed stress. The Kawanishi robot moved out of sequence and hit Mito because he was standing too close. The Zecom robot could not physically have hit Nakamura if he fell in the way we found him."

So Sakaki was off the hook. His guilty act must be about his debts.

They drove off the expressway, down into the narrow canyons of back streets festooned with electric lines and billboards, filled with cars and bicycles and people. A bit like ground-level Tokyo but with fewer Chinese, more Koreans and Russians. The car crawled, but if they walked, Ishihara would have to watch McGuire as well as his own back.

McGuire stared wide-eyed at the street. "I've never been in this part of town," she said. "It doesn't look very safe."

"It isn't." Ishihara steered between a noodle delivery bike and three men either stealing or moving a tall vending machine.

McGuire looked directly at him. "Thank you for bringing

me along. Is this expert one of your"—she struggled with the word—"informants?"

He kept his eyes on the street. "Not really, although he does give me information. He used to be a member of one of the late-twentieth-century New Religions." He didn't say Soum. The word created an instant reaction of distaste in most people's minds.

"He left them and went back to orthodox Buddhism." Well, closer to orthodox Buddhism than to anything else. "He used to be affiliated with Daitoku-ji temple."

"So he really is a priest?" she said.

"Kind of a lay priest."

She was silent again, and Ishihara concentrated on driving. The road cleared as they passed the crowded area around the station.

"Assistant Inspector?"

"What?"

"If Mari is being kept with this group against her will, what can we do to get her away from them?"

She was looking directly at him again. Ishihara braked at traffic lights and met her eyes. Their round foreignness still shocked him.

"If you have reason to think she's being physically restrained from leaving," he said, "you can request a Custody Officer from the local police station to go with you. You have a right to ask to see her, and she has to tell you in person if she doesn't want to go with you."

"What if they coerced her into saying that?"

"If you've got reason to believe they're coercing her—and that's why you take a disinterested witness—you can make a formal complaint, and the police may take out a warrant to investigate the situation."

She mulled that over.

"What you can't do," he said, "is barge in without a warrant and demand the group give her back. We end up having to arrest you, not them."

"Has that happened before?"

He nodded. It happened, even to experienced policemen who should know better. The stupidest thing he'd ever done. In a moment of desperation, he'd wasted his last chance to see Junta, if the boy had ever been there. By the time he returned legally, the whole group had gone.

"Here we are."

エレナ

Eleanor hesitated, then got out of the car. She'd be safe with Ishihara, surely. She hurried a couple of steps to catch up as he stalked away, keeping her eyes on his stooped back.

They were parked in a narrow street shaded by two- and three-story buildings. Ishihara had stopped right next to the building wall, but still there was barely room for another car to pass. The gutters were black with dirt and concrete walls bled dark lines of pollution. Flaking blue plastic bins were chained in a line. Overhead, electricity lines buzzed faintly. It could have been a scene from the 1980s.

Ishihara ducked inside a narrow entry. When Eleanor followed, she realized it was a path between buildings. She pinched her nostrils against the smell of mold and urine. The path opened up into a small courtyard, flanked by an old single-story block of flats sandwiched between the higher buildings in front, rear, and sides.

Each flat was entered by a short path off the courtyard. The building must date from the 1970s at least, with dirt walls and wooden frame. Eleanor had lived in one of these places when she was a student in the 1990s. It had been an anachronism then. How could this one have survived for so long?

"Stubborn landlady," said Ishihara, seemingly reading her mind. "She left it in her will that all tenants had to freely agree to rebuild before the developers could do anything."

They passed the first doorway, which was surrounded by neat rows of potted plants. A flowery-lettered sign hung over the second doorway. CHURCH OF THE SERENE MIND.

Ishihara rapped on the flimsy wooden door. The only plants near the second doorway were a couple of aloes thrusting their prickles outward as if trying to hook passersby. Nobody answered Ishihara's knock, although a curtain in the window of the far flat twitched.

Ishihara rapped again, louder this time. "Open up, priest," he yelled.

Another pause. Then the door opened to the length of a fifteen-centimeter chain.

"What?" said a throaty, suspicious voice. The smell of incense wafted out the crack.

"It's me, Ishihara. You remember."

"Cop Ishihara?"

"Yeah. Open up, I brought you a visitor."

The door shut, then opened again. In the dim interior a small man stood blinking at the sunlight. He wore a threadbare cotton kimono that had once been indigo, open over a gray undershirt.

He glanced up at Ishihara, then peered at Eleanor. "Ooh, a gaijin-san. I've only got green tea, y'know."

"This is McGuire-san. McGuire-san, this is Gen. He's a bastard priest."

The "bastard priest" cocked his head on one side and kept his eyes on Eleanor. "By that, he means both my parentage and my sect."

His gaze was quite impersonal, and Eleanor relaxed a little.

Ishihara held up the plasbag he'd been dangling in one hand. "We brought snacks. Picked 'em up on the way."

That got him a gap-toothed grin. "Come in, then."

Except for the reek of incense and the prominent altar on one wall, inside the flat was very similar to Eleanor's memories of her student days. Dark, because both side walls had no windows, and with the musty smell of unaired tatami. At least it was cooler than outside. There was another smell, too, that reminded her of sushi.

Ishihara, too, sniffed rudely before sitting on the proffered cushion.

From the kitchen on the other side of the patched shoji door, Gen chuckled. "You came on my bath-cleaning day. It's vinegar."

Eleanor knelt formally on the other side of the square table. It was the only item of furniture in the middle of the room. A low bookcase stood beside the altar. She couldn't read most of the kanji on the spines, although jammed in between the difficult-looking titles were a few comics.

Presumably Gen had so few belongings they could be stuffed with his futon into the cupboard, behind the sliding doors papered with a faded water pattern. Tears in the paper had been repaired over the years with a patchwork of picture postcards.

"Here you go." Gen shoved the shoji impolitely aside with one foot and put a teapot and three cups on the table. He took the plasbag from Ishihara and opened it with "mmm"s of delight.

"My favorite, kusa-mochi."

"I know," said Ishihara. "You remind me every time I come."

"You haven't come for a while."

Eleanor was conscious of Gen's small, bright eyes flicking over her face and hands. She tried not to stare back, but curiosity won. A puckered, bulbous nose dominated his wrinkled face. The unevenness of his face contrasted strangely with the smooth, shaven surface of his scalp. She couldn't tell how old he was—any age between forty and seventy.

"Tell us about the Silver Angels," said Ishihara.

Gen finished pouring the tea without a sign that he'd heard. He put one cup in front of Ishihara and one in front of Eleanor.

"Why them? They're not a religion." Gen blew gently on his tea as he spoke.

"Never mind why. We want to know more about them," Ishihara said.

"If the mighty Religious Affairs Department doesn't know who they are and what they're doing, how should I?"

"He bears a grudge because we had to investigate him once," Ishihara explained to Eleanor. He recrossed his legs into a more informal pose and picked up his tea. "We know what they're doing. You can explain why."

Gen blew on his tea again and sipped it thoughtfully. Ishihara slurped his.

Eleanor burned her tongue on her tea. She didn't think Mari and her friends would have anything to do with Buddhism. To them, it would be associated with the dead; with constricting clothes and enforced silence; with priests around whose visits the year was organized and to pay whom everyone went a little short; with sickly sweet incense—with a world that was nearly gone.

"The Angels," said Gen slowly, "call themselves the Third Children. Nobody knows about them. Yet."

There was a short silence, filled with his last word. Somewhere nearby a vacuum cleaner droned. The room didn't seem cool anymore. It was hot and still.

"Somebody knows about them." Ishihara's voice grated harshly in the quiet. "And four of those are dead."

Eleanor's hand shook tea onto the vinyl table surface. If it had been Mari . . .

"They tried to connect themselves to computers. At least, that's what it looked like," Ishihara said.

"I know someone in the group," said Gen. Before Ishihara could speak, he added, "And no, I will not tell you who. He is a minor member only."

Ishihara settled back, frowning, but said nothing.

"They have one guru. He calls himself Adam."

"We know that," grunted Ishihara.

"Adam controls several main disciples who give themselves angel names. Samael, Iroel, Gagiel, Melan."

His precise, un-English pronunciation gave the archaic names a curious solemnity.

"You can get all this off the Net if you know where to look," he added, breaking the spell. "Adam preaches . . . do you want the long version?" Gen cocked a nearly hairless eyebrow at Ishihara.

"No, thanks."

Gen rolled his eyes and included Eleanor in his long-suffering look. She felt obscurely pleased.

"Adam preaches a kind of asceticism. He advocates merging the human soul with technology to achieve denial of the body in an attempt to deny desire. Desire being the root of all suffering," Gen added in an aside to Eleanor.

Ishihara helped himself to another kusa-mochi, but his body was tense with concentration.

"So he is Buddhist?" Eleanor said, confused. Wasn't Nirvana the goal of Buddhists?

"They use Buddhism, but basically they despise things of the body. You know, blood, spit, shit, wrinkles, dirt." Gen smiled at her as if to soften the bluntness of his words. "They flush these things away or hide them. It's shameful even to speak of them. They use the excuse that the body gets in the way of transcendence."

Eleanor remembered a moment of horrible embarrassment as a child, when she had invited one of her Japanese friends over to play. The child's mother had whispered obviously that *foreign houses are too dirty, invite her over to our place.*

"Adam scares his followers with talk of a plague that will wipe out the human race. Only those with inorganic bodies will survive. That's why they try to connect themselves to machines." Gen looked at Eleanor shrewdly. "They like machines because machines are clean."

"Not if you're a maintenance engineer," she said.

Ishihara chuckled.

"Machines do not decay," Gen said. "The Angels fear dirt and sickness because it reminds them that they are mortal." He picked up another kusa-mochi and examined it. "They fear death, that's all." He popped the sweet into his mouth with relish.

"We all fear death," grunted Ishihara. "But we all die sometime."

"Yes, and these children don't understand that the present is our only defense against the fear of death," said Gen, licking the sugar dust from his fingers. "They've never learned to live in the present. All their lives they've been told to study for the future, and their parents did the same."

"Look where it got them," said Ishihara.

"Exactly. The children see their parents and think, not me. They worked so hard for the future, but in the end, all the future holds is death. Only the present holds life."

Eleanor felt sick. She had an awful vision of Mari lying like Nakamura in a pool of blood. *All the future holds is death.*

"'Scuse me," Eleanor muttered. She stood up, wobbling. Her leg had gone to sleep. "Need to go outside."

She stumbled through a tiny kitchen, down a step, into a corridor lined with bundles of old newspapers tied with string. She'd come the wrong way. But no, here was a wooden sliding door that rattled when she slid it open onto outside air.

A couple of meters away, a crumbling concrete fence

stood between the flats and the side of the next-door apartment block. The tall building shut out sun and view, but in the tiny courtyard she could breathe easier than inside.

Ornamental bamboo bulged the sides of a faded blue bucket used as a pot. Beside it sat a large, reddish stone surrounded by dandelions and other weeds. And dirt, raked in a spiral pattern. This brown dirt wasn't as effective as the white sand of Ryoanji temple, but the principle was the same. You followed the lines with your eyes and didn't have to think about anything. Rather, you followed the lines with your eyes until you successfully thought of nothing.

"Do you like my garden?" said Gen's voice at her shoulder. "I'm particularly fond of the rock. I stole it from the construction site one night when they were filling in our local river." He sighed. "That river was there since before Osaka became a town. No good will come of all this." He waved his hand upward and outward, indicating everything beyond the concrete blocks.

"The garden is restful," said Eleanor, and meant it. She felt better. "What can I . . . if my niece is with the Angels, how can we persuade her to come home?"

He looked at her, then let his gaze drift out to the rock. "I can't imagine that a child of her generation will feel it's her duty. I suppose you will have to persuade her that she'll be happier at home."

If Mari had been happy at school or at home, would she have joined the Angels in the first place?

"It is indeed a challenge," said Gen, as if she'd spoken aloud. "She has been taught that happiness means possessing many things and having a good time. Then she discovers that this is not so. In her confusion she turns to someone who offers her a different way to happiness. This involves becoming part of a close group, of trusting others—perhaps with her life—and of doing new things."

"But . . ." Eleanor found she had nothing to say.

"I don't have to ask you which one she would choose."

Ishihara's footsteps sounded heavy on the kitchen tiles. "Nice try with the rake." He looked over Eleanor's head. "Be better with another rock, though."

"Perhaps you will volunteer your head?" said Gen politely.

Ishihara laughed loudly.

Eleanor pushed past him back into the main room. She must do something to find Mari.

"Can we go?" she said.

"Wait a minute." Ishihara turned to Gen. "Do you think the Angels could be dangerous?"

Gen grimaced noncommittally. "I don't know. There are only a few of them, but they have significant technical know-how. And I don't think Adam is stable. He could suddenly decide society is out to get him and strike first."

"Like Soum in the nineties," said Ishihara. "Do they have a commune?"

Gen shook his head. "I don't think so. They communicate electronically." He caught Eleanor's eye to include her in his audience. "There are no shortcuts to enlightenment. You must live, create karma, die, and repeat this until you become Buddha. All souls will eventually achieve this. Anyone like Adam who wishes to be immortal is to be pitied, for immortality does not mean escape from the Wheel. Remember the Enlightened One's dying words— 'All that has form, dies.'"

There was a moment of silence, the only sound the susurration of her own breath and the thud of her own pulse.

"All right, let's go," said Ishihara. "Thanks, Gen. Don't come out."

"I won't." Gen smiled at Eleanor, an expression both innocent and lecherous. "I get a sunburned head."

Eleanor and Ishihara walked back past the other flats to his car. The sunlight sizzled on Eleanor's skin. She could almost feel the freckles popping out.

"I dunno if that helped." Ishihara glanced at her as they

got into the car. "Don't believe everything the old fellow says. He gets a bit mystical sometimes."

Eleanor was touched by his concern. Gen hadn't given her any idea how to find Mari, but at least she knew what kind of nuts the girl was involved with.

"I'm an engineer," she said. "Mystical isn't my thing."

He grunted in amusement. "I'll drop you back at the subway." He pressed the key into the start button. "You'll be wanting to get back to work, eh?"

"I suppose so." She stared out the window at the greasy gray concrete.

Neither of them said anything more until Ishihara dropped her at the station.

She didn't go to work. After Ishihara's car disappeared around the corner, she walked away from the subway entry. Along the narrow footpath she dodged people running for trains, bicycles leaning against poles and shop fronts, women pushing prams, automatic vending machines and the occasional robot hawker, chained firmly to its shop to discourage casual thieves.

Her feet seemed to know where to go. She'd been here before, must have been a long time ago, probably when she was a student. The buildings around the station didn't seem familiar, but the small park in front of the station was distinctive. So, too, were the roads leading off from the park like spokes from a hub. She remembered the bus stop, tucked under a large tree—rare in Osaka—by the side of the tracks.

She should get back to Tomita, but she was overcome by a desire to see if the whole memory remained. After her accident so many memories were left as fragments that sometimes she tried to forget the lot. She didn't like to think about the memories that were lost completely, the ones she'd never know because she didn't realize they were gone.

If she'd been here as a student, she would have waited for

the bus or walked. She'd never had enough money in those undergraduate years. Her father was dead by then, and her mother had expected Eleanor, when she thought about her at all, to work like her sister. None of them approved of her going back to Japan, and they couldn't afford to support her.

She worked, teaching English, waitressing, whatever. Not bad money, given gaijin wages, but she hated every minute of it. Thank god she had enough money now, enough to live in security.

She stopped and stared into a bookshop window. *Seikai—Are We Building Big Enough?* asked the latest best seller.

She and Masao couldn't afford the loss of her present job, whatever he thought about her working too hard. His teaching gave them enough to live on, but not enough to pay off the huge debt of Betta residency. If they sold their Betta apartment, they'd have to start from nothing again.

Did Masao really think she'd be happy running a small business—no infrastructure, no economies of scale, no knowledge base . . . ? She supposed it might be fun to find a new product that could bring Kazu and Grandpa out of debt . . .

She kept walking, past a hairdresser with pinkish faded posters of forgotten pop stars in the window. Past a display featuring a huge vase of ikebana centered on lilies. NAKANO & SONS, FUNERAL ARRANGEMENTS. PLEASE DO US THE HONOR OF INQUIRING WITHIN.

Gen's words echoed, unwanted, in her mind "All the future holds is death."

She kept thinking of Nakarnura's smashed head. She wished she'd looked at it properly, because now her imagination kept trying to supply details. Nakamura had been such a thoroughly unlikable person. Yet now he wasn't anything. Like her father, one minute sobbing in lachrymose resentment at her mother and life in general, the next curled up and motionless on the old sofa in the garage, flies drowned in his half-empty glass.

Death was so very definite. A person was here, then not here. As though a switch had been turned off. Like a robot, but final.

If the Silver Angels thought they could use technology to cheat death, they were mistaken. They would merely exchange one kind of off switch for another.

Just forget it. She strode on, angry now at herself for not going straight back to work, at Ishihara for taking her to see Gen, at Mari, at Tomita . . . It was hot work, striding. Sweat soaked her blouse, and the skin of her nose and cheeks burned.

She turned a corner about three blocks along one of the main "spoke" streets. There was a post office on the ground floor of the corner building, perhaps that had given her subconscious the sign. Halfway along the next block she remembered, with a feeling of release. Another memory that could be salvaged from the accident.

This was the way to the Manga Museum. She'd come here in her first year of university with some friends. They all wanted to recapture the magic of comics remembered from childhood. Or maybe they simply wanted to escape from the unfamiliar pressures of university. In any case, the trip wasn't a success. Eleanor's memory supplied dark rooms and colorless exhibits, overlaid with a musty smell of disappointment.

The sign over the gates looked more than twenty-one years old. It was almost covered by tall camellias on both sides. Eleanor turned in the gate with a sigh of relief at their heavy shade. The rest of the small front yard was shaded, too, by pine trees that spread branches right over the two-story wooden house. And by the tall buildings on either side.

That was one reason she'd been disappointed, she remembered. Because the old-fashioned reality of this house and the colorful, dramatic, high-tech world of the comics seemed so far apart.

It didn't bother her now—she was grateful for the shade. She wasn't interested in seeing inside, either. Her subconscious had taken advantage of her while she was preoccupied with Nakamura's death and the problem of Mari, that was all. She'd sit on the bench next to the main doorway for a few minutes until she cooled down.

As soon as she sat down, the door opened and a wrinkled sallow face like a dry tangerine peered out, accompanied by short *phut-phut* sounds.

"Are you wanting a ticket, then?" the elderly woman asked.

She opened the door farther, and Eleanor could see that the sound came from a round paper fan flicked energetically.

"Not really. I just want to sit in the shade," said Eleanor. She stood up politely, but the old woman must have taken that to mean yes, or she hadn't heard Eleanor properly.

"It's five hundred yen to get in," she said. "We keep it cheap because of the children. Most of them don't have enough pocket money for more."

"Thank you. But I'm really not interested," said Eleanor.

"In you come, then." She swung the door right open and disappeared down a corridor, *phut-phut*ting the whole way.

"Excuse me," called Eleanor. "I'm not . . ." What the hell, she thought. I can afford five hundred yen. And at least she didn't compliment me on my Japanese.

The illusion of coolness was no more than that. The house wasn't air-conditioned, and, as in Gen's rooms, the air stayed motionless and suffocating. Eleanor wiped sweat off her upper lip and vowed not to complain about how cold Masao set the air conditioner at home.

The corridor's dark wooden walls were covered with posters old and new, although she had to peer closely in the windowless gloom. *New Treasure Island, Dash, Mighty Atom, Tomorrow Joe, Sazae-san, Space Cruiser Yamato,*

Tale of Kamui, *Rose of Versailles*, *Totoro*, *Pat Labor*, *Evangelion* . . . The newer ones gleamed, the old ones blended into the walls.

The sound of the fan came from a room halfway down the corridor. On the other side of a waist-high divider, the old lady perched like a bathhouse attendant on a high stool topped with a cushion.

"Five hundred yen, yes?" She held out her hand for the money and passed Eleanor a pamphlet in exchange.

"A guided tour is five hundred extra?" she added hopefully, but Eleanor shook her head firmly.

"No, thank you."

The woman looked away sulkily and picked up her fan.

Eleanor walked along the corridor to where some light was coming in from the next room. The museum rooms were now divided by theme, unlike the historical progression she remembered. She headed for the third door along, the one that said ROBOTS.

Talking robots, helping robots, fighting robots—lots of the latter. Working robots, cyborgs, human/robot interfaces . . . from the walls lined with bulging bookcases to the open comics in glass display cases, robots of every size, shape and intent.

If the Silver Angels wanted material for human-machine dreams, they need look no further. But Mari wasn't a fool— if the Angels had offered her only a cartoon, she would have laughed at them. What more did they have?

She stopped at one of the glass cases. Inside, an early *Journey to Life* episode lay open, the one in which the robot protagonist Sam Number Five meets the second of the enigmatic figures of the Masters, who propel him on his quest and protect him from the shadowy pursuing figures of Kaisha. In this chapter, Eleanor remembered, Sam Number Five first considers why he wants to become mortal. Until then, he had sought replacement organic parts for his artificial body without really considering the reason he yearns to be flesh and blood.

Sam Number Five has a barrel-like body topped with a flat screen that shows a holographic face, but human arms are attached to the metal torso and human legs sprout beneath it. Both arms and legs seem to be from a child.

He stands at the bottom of a space that has mecha parts instead of walls and an abattoir instead of a ceiling. Frost-rimmed pipes form a maze among the bio parts hanging above. Arms, legs, paws, claws, tails, torsos, heads of many species . . .

Hello, says a grotesquely wrinkled human being, leaning into Sam's visual pickups. *I've been waiting for you.*

Is this the Second Master? Sam isn't sure. This tiny person in his museum of mutilation is not at all like the First Master.

You want a face, don't you? says the human.

Only a Master would know that.

Yes, says Sam Number Five.

Why? asks the Second Master.

Because I'm programmed to want to be human, says Sam.

Are you sure? Did Kaisha program you to run away and hide from them?

Of course not, Sam retorts. The Second Master must mean he has risen above his programming. This craving to be human is all his own.

What do humans do? says the Second Master.

Sam ticks off on his fingers, enjoying the feel of them. *Be born, live, eat, drink, work, have sex . . .*

A shiver runs through all the bio parts hanging above them.

Die, says the Second Master.

Eleanor stepped back from the case. This was too close to her own thoughts. The Manga Museum was no longer a quaint anachronism. The comics, far from being childish flights from reality, now held reality hostage to unguessable ends.

She must find Mari.

She left the room, swept past the ticket office with a curt thank-you, and strode through the white-flowered shade into the baking street.

On the way, she stopped at a secondhand bookstore and bought a copy of the last episode of *Journey to Life*. It was a link between herself and Mari, however small.

Mari's apartment was on the third floor of a residential block near the university, but not inside the Betta that housed many of the students. Eleanor had visited the area once with Masao, as the Buddhist University where he worked was part of the "academic town" area.

The apartment block corridors were neatly swept, and well-tended potted plants decorated the elevator lobby. Clean, bright, and new, it was the type of residence to appeal to young women living away from home.

The door of apartment 305 opened to reveal a tousled female head leaning over from the entry step to open the door. For a second, Eleanor felt a thrill of delight. Then she saw that the hair was too light to be Mari's.

"Oh." The girl stared at Eleanor. "I thought you were a friend. He's got dyed hair." She blinked at Eleanor's head and giggled. She was wearing a tank top and long underpants, or maybe short shorts.

"I'm looking for Mari," said Eleanor quickly before the girl could shut the door. "Mari Kitami. I'm her aunt."

The girl stepped down into the narrow entry and crossed her arms defiantly. She was much shorter than Mari, a thin creature dwarfed by a mop of bleached straw hair.

"She moved out. There was three months' rent left, so she let me stay here. What's wrong with that?"

"Nothing, nothing," soothed Eleanor. "It was good of you to help her out."

Mollified, the girl uncrossed her arms and leaned against the doorframe. "Yeah, I keep the place nice."

A glimpse of clothes-strewn floor behind her suggested otherwise.

"Trouble is, I've got some discs to give Mari, but she didn't tell me where she'd moved," said Eleanor.

"Try mailing," suggested the girl. She twisted a strand of hair around her finger and stared unself-consciously at Eleanor's face and clothes.

"I did, but she's not answering."

"Sounds like she doesn't want to talk to you."

Eleanor shrugged. "Maybe. But I'd like to at least leave these discs at her new place for her. They're too good to send over the Net."

The girl straightened up. "What are they, music? I'll give them to her."

"I'd rather do it myself," said Eleanor. "We could go together?" she added, willing to put up with the girl if it meant finding Mari.

"Ooh, no, it's too hot." The girl's lip curled. "I don't go out during the day in summer."

"Do you know the address, then?"

She hesitated, then stepped back into the room. Something thudded to the floor.

"Here you are."

In round, childish characters—one of them a mistake— on the back of an old receipt, the girl had written an address in the south of Osaka. Eleanor sighed. Back in the subway again.

"Thank you."

"S'all right. I don't usually open the door to strangers, you know." She seemed to think it was important. "But I saw you in the security camera . . ."

Eleanor nodded. "I know, you thought I had dyed hair."

The girl leaned forward. "Is it real? The color, I mean?"

Eleanor was so pleased to get Mari's address she didn't care. "It's real. Some gray in it, though."

"Gaijins go gray, too?" The girl patted her own hair as if to reassure herself it was still unnatural and ungray.

"Sure do." Eleanor waved. "Bye."

"Bye-bye." The girl waved back cheerfully.

Masao didn't answer his phone, he must be teaching. She left him a message, saying that she was going to meet Kazu at what might be Mari's new address. She hesitated to call the police yet—if the address was wrong, she'd look pretty silly. And if she did find Mari, the girl certainly wouldn't talk with policemen in the background.

Mari's new address lay in a southwestern inner town, Ashigawara. Eleanor had to ask one of the station staff how to get to the address. The area around the station was a mass of people, bicycles, buses, and stalls. It reminded her of the area near Gen's flat, but newer.

This wasn't the Japan she knew. It was as far from the pristine surfaces of the Bettas as the stubborn ordinariness of Hirano, where the Tanaka family lived. Canyons between buildings rose in tiers of electricity lines and advertising banners, garlanded with lights. The asphalt below was almost invisible under passing feet, and makeshift hovels against every blank wall were covered with blue vineel sheets.

The shop fronts looked authentic—Golden Pagoda Chinese Restaurant, Aquarium Karaoke, Fun Phones, more karaoke—but the interiors were dark, and bouncers guarded many of the entries. Groups of teenagers gathered everywhere, talking, comparing phones, and punching game machines. Many of them wore garish clothes and implants, or had shocks of dyed hair. Their faces carried more definite expressions than she was used to, and many of their gestures were unfamiliar and un-Japanese. It made her uneasy, as though she'd strayed into a foreign country where the people were unpredictable and potentially dangerous.

Free from the constraints of the double hegemony of big companies and government, small companies vied desperately for consumer attention. Icons flashed in her eyes, vidscreens and billboards leaned from every wall, and recorded voices assaulted her ears. Buy *me!* Buy *me!*

Her heart beat uncomfortably fast, and she remembered Ishihara's comment about the streets being unsafe. But she'd come this far and—the irony gave her courage—her foreign features blended in quite well. She followed the stationmaster's directions into side streets, past a grassless park crowded with blue tents like an army bivouac, and found Mari's new address. The two-story concrete building looked nearly as old as Gen's block of flats. It stood out from the other buildings because of the cats.

At least a dozen of the scrawny creatures stretched in the shade under the stairs or wandered between the house and the side of the road. When Eleanor approached, these wanderers meowed and tried to wind around her ankles.

Stepping between them, she peered at the names on the doors of the first-floor apartments. Most of them were barely decipherable. Takeda, something-guchi, Ikuno, Acupuncture Specialist.

Should she wait for Kazu to arrive? He said he'd ride the delivery motorbike, but it would depend on traffic how long he took. She might as well confirm whether this was the right place or not.

She climbed the iron staircase that probably doubled as a fire escape. Two of the top-floor nameplates were new and not Mari's. The far apartment's windows were boarded up, and advertisements clogged the mail slot. The remaining apartment had no nameplate, but she thought she heard voices inside. Three mangy cats bumped their heads against her ankles, meowing plaintively.

She knocked. Whoever was inside must know she was there, from the racket the cats were making. Someone moved behind the closed window next to the door. She knocked again. Should she call out?

Before she could decide, the door opened. Mari stood there, holding a roll of packing tape. She wore jeans and a T-shirt, and looked more relaxed than on Sunday.

"Aunt Eleanor—what are you doing here?" Mari stepped back in surprise.

Eleanor shooed away the cats and stepped in. "I came to see if you were all right."

"Of course I'm all right," she said. "Why shouldn't I be?"

"Your parents can't contact you, you haven't called. We were worried."

There were only two rooms in the apartment, the tiled kitchen and the tatami back room. From where she stood in the entry, Eleanor could see a couple of monitors and a slim, portable hard drive placed directly on the tatami against the wall.

"Who's that?" said a voice. A young man, no more than twenty, with a dark, arrogant face, emerged from the back room and took the tape from Mari. He stared rudely at Eleanor.

"This is my aunt, the one I told you about." Mari glanced anxiously at him.

The boy ignored Eleanor after that first stare. "What's she doing here?" he said to Mari. "I thought you didn't tell anyone."

Mari avoided his glare. "I didn't. Well, only Chee."

"Good thing we're leaving then." He went back into the other room.

"Where are you going now?" said Eleanor. "You need to

let your parents know what's going on. They're worried sick."

"Come and get your stuff," called the boy.

Mari looked at Eleanor, her expression unreadable, then turned and went into the other room.

"They're not worried," she said over her shoulder. "They just don't want the rest of the world to know they failed as parents."

She knelt in front of a long table and began to put things into a cloth bag—a hairbrush, some books, and a Buddhist rosary. The boy put the hard drive into a cardboard box and began to tape it shut, pulling the tape out with a sharp, tearing noise.

Eleanor felt a flush of irritation. She would have to argue with a stubborn teenager. Where was Kazu? She knelt at the table, too, and dumped her own bag on it.

"Mari, the police have been to your home. They say you might be involved with some pretty strange people. Is this true?"

The boy narrowed his eyes at her. "What did the police say?"

"Do you mind?" Eleanor said coldly. "I'd like to talk to Mari, please."

He opened his mouth to retort, but Mari reached over and patted his leg. "Taka, please." She turned back to Eleanor. "Tell them I'm going away with friends."

"Why don't you tell them where you're going?" said Eleanor.

"Because it's none of their business. It's none of your business."

Eleanor looked around the bare apartment. Dust coated the sides of the old tatami, and one of the grime-dark windows had long ago been taped shut.

"What do you really know about these 'friends'?" she said. "Did you know that four students died? They fooled around with implants. Are you going to do that?"

Mari dropped the bag on the table and the contents spilled out. "Implants?" She turned to Taka. "But you said . . ."

"It was an accident," he said. "These are new techniques. She wouldn't understand."

"Don't patronize me," snapped Eleanor. "I was wiring circuits before you were born." She leaned closer to Mari. "They failed, and now they're dead. Do you want to be like them?"

"It's too late now." Mari reached up and pulled at her fringe. Her hair came off neatly, leaving her with a wig in one hand. Her shaved skull shone softly. On the side of her head, an implant reflected the light with a colder gleam. It looked like the new compound type, with both retinal and cochlear attachments.

"You see?" Mari was almost pitying. "Mother and Dad wouldn't understand."

"Don't tell her any more." The boy reached past Eleanor roughly, and pulled Mari up. She fitted her wig and bent down for her bag.

"Sorry, Aunt Eleanor. Say hello to Uncle Masao for me."

"Wait," said Eleanor. She had to keep Mari here until Kazu came. "Please don't go yet."

"Why, so you can call the police?" sneered Taka.

Eleanor stood up, too. "Her father's on his way. At least let him see you're all right," she appealed to Mari.

"He's coming to see me?"

Eleanor nodded. "He only wants you to be safe." She reached for Mari's hand, willing her to stay.

Taka shoved Eleanor backward. Her foot caught on the table. She lost her balance and fell backward, her head and shoulder hitting the corner of the table with a crack that filled her vision with bright dots and set her ears buzzing.

"Taka!" Mari cried.

"We don't want parents or cops here." He went to the kitchen and picked up the box.

Mari's face blurred in front of Eleanor's eyes. "Are you okay?"

Eleanor sat up unsteadily. "Don't go. Please."

"Mari, hurry up!" Taka called from the doorway.

Mari shook her head. "I have to do this. I know you don't understand but . . . Look, when I was little, I used to have this strange dream. I was falling into a huge white *nothing* that swallowed me out of existence. Then I'd wake up screaming." She paused, her eyes focused on something not in the room. "I think that's what dying's like, and it scares me. If there's a way not to fall into that nothing, I want to try it."

"How can I contact you?" called Eleanor.

"You can't." She picked up a book that had fallen off the table and slipped it in her bag.

"Mari, come on!" Taka reappeared in the doorway and glared at Eleanor.

"Sorry, Aunt Eleanor. Tell Dad I don't really think it's his fault."

She left without looking back. The door closed, and Eleanor was left alone with the peeling wallpaper and flat, gray screens.

石原

Ishihara frowned at the blank computer screens, willing them to show him something useful. Two forensic teams, one from West Station and one from Taiho Ward, swarmed over the dusty apartment room. McGuire had called him at West Station, and this incident was linked to one of their cases, but the apartment itself was in Taiho Ward territory, which meant ward police got called, too, as courtesy. A couple of their detectives had dropped in at the apartment, then rushed off on another case, leaving the forensic teams and the West Station detectives to get what they could from the empty rooms.

"You looked at the computers, I suppose?" he said.

McGuire raised her eyebrow quizzically. "They're only monitors, generic hardware available at any retailer. The kids took the hard drive."

He cleared his throat in embarrassment. "Ah, yes. I meant, if you touched anything we'll need your fingerprints. For comparison," he added, seeing her expression.

"They're in the Immigration database," she said.

"I know, but that one's hard to access."

"It's linked to NDN."

"The police can't just poke into anyone's affairs," he said, stung. The public seemed to think that database was solely for police convenience.

"Not unless we've done something wrong?"

"Exactly." He wondered why she grimaced at his reply.

"Assistant Inspector." The man next to McGuire, the missing girl's father, Kazu Kitami, blinked his prominent eyes nervously and held his motorbike helmet in front of him like a shield. "Do you have any idea where my daughter might have gone?"

Ishihara kept his face bland. He hated doing this to people. "We don't have any information at present."

Slow footsteps clanged on the iron stairway and Beppu panted into the flat. The man needed to diet.

"No sign of them." He wiped his upper lip and forehead with an already-soaked handkerchief. "Two constables are doing a house-to-house. Why didn't you keep them here?" he reproached McGuire.

She glared back. "They're both bigger and younger than I. What was I supposed to do—lock the door and swallow the key?"

"Aren't you smarter?" retorted Beppu.

Before McGuire could answer, Ishihara's phone buzzed. The text message said Prefectural Office detectives were on their way over.

"Are you sure she went willingly?" Kitami asked McGuire. The man looked stunned. It was always difficult for the family to accept that their loved one might *want* to join the cult; might want to leave them. He still had trouble believing it himself.

"You can go now," he said gently. "We'll contact you if we hear anything."

"Do you need me here?" McGuire said.

"No, we've got your statement," said Ishihara. "The kids didn't say anything about where they were going, right?"

"No."

"You mean, they did say something?" said Beppu, puzzled.

"No, I mean they didn't." McGuire was puzzled, too.

"Why didn't you say yes, then?"

"Because they didn't say anything." She eyed Beppu warily, then inclined her head in farewell to Ishihara. Kitami bowed low over his helmet.

"Please tell us if you hear anything, Assistant Inspector."

"We will. Next time, call us earlier," he said to McGuire.

Her face clouded, and she nodded, unexpectedly contrite. "I will. I'm sorry."

He was so surprised she should be sensible that he didn't push the point, and the two of them left. He could hear Kitami's voice as they walked away, apologizing for not getting there in time to . . . Nice bloke. He didn't deserve to lose his daughter like this.

"Bloody gaijin, can't understand what they mean half the time," grumbled Beppu.

"Shaddup," said Ishihara.

The Prefectural Office detectives got there in an amazing twenty minutes. This alone would have convinced Ishihara that the Silver Angels were bigger game than he'd been led to believe.

Which pissed him off in a big way. If he was expected to provide backup for these hotshots, the least they could do was tell him what the stakes were. The old priest Gen hadn't given him any practical information, although his philosophical rambling was sometimes useful.

Inspector Funo came into the kitchen, peeling off her platex gloves with a frustrated snap.

"We got a statement . . ." began Beppu.

"Why didn't you call us earlier?" she interrupted.

"We called you as soon as we confirmed it was genuine," said Ishihara. He was on solid ground here, playing by the rules.

"And why didn't you keep the informant here until we came?" Funo wasn't playing.

"We got a statement," Beppu said again.

"Inspector, what are we doing here?" Ishihara said politely.

"You're following orders," she snapped.

"The information I've been given access to," continued Ishihara, "indicates that all we've got is a group of runaways who get off by painting themselves silver and using people's empty homes. Surely it's a problem for Missing Persons and Juvenile Crime?"

The western sun turned the light in the closed kitchen to bronze, and it felt like a sauna. Funo patted her upper lip with a neatly folded handkerchief. "It's classified. I couldn't tell you if I wanted to."

"How can we assist PO if we don't know why we're doing it?" put in Beppu reasonably.

Funo looked from one to the other. She doesn't want to do anything without permission in case it affects her career, thought Ishihara in disgust. This is what's ruining the police force. Lack of initiative.

"At least give us a hint of what we're after." Beppu gave Funo his best competent smirk. "It's not like we're going to blab about a case in progress. Give us credit for a little professionalism."

The three of them waited as the forensics team trooped past them and out of the apartment. They sounded like shod elephants on the iron stairs. The apartment seemed very quiet once they'd gone.

"Remember how the four kids got into the Betta?" said Funo finally. "We're worried they might have a hacking technique that can bypass Betta security."

"Or they've got someone on the inside," said Ishihara. He still suspected the Betta manager of knowing more than he let on.

"Possibly," conceded Funo.

"What did you find in those computers?" said Beppu. "The ones the kids were wired to?"

"Enough to worry the experts," said Funo, then relented. "They found a completely unknown program. Some kind of indoctrination, I'm not sure of the details myself."

"Computer crime is white-collar work," said Beppu. "Nothing to do with us."

"Not anymore." Funo seemed on firmer ground. "We're assembling multitasked response units for this kind of crime now. Got to move with the times."

It made sense. If terrorists and gangs played the stock market to finance weapons, for example, there was no point in the police having two or more departments trying to deal with it.

"This person who called from here," said Funo. "Any chance it's a hoax? Or a deliberate attempt to confuse us?"

"No," said Ishihara. "This same expert gave us an opinion on a different case, quite reliable."

"We'll have to talk to him. We should give him a quick-response number to call in case the daughter . . ."

"Niece," corrected Ishihara.

"Niece contacts him again." She put her handkerchief back into her handbag. A square, black box that looked big enough to contain an entire scene-of-crime kit plus folded laser rifle.

"We might even put a tracer in his phone," she considered, then more enthusiastically. "Has he got a phone implant?"

"No," said Ishihara.

"Er, it's a 'she,'" put in Beppu. "A foreigner."

Funo's eyes widened. Ishihara could see the fine, pale line of her corneal enhancement scars under the real line of her eyebrows.

"Well, well. We didn't think the Angels had any foreign connections."

"No," said Ishihara loudly. "The woman is foreign. She

has no connection with the Silver Angels except for this niece."

"All right." Funo looked at Ishihara speculatively. "Your informant, you handle it. But I still want to do a background check."

"Do what you like." Ishihara turned and stomped down the stairs. He'd never get anywhere with her.

At the bottom he halted. McGuire had asked him for help in getting her niece back from the cult. So far he'd done nothing. He needed more information, but to get that, he'd have to use McGuire as a bargaining chip. There was a nice irony there, one he was sure McGuire wouldn't appreciate.

"Adam first surfaced in 2008." Inspector Funo placed her handbag primly on the low table in the tatami mat room. "He didn't call himself Adam, he was just The Guru. He had a Web site where he posted all sorts of neo-Buddhist mystical proposals for self-enlightenment. Gradually the stuff got more and more over the top, and after three servers banned the site, it disappeared in 2012."

"What do you mean by 'over the top'?" Ishihara lit a cigarette, ignoring her disapproving eye. He and Beppu leaned on the peeling wall.

"He predicted a massive plague that would wipe out most of the human race and welcomed this. He actually offered a prize to anyone who could come up with a new disease."

Beppu snorted. "What was the prize—a posthumous fortune?"

"He offered to tutor the winner in techniques that he claimed would make them invulnerable to any disease."

"Some kind of out-of-body meditation technique?" said Ishihara, puzzled. "How would that protect you from a plague?"

Funo pursed her lips. "Out-of-body in a way. We're not sure, but we think he meant some kind of downloading of consciousness."

"Download? You mean, into a computer?" Beppu grinned. "Who'll keep the electricity flowing into the computer if everyone's dead? That's the trouble with these messiahs, they don't think things through."

"We know from this," Funo raised her voice a little, "that three years ago Adam was involved with advanced digital research. You can see why we were concerned to find that new program."

It certainly fit in with the four dead children wiring themselves to computers.

"We lost track of him after the Web site was banned," she said. "But now he seems to have gathered a group of believers, and he's got private funding from somewhere."

"Not from the believers," put in Beppu.

Otherwise, they'd have to register as a religion.

"It all depends on the people close to him, doesn't it?" said Ishihara. "We've all seen this before—charismatic leader, message that gets through to some people, funding that allows them to build places to worship, etc. But unless his second- and third-in-command are willing to carry out dangerous orders, the group is no threat."

Funo nodded. "The so-called Soum army wouldn't have been much of a problem with just the leader. It was his ruthless disciples who allowed things to get out of hand."

Beppu belched reflectively. "What we need is someone on the inside."

"Or someone who's lost a friend or relative to the group and knows something about them." Ishihara stubbed out his cigarette in the dusty sink. He thought of McGuire's niece. Maybe she could have been persuaded to defect. If they'd got to her first.

"Or luck," said Funo unexpectedly. "Like the newspaper delivery boy who noticed the Happy Universe truck before the timer went off."

Ishihara didn't want to think of the Silver Angels as a ticking bomb. "What do you want us to do now?"

Funo picked up her bag and swung it over her shoulder. "Continue the background checks for those students who had any connection with the dead and the geography club. Send on all the information you find. We'll correlate it with our data."

They locked the door, put a police seal on it, and clattered down the iron stairs. It took Beppu and Ishihara ten minutes to get all the cats out from under Funo's car.

Later that afternoon, Ishihara waited for McGuire's description of her niece's boyfriend to be processed into a format he could run through the NDN and tidied the piles on his desk from the Kawanishi Metalworks case. That morning he'd heard about Sakaki's gambling debts and thought it might provide a motive for Mito's murder, but McGuire assured him that Sakaki couldn't have used the robot.

Yet his intuition said the man was involved in Mito's death somehow. He stubbed out his cigarette and left a message for Beppu that he was going to tidy up a loose end in the Kawanishi case. One more little chat with Sakaki.

エレナ

Eleanor reached the company about three o'clock. She nodded vaguely at the department admin assistant's cheery "good morning," threaded her way between the four rows of desks to her own little alcove in the corner of the room, and sat down with a barely suppressed groan. Her feet hurt from the unaccustomed walking, and her head ached where she'd hit it on the table when Taka pushed her.

She'd taken Kazu for a cup of coffee after they left Mari's abandoned apartment and lent him her phone—he'd forgotten his in his rush to get there—so he could call Yoshiko and tell her Mari wasn't coming home yet. He'd looked so miserable, and she had so little to say to comfort him, that she tried to think of another topic. The only thing she could think of was to apologize for getting him in trouble with Grandpa on Sunday, which sounded inadequate, for the normalcy of the workshop and the Tanaka house seemed far away.

Kazu said merely, "You don't need to apologize. It's between Grandpa and me."

"I didn't mean to . . ." she hesitated, unsure of how to

phrase it tactfully ". . . to bring back any unpleasant memories for you."

He waved away the idea. "That's fine. But I don't suppose you've changed your mind?" He sat on the edge of his seat, his faded, stained work clothes out of place in the bright cafe.

"I can't . . ." *change jobs*, she intended saying, but instead said, "decide just yet. Give me some time."

"We could make you a partner." He looked at her directly, and said in a rare burst of honesty, "We need to get the factory back in competition. All we do now is take the same old orders from the same old companies, for less and less money. If we don't make more profit, we won't be able to repay the debt."

She remembered Masao talking about Kazu's failed business venture. "You mean from livelining the old factory?"

He nodded miserably. "We need an edge. I was hoping you might be it."

Tomita obviously doesn't think I'm an "edge" anymore, she thought. "Kazunori-san, I don't know if I can make such a huge change."

"We're not going anywhere, if you change your mind." He left abruptly after that, saying he had to get back to the workshop. He was so flustered he let Eleanor pay the bill.

She should have called the police before she went to the apartment, she realized. Especially after seeing the frustration in Ishihara's eyes when she told him what happened. His restraint about it only made her feel worse.

She eased off her outside shoes and slid her throbbing feet into the comfortable old sneakers. On the other side of the filing cabinets, shelves, and potted plants that formed her little alcove, the main office hummed with muted conversation and computer noise. All very familiar and, just then, unreassuring.

Although she hadn't said so to Kazu, she felt better about Mari's disappearance after seeing her. Before, she'd imagined Mari as a helpless victim spirited away by outlandish kidnappers. The worry was still there, but it was tempered by the glimpse of Mari very much alive and well, and rebellious. Short of dragging her away physically, there didn't seem much they could do to bring her back.

In the coffee shop earlier Kazu had kept repeating, "Why didn't she tell us? What does she see in these people?" Eleanor could find no answers. She didn't know who "these people" were. What had Gen said? The Silver Angels are afraid of death and decay. And Mari said something about a "white nothing," but Eleanor had been feeling woozy at that point and didn't remember clearly.

She leaned her forehead on her hands and stared blankly at her personal com screen. How do we convince Mari that this is the wrong thing to do? Hell, how do we know it *is* the wrong thing to do? Is our way of life so wonderful? She heard Masao's voice, *I never see you.* She'd worked fifteen years for a company that now axed her best work.

If this Adam guru had found a way to cheat death, how could she tell Mari not to join in? Gen's Buddhist reservations aside, she would be interested herself . . . Or would she?

It's not death itself that frightens me, she decided. It's saying good-bye and knowing there will never be another meeting. Good-bye to the child Mari used to be. Good-bye to her father and mother and all the things she should have said but didn't. Someday, good-bye to Masao. Then she'd regret all these hours spent at work.

The truth hit her as though she'd swallowed a lump of ice.

It's not the most important thing in the world.

She gulped the jagged lump and activated her computer automatically, pushing her bag to one side. It felt heavier than usual. A strange coincidence . . . In the apartment earlier when Taka pushed her, she'd knocked her bag onto the floor, and the manga she'd bought earlier must have fallen out. Mari had picked it up instead of her own book and taken it. Eleanor found Mari's book farther under the table. The shop covers were similar, and Eleanor might easily have mistaken them herself. So Mari now had her copy of the last volume of *Journey to Life*. And she . . .

When she opened Mari's book she couldn't help laughing. She now had a copy of Volume One in the same story. Perhaps Mari remembered their conversation on Sunday. The thought comforted her. She had reached her niece, in a small way.

She realized she was staring at mail from Akita.

```
Sender: A
Subject: Re: Discussion
McGuire-san
I am delighted that you have decided
to meet with me. Please do not be con-
cerned about your response to my ear-
lier query. We shall discuss this further
when we meet. I suggest tonight at six.
I will book a table at the restaurant
Higo beside the games plaza 3 at Umeda.
    A
```

Eleanor didn't want to meet Akita that night. Why couldn't the man phone her? And she found the tone of the mail overbearing, without being able to pinpoint anything. Still, if they met at six, she'd be home by nine, which would please Masao. He said he'd call her if he heard anything about Mari.

She sighed and replied that she'd be at the restaurant at six. Akita had always been abrupt. In their first days at the company he had been the only other new recruit who gave her no concessions or even special looks because she was a foreigner. He treated her, like he treated everyone else, as a potential rival or, if they turned out to be unworthy of rivalry, with disdain. Eleanor was able to keep up with him and therefore received grudging acknowledgment that deepened into tolerance.

Voices rose in the main office, then dropped again. Something sounded wrong. She poked her head around the filing cabinet.

The five members of the Robotics Department who weren't in the lab gathered around Kato's desk, Kato's thin neck and shiny scalp just visible in the middle. The admin assistant, a young woman named Kimura, perched on the desk corner. Kimura wore the demure blue uniform required of administration employees, but she still managed to look frivolous.

". . . left the year I was recruited," Kato was saying. He looked up over and saw Eleanor. "Chief, you knew Nakamura-san, didn't you?"

Eleanor opened her mouth, shut it again while she gathered her thoughts. The others waited expectantly.

"It's been in the news?" She left her alcove and came to stand with them.

They all nodded.

"It must have happened just after he called you on Monday night," said Kato.

"Oh, that was Nakamura?" One of the others in the Sam team wrinkled his forehead with the effort of remembering.

Eleanor hadn't told them she went to Zecom, and she didn't think the police would want her to start now.

"The news said it was probably an intruder," said Kato, glancing at the screen.

"Their security can't be up to much," grunted someone else.

Kimura touched a handkerchief to moist eyes. "He was always willing to stop and chat," she sniffed. "Even after he left here."

That's why he never got any work done, thought Eleanor. Then Kimura's second remark registered. "What do you mean, 'after he left here'?"

Kimura lowered her handkerchief and stared back at Eleanor with mascara-smudged eyes. "When he came to get his mail."

"What mail?"

Kimura glanced at the others as if asking what the fuss was about. "The letters and stuff that got sent here. He didn't want us to forward them on, so he came to pick them up. He always brought some sweets or crackers for the mail room staff, and . . ."

Eleanor blanked out the rest of Kimura's words as she reached over and opened a line from Kato's desk.

"Mail room? This is Supervisor McGuire, Robotics Department. Do you have any mail kept for an ex-employee named Nakamura Shigeo?"

The mail room clerk said he'd check.

"You think the police might want to see those letters?" ventured Kato.

"I'm sure they will," said Eleanor. And so did she.

石原

Ishihara hadn't expected Sakaki to run.

The manager pointed out Sakaki's skinny, overalled figure on the other side of the factory, walking toward the exit. The manager shouted his name and waved. Sakaki started running. Ishihara cursed and sprinted after him down one of the aisles, found his way blocked by machines, and fumbled for his phone. Sakaki disappeared out the loading bay doors.

Ishihara's phone was buzzing already.

"Ishihara here."

"This is Constable Taji. We're holding one male who was running out of the building. Is he connected with the case?"

"Hold him there, I'll be right out." Ishihara let out a breath of relief and picked his way between benches and machines, wiping sweat from his face.

"What's going on?" said the manager beside him. He was a thin, middle-aged man with the expression of one who expects and gets the worst.

"Your man Sakaki has a guilty conscience."

"Can I do anything?"

"Not now." Ishihara inclined his head to soften the directive and closed the door firmly behind him.

Sakaki stood in the parking space in front of the building, between the local constable, who'd met Ishihara when he arrived, and the constable who came in the car with Ishihara. A truck was just pulling out, leaving the air thick with exhaust fumes, which seemed worse in the heat.

The sun seared their necks and shoulders, but Ishihara didn't suggest they go inside. The less comfortable Sakaki felt, the more likely he was to talk.

The manager peeked out the doorway, but Ishihara waved him back inside.

"We'll be there in a minute," he called. Then to Sakaki, "Why did you run?"

Sakaki kept his eyes down. He looked worse than he did on Saturday—his face was drawn and unshaven, and his blue overalls were filthy. He hunched his shoulders and thrust his hands deep into the overall pockets. "Didn't want to get into trouble."

Ishihara lit a cigarette and, as if on second thoughts, offered one to Sakaki. The beat constable looked on, interested, while the West Station constable stared into space.

"Why should you get into trouble?"

"I was here when Mito died." Sakaki accepted the cigarette. His hands shook. "I came in that night to ask Mito for a loan. I knew he wasn't likely to give me one, but I had to try. He never spent money, the tight bastard. I stayed behind in the locker room after my shift finished, thinking what to say to him. I must have fallen asleep."

"For how long?" said Ishihara.

"Until after three-thirty . . . All right, I had a couple of beers. I thought I needed some help before talking to Mito. You don't know what a self-righteous bastard he was."

Ishihara had met a lot of Happy Universe members and thought he could guess, but didn't say so.

"Anyway, I washed my face and went to talk to Mito. He wouldn't lend me anything, then he had the cheek to give me a sermon. At five o'clock—I noticed the time because I could get breakfast near the station—Mito looked at the monitor and said something like 'that's funny.' I said 'what's up,' and he said 'hang on, the welder's stopped, I'll be back in a tick.' He went over to the welder . . ."

"Which one?"

Sakaki stared. "The one that hit him, of course. I was nearly at the door by then because I wanted to get away from him. He was looking at the controller. When I next looked around, he was on the ground, and the welder's arm was shaking."

He took a pull at the cigarette, then another. "I hit emergency stop on the line and ran to see him, but he was already . . ." He threw the cigarette on the ground and swallowed several times.

"Didn't any of the alarms go off?" said Ishihara.

Sakaki shook his head.

"What did you do then?" Ishihara said. A pity there weren't any witnesses to back up this story.

"I left. I couldn't do anything for Mito, could I?" said Sakaki defiantly. "I didn't want anyone to see me there."

Ishihara ground his cigarette butt out on the concrete with his heel. "Why didn't you tell us this before? You could have saved us a lot of trouble. I could charge you with obstructing an investigation."

"Who cares?" said Sakaki. "Telling you isn't going to repay my loan."

"You shouldn't take out loans if you can't repay them," said the local constable disapprovingly.

"That's what Mito said." Sakaki glared at them all. "Everyone knows that, but nobody tells you how to get out of repayment hell once you're in there." The words burst from him. "You don't know what it's like. I borrow from A to pay B, then from C to pay A, and it never ends."

He folded onto a concrete block, as though his legs had given way, and put his head in his hands.

"Declare personal bankruptcy," suggested Ishihara. "It's about all you can do."

Sakaki didn't look up. "Some of my creditors don't listen to the courts."

Ishihara sighed. "You're sure the robot moved by itself?"

"I'm sure." Sakaki's voice was muffled.

"Take him to the station," said Ishihara to the constables. "He'll make his statement there."

In the tiny office, the manager was talking on the phone, no video. Ishihara sank into a chair beside a low table without being invited and breathed the cool air with relief.

Certificates and group photos covered the walls, most of the photos taken in front of the factory. Three desks were crammed into the narrow space. A door at one end bore the sign PRESIDENT'S ROOM.

"A man called Noda," said the manager to the other end of the conversation. He raised his eyebrows at Ishihara, who opened his palm in a go-ahead gesture.

"No, we hadn't seen him before," continued the manager. "His rego number was . . . hang on." He tapped the keyboard beside him and read a number from the screen.

Short pause.

"Well, we couldn't know that. I suppose it's a matter for the police, then." He looked over at Ishihara, then continued. "There's a detective here now."

Ishihara pointed to himself and raised his eyebrows in query.

The manager offered him the handset. "It's an engineer from Tomita Electronics. She says someone from another company sabotaged their robot the other day, when it hit Mito."

It was McGuire. "Nakamura was the technician who serviced the Zecom robot the week before the accident," she said. "He gave a false name, and when he serviced the Zecom robot he attached the device to our robot. I think that allowed him to send a signal and operate it long-distance."

"How do you know?" said Ishihara.

"We found one of his backup files." She didn't sound as pleased as he'd expected.

"Does it tell you how he did it?"

"Not in detail, but it might tell you who killed him."

"Are you at Tomita?"

"Yes."

"I'll be right over."

He cut the connection and turned to the manager. "Thanks for your help. We may soon know more about Mito's death."

The manager ran his hand over his balding head. "It's not going to stop the line again, is it?"

"Not as far as I know."

"And what about Sakaki? Is he under arrest?"

"No, but you should know he's heavily in debt," said Ishihara.

The manager grimaced. "We know that. And we've been missing petty cash for a while now. But we've got no proof, and I don't like dismissing a man who's obviously in trouble."

No wonder the company was going down. Soft, that was their problem. They should have got rid of Sakaki years ago.

"I'll be sending a detective over here with some photographs," he said. "He'll ask your staff if they recognize the technician from Zecom."

"Right." The manager half raised his hand and turned away, preoccupied again.

Ishihara read the first three lines of characters on the screen and reached for his phone. Beside him, McGuire swiveled her chair and exchanged glances with her boss, who stood inside the doorway of the lab.

"Hello, this is Ishihara of Osaka West. Put me through to Inspector Mikuni."

The constable on the other end of the line didn't argue.

"Mikuni. What's up?"

"Your Zecom murder. We've got a suspect."

Mikuni's fuzzy image lunged for a pen, knocked a wad of paper to the floor, and cursed. "Okay, go ahead."

"I'll send you the evidence by courier. Basically, Nakamura was blackmailing his boss, Yui, about something called a . . ." He squinted at McGuire's computer screen.

"Integrated interface system," supplied McGuire.

"Integrated interface system. It looks like Yui got the basic research for this system from someone else, then used it or was planning to use it in Zecom products. Nakamura found out and blackmailed him."

"That would explain the post office account," said Mikuni with satisfaction. "Nakamura had a savings account. But he didn't carry a card or account book, so we only found out when the NDN search pulled all his data together."

Beside Ishihara, McGuire swung her chair restlessly, then began to scroll down the document on the screen.

"This account has regular pay-ins," continued Mikuni. "We won't be able to trace the payer, if it was done in cash."

"Worth seeing if staff at post offices around Zecom recognize a photo of Yui."

"Yup. Can you get that evidence sealed and sent over?"

"Will do. You'll never believe it. He sent it to himself by post, care of his old company." Ishihara glanced at McGuire, but she kept her eyes on the screen.

"He turned up here bold as a monkey every couple of months to collect his snail mail."

Mikuni whistled. "No kidding. How long has this been going on?"

"Nearly two years, according to the mail room." Ishihara had already interviewed the mail room clerks and one of the administrative staff, Takako Kimura.

"We'll get started on Yui's alibi and background," said Mikuni. "Thanks."

"No problem." Ishihara ended the call.

McGuire tapped the keypad, ignoring him. Her shoulders were hunched in a tight arc of tension.

"Why did your mail room accept packages for Nakamura?" said Ishihara. "He quit years ago."

"We're looking into that," said Izumi. The head of the Mechatronics Division reminded Ishihara of his own superintendent, but with more class. He'd be in middle management till he retired—didn't look nasty enough to rise any higher.

"If an ex-employee's mail is sent here, we forward it on," he continued. "And ask them to notify the post office. In Nakamura's case, there was probably some misunderstanding."

Or some particular understanding between Nakamura and the mail clerks, Ishihara thought, but he let Izumi save face.

"There are four discs," said McGuire, with an air of wanting to get the interview over. "Two are updates of the others, and are dated as such. One pair contains technical files. The other contains copies of mail and dated notes."

"Does he tell us how he got the information, or where Yui stole the research?" said Ishihara.

McGuire frowned at the screen. "No. In the notes, dated July 21, he says, 'the second part of the core studies is in the folder named Puppet in the Zecom backup drive. Access to this folder is unavailable even to sysadmin, which is why I assume Yui put the files in there.'"

"Does he say how he found out about it?" said Ishihara.

"Not here. This is probably one part of several documents, and he was confident nobody would find it. I think it was a kind of insurance."

"Against what?" said Ishihara.

"If Yui found all his other backups, or threatened him, he could say, "'Uh-uh, I've got evidence you don't know about.'"

"Maybe he was going to confess to you," suggested

Izumi, polishing his glasses with the end of his tie. "You used to be his supervisor."

McGuire frowned. "I don't know. This is the last entry in the notes, dated August 8. Here's where Kawanishi comes into it." She opened another file and read from the screen.

"'I have set August 15 for the first trial run. I've decided on Kawanishi Metalworks as the place, because the maintenance check for our robot there is on August 12, which means Y will be out of the country.'"

"He was scared Yui would catch him," said Ishihara.

McGuire nodded, and continued reading. "'Also, the Tomita T56 at Kawanishi is still more advanced than the old TiX6 in Suita, which means it will be easier to set the translator.' That's the device I told you we found on our robot," she added.

Izumi shook his head sadly.

McGuire continued reading. "'Once I understand how to work the interface, I shall call Tomita. I'm looking forward to seeing the expressions of that arrogant fat Matsuki and the smart-aleck gaijin.'" Her voice didn't change on the last words.

"No mention of Mito," said Ishihara.

McGuire looked up at Ishihara over her shoulder. "I don't think Nakamura meant to kill Mito. He wanted to test this long-distance interface, then bring it to us as his own work."

"Why call you to Zecom then?"

"Maybe he thought it was his last chance to show me this interface. Once Yui came back, he might not get a chance to come to us."

Nakamura probably thought Yui had gone home and was resting after his overseas trip. Of course, Yui said he *did* go home.

"Very sad." Izumi sighed. "If only he had concentrated on doing his own research . . ."

There was a loud knock on the door, and a young man wearing heavy-rimmed spectacles poked his head in.

"I'm sorry to interrupt, but Chief Matsuki would like to see Division Head Izumi immediately." He inclined his head formally to Ishihara and nodded cheerfully at McGuire.

Izumi settled his glasses. "Very well." He bowed to Ishihara. "My apologies for the interruption, Assistant Inspector. I think the matter is in your hands now. We would appreciate a short explanation of the involvement of our robot, however, once the case is solved."

Ishihara bowed back. "Your cooperation is appreciated. We'll keep you informed as much as possible."

"McGuire-san will see you out," said Izumi. "Please ask her if you require anything further." He bowed again and left with the bespectacled young man.

McGuire avoided Ishihara's eyes and swung her chair back to face the screen. "Mito must have seen that the robot wasn't working properly and gone to investigate. But I don't understand why it took him so long. The logs stop at four-thirty."

Ishihara reached for his cigarette packet, remembered where he was, and shoved it back in his pocket. "Sakaki says Mito didn't notice anything wrong with the welder at first because they were talking."

She looked up at him properly at that. "Was Sakaki there?"

"He didn't see the robot actually hit Mito, but he says there was nobody else there. He says he looked to see if Mito was alive. When he saw not, he ran away."

She ran her hand over her hair, her face tightening in distress. "Why didn't he call an ambulance?"

"He didn't want anyone to know he'd been there after hours."

She stared at the screen again. "Do you believe him?"

"If you're right, and Nakamura did it with some long-distance control method, his story adds up. Anyway, you said Sakaki didn't have the expertise to tamper with the robot."

"No."

"What's the matter?" he surprised himself by asking. "I thought you'd be pleased the case is cleared up."

"It's not cleared up," she retorted. "That's the trouble."

Her vehemence shocked him with its foreignness. She looked away, took a breath, and continued more calmly. "I . . . we still don't know the details of this 'interface' and where Yui got the research it's based on."

"When they catch Yui they'll find out."

"But if Nakamura had proper control of the robot, it shouldn't have hit Mito. If the interface had worked properly, Nakamura would have contacted us before Yui got back."

"Nakamura saw Mito's death in the news, realized what had happened, and got scared," said Ishihara. "But then he got worried about Yui, too, which is probably why he called you to Zecom."

"The device is made of biometal and looks like a liveline converter. But the factory only has one connection to liveline, and that's through the main switch, so you wouldn't need a converter on the robot. I can work out from Nakamura's notes"—she waved at the screen—"that he attached the device because he thought it would allow him temporarily to override the robot's ID, replace it with the ID of a Zecom robot, and thereby allow Nakamura to control it like virtual reality."

"You mean the robot in the factory would move the same as a robot in his lab?"

"Uh-huh. Our robot at the Kawanishi factory went to halt after hitting Mito because it was moving on a different sequence, the one that Nakamura was using on his Zecom robot. The converter decodes signals sent via liveline through the switch. But he doesn't give me enough detail in these notes!" She closed the screen with an angry slap on the keyboard.

Ishihara shifted impatiently. "What does it matter to

you?" he said. "It's clear that even though your robot was involved, there was no negligence by Tomita. Nakamura tried out some new technology and killed Mito by mistake. Yui killed Nakamura because he was being blackmailed."

"I need to know how it was done and where Yui got the research."

All she worried about was the research. It didn't seem . . . decent, somehow, for a woman.

"I'd like to say we'll pass on the information if we find it, but . . ." He didn't finish. She must know the police wouldn't release evidence. And they'd already arranged to take Nakamura's device.

"Here are the discs." She passed him a case.

He turned it over. Mito's death was an accident after all. But how he was going to explain it in his report . . .

"I can't believe I missed where Nakamura was sending his backups." McGuire sounded both amused and annoyed. "It's about the only place Yui wouldn't think to look."

"And so low-tech, too." Ishihara couldn't help teasing.

She glared at him, but without real heat.

He turned to go, but there was such misery in her hunched shoulders that he paused. "How's your brother-in-law taking it?"

"He's devastated. We all are."

"If we find out anything about the group, all the families concerned will be informed." That sounded pompous and official. Just the sort of thing he hadn't wanted to hear when Junta went missing. "Good-bye."

McGuire just nodded.

エレナ

By the time Ishihara left it was five o'clock, time for Eleanor to go and meet Akita for dinner. Possibly the first time I've left the office this early, she thought, a little grimly. Masao waited most nights at home for her. Instead, he'd be waiting for a call from Kazu or the police.

She was grateful to Ishihara for not giving them false reassurances. Nothing worse than being told, "everything will be all right." His blunt professionalism was almost a comfort in itself. She hoped he was handling the case. She could just about bear to receive bad news from him if . . . she shook off the thought.

As for the Kawanishi case, she wasn't surprised that Nakamura was blackmailing Yui. What did surprise her was that Nakamura would be bold enough to plan to double-cross Yui and bring the research to Tomita. And where did Yui get the information in the first place? From one of Zecom's foreign connections, as he'd just been overseas, and probably went several times a year. But if that were the case, the information should have been available to Zecom anyway.

Which left domestic sources or an overseas source not

affiliated with Zecom—a competitor, or a university lab. Eleanor thought Yui had probably been given or bought this information, whatever Nakamura said about stealing. He was in a position to offer many things in exchange: money, Zecom shares, insider trading information, research data, manufacturing data, even actual machinery parts . . . but if he didn't steal it, why would he worry about Nakamura threatening to reveal him?

She shook her head as though that could dislodge the key to the problem and ran her chair back from the desk impatiently.

Dinner with Akita. She had put together a short report for him, explaining the stage her own research had reached without giving away too many details. Tomita management might just agree to a new project. Akita's ability to carry out his brilliant ideas had never been as good as hers. But he did have some great ideas.

She folded the hard copy of the report and put it in her handbag, followed by her phone. Akita hadn't included a number with his e-mail, she noticed with annoyance. She wouldn't be able to call him if she was delayed, only text. She called Masao, though, and left a message for him. She even remembered to call home and set the oven to unthaw one meal ready for heating.

Smoothing her hair, she glanced in the little mirror on top of the filing cabinet. *I wonder how Mari feels without her hair?* That glimpse of Mari's naked head, more than anything else brought a great sense of loss to Eleanor—her niece was changing in a way that Eleanor could not understand.

She bent down to hook her outside shoes from under the desk and felt someone's eyes on her back. But when she straightened up again, nobody was there. In the main office only Kimura remained at her desk, patting makeup onto her cheeks using a handheld mirror. A cleaning robot hummed across the floor between the rows of desks.

You really need a break, she said to herself. Soon you'll be seeing things.

She found the restaurant on time. It was sandwiched between a vidgame arcade thronging with excited children and a pachinko parlor blaring a continuous loop of advertising jingle over the crash and jangle of the machines. Just the place for a quiet chat.

The racket cut off as soon as the restaurant door closed behind her. Half a dozen people sat on stools at a long counter, and there were low tables at the back, on tatami mats. It reminded her of the bar she visited with Ishihara, expanded several sizes.

As usual, she had no trouble catching the barman's attention—every pair of eyes at the counter turned to her as she stepped in. The barman paused in slicing sashimi.

"Irasshei," he said uncertainly.

"I have a booking in the name of Akita," she said.

The barman nodded, relieved. "Up the back."

She squeezed past the stools, past a large fish tank where much of the menu swam, and slipped off her shoes to step up onto the tatami.

"McGuire-san, over here," said a deep voice.

A heavyset man in a cheap business suit sat cross-legged at the far table. "You look much the same," he said, as she knelt at the table.

"You've changed a bit." She saw a man's face, rather than a youth's. Heavy jaw and high cheekbones, flesh starting to sag, slightly drooping eyes. He was heavier through the body, too. If not for his hot, restless eyes and stubborn mouth, she might not have recognized him.

"We all grow in different ways." He raised his voice and called for sake.

The barman's assistant hurried over with a tray containing small china bottles, tiny cups, hot towels, and some kind of seaweed pickles.

"You will join me in some sake." He poured her cup, then poured his own without waiting for her to offer. She noticed with a start that he was wearing dark gloves.

"Only a little, please." She wiped her hands on the towel. "I came to talk about work."

"Of course." He saw her gaze on the gloves. "An affectation, I'm afraid. We develop them as we grow older." He raised his cup. "Kampai. To renewed acquaintances."

"Kampai." Eleanor sipped the sake. It was cold and smooth. "Where exactly are you working now?"

"I'm on leave at the moment. Summer holidays. I'm staying with a friend in Okayama."

She'd been in Okayama on Monday, at Zecom. It was close enough for Akita to get to Osaka easily tonight. She'd had the impression his teaching job was farther away.

"Akita-kun." She used the peer-group suffix without conscious thought. He didn't seem to mind. "I was surprised when you contacted me after all these years. You haven't published anything in that time; I thought you'd gone to a different field."

"You, on the other hand, have been as active as always, McGuire-san, according to the Institute of Engineers database. How is everyone at Tomita? Did you get funding renewed for your integrated response project?" He shifted uncomfortably in the gray suit, which looked too tight across the waist and shoulders.

"How did you . . . No, it doesn't look like they'll renew funding." She felt curiously reluctant to admit that her project might meet the same fate as his had, so many years ago. "They decided it had too few practical applications in the near future."

"I'm sorry to hear that," he said, but his eyes lit up.

"But Chief Izumi—you remember him? He suggested I propose a m . . . more development-based project using my previous research. I, um, was wondering if you'd be interested in a form of collaboration." She hadn't intended blurting out the object of their meeting so quickly, but there, it was done.

A flash of something like elation crossed his face. "Do you mean collaboration involving the artificial synapses I referred to in my mails?"

"That's right. I was thinking, if we could concentrate on getting the neural network connections stable, then we could integrate them with the robot system at a later stage."

Akita nodded, but she had the impression he wasn't really listening.

He drew his hands apart, then brought them together. "I am so glad we have the chance to bring our paths together again. Many are the paths but all converge on the Way." The archaic syllables sounded vaguely familiar.

"Ancient Chinese," he added smugly. "One of the Taoist sages."

"So you are interested? I can't tell you what kind of a consultancy fee Tomita will pay you . . ." She handed him the pages from her bag. "Here's an overview of what we've been doing."

The barman's assistant knelt beside the table and placed before them several dishes: raw tuna and trevally, steamed eel, shellfish boiled in their shells, and miso soup with tiny clams.

Akita nodded thanks. He took the pages from Eleanor, but barely passed his eyes over them before placing them on the mat beside him. "I am interested in working with you again, McGuire-san. You have a great talent for the mechanics of research."

"Thank you . . . I think." She took a mouthful of sashimi to cover her confusion.

"But I must say I consider it my duty to wean you from this immature desire to create a humanlike robot." He touched his chopsticks on the little ceramic holders shaped like blowfish. "McGuire-san, why do you think we still have waiters to bring us our food?"

Eleanor grimaced sourly. "I know, you don't think humanoid robots are the way to go, but . . . ."

"Because humans do it better than we can build a machine to." Akita looked at her, head on one side. He had a fleshy nose, large for a Japanese, and very dark brown eyes, almost black. The whites were bloodshot, as though he'd been swimming in an overchlorinated pool. "You have not told me why you want to build your perfect robot."

"I suppose because nobody has ever done it before," she said.

Akita smiled, an expressive, un-Japanese smile. It shocked her more than anything he'd said. "The *Guinness Book of Records* is full of things that people do for the first time."

"I mean, it offers a significant challenge," she said, scowling.

"Some might say an impossible one."

"So you've gone over to the short-term view as well? That humanoid robots are a waste of time and resources?"

"No. I take an extremely long-term view." His hands clenched and opened on the tabletop. "I think you want to build a humanoid robot to get closer to God."

Eleanor began to have doubts about collaborating with him. "If God built like we do, the world would have fallen to pieces long ago."

"I didn't say play God. By creating a being in humanity's image, but a being that is perfect and immortal, you honor humanity and therefore honor its creator."

"I don't try and improve on humanity."

Akita sat up very straight. "If you could, what would you have your robot do—walk?" He waited until Eleanor nodded. "Interact with humans?" Nod. "Manipulate any material in a normal environment?" Nod. "React to the environment?"

"That's the aspect of the project I was hoping we could . . ."

"Please, do not escape into the practical," interrupted Akita. "I am talking of the great generalities here. I mean you would like your robot to see, feel, and decide on action, wouldn't you?"

"Of course, but . . ."

"And is the ultimate use for your robots to be slaves to humanity?"

Ishihara had intimated the same thing. That's the question, isn't it? We're talking self-awareness. A self-aware machine isn't going to want to stand in a department store elevator and say "welcome" all day. It won't be used as a museum guide or novelty toy.

"By dealing with a machine's self-awareness," she said, "we have to face our own self-awareness."

"Exactly," said Akita. "And that's not a goal that the rationalists can or want to comprehend. No wonder they cut your funding."

He made it sound like a conspiracy.

"Look, I just want to make something that works," she said.

He smiled at her again, in a way that made her neck hot with discomfort. She ate some eel, annoyed at her reaction. She really needed Akita's help; she should try and understand him.

"What do you see as the future direction, then?" she said finally.

"This." He glanced over at the other customers before stripping the glove from his right hand.

The hand was a prosthetic. No, "prosthetic" was the wrong word. The hand was obviously artificial. No false skin covered the biometal bones and polymer sinews. They shone bone white and silver and gunmetal gray. As he opened and closed his fist she could see the intricate tangled balls of microfibers in their mucoid casing.

His eyes watching her reaction, Akita opened the hand wide. From first and second fingers sprang long, flexible tubes that explored the surface beside his arm. The slim white tongues licked the table and traced the outline of the sake bottle.

Eleanor realized her mouth was open.

Akita chuckled and, with another glance at the counter, retracted the tubes and replaced his glove. "I've made some improvements to my original design. I don't need it to look like an ordinary hand. That used to frustrate me, you know? How people wanted their artificial hands to look like everyone else's. Such a waste of potential."

Eleanor found her voice. "Did you have an accident? Where did you get it done? Why haven't we seen reports of this?"

"A friend of mine is a surgeon. He did it because he has an interest in the field. But he is sadly in the minority." His eyes shone with the passion she remembered. "You will be interested to know that its function is not solely manipulatory. It incorporates a direct silicon interface."

Eleanor caught his excitement. "That's amazing. You can activate a computer directly?"

"Something like that."

"It's not commercially viable though, is it?" She imagined the cost and the social problems associated with implants— lack of acceptance, medical and insurance complications . . .

He smiled again. "Ever practical, McGuire-san. At present, no, it is not being developed in a commercial direction. Although a greatly simplified VR version is possible."

"What kind of modifications do you need on the hardware?"

He poured them both more sake. "You are welcome to come and see the results of my research anytime you like. I have a working model with me in Okayama. However, tonight we should consider the problems you are experiencing in your research and how we may solve them."

"Kampai," he added, raising his cup. "To the future."

"To the future." This time she clicked their cups together.

*   *   *

Eleanor's pleasure at talking to Akita about her research—it wasn't often she had the chance to discuss it with someone outside Tomita who actually understood—dissipated soon after she left him. The whole evening seemed slightly out of focus. That hand of his . . . an amazing thing. She had so many questions about it that she couldn't begin to put them in order. She would definitely go and see what he'd been doing, and soon.

But something about him made her edgy, something personal. Was he attracted to her? He didn't behave like any of the men she knew who had professed to being fascinated by a gaijin. They had all made their "fascination" plain by the end of the first few drinks.

Even when she arrived at the Betta's cool, comforting passages she didn't feel settled. Ridiculously, she kept looking for the wayward cleanbot that she'd spotted twice before, but all the robots were behaving normally.

As she reached her doorway, a voice called her name from the direction of the elevator. It was Akita.

"I forgot to give you this," he panted, out of breath, presumably from chasing her along the corridors. His face was quite red. "This" was a business card, but without the usual digital code on one side. She would have to input the number instead of swiping the card in her phone.

"It's the number of the friend I'm staying with," he explained. "He didn't want me to give it to just anyone." The name on the card was Yusuke Hatta, the address a number in the Zecom Betta.

"How did you get in?" she said. "You're supposed to call me from the front entry. Unless you're chipped as a resident, the elevator won't take you up."

He smiled. "McGuire-san, you're still more Japanese than we Japanese are. You know very well how such ID systems can be bypassed or adjusted for new users." He bowed, then turned and waved over his shoulder. "Nothing is un-crackable."

She watched him disappear around the corner. The lift doors swished open and shut. Nothing, indeed.

"I met Akita-kun today. Do you remember him?"

Masao nodded around a mouthful of noodles. "Big, sulky-looking man. I thought he quit Tomita?"

She laid her chopsticks on the top of the bowl, which was still half-full. She'd told Masao she didn't want a late snack.

"He did quit, years ago. He went on to Zecom, then he quit there, too. Seems like he's teaching in a rural univer-sity." Which one, he didn't say.

"Why the reunion?"

"Izumi thinks if we put together a research proposal on a particular area of the Sam project, there's a chance it might be implemented. One of the most promising areas is sensory processing, which is something Akita used to work on and still seems to be. I wanted to know if he was open to collab-oration."

"Is his university open, you mean." Masao finished his noodles. He picked up his own empty plate, tipped the con-tents of Eleanor's plate into the recycler, and left both plates in the sink for the automatic washer to finish.

"You think his university might not want him doing an-other job?"

"If it's anything like our place, it's possible." Masao stood behind her and massaged her neck absentmindedly. "Was he changed?"

"He was, a bit. Intense in a different kind of way. Mmm, more to the left . . . he's got an artificial hand."

Masao's hands paused for a second. "My God, what hap-pened?"

"He wouldn't say. Funny—he used to work on prosthet-ics, and now he has one."

"He always was pretty intense, wasn't he? You were

always complaining how he didn't share computer time fairly."

"I'd forgotten that." Masao's fingers reached under her hair and she half-closed her eyes in pleasure.

"I asked if he'd changed," he said, "because I ran into a man the other day that used to work in Islamic history. He's gone off to farm oranges in Shizuoka. Says he realized what he had here wasn't what he wanted." He sat down. "Your turn."

Eleanor sighed and stood behind him. Massaging Masao always left her hands sore—his back and shoulder muscles were a dense surface impervious to pressure.

"We're getting to that age when you never know if people are going to stay in their groove," he went on. "You talked the other day about leaving Tomita and working with Kazu. You'd never have said that a couple of years ago."

He was right. She dug in her fingers with more force than usual. She could taste an unaccustomed panic at the thought of the year ahead of her at Tomita, then another, then another. All those years, and what to show at the end of it— more canceled projects? *The past is dead, and the only thing the future holds is death.*

"Masao?"

"Hmm? A little lower."

"Do you believe people have souls?"

His muscles tightened under her hands. They hadn't talked about religion for years. Or love, or desire, or happiness, she thought with dismay. She'd been too damn busy.

"I know that Buddhism says we aren't reborn as the same individuals," she kept going, a little nervous now. "We're reborn as new, right?"

"According to what we've done in previous lives, yes." Masao kept his gaze ahead.

"What about our memories?"

"Do you remember your previous lives?" She could feel him grin.

"Oh. But what are we if not our memories, our experiences?"

"Our actions," he said softly. "That's what karma is—what we do. Anyway"—he swiveled in his chair to face her—"if what you mean by 'soul' is the thing that's reborn, then not only people have souls. All living things die and are reborn."

"All that has form, dies," she said softly. "Even robots. Even Sam Number Five in *Journey to Life*. It didn't matter that he wasn't human. If he had consciousness, he could achieve rebirth."

He swiveled in his chair, surprised. "That's right. Why the sudden interest?"

She shifted awkwardly. "I was doing some research into that group Mari's with—the Silver Angels. And I started thinking about . . . other things."

He chuckled and drew her to him, pulling her down onto his lap. How long had it been since they last sat like this?

"Ellie, if you get one of those moving-out-of-the-groove impulses, don't ignore it. Change is a good thing."

"It's nothing to do with work."

He hugged her so hard that her elbows dug into her sides. "That's what you think."

She slept badly that night. She had a dream that there'd been another earthquake, only this time it was everywhere. Smoke rose in a haze over the horizon as she stood in front of the rubble of the Betta with Masao. These were supposed to be quakeproof, she said. What happens now?

And her eyes opened. She lay still until her heart stopped thudding and wondered if the Bettas were as safe as they were supposed to be. One of the main causes of damage in the Great Quake and the Kobe quake before it in 1995 was the way construction companies had cut corners to finish buildings in time for deadlines, leading to weakened structures. The Bettas were supposed to have stricter controls, but she wondered.

Look how easily Akita entered. Theoretically, the fingerprint and retina ID systems were possible to crack, and the microchip recognition even less secure. But it required inside knowledge of the overall system, and the Bettas were supposed to have layers upon layers of security redundancies to protect that. If Akita could do it, anyone with specialized system knowledge could get in. They could interfere with the environmental systems, stop the air conditioners . . . or, more insidiously, reprogram it to include toxic gases.

Masao breathed as calmly as always beside her, but she felt no peace. The cool, smooth walls seemed like a prison. Her chest felt tight, and she was sweating. Could the windows be opened? She'd never tried. Surely there would be emergency latches, in case of fire.

She rolled out of the futon, taking care not to disturb Masao, and padded to the window. The glass was dimmed in preparation for morning glare, so she couldn't see anything outside except a few blurred lights.

There *must* be an emergency catch. Her fingers, shaking with urgency, scrabbled along the line of the lower sill. Betta safety and security closed in like a vice. Akita's voice in her head, *Nothing is uncrackable*. Sweat soaked a line down the center of her back.

Where was the damn catch? If there was a fire or an earthquake, how would people find . . . with a moan of relief, she felt an indented area in one corner under the sill. Under a hinged cover was a tiny leverlike device.

It wouldn't open, she didn't have the strength. Was the air really growing staler or was it her imagination?

"Ellie? What's the matter?" Masao's voice from the floor.

"Open this. Please."

The futon rustled, his feet slapped on tatami then his comforting bulk was beside her, his hand warm on her waist.

"Open what, the window?"

"Yes."

"Why? We'll get fined."

"Please." She tried to take deep, long breaths but they got caught halfway in.

Masao's hand left her waist and with a click-clunk, the window slid outward about ten centimeters. Tepid, moist air touched their stomachs. A warning light on the wall above began to blink, and if Eleanor had not canceled the apartment's vocal function after they moved in, a voice would now be asking them to close the window.

She relaxed immediately, and almost as immediately began to feel a fool.

"What was all that about?" Masao put his arms around her. "You're sweating. Are you sick?"

She shook her head and allowed herself to almost fall into him. They subsided onto the floor under the window, breathing humid air laden with the exhaust of countless air conditioners.

Her safe house was no longer safe.

石原

Thursday morning. Ishihara stretched his legs the full width of the passageway and lit another cigarette. New regulations said he couldn't smoke in the office and had to use a segregated section of the corridor. He'd damn well use the whole section, then.

He wondered how Mikuni was proceeding with the Zecom case. Ishihara didn't pretend to understand the contents of Nakamura's files, but as far as the police were concerned, if Nakamura had been blackmailing Yui for money or anything else, Yui had a motive for killing. And at the moment he was the only suspect.

Nakamura might have threatened to reveal that Yui copied research from . . . wherever it was. Nakamura hadn't been specific, which was what infuriated McGuire. Maybe Nakamura wasn't sure himself. It didn't matter, as long as Yui thought Nakamura knew.

Ishihara shifted from one side of his bum to the other on the hard bench. Both sides were equally uncomfortable.

Nakamura decided he would take the credit for the new system by taking it to Tomita. He made a mistake when testing it and killed Mito. The day manager at Kawanishi

Metalworks had identified Nakamura as the technician who had serviced the Zecom robot on August 12. Nakamura must have planted the device on the Tomita robot then.

Yui found out Nakamura was going to double-cross him and killed him. As far as Nakamura's murder went, all Mikuni could do was try to crack Yui's alibi. Okayama police certainly weren't going to bring him in for voluntary questioning yet. Zecom was far too important to the prefecture's economy to offend without evidence.

The cigarette burned down to the filter. Miserable short things they were, these days. He ground it out on the leg of the bench and tossed it in the ashtray, then went back to the office. He told his computer to open the folder labeled Zecom.

Yui had a level of security clearance that made it possible to tamper with the security system to show nobody in the building. He said he'd gone straight from the airport to Zecom, met the president, then went home. President Tatsumi confirmed he met with Yui at five-thirty. The clock-in records also confirmed it. Yui then went home, two stops on the Zecom maglev line, and arrived "in time for dinner" according to his wife.

She seemed startled, Mikuni had added. Doesn't sound like they eat many meals together. Mikuni had detailed a constable to track down the train records for that evening.

Something bothered Ishihara about Yui's statement. A déjà vu thing with the words. Was it the times? But Ishihara had only spoken to Yui once, at Zecom the night Nakamura died. All the other details had come secondhand via Mikuni. That time at Zecom, Ishihara was sure Yui said something about getting home at eight o'clock. Maybe Yui wasn't conscious of the exact time he got home, then later his wife reminded him. The man had just returned from overseas, after all. On the other hand, Yui might have let "eight o'clock" slip when he thought the police didn't suspect him. Then he

would have revised the time he got home to provide an alibi
for the time of Nakamura's death. They knew for sure that
Nakamura had been alive and talking to McGuire on the
phone at 7:30. His door card was last used, presumably by
the murderer, at 8:05.

Yui killed him, for whatever reason, removed the discs,
cut power to the computer to wipe it, fixed the internal security cameras so he wouldn't show up, let himself out with
Nakamura's card, opened the toilet window downstairs to
make it seem like an outsider got in, and left. He could then
walk around to the Zecom subway entrance . . . no, too
risky. Someone would see him, or he could be caught on
camera.

Ishihara made a bet with himself that the train records
wouldn't show Yui. It wasn't an issue as far as evidence
was concerned, because the visual records weren't admissible in court. Too great a chance of wrong identification,
they said.

The Zecom Betta records, though, should show the time
Yui entered. Ishihara flicked through screens of Mikuni's
notes and found . . . 7:35. Betta records showed Yui had entered his usual elevator from the subway. Ishihara clicked
his tongue in annoyance. These records *were* admissible as
evidence. He must have heard Yui wrongly. Yet he could
have sworn . . .

He put in a call to Mikuni, who was in a meeting and inclined to be irritable.

"What? No, nobody saw him outside the station."

"Did you ask the people in the houses around the Betta?"
Ishihara persisted.

"Why? He went in the Betta from the subway entrance."

"Is that on visual?"

"No, but his chip signal's in the record. Look, I gotta go."
Mikuni dropped his voice. "We put out a call for anyone
who saw anything suspicious to tell us. Okay?"

"Yeah, thanks." Ishihara didn't have much faith in the

public's spirit of cooperation. Either they'd get no response, or a lot of calls from a few weirdoes.

"Don't you have any cases in Osaka?" was Mikuni's parting shot.

Ishihara did have a case, and afterward he wished he'd looked at his mail sooner.

"The silver paint was deliberately poisoned," said the chemicals expert. He was a dapper young man with slick hair, wearing a Toramon T-shirt instead of the usual white coat. He rolled his chair from one side of a long desk to another, and the pickup changed to a different angle.

"So it's homicide." Ishihara thought with dismay of the time they'd wasted.

"This isn't a poison you'd expect to find in paint," the expert said, his eyes on a computer screen. "It's called 'fujirin,' after Daisuke Fujita who first synthesized it in the 1990s. At the time, he was working for one of the big pharmaceutical companies that later went bust after the Quake . . ."

"Can we have the gist, please?" said Beppu, who was crowding Ishihara so he could see the small screen.

The expert shrugged gracefully. "Whatever you like. Basically the victim dies of anaphylactic shock. Suffocates, you know. Fujirin can be absorbed through the skin or respiratory system."

Bloody sarin all over again, thought Ishihara. If this is what Prefectural Office is worried about, why didn't they tell us?

"Where would they get it?" said Beppu.

"I put a list of places in the report." The expert finally looked up from his screen. "A few research labs handle the inert form used for cancer treatment. Otherwise, you'd go to the black market. That means international."

"How much of this stuff exists domestically?" Ishihara asked.

"Not much. A few grams in each lab."

Both detectives relaxed.

"But you only need a fraction of a milligram for treatment. There would have been less than that diluted in the paint."

Ishihara rolled his eyes at Beppu. "So we're looking for someone who knows what he's doing."

"Oh, yes." He beamed. "I nearly missed it myself."

"Thank you." Ishihara reached to cut the connection.

Beppu put his hand out to stop him. "Is it possible these kids put the poison in the paint themselves because they thought it would help them connect with the computer? Does it work on nerves?"

Nice one from Beppu. That one hadn't occurred to him.

The expert ran his chair in and out from the desk a couple of times. "I doubt it," he said. "Firstly, because of the general unavailability of the substance. Secondly, because it's almost unknown except to the people working with it. The general medical community doesn't know about it, and it hasn't been adapted for military use overseas because of manufacturing difficulties."

"It's not available as a gas or anything?" said Ishihara.

"Certainly not." He began to look exasperated. "I really must go now."

"One last thing," said Ishihara. "Have you sent a report to our Prefectural Office as well?"

"Of course. First thing this morning. Good day, Officers."

"Thanks for your help," said Beppu, but the screen was already blank.

They looked at each other.

"PO probably already know a Silver Angels suspect working in one of those labs," said Beppu. "You'd think they could keep us updated."

Ishihara lit a cigarette, ignoring a number of pointed coughs from across the room. His hand shook slightly with annoyance. "Bloody hell. If PO don't tell us what they're doing, this is going to end up a mess." He thought of McGuire and her niece, and the dead children, silver-painted and gone to join the angels. And of what crackpots could do with access to a poisons lab. "We can't risk that."

"They haven't called us to a meeting since Tuesday," said Beppu. "When you weren't here," he added reproachfully.

"Yeah, sorry. I was catching a couple of hours' sleep after spending the night in Okayama." Ishihara pushed his chair back until it crunched on the desk behind his. "When did this report come in?" He pointed with his cigarette at the screen.

"An hour or so ago. I went to dinner, came back, there it was."

And Beppu had come and interrupted Ishihara's musing on the Zecom and Kawanishi cases to tell him to check his mail.

"We need to talk to the super about Funo." Beppu eased his backside off the corner of Ishihara's desk.

"You bet we do." Ishihara dropped his cigarette in a half-empty coffee cup and grabbed his phone.

They trudged up the hill from the subway station to Osaka Prefectural Police headquarters. There was no underground connection, for security reasons.

West Station's superintendent had been less than sympathetic. "Get over there if they won't come to you," he snapped. "You can't expect them to keep calling you with updates. Especially when they don't want us getting any of the action, anyway," he added. But he did agree they should do their damnedest to stay part of the investigation. "If those kids were killed on our beat, we'll find out who did it."

Ishihara and Beppu swallowed their indignation and went.

It was hotter than the day before. Looked like another summer of record temperatures. They passed the stump of an ancient gingko tree that used to shade the footpath before it fell, just before the Great Quake, its white sacred ribbon still girdling the stump. The tree falling had been a warning of the Quake, people said, a sign from the gods.

The only thing Ishihara liked about police headquarters was that you could see Osaka Castle from the east-facing windows, its green copper roof glinting in afternoon sun, crouching sullen and forgotten by all but a few tourists in its refuge of moat and trees. The seventeenth-century building had been restored in the 1990s. Police headquarters, also built in the 1990s, reminded him of the castle, being a squat nine-story box with defensive, inset windows. The first- and second-floor walls angled outward like castle walls, and a moatlike ditch in front ostensibly gave light to belowground offices.

The air inside the lobby almost cut his skin with the shock of coolness. Their sweaty shirts changed instantly to clammy shrouds. They nodded to the constable on the information desk, then went to the security booth beside the elevators and let the system scan their Betta chips, palms, and eyes before it would let them any farther into the building.

On the third floor they saw Funo coming out of the incident room. She was reading a printout on a clipboard and nearly ran into Ishihara.

"I was about to call you," she said without surprise at seeing them. "Follow this up." She thrust the clipboard at Ishihara and kept going past them down the corridor.

"Inspector . . ." Ishihara managed to get out, but by then she was talking to someone else. "Damn."

"Doesn't matter." Beppu peered at the clipboard. "What's the lead?"

One of the dead girls, Lissa Takada, and McGuire's niece, Mari Kitami, had given the same person as guarantor when they paid the contract money for their rooms. In Mari's case, for her second room.

"Footwork," said Beppu distastefully.

"You need the exercise." Ishihara went into the incident room and asked one of the detectives he knew for an update.

The case was now officially a homicide. Detectives had been sent to the two companies in western Japan and the three in northeast Japan that produced the poison found in the silver paint. They would cross-check the companies' personnel records and check their safety regulations compliance. Inspector Funo was liaising with Tokyo about the Silver Angels.

Ishihara and Beppu were to report to Assistant Inspector Ube, of Prefectural Office, as his team was following up the backgrounds of the dead kids.

"So who do you think did it?" said Beppu, as they walked back up the corridor. "A rival group?"

"Dunno," Ishihara grunted. He still felt Funo should have kept them more in the loop. "More likely they stepped out of line, and the group got rid of them."

"True." Beppu considered this gloomily. "Plenty of precedents."

"Assistant Inspector Ishihara." Funo's voice and tapping heels came from behind them. "About our international connection," she said as she caught up. "The other possible sources for the toxin used in the paint are all overseas. I think we should follow up your foreign contact, especially as she has family connections with the Silver Angels."

Ishihara realized she was talking about McGuire. "It's a waste of time . . ." he began. But as the guarantor lead meant following up McGuire's niece, it was kind of the same thing. "I'll get on to it," he finished.

"I'll get a level-two check on her, e-mail, phone, the lot," said Funo. "Particularly any international contacts."

"Is this poisoning what you meant when you said the Silver Angels had terrorist potential?" said Ishihara.

"We thought it more likely they'd disrupt network communications, but you never know." She looked at them as though they were cleaning robots away from the herd. "Get on with it, then."

"Ishihara." Funo waited until he got five paces away.

"Yes?"

"I'll decide what's a waste of time and what isn't."

Ishihara inclined his head.

"Ice queen," muttered Beppu. But he waited until they were in the elevator before saying it.

The name of the mystery guarantor was Tomonaga Ikujiro. Address: 501-3-16, Muko-machi Betta, Amagasaki. There was no such person at that address, of course, and the owners of the flats hadn't bothered to check. There was no such person on record anywhere and no record of the same alias being used before. The flat owners hadn't seen the man, so the police couldn't get a description.

"No wonder people get ripped off," Ishihara said disgustedly. "What do we have this national database for, anyway? All they need to do is touch the screen to check an address."

They had bought take-away eel for lunch on their way back to West Station.

"I reckon it's the same bloke." Beppu picked his teeth reflectively. "He must be connected with the Angels. The whole point is to get these kids away from their families and former lives, right?"

"The girls gave his relationship as 'tutor.' Maybe he was, but his real name's not Tomonaga."

Beppu flipped open his notebook, and told it, "Check tutors and teachers in common, Lissa Takada and Mari Kitami."

"Could be a boyfriend."

Beppu paused. "Then it's more likely to be two men using the same alias."

Ishihara pushed his empty styro box over the side of the desk into the waste bin. "There might not have been a man at all. The girls could have bought the seal and written the name themselves."

Beppu shook his head. "They'd have someone ready in case the flat owners got fussy."

Ishihara wasn't so sure, but they had to follow the lead. "I'll go to the university." He pocketed a pen and his cigarettes. "You check out the neighbors of the flats. Get a description of any man the girls were seen with and see if it matches up."

"See you later." Beppu went back to his own desk and started collecting his things.

University administration was icily cooperative. Ishihara got the message clearly—they'd talked all this over with the police already, but they would make one last effort.

A polite young clerk sat with him in front of a computer screen and compared Mari's academic record with that of Lissa Takada.

Mari and Lissa had taken three common subjects: English, western history, and communications theory.

"But their teachers are all different?" Ishihara asked the clerk.

"English is divided into several areas." He flicked to another screen that showed a class schedule in table form. "Lissa took English IIA, which is reading comprehension. Mari took IIC, which is travel conversation."

He flicked to another screen that showed an example of a timetable. "As you can see, Mari would have taken west-

ern history in first period Tuesday, because it clashed with
her prac classes. Lissa took the same subject in first period
Wednesday, but with a different teacher because the professor has a senior seminar at that time."

Ishihara left eventually with a printout of the girls' subjects and his head spinning with curriculum details. No wonder university students spent most of their time playing
around—by the time they worked out their timetables,
they'd be too tired to study.

He'd arranged to meet one of Lissa's friends in the
Student Welfare Office. She said she was at the library
studying, in spite of the holidays. The woman in charge of
the Student Welfare Office had sounded properly protective
and insisted on being present.

He stopped to buy a can of orange juice from a vending
machine near the main courtyard. Shade from chestnut and
gingko trees dappled the flagstones and benches. His
imagination peopled the courtyard with girls, chattering
and giggling, adjusting their makeup or eating slivers of
the latest fad food. He tried placing Junta with them,
laughing at whatever they laughed at because they were
girls and pretty.

He swallowed the last of the juice. The courtyard was
empty. Junta would be twenty-seven now, and beyond
eighteen-year-old girls.

Ishihara crumpled the juice can, all his strength going
into the simple plea that wherever his son was, he'd be
happy.

At the Student Welfare office he talked to Lissa's friend.
She seemed puzzled, more than anything, at Lissa's death. A
detective from Prefectural Office had already interviewed
her, so she seemed relieved that Ishihara only wanted to
know about boyfriends, and whether Mari and Lissa had
been friends.

"When she was still talking to me, Lissa didn't have any
steady boyfriend." The girl looked down at her hands,

folded in her lap around a pink handkerchief. She was thin and conservatively dressed in a knee-length skirt and cotton shirt. "But after she stopped telling me things, I don't know."

"When did she stop telling you things?" Ishihara tried to keep his tone gentle, but the burly head of Student Welfare kept glaring at him from her seat in the corner. A small air conditioner on the wall rattled ineffectively against the heat.

"About November last year. I was busy with exams, so I didn't worry too much. Then when we came back after the New Year break, she seemed like a different person."

"Was that when she moved apartments?"

"Probably. I didn't find out until I went around and found she'd moved."

Lissa had moved in early March.

"I don't suppose you know who she asked to be guarantor for the key money at her new place? She couldn't ask her parents, of course."

"No."

He hadn't expected it. "If you do remember anything, especially about any teachers Lissa might have confided in, give me a call. Thank you for talking to me."

He passed the girl his card, a cheap plasper one. She took it with small, tapered fingers.

He called Beppu from the courtyard. Beppu had got nothing from Takada's neighbors.

"I'm about to try Mari Kitami's lot," he said. "Meet you there?"

"Right." Ishihara could as easily take that line on his way back to the station.

The landlady's strident voice reached him before he turned the corner from the street.

". . . don't think I don't know what you're up to. I seen it on TV. You suss out where everything valuable's kept, then one of your thieving mates breaks in. You only pretend to try and catch him, and split the lot."

Beppu caught sight of Ishihara and waved, relief all over his face. The landlady peered at Ishihara from her seat halfway down the metal fire escape stairs. She wore a dirty apron over a frayed nylon dress that dated from the sixties. She reminded Ishihara of a character from an early *Sazae-san* comic.

"Here's your accomplice, then?" She whined.

"Don't shoo away the cats," Beppu muttered to Ishihara. "That's what set her off."

The landlady hadn't seen any men upstairs at Mari's, but if she had, she would have kicked them out.

The kitchen window of the downstairs flat rattled open. An unshaven face growled at them to shut up, some people gotta sleep during the day.

"Pardon me," said Beppu swiftly. "Our apologies for disturbing you, but we'd like to ask a couple of questions. Did you know the young lady in the upstairs flat?"

"Get fucked," said the face. The windows rattled shut.

"You're disgusting," yelled the landlady. Then to Beppu, "He wouldn't know her, he only just moved in."

"Is anyone else home?" said Ishihara to Beppu.

"No," said the landlady.

The two policemen bowed and retreated.

Beppu wiped his face with an already-damp handkerchief. "I've always felt it important to gauge when information is likely to be forthcoming and when not."

"It's too bloody hot," agreed Ishihara. He didn't think the landlady would have forgotten to tell Prefectural Office detectives such juicy details as men in Mari's room.

"I found a bit of extra information." Beppu paused in the shade of a hairdresser's awning when they reached the main road. See that coffee shop over there?" He nodded at the tiny lounge with a sign that said COFFEE AKEMI.

"The owner reckons Mari went in there a couple of times with two different men. With each of them at different times, I mean."

"Did she recognize a photo?"

"Picked Mari at once. One of the men sounds like the boyfriend your gaijin saw." He grinned at Ishihara's expression. "The other one sounds a bit older, maybe late twenties. Conservative dresser, a salaryman maybe."

"That's all the description we've got? It only fits about a tenth of the population of Osaka."

"Yeah, I know."

As they trudged back to the subway entrance Ishihara's phone buzzed. It was Lissa Takada's friend.

"Assistant Inspector? I just remembered that I think Lissa had a class with Mari Kitami. Geography, maybe."

"Are you sure?" Ishihara tried to unfold the schedule printouts with one hand.

"I think so. But I couldn't be certain . . ." Her voice trailed away.

"Thanks for calling," Ishihara remembered to say.

The brightness of the sun reflecting off the printout made them both squint. None of the girls' classes coincided.

"She made a mistake. Never mind." Ishihara refolded the paper.

"Hang on," said Beppu. "Mari didn't take geography." He slapped a fist into the other open hand with a damp smack. "Not a geography class—the geography *club*. The man must be connected to that club."

"You're a bloody genius." Ishihara reached for his phone.

"I know," smirked Beppu. "Got a dry handkerchief I can borrow?"

At 3:00 P.M. Ishihara and Beppu went off to question Kiichi Harada, alias Ikujiro Tomonaga, the man who had acted as guarantor for McGuire's niece and Lissa Takada.

Harada was a research assistant in the electrical engineering department at Osaka Engineering University.
According to the geography club convener, Harada joined
the club in autumn last year and usually directed one of the
bimonthly Sunday walks.

"He's very sound on the infrastructure of the town," said
the convener. "You know, how the electricity reaches us,
where the main broadcasting stations are, where the sewers
run, that sort of thing. It's good for the students to learn
about this as well as the usual historical sites."

The university informed Ishihara that Harada was on
leave for Bon and wouldn't be back until August 25. They
told him Harada's Osaka address reluctantly, and his home
address in Gifu Prefecture only after confirming Ishihara's
identity with West Station.

Ishihara grumbled at their caution, and the two detectives
caught yet another train south to Harada's apartment, in
Kuramachi, Hirano Ward. He didn't live in the university
Betta. Administration had explained shortly that a research
assistant didn't qualify for Betta residence. Harada obviously couldn't afford the rent near the university, either, because the address was an old-style block on the east side
away from the city center.

Ishihara mentally called these areas the "dough in the
doughnut." Years ago in the nineties, before the Quake and
the Seikai reforms, a lot of fuss was made about the "doughnut phenomenon" of cities. Experts sat solemnly in front of
TV cameras and predicted how residences and services
would flee the city center, leaving an empty hole of illegal
residents and lawlessness.

They didn't predict the Bettas, or the maglev trains, or
the networks. Business in the center of the city was as
healthy as ever. The Bettas sat happily in the suburbs, each
connected to the center by transport and service networks
that spread like the spokes of a wheel.

The wheel was a better metaphor, really. Into the empty

space between the spokes fell the poor, the homeless, illegal immigrants, shady businesses, and illegal entertainment of all kinds.

Harada's apartment building sat squarely between the spokes. It had been built in the eighties, when eccentric small buildings were in vogue. Now graffiti covered the red-brick walls, and the residents had put a wire fence around its quaint courtyard entrance because it was such a good place to ambush people.

The manager's door bore a sign. "Out shopping, back about 4:30."

Guests had to call residents on the intercom and get them to open the main doors. Harada's name was written beside Apartment 4B's intercom button.

Ishihara picked his way around trash and abandoned bicycles stacked at the side of the building, and found a fire escape at the back. He waited there until Beppu signaled him with his wrists crossed—no good.

"If he's there, he's not answering the intercom," Beppu said across the bicycles.

Ishihara looked up at the flimsy metal fire escape. They could try going in that way, but he'd bet the windows were locked.

"Let's wait until the manager gets back," he decided. "Then we'll know if he's here or in Gifu."

"We could call Gifu," Beppu pointed out.

"Better not to alert him if he is involved."

They waited, sweating even in the shade of the brick wall. "We should have checked the geography club first," grumbled Ishihara. "We knew the kids all went there."

Beppu mopped his forehead. "Can't help it. We didn't think a teacher was involved. And you know how it is—you get caught up in one line of investigation and forget the others." He pointed across the road at a small park with spindly trees and a water bubbler. "Drink?"

They crossed the road and drank at the bubbler. Typical Osaka water, tasting mostly of chemicals.

A young woman sat pushing a pram backward and forward. She kept one eye on a toddler who sang softly to himself as he played in the dirt with an empty yogurt container and bottle lids.

Beppu greeted her cheerfully. "Good day. We're waiting for Harada-san from the fourth-floor flat over there." He pointed at the brick building. "I don't suppose you know when he usually comes in?"

The young woman blinked tiredly at them. Her T-shirt was covered with food stains. Beppu gave her his best avuncular smile and peered in the pram.

"There's a cutie," he said. "Is she a good sleeper?"

The girl relaxed a little. "Not bad. She keeps him awake though." She nodded at the toddler.

"They'll settle down soon," said Beppu. "It's the heat."

Ishihara waited for him to mention Harada again, but before he could, the girl nodded across the park.

"There's Harada-san coming now."

Two things happened simultaneously. Beppu straightened up from the pram, both he and Ishihara staring in the direction the girl indicated.

The man walking past the park paused, looked across at them, and ran back the way he had come.

Ishihara cursed and chased Harada. He could hear Beppu panting into the phone behind him but the sound soon faded. Harada ran down the shopping street, dodging people, bins, and bicycles. Ishihara followed, pacing himself. If he could keep Harada in sight while Beppu called for backup, they'd get him. There was no subway entrance in this direction for a kilometer or more.

Harada swerved left by a shoe shop, off the shopping street. Ishihara sprinted. Catcalls and cries of annoyance followed him. His side hurt, and sweat stung his eyes.

Around the corner . . . yes, Harada still ran ahead. He was limping now, he must have hit his foot on something.

Ishihara put on a final, desperate spurt. Visions of himself actually making the emergency arrest and bringing in the key to the whole case flashed through his mind. His last arrest.

Harada stopped and turned right into what looked like a wall.

Ishihara was staring so hard that he failed to notice the shopping cart being pushed out of a grocery store by an elderly woman; he skipped out of the way at the last minute and crashed into a parked bicycle at disastrous speed.

The world spun and hit him from many angles. He disentangled himself and hobbled on to where Harada had disappeared—a door set between buildings, now locked.

Ishihara rattled the door ineffectually. He couldn't see another entry anywhere along the road. He knocked at the entry of the building next to the locked door, but nobody responded.

Finally, he sat down on the curb and lit a cigarette with shaking hands. Probably the last thing his aching lungs needed at the moment, but what the hell. When he thought his voice would be steady, he dug out his phone and hit Beppu's number.

"I'm at"—he glanced up at the nearest direction sticker on a pole—"Kireda four-thirteen-twenty."

"Yeah, we followed you on survey camera until you left the shopping street," said Beppu's voice. "I'm in a car from the local police box. We'll be there in a minute." He paused. "Did he give you the slip?"

"What do you think?"

Beppu wisely didn't answer.

They left the local police doing a house-to-house. By the time they got back to West Station it was nearly five and the house-to-house hadn't found Harada. Ishihara wanted a bath and bed. Damn Harada for being young and fast. The vision of an arrest mocked him.

Beppu took a call from Prefectural Office as they finished their report over a cup of tea.

"The ice queen wants to see us at a nine-thirty meeting. Looks like the toxin lead might be breaking."

Ishihara groaned and reached for his notebook. They'd missed Harada, but at least they had made a positive ID. He would be picked up sooner or later.

エレナ

Eleanor spent Thursday packing away a dream. The budget committee had recommended that the Sam project be shut down in order to "divert resources to more flexible projects with wider applications." All current experiments were to be completed at the earliest opportunity or simply abandoned, reports written, and the lab cleared away.

Eleanor made a formal protest to Division Manager Izumi and, although she knew it was futile and might damage her reputation, to the executive director, Matsuki. She had to do *something*. Never had she felt so much like a very small and dispensable cog in a large machine.

The other members of the project team were at first loudly disappointed, but when Eleanor returned from Matsuki's office silent and withdrawn they, too, began to work in silence, darting worried glances at her. Eleanor knew she should talk to them about it, but she didn't trust her voice to stay steady or her eyes to remain dry. She immersed herself in the tasks, and the day passed in a kind of dreary disbelief. It wasn't as if the project had to be cleared away that evening. They still had experiments to write up, conclusions to draw. Two of the team had a paper to write for a conference the following month. The Sam robot still stood in the lab, connector rod stuck in the wall as it recharged its battery ready for the next challenge. Only there would be no more challenges.

Eleanor sat at her desk in the office and stared blankly at the monitor screen. She tried to tell herself that she wasn't angry, that she was an adult and these things happened, that she could cope with this rejection of everything she'd worked on for nearly a decade.

What would they do with Sam? Probably take it apart and use the components. She felt an almost physical pain at the idea, although she knew that to be ridiculous. It was only a robot. She could build another.

Yet it still hurt. All that work on Sam, and for what? For what, indeed. *What are your goals? What use are they?* To create something that worked. Why did she choose the humanoid robots—because they were the greatest challenge? But they'd always be less than human.

"Are you coming for a drink, Chief?" Kato, who had worked with her on the Sam project, poked his head around the filing cabinet.

"Now? It's only five-thirty."

"We don't want to hang around much, tonight," he said with embarrassed defiance.

They would go to a bar and commiserate with each other over a continuous flow of beer and whiskey, spilling all the complaints they couldn't voice at work and reminiscing on how they'd come this far together.

Eleanor couldn't face it. She wanted to do something, anything. Even start work on the new research proposal, now that Akita had agreed to collaborate . . . Akita's artificial hand flexed in her memory. That's what she could do— go and see for herself what he'd been doing.

"I think I'll pass tonight, Kato-kun. I'm sorry."

He looked both relieved and disappointed. "Are you sure?"

"Yes, I'm a bit tired." She dug a ten-thousand-yen note out of her handbag. "Have a couple of drinks on me."

"Thanks, Chief." He grinned and left. She heard the six members of the team go, leaving the office quiet.

The number Akita gave her had an Osaka prefix, but after it rang twice she heard a double click as it diverted. It rang four more times, then connected. "Audio only," her darkened screen informed her.

"Hello, McGuire-san." Akita's voice.

"Hello." She felt awkward. "Thank you for your hospitality last night. You gave me this number if I wanted to see more of your research."

"What good timing. I was just thinking about you."

She couldn't think of a polite follow-up to that one.

"I knew you'd want to see more," he went on. "I shall give you a demonstration. What time can you leave work?"

Eleanor was about to say seven, which was normally the earliest she'd get away. But things weren't normal.

"I can leave sometime in the next hour," she said. "Where's your lab?"

"I've got some equipment at my friend's place. Why don't I meet you at the fast train station?"

"Okayama Central?"

"No, the Zecom line, first station, Betta East." Akita sounded almost cheerful. "I'm staying close to where I worked before. Funny, isn't it."

Very funny. But why shouldn't Akita have a friend who worked at Zecom? Lots of engineers did.

"I'll get there about seven."

"I look forward to it. Oh, and McGuire-san?"

"Yes?"

"Did you know the police are bugging your phone? You should invest in some protective software. I have one that's very effective."

"I'll, um, look into it."

She stared at the blank screen. Bugging her phone, were

they? It wouldn't be difficult. Rumor had it that the police and domestic security forces monitored all hand phone frequencies as a matter of course. The old cable used in the Tomita lines was open to surveillance, too. The only totally secure wiring was liveline, which was why they were used in the Bettas and new areas of Tokyo, including the NDN. Nobody had, officially at least, found a way to penetrate its biometal sheath.

She dictated a terse e-mail to Assistant Inspector Ishihara, asking if the police were tapping her phone and if so, why. She felt obscurely betrayed by Ishihara, with whom she'd just begun to feel comfortable. So much for the "honest cop." And she called Masao and left a message that she was going to meet Akita and would be home between eight and nine.

She glanced sharply at a cleaning robot in the outer office, but it was ticking over harmlessly in a rest cycle and showed no sign of following her.

The Zecom line was a short local train line off the main fast train track. The first two stations connected to the Zecom Betta, the third to the factory where Eleanor had come to see Nakamura last Monday night.

Akita waited just outside the ticket gates. He blended into the gray-suited crowd of homecoming salarymen and women as though he was still one of them. When he saw Eleanor he raised his gloved hand in greeting and smiled as she approached.

That slightly vacant, un-Japanese smile didn't help Eleanor's nerves. She'd never felt this physical unease with the old Akita. Was she being oversensitive?

They walked down the wide, clean passage. Homecoming workers were only just beginning to fill the space.

"What department does your friend work for?" said

Eleanor. The walls shifted in green-and-pink abstract patterns, and Bach tinkled softly from invisible speakers.

Akita nodded in time to the music. "My friend is the systems manager at the Betta. He lets me use one of his storerooms to keep my equipment in."

"But you must have had access to an advanced laboratory to do the work on your hand . . ." Eleanor began, but paused. A cleanbot—one from a Zecom line, of course—was following them. There was no other word for it. The round, wheeled shape hugged the wall behind them, staying an even ten meters back. There were no other cleanbots in view.

Akita noticed her gaze. "Is something wrong?"

"I don't know." Eleanor kept walking, and looked over her shoulder as they turned a corner toward some elevators. The cleanbot came to the corner and plunged across the corridor, zigzagging frantically to avoid human legs. Then it settled down against the wall again.

If she said *I'm being followed by robots,* he'd probably call a psych counselor.

Three other people also waited for the elevators. Akita waved his card in front of the sensors, and the down light went on. The other people moved on to the next elevator.

Welcome to Zecom Betta East, said the elevator in an attractive female voice.

"I've got your visitor's chip," said Akita. He handed her the card, which she passed in front of the elevator's internal sensors.

Thank you, said the elevator. As the doors closed she could see the cleanbot motionless against the wall.

Eleanor watched the numbers drop by two.

Lower ground floor, authorized personnel only.

"Here we are." Akita led the way to a door labeled MANAGER, close to the elevator. "My friend's away until later this evening," he said.

The apartment was large and Western-style, with bare

walls and square black furniture. Two extra doors in the living room were labeled SECURITY and SYSTEMS.

Akita noticed her glance. "The manager's got access from here as well as through the main office. In case he needs to be contacted after hours." He gestured at the low sofa. "Have a seat."

Eleanor sat on the edge of the sofa, shoving her handbag behind her feet. She did hope she'd been right about Akita's interest being purely platonic. "Where do you keep your research equipment?"

"Mostly in there." He sat down heavily in one of the armchairs and pointed at an unlabeled door that Eleanor had assumed led to a bedroom. It didn't reassure her.

Akita leaned over and spoke into the arm of the chair. "Bring two drinks to the living room." His pronunciation was so slow and clear that he must be talking to a Betta system.

Sure enough, a few seconds later there was a whirring sound from the kitchen, and a squat, flat-topped helpbot hummed across the floor toward them, carrying a tray on its head. A shiny silver cylinder with multiple retractable appendages, it moved a little jerkily. Perhaps it needed a sensor upgrade. Or the room might have recently been rearranged, and that was confusing its navigation system. When it got to the sofa it stopped.

Please take your drink. It sounded familiar, a synthesized version of Akita's voice.

She took one of the glasses of iced tea. "Nice touch."

"I think so." He peeled off his gloves and took the other drink, letting her see how the artificial hand worked; the fingers held the glass, but the long, tonguelike appendages were free to manipulate other things, in this case a straw.

"Can I, um, see the specs for that?" Eleanor stared unashamedly.

"Of course." Akita nodded seriously. "I am so glad you have decided to join me."

"Join you . . . ?" Eleanor was being distracted by the helpbot. It seemed to be looking at her. How something with only a flat screen as an interactive surface could "look" at anything, she didn't know. "Akita-kun, is there anything wrong with this robot?"

He smiled. "It is different. Watch." He clapped his hands, and the helpbot swiveled slightly, giving the impression that its attention had shifted to him.

"Draw me the shape that has no end," he said.

The helpbot zoomed over to the middle of the room and ran slowly in a circle, leaving its vacuum appendage down so that the trail remained in the carpet pile. The circle was slightly egg-shaped.

"That's an impressive recognition program," Eleanor said, and meant it. A helpbot was normally programmed to process only a handful of simple commands, certainly not metaphors.

"It's not a program. Tell it to do something."

"What . . ." Eleanor frowned at Akita, certain he was teasing her. "All right." She clapped her hands. "Dance. You choose the step," she added.

The helpbot didn't move for a moment or two. No way it could process an unspecific and arbitrary command like that.

Then it began a jerky series of movements, slowly transcribing an arc. Seconds later, the apartment's audio system activated, and the sounds of "The Blue Danube" echoed softly. The robot's movements were in three beats.

Akita laughed at the look on her face. It was a superior laugh, and Eleanor set her teeth.

"What kind of processor have you got in there?" she demanded. Then to the robot. "Stop."

The robot kept dancing.

Akita spread his hands wide. "An effective demonstration, you must agree, McGuire-san. As I told you, it is not a program." He called to the robot. "Enough, Ken. You may finish now."

The robot stopped, and the music faded.

"This way." Akita rose and opened the door marked SYS-TEMS. The room was filled with wall-to-wall monitors and consoles that spoke of the complexity of the Betta. At a desk in the middle of the room sat a man, with wires connecting his bare skull to a large console on the desk. One of his hands seemed to be stuck inside part of the console, via a huge glove that reached to his elbow. He wore shorts and an undershirt, and his body gleamed with sweat.

The man shook his head as though waking from sleep and reached up with his free hand to disconnect the wires on his head. Then, very slowly and with many stops and starts, he withdrew his hand from the glove. His hand wore another glove, this one black with the shine of metallic thread.

"Well done, Ken," Akita said. "This is McGuire-san, but you two have already met. McGuire-san, this is one of my associates, Ken Fujinaka."

The man turned in his seat and looked their way with thin, slanted eyes above high cheekbones. His eyes were slightly unfocused. The smooth, muscular shoulders in the dark undershirt were those of a young man, but his face was sallow and drawn. There was a line of drool down his chin, which he wiped with a shaking hand. He mumbled something at Eleanor and turned back to the console.

"Ken will join us in a minute," said Akita with a patriarchal air. "He is still learning. There is a certain lapse between in there and out here."

He pulled the door of the room closed again, forcing Eleanor to step backward into the apartment living room again. But she went no farther.

"What *is* that?" She folded her arms and set her feet, not intending to budge until she got some answers. "What do you mean by 'in there'?"

Akita loomed closer. He was almost as tall as Detective

Ishihara. But Ishihara had never intruded into her space like this. She could feel the warmth from Akita's thinly shirted chest and smelled unwashed sweat and another, sweeter scent, like incense. He bent forward to speak, and she had to step back.

"That, McGuire-san, is my new interface. It enables the user to control elements of a system from the inside."

He kept stepping forward as she retreated, until the back of her knees hit the sofa, and she had to stop.

"Fujinaka-san could hear what we said and made the helpbot move? And he must have made that cleanbot move in the passage outside . . ." She still didn't believe it. "A direct interface? But you'd still have to go through the programs. That would take hours, days."

"My interface is an intuitive thing." Akita finally left her some space. He returned to his chair and finished his drink.

Eleanor sat down again reluctantly. She wanted to examine this so-called interface for herself. Part of her had started to be excited at the possibilities, but she couldn't let go of caution. It was probably an elaborate fake.

"What do you mean by 'intuitive'?" she said.

He leaned back in his chair and raised his artificial hand in front of his eyes. With a theatrical gesture he smiled, turned the hand this way and that admiringly. The pale biometal flexed like a cluster of strange coral in an ocean current.

The biometal converter on the Kawanishi robot . . .

"It was you, wasn't it?" Things began to fit together. "You sold this new interface to the director at Zecom—Yui. That's what Nakamura was testing."

Akita looked puzzled. "Nakamura? I don't know who you mean. And I did not sell my interface to Yui-san. I merely provided him with some ideas that could lead to Zecom developing a watered-down virtual-reality version of my interface. He provided me with a reference for this job and certain other . . . privileges."

"And Nakamura blackmailed his supervisor Yui, then tested the interface using my . . . Tomita's robot at Kawanishi Metalworks, which killed Mito by accident when he investigated."

"I don't know what Yui did with my ideas." Akita was back at admiring his hand. "I imagine it is plebeian and commercial."

"Commercial means you get money to do the research properly." Eleanor was stung by his implied criticism of her own work.

Akita shot her a shrewd look. "Or not, in your case."

"How did you manage to afford that, then?" She pointed at the systems room.

"My work inspires a number of people who are glad to offer assistance." He leaned forward, suddenly intense, his dark eyes fixed on hers. "I have discovered something more than another technological fix. I have discovered a way to give people hope."

"Hope for what?" She didn't really care what Akita had dreamed up to justify begging for funding. What she did want to know was how the interface worked.

"Hope for a different life. McGuire-san, you must see how we Japanese are tired of this relentless balancing act to maintain our economy."

"Yes, yes, development is blamed for everything from the breakdown of family life to new diseases," said Eleanor restlessly. "I'm aware of the arguments on both sides. Can you get back to how it works?"

He didn't appear to hear her. "You see, in ancient times people believed in the unity of the physical world and the divine world. The divine cosmos, the Macrocosm, was a living manifestation of God. That is why our ancestors paid homage to spirits in trees, stones, and the weather.

"Within it was the Microcosm, our physical world that reflected the divine cosmos and was ruled by it. Our own bodies, like those of every living thing, are also

Microcosms. We are a reflection of the divine. We are simulacra of God."

Eleanor picked up her handbag. Interface or not, she had better things to do than listen to this.

"With the domination of rationalism," continued Akita, "we lost the knowledge of God and the divine world. We only know the physical world, and we think that is all there is. But if we do not know the divine for what it is, we can never become God."

Eleanor cleared her throat. "I, um, think I'd better go now."

"In my research I discovered a way to use science to become part of the Macrocosm ourselves, and thus divine. We are no longer reflections. That is why I said to you that your robots are no longer necessary. They are merely puppets, simulacra."

She stood up. "Akita-kun, I came to see an example of your research, in the hope this might lead to us collaborating. But if you can't show me something more than an unproved demonstration and this ranting, I shall leave."

He looked up at her, his heavy eyebrows crooked in puzzlement. "I am explaining."

The door to the systems room opened, and Fujinaka stepped through, shutting the door behind him. He looked more composed now—he'd put on a collared shirt and had wiped his smooth head and face. His scalp was marked in places by the flat shine of the implants where the wires had been connected. He still wore the black glove on his left hand.

"Nice to meet you, McGuire-san." He looked her up and down in what Eleanor recognized as the Bold Young Man Sizing up Foreign Body stare.

She ignored the look, as usual.

"The Boss here"—Fujinaka pointed with his chin at Akita,—"has told us so much about you." He sat down in the chair opposite Akita, so they flanked Eleanor.

"Like what?" she said, momentarily distracted.

"How you and he were the bright young hopes of Tomita Corporation." Fujinaka grinned. His long eyes almost disappeared into his cheeks. "Before the Boss went freelance."

"I was not appreciated," Akita said.

"So you don't work at a university?" Eleanor's unease grew.

"Academics have been particularly critical of my work." Akita frowned. "They'll regret that."

"The Boss has high hopes for you, McGuire-san." Fujinaka tried another version of the Stare.

To avoid his eyes on her crotch, Eleanor sat down again. "High hopes?"

"With our new interface." Fujinaka jerked his chin at the systems room. "The Boss is always telling us we need to study more about the Betta systems so we can use it properly, but none of us know enough. He reckons you're an expert."

"Not on Betta systems as such," protested Eleanor. "On some of the robots, perhaps. Tell me, how did you make the robot respond so quickly to my order to dance?"

Fujinaka looked at Akita, who nodded. "I thought about dancing," said the young man. "Only I couldn't find a step you old fogeys would recognize for a while."

"It seemed like a while to him," Akita put in, stroking his artificial hand with the other as he leaned forward. "To us it was much quicker. There is a time lag between our perceptions in the Ma . . . in the interface and our perceptions outside it."

Eleanor looked at Fujinaka's gloved hand. "The synaptic connections are made through the nerve endings in the hand?"

Akita nodded. "Sensory nerves. How ironic that we should be using those supreme servants of the body to conquer it."

Eleanor didn't pay attention. She was trying to understand how it might work. You'd have to translate the electrical signals from the human brain into electrical signals that a computer could process . . .

Fujinaka sat upright and put his hand on the large implant above his ear, listening. "He's here," he said to Akita. He glanced at Eleanor, and added cryptically. "You know, from the south."

"Where is he?" said Akita.

"On his way up now. Something's wrong." Fujinaka glanced at Eleanor again and slid a phone out of his shorts pocket. "Do you want him to wait?"

Akita smiled at Eleanor. "Of course not. We have no secrets from McGuire-san. She has decided to join us."

There it was again, the "joining" thing. As if Akita was talking about some special club. Mind you, if it was a club devoted to researching the new interface, she'd join.

"If you'd like me to come back later . . ." she began insincerely.

The front door of the apartment banged open. A slim man stood in the doorway, breathing heavily. He had a thin, ascetic face and was carrying a bulging briefcase. He strode forward, his eyes on Akita.

"Adam-sama, we have a problem."

石原

At 8:20 Ishihara's desk phone buzzed. Mikuni's face appeared on the screen, stretching sideways, then snapping back into proportion as the image stabilized.

"Ishihara, I owe you an apology about the Zecom murder. We found a witness who places Yui outside the Betta at eight o'clock. I don't know how the Betta records can show him going in at 7:35, but we brought him in for an interview."

"Not an arrest?"

Mikuni grimaced. "We couldn't go that far. His DNA's all over the lab, but you'd expect that. His fingerprints aren't on Nakamura's workstation, but there are plenty of gloved prints, very recent. We also got glove prints from the downstairs toilet. We brought him in mainly so that the witness could try to identify him."

"And?"

"I'll run the tape for you." Mikuni's face disappeared from the pickup, leaving a blurred image of his office. Then the screen darkened, and lightened again to show Mikuni talking to Yui over a desk in a bare interview room. A constable sat in the corner, monitoring the recording at a small computer.

Yui was ticking items off on his fingers with exaggerated patience. If anything, Mikuni looked more uncomfortable than he did.

". . . I sent my suitcase home by courier from the airport. Then I got on the fast train to Okayama. When I reached the Zecom stop it was nearly five. I clocked in, greeted my assistant, then went into my office and checked my mail.

"Then I met with the vice president and the managing director of the Marketing Division to give them an informal report on our situation in Jiangsu," Yui went on. "After that I returned to my office, sent a couple of e-mails, then went home."

"That would have been about seven?" said Mikuni.

"Probably a bit after." Yui sighed. "I'm sure you confirmed that my assistant went home at seven."

"So you say you got in the monorail at the company, got out at the Betta West stop, and went straight home?"

"That's what I said. Shall we replay the recording so you can listen?" Yui drummed his fingers on the table in a show of irritation. It must be only show—Yui was far too cool to get flustered yet.

Mikuni leaned forward. "Would it surprise you that the station videos show no record of you catching a train that night?"

Yui raised his eyebrows. "No, it would not surprise me. Approximately seven thousand people live in the Betta and catch that train every day. What would surprise me is getting a clear image of everyone." He regarded Mikuni almost pityingly. "Inspector, surely you aren't trying to build a case around this?"

Mikuni shook his head and smiled. Ishihara could see the nervousness behind it.

"I assure you, we're merely making inquiries with regard to the Nakamura case. Nothing more." He blinked and looked down for a second. Ishihara suspected the witness's positive ID was being conveyed through Mikuni's aural receiver.

Mikuni looked up. "However," he continued more confidently, "we appear to have a slight problem with your timing. You're sure it was 7:20 you caught the train and 7:35 you got home?"

"I think we've made that clear, Inspector. You spoke to my wife, you saw the Betta entry records."

"Nobody saw you at the station," said Mikuni. "But somebody saw you outside the Betta at 8:20."

Ishihara wished he could see Yui's face better.

Yui looked bemused. "It's a mistake."

Mikuni leaned back in his chair, but his eyes never left Yui's face. "As Nakamura talked to someone on the phone at 7:30 and was discovered dead at 9:03, you can see why this witness interests us."

"He or she must be mistaken. I had no reason to wish Nakamura any harm. This whole interview is ridiculous." Yui pushed his chair out from the table.

Mikuni put his hands up in a calming gesture. "Please, a couple more minutes, if you don't mind. Firstly, we'd like you to explain why you have been making regular large withdrawals from your bank account for the past six months."

Yui drew his chair under the table again. He straightened his glasses, looked at the observation wall, then back at Mikuni.

"I think I'll talk to my lawyer now," he said.

The screen darkened, then Mikuni's face snapped into focus.

"As you can see, we got a positive ID from the witness." He sounded satisfied.

Yui insisted he'd used the money to gamble and lost all of it. It was a coincidence that the amounts were the same as payments going into Nakamura's account. As for the research on interface systems, that was the result of a former collaboration. They were welcome to check the people he'd collaborated with.

"And?" said Ishihara.

Mikuni shook his head. "One of them is a professor in Sweden, one left the field and works as a journalist, and the other one left with no forwarding address."

"It doesn't sound like they kept in touch with Yui."

"No. We'll check his mail just in case. We've got analysts looking at the research Yui mentioned, but it will take them a while to work out if it could be used to do something like whatever Nakamura did. And you know the file Nakamura mentioned? The one named 'Doll' or something?"

Ishihara remembered McGuire saying it was probably the file with Yui's core research. " 'Puppet,' " he corrected.

"Yeah, well it's not there."

Damn, he would have liked to give McGuire a look at that file. "When did Yui come in tonight—seven o'clock? Can you get a search warrant to go through his files before one o'clock?"

Mikuni would have to apply for an arrest warrant before he could arrest Yui, as Yui had come in on voluntary appearance. That would have to be done within six hours, or they'd have to let him go and pick him up again. Ishihara doubted the magistrate would approve a warrant so quickly, especially as Yui had shown no signs of being likely to run. Mikuni's superintendent, though, could issue a search warrant, and if they uncovered evidence, he could then make an emergency arrest without a warrant.

Mikuni took off his glasses and massaged the bridge of his nose. "I'd feel better if we only had the wife's word on when he came home. The Betta records evidence is too strong. We'll need a confession to beat it."

"Talk to the wife again," suggested Ishihara. "Does she know about the payments to Nakamura?"

"Good point."

Ishihara checked the time. It was 8:45. "I gotta go."

"Something big?"

"Not sure. Prefectural Office is being cagey."

Mikuni shook his head sadly. "They're always like that. See you later."

The Prefectural Office incident room was rowdy with the noise of half a dozen conversations being held at the same time on different phones. The air smelled of smoke and Korean take-away. Four detectives he didn't know tapped keyboards in front of computer screens. Inspector Funo was talking to two of them at the far end of the room. She saw Ishihara come in but didn't nod.

Beppu beckoned to him from one of the desks closest to the door.

"You took your time," he said. "I had to explain to her ladyship that you were tidying up a case in Okayama. Meeting's postponed until we hear from the chemical lab in Shikoku about that poison found in the paint." He pulled over a chair from the neighboring desk. "Siddown."

Earlier that evening, two detectives from Osaka had gone to interview management of a research lab in Tokushima on Shikoku Island, one of the few places that stocked the fujirin chemical used to kill the four Silver Angels members. The two detectives would be there by now, and were to send word if any of the stuff was missing.

"The thing that got everyone a bit excited," concluded Beppu, "is that a few minutes ago we had a call from Takamatsu. Guess who the station cameras picked up on the platform of the fast train from Osaka at four this afternoon?"

"Who?" Ishihara picked up an untouched box of food from the other desk. It was lukewarm, but he was hungry again. The less sleep he got, the more food he ate.

Beppu groaned. "You could at least act interested. Harada, that's who. Our tutor from the geography club. If he was involved in the poisoning . . ."

"No wonder he ran," said Ishihara, his mouth full. Takamatsu was the first stop after Okayama, through a long tunnel under the Inland Sea and into Shikoku. "Have Takamatsu police picked him up yet?"

"Not yet," said Inspector Funo behind them.

Beppu swung his chair to face the desk properly and Ishihara put the box and chopsticks down. One of the chopsticks tipped off, flicking spots of kimchee onto Funo's dark blue trousers. She didn't notice.

"How kind of you to join us, Assistant Inspector."

Ishihara had half expected a reprimand for failing to bring Harada in.

"Harada and his friends are too savvy," she said. "They don't carry phones, they either don't have Betta chips or they've removed them, and they manage to avoid public cameras."

"Makes it hard to track them," Beppu said sagely.

Funo raised her eyebrow. "To state the obvious, yes. It also interests me how they communicate with each other."

"Telepathy?" said Beppu carelessly, then caught Funo's eye. "You'll be wanting that train timetable . . ." He passed her the printout quickly.

"He might come back by car," said Ishihara.

"I hope so," she said. "We've notified all rental companies, and Shikoku is easy to roadblock. Now, we're bringing in all the known Silver Angels we can find for interviews. I'll need you both soon for that."

"We're looking for information about the group's plans?" said Beppu.

"I doubt the ordinary members know the group's plans." She frowned. "Mostly we want to know where Adam lives, preaches, works, anything. Even the smallest clue."

"Quiet!" yelled a detective from the other end of the room. He cupped both hands over his ears, nodding, then jumped forward and ran his eyes over a monitor configured for visual input.

"Inspector Funo?" he called. "I'm routing this to the super's office."

Funo swept out, her face tense, her heels tapping.

Everyone else in the room turned to the detective who'd taken the call. He was lighting a cigarette, his face somber.

"From the lab at Tokushima. They found a discrepancy between the actual amount of toxin in storage and what's on record." He met their eyes in turn. "And the person in charge has disappeared."

"Shit," said Beppu. "Not another runner."

"That's not all," said the detective, his voice lower. "When he left, he took a batch of rescopal with him."

Beppu and Ishihara looked at each other. Rescopal, like sarin, was one of those substances well-known to police all over Japan, and for a similar reason. A group calling themselves Swords of God had used it several years ago to gas almost an entire block in Tokyo, with thirty fatalities.

The fax machine and two networked printers whirred into life.

"That'll be the background info now," said the detective.

"When did this person leave?" Ishihara asked. It was nearly ten.

"The last anyone saw him was about five o'clock."

Silence, as everyone realized the man and the poison could be in Osaka or Tokyo or even Hokkaido already.

When he first became a detective, Ishihara had worried constantly about every detail in each case he worked on. He tried to see the whole picture, to second-guess what had to be done by everyone in order to solve the crime. Now he found it comforting to know that all he needed to concentrate on was his own particular corner of the crisis.

So while a national police and public network alert went out for Harada and the man from the chemicals lab, Yasuo Inoue; while public transport authorities and national organizations went into high-security mode; and while police toxicologists contacted hospitals and advised them how to treat rescopal poisoning. Ishihara and Beppu interviewed the pitifully few Silver Angels members whom the police could find.

Most of the Silver Angels were missing, including McGuire's niece and her friend. They'd tentatively identified the boy, however. Based on McGuire's description, the geography club convener thought it was Shin Takagi, who'd been once or twice to the club with Mari Kitami. The convener didn't know anything about him except that he'd made everyone uncomfortable.

The National Data Network found several Shin Takagis between eighteen and twenty-five living in Osaka. Phone calls accounted for all but one, the son of a small factory owner who'd committed suicide six years earlier, when Shin was fourteen, after the business was bankrupted by a cartel of larger companies.

The widow, Shin's mother, didn't know where her son was. He moved between jobs, never settled down, and only came home occasionally. The last she heard, he was working as a courier based in Sakai, south of Osaka.

The courier company said Shin Takagi quit in May and left no forwarding address.

Of the four suspected Silver Angels the police did find, one couldn't be questioned because she was an anorexic girl of seventeen who collapsed in panic when she saw police uniforms and had to be rushed to hospital.

Of the other three, one worked as an intern at Osaka Central Hospital, one studied at the same university as the two dead boys, and one was the girlfriend of this student.

Ishihara interviewed the intern and Beppu the student. Afterward, they compared notes.

The intern was brought in because he'd talked about the Angels by name in a well-known chat room, using his real name backward as an alias. Unfortunately, he wasn't a

Silver Angels member—he'd only heard about the group from a friend, another doctor who couldn't be found.

The student knew a bit more—he recognized Harada's photograph from his one visit to the geography club. He liked the ideas some of the members were talking about, such as meditation and renouncing consumerism, but he thought the bit about Adam saving the world seemed weird. He thought they might be stuck in a role-playing game that got too real. He didn't know where any of them lived.

"Neither of them has met Adam." Beppu tossed the disc with the recorded interviews onto one of the desks. "And neither of them knows how to contact him. Waste of time bringing them in."

The incident room was peaceful again. Headquarters for the investigation had moved upstairs, and the superintendent had taken direct control. Funo was coordinating alert status in Osaka public areas.

Beppu stretched and wriggled his shoulders irritably. "Do you want to do the girl?"

Ishihara nodded. "Might as well. It shouldn't take long."

"I told my boyfriend he'd better avoid them." The girl wound a strand of long, bleached brown hair around her finger as she spoke. "They gave me the creeps with their fancy implants and shaved heads."

"Shaved?"

"Yes, even the girls." She flicked a long purple fingernail through the strand of hair as if looking for nits. Her small, thin body hunched in the chair and bright button eyes reminded Ishihara of a monkey.

"They only talked about stuff like meditation and self-cleansing and computer games."

Ishihara swung the monitor to face her across the desk. He ran through several photos—Harada, the four dead students, and the chemist Inoue. Harada's photo came from university files, and Inoue's from his driver's license photo in the national database.

The girl shook her head at Harada, Inoue, and one of the girls, but correctly identified the other students.

"Can you go back?" she said.

Ishihara replayed the photos in the opposite direction.

The girl pointed at Inoue. "Maybe . . . maybe not."

Ishihara had an idea. "Wait a minute." He fiddled with the image controls and finally produced Inoue without hair or glasses. The studious-looking young man with longish hair and a vague expression was transformed into an ascetic priest. Even his expression seemed more intense.

The girl reacted instantly. "Samael, that's what they called him. I remember because he came to Tsuneo's room once, and they all practically kissed his feet. Pretty dishy he was."

Samael. Wasn't that one of the names the old priest Gen had mentioned when he and McGuire visited? One of Adam's disciples.

"You found him attractive?"

"Not really. He looked an S and M type. Not my thing." She grinned at Ishihara's expression. "Uncle, you're a bit old-fashioned for a cop."

Her casual "Uncle" made him feel about eighty. He asked her a couple more questions without getting any further useful information, then sent her home.

"Samael, huh?" Beppu added the name to the Inoue file.

Ishihara's phone buzzed.

"Constable Aratani speaking. I'm in Tachibana North Betta, Amagasaki. I have a bit of a problem with one of the other voluntary informants. The, er, person involved will only talk to you."

Ishihara shook his head irritably. "What are you talking about?"

"When I went to ask McGuire-san to come to the station . . ."

"Why?" Ishihara interrupted. "What's this about?"

"Inspector Funo wanted everyone with a possible Silver Angels connection . . ."

"Brought in, I know." Ishihara looked at Beppu.

"Maybe because of the niece?" Beppu guessed. "Or the foreign connection?"

"What's the problem?" Ishihara asked the constable. McGuire was probably demanding an explanation or refusing to move. Funo should have told him.

"McGuire-san's husband says she hasn't come home yet. He wants to talk to you about where she might be." The constable nervously overlaid two mutually exclusive polite expressions.

"Tell Tanaka-san he'd better come over to the station."

"He's already waiting in the car," said the constable.

エレナ

Eleanor didn't grasp the slim man's words for a moment, why he was calling Akita "Adam." Then she remembered talking about the Silver Angels to the old priest Gen with Ishihara, and it made sense. Akita was Adam, and these young men were part of the cult. Shit, and Akita thought she'd joined them . . .

She might find Mari this way. The thought formed itself without warning and held her to her chair instead of obeying her first impulse to run out the door.

"I had to discipline Niniel. He has endangered us all." The new arrival's words spilled out quickly, as if he'd been waiting desperately to tell someone. His voice was quiet, but the precise way he said "discipline" made Eleanor shiver.

Fujinaka had stood up immediately when the other man entered. He cleared his throat and gestured at Eleanor.

"We have a guest," he said.

The slim man put the briefcase down and strode closer to stare at Eleanor. "Is this the foreigner you talked about?" he asked Akita.

They won't let you leave, Eleanor told herself. You've seen their faces. You can stay as a prisoner or you can try and bluff the other way. She grabbed a business card from her bag, stood up, and offered it to the new man with a bow.

"Eleanor McGuire, from Tomita Electronics. Glad to m . . . meet you."

He stared at her, mouth half-open. Closer up, he was a striking young man, with sharply angled eyebrows and large, clearly lidded eyes. His collar-length hair was curiously flat and black, probably a wig.

"I'm . . ." He glanced at Akita, who nodded happily. "I'm Samael."

Beside her, Fujinaka murmured discontentedly. Did he suspect her? She sat down again, trying to look relaxed.

"Settle down, Samael." Akita pointed to the kitchen. "Get yourself a drink. You look hot."

Samael didn't budge. "We must implement Operation Debug immediately. I have had to leave the lab permanently, due to Niniel's carelessness in using the fujirin to discipline his acolytes. They will eventually trace the connection between you and me, and find you here."

Akita received this news with an impassive face, but Fujinaka cursed and took out his phone.

"I'll need help setting this up." His thumb danced over the keys.

"You'll be fine," said Akita calmly. "Just do as you practiced."

Samael paced nervously beside the kitchen. "What about her?"

"She comes with us." Akita sounded surprised to be asked. He smiled at Eleanor in what was probably supposed to be a reassuring way.

Eleanor tried to smile back. She felt sick, and her heart wouldn't stop racing. "What's Operation Debug?" she said brightly.

"We leave here and regroup," said Akita. He leaned back, comfortable to let Samael and Fujinaka do the work. Fujinaka had gone into the kitchen and was talking to his phone. Eleanor could hear isolated words such as "transport," "detonator," "masks," and "synchronize," that didn't make her feel better. What did Ishihara say . . . that the group could be dangerous if pushed too far?

"Are you taking the interface hardware?" she asked. "That's a delicate job. Shall I help?"

"No," said Samael sharply. He was tapping a message on his own phone. "You will go in the first van." He snapped the phone shut and bent down to the briefcase, behind her.

"It's not that we don't want your help." Akita leaned forward. "We must keep our destination a secret, that's all."

Despite what she knew about him by then, she wasn't frightened by his nearness. His bloodshot eyes were desperately sincere, and his rather petulant mouth twisted in another emotion, she couldn't quite tell what. It certainly wasn't sexual attraction—looked more like guilt.

He looked up at something above her head, then lunged forward, grabbing both her arms at the elbow, his knee across her thighs so she couldn't move her legs.

The attack was so sudden that Eleanor had barely sucked in breath to scream when she felt a hand on her neck and a sharp pain in the muscle of her shoulder. The scream came out as "Ow!"

Samael chuckled behind her.

Akita let her go. "My apologies, McGuire-san. I will show you the wonders of the Macrocosm, but not tonight."

Eleanor scrambled off the couch and pushed past him, but her knees gave way, and she dropped to all fours on the carpet, then slumped on her face as her knees and elbows gave way as well. The bastards had drugged her.

She could see the pattern on the carpet—a brown fleck interwoven into a cream ground—and hear the men's voices, but she couldn't move at all. She didn't even know if she was breathing or not. Perhaps she was dead, and that was what Akita meant by "wonders of the Macrocosm." If she was dead, though, she should be able to see something

more than this damn carpet and hear something more than
the three voices . . .

"Where's the hand?" said Fujinaka.

"In the verandah freezer." Akita sounded unconcerned.

". . . set the recording for the cops." Fujinaka's voice,
coming from a different room.

"I'll take Adam-sama and the equipment." Samael.

The door swished open. A babble of voices, male and female, just out of hearing. The carpet blurred, darkened. All
sounds faded away.

石原

Ishihara expected McGuire's husband to be a Westernized scholarly gentleman. Instead, a stocky figure in T-shirt and jeans smacked a hand like a farmer's onto the reception desk and demanded Ishihara find his wife. The only scholarly feature about the man was his thick glasses, which continuously slid to one side of his nose and had to be pushed straight again.

"Whatever trouble she's in, it's your fault." Tanaka glared at Ishihara and Beppu impartially.

"When did you hear from her last?" Ishihara led him to an interview room, away from the desk clerk and the curious stares of a couple of teenagers thumbing their phones while they waited on the benches.

The room had three chairs and a desk. Ishihara pulled up one chair and Beppu sank into another. Tanaka paced up and down.

"She called at about five-thirty and said she'd be home at eight or nine. I heard the message when I got home at seven."

He glanced at Beppu, who was jotting times in his notebook, and waited before continuing.

"She said she was going to see an old friend. She didn't call and her phone is turned off, but lately she's been out at all hours on police business"—a pointed look—"so I thought maybe something had come up. But now you say she's not here, and she's not at work."

"Where was she meeting the friend?" said Beppu.

"She didn't say."

"I haven't seen McGuire-san since . . ." Ishihara took a moment to remember. "Since this morning. I went to Tomita to pick up some evidence."

Tanaka frowned. "And what's all this about the Silver Angels? Eleanor's got nothing to do with them. It's my niece who may be involved with the group."

"I'm not sure why the inspector wanted to talk to McGuire-san," said Ishihara. He knew Funo thought McGuire had gone to ground with the rest of the Silver Angels. But Ishihara was sure McGuire wasn't part of the cult. If she was in trouble, he might need Tanaka's help to find her.

"We think the Silver Angels may be about to attack the public," he said. "Most of their known members have disappeared."

He glanced at Beppu, who tilted his head as if to say *It's your call if you want to tell him anything.*

Ishihara continued. "Do you think it's possible your wife went looking for your niece and got dragged into something?"

Tanaka frowned again and pushed his glasses up hard against his forehead. "She didn't say anything about it. If it was family business she usually told me."

"What about this friend?" put in Beppu. "Did you try to contact him, or her?"

"I don't have a number for him and he's not listed," said Tanaka.

"What's his name?" said Ishihara. "We'll see if we can track him down here."

"Akita . . . I think his first name is Nobuyuki or Nobutaka, something like that. He used to work for Tomita years ago, when Eleanor first joined them."

"I'll get onto that." Beppu left.

"Assistant Inspector," said Tanaka thoughtfully, "have the Silver Angels given you any demands?"

"No."

"No declaration or communication of any kind?"

"No, why?"

"I'm not an expert on this kind of group," Tanaka said. "But if they shift into a mode of public activity, I'd say either they want something from the rest of society, or they're trying to demonstrate something."

"Such as?" said Ishihara.

"It depends on the group. The action might be something relatively harmless, like beating drums in the street and telling the emperor that their god would grant him an interview."

Tanaka smiled at Ishihara's puzzled expression. The smile softened his blunt features. "A much earlier case. Or the action might be violent, like Soum deciding it's time to release all our deluded souls by flooding the subway with sarin so we can ascend to heaven."

"Don't tell Beppu that," said Ishihara. "He was a rookie in Tokyo in 1995. It still gives him the creeps."

"The reason I'm asking is that if they contact you, at least we could tell what they want, however strange it seems to us. And it might give us an idea how likely they are to become violent."

"There's been one violent incident we know of," said Ishihara.

"The kids from Mari's university? That sounded like an internal problem to me."

Ishihara stood up. Maybe the incident room upstairs could use another expert.

"You'd better stay here until we find out this Akita's

number or address," he said. "That's our best lead." He hesitated. "I should warn you that our boss might think your wife is part of the cult."

"Don't be ridiculous," Tanaka snapped.

"We'll find her," said Ishihara, with as much decisiveness as he could manage.

"I hope so." Tanaka folded his arms defiantly. "You got her into this in the first place."

Ishihara had the uncomfortable feeling he was right.

Mikuni called him an hour later. He looked much brighter than before, in spite of the time.

"We've had a breakthrough here, you'll be glad to know."

Ishihara eh-really'ed encouragingly, but kept one eye on the other desk monitor. It showed the updated list of suspected Silver Angel members and their details from the NDN. The Zecom murder case seemed a long time ago and a lot less urgent now.

"We took out a search warrant on Yui," said Mikuni. "I tell you, I was pissing myself in case we didn't find anything. We went to his house. His wife wasn't too happy but she stuck to his story. We asked her where the clothes were that Yui was wearing Monday night. She seemed genuinely surprised. Said she sent the shirts and trousers to the dry cleaners today. Usually she sends them on Saturday, but he brought all his washing back from overseas. And she remembered that one of the shirts had a stain that he'd tried to wash himself. She thinks it was red wine."

Ishihara whistled appreciatively. If they found Nakamura's blood on Yui's shirt . . .

Mikuni grinned. "To cut a long story short we went to the dry cleaners—it's in the Betta shopping center—and they'd started on Yui's stuff. We only just got the shirt in time." He sat back in his chair. "The stain's being analyzed now. I hope to hell it doesn't turn out to be wine after all."

"Bet it isn't," said Ishihara. "You always were a lucky bastard. Don't forget to find out where he got the research from," he added, thinking of McGuire.

"Yeah, talk to you later." Mikuni cut the connection.

In the incident room, sighting reports of Silver Angels suspects and tip-offs of any suspicious activity poured in from all over the country, none of which had been confirmed. Arrest warrants had been issued for Inoue/Samael and Harada—they were the only names the police had—but all stations were authorized to make emergency arrests of any suspected Silver Angel members, including McGuire.

The only bright spot of the evening had been the look of scorn Tanaka gave Inspector Funo when she asked him about McGuire's involvement with the Angels. Apparently McGuire had made a call that afternoon from her office that the police couldn't trace. It was diverted through some kind of interference. All her other calls were routine, and Ishihara had to admit that Funo was right to regard this diverted call as suspicious. It must be the call she made to arrange to meet Akita, whoever he was. But that didn't necessarily mean she knew the call was shielded.

When Tanaka was told their apartment would be searched, Ishihara thought he would spit in Funo's eye. But all he said was, "I suppose this is under the Internal Security Law." They found nothing incriminating in McGuire's apartment, of course, and Tanaka returned to the station with them. He was now helping the profilers put information about the Silver Angels into order.

There was a growing air of exhausted frustration in the main incident room. Detectives hunched over computers or argued on phones. Cigarette smoke hung in a blue haze on the ceiling despite the background moan of air conditioners.

Beppu beckoned to him from a desk across the room.

"I think we've found Akita," he said, when Ishihara was looking over his shoulder. "And Funo needs to know." He pointed at the screen, which displayed multiple windows of matches. One of them was flashing red.

"Inoue formed a software company with Nobuyuki Akita in 2012," read Ishihara. "Shit." Too much of a coincidence. Akita must be involved with the Angels, too. And McGuire was with him. "The company declared bankruptcy earlier this year." Which didn't necessarily mean it was in trouble. Directors of small companies who got sick of the struggle to survive often exploited the bankruptcy option.

The software company was based in Tokyo, but Akita's address was given as a small town in the northeast. They'd have to ask the local police to check it out. Inoue's address was in Shikoku, where the police had already found an empty apartment.

Akita had worked at Tomita Electronics after leaving university, as Tanaka said. He spent only three years there, then moved to Zecom. The familiar name prodded Ishihara's intuition. But Akita left Zecom after five years, then didn't appear to have worked anywhere until 2012, when he teamed up with Inoue. More likely he did casual or illegal work that wasn't linked with the main employment database. He had no police record or anything else suspicious, not even tax evasion. He also carried no credit cards, bankcards of any description, and his health card hadn't been used for ten years.

The last visual record of Akita was from 2008, the year he left Zecom, when he renewed his driver's license. Ishihara sighed. Digital technology was supposed to improve things like license photos, not produce a blurred likeness of what appeared to be a surprised gorilla. The only useful information was that Akita was tall and heavily built, which might help him to stand out in a crowd.

Inoue was only thirty—he'd taken the elite course of top high school—top university—top company. He'd been in the same company since 2007. No police record, but he did have credit cards, a couple of bank loans, and the other trappings of a normal life.

"That's a good lead," Inspector Funo said, taking Beppu's place at the desk. She had removed her suit jacket and a couple of hairs were out of place in her neat bob. It didn't make her any more approachable. "We'll see if the local police can find anything at Akita's address. Possibly McGuire and Akita are meeting Inoue somewhere."

"She said she'd be home by eight or nine," grunted Beppu. "Can't be too far away."

Funo looked at him pityingly. "You believe what she said?"

"Her husband does."

"We have to consider that she might be a prisoner," said Ishihara. "As a possibility," he added, with an eye on Funo's frown.

"Agreed." Funo stood up again. "But try and keep an open mind, you two. The women are often the worst in these groups."

Even Beppu didn't have an answer for that.

The report on Akita's address came in an hour late from the local police. The apartment building had been pulled down the year before, and nobody of that name lived in the new building. The police were interviewing all residents, but so far nobody resembling Akita had been found.

"It's a fake," said Ishihara. "The bastard's somewhere else entirely."

"I thought you couldn't do that with the NDN. It cross-checks, doesn't it?" Beppu yawned. He sat on a cot in the downstairs incident room. They were supposed to be getting a few hours' sleep.

Ishihara smoked morosely at one of the desks. He had a bad feeling about this.

"We don't have any more leads where he might go. He's probably using a fake name here in Osaka."

"Can't do that, either." Beppu lay down with a groan.

Can't do this, can't do that. The NDN, the Bettas, and other post-Quake networks were supposed to be tamper-free. Something about the liveline cables protecting the information. But if somebody invented those things, he believed somebody else would eventually come up with a way to get into them.

He accessed the information about Akita and Inoue and ran through it again, sipping lukewarm coffee in a plastic cup with a soapy smell. There was no new information from the system about either man, and nothing fresh suggested itself from the screen. He placed Inoue's license photo beside the one he'd touched up for the witness, so that Inoue had no hair or glasses. He looked believable enough as a fanatic. Akita, on the other hand . . .

Ishihara dragged Akita's photo beside the others and told the computer to make it clearer. Akita looked more like a motor mechanic or a plumber. A totally ordinary face except perhaps for the intensity in the deep-set eyes. You might guess at a drinking problem, too, from the high color and bulbous nose. Even doctoring the photo to remove his hair didn't make him look much different.

Akita might have helped the four dead kids get into the Betta where they died. Was it possible to use specialized knowledge of one Betta to get into another?

Beppu snored.

If McGuire suspected Akita was anything to do with the Silver Angels, she wouldn't have gone to meet him. Her contrition at not calling the police to her niece's apartment on Wednesday had been genuine, he would swear. McGuire always called her husband if she was going to be late. She hadn't called, so she must have walked into a trap.

He rubbed his face, suddenly tired and stupid. Better take the rest while it was offered. He pulled the cotton blanket off Beppu and made a pillow on the desk. It felt as soft as goose down.

"Ishihara." Funo's voice in his ear. He sat up, his eyes smarting, but the voice came over the interoffice phone, which functioned as an intercom.

He fumbled the return switch. "Yes, I'm here."

Beppu stirred behind him.

"Get up here."

He groaned and went to the hand basin, where he sloshed water on his face and wiped it off with a paper towel. It was nearly five.

"Get up." He poked Beppu as he passed and took the elevator upstairs.

There were tired smudges around Funo's eyes but she moved as briskly as ever. "Take Beppu and Fujita and meet the local police in Okayama. Your mate Mikuni thinks they've found Akita."

Yui had confessed to Nakamura's murder and given them the information to reduce his sentence. He said that he'd got the research data from Akita, who was working as systems manager at the Zecom Betta under another name. Mikuni, knowing Osaka police were looking for information about Akita, called immediately.

"We checked McGuire's e-mail, too," said Funo. "She's been communicating with Akita for months."

"About what?" Ishihara still didn't believe McGuire was guilty.

"Technical stuff only," Funo admitted. "Oh, and an e-mail to you yesterday, asking why we're tracing her calls. How did she know that?"

Ishihara cursed himself for not checking his e-mail last night. Not that it would have made any difference.

"I think if you find Akita, you'll find McGuire there, too," she said.

"It's possible Inoue is there, as well," he said gloomily. "And the rescopal."

The shadows around Funo's eyes deepened. "I know. We've told emergency services to stand by."

*   *   *

Ishihara, Beppu, and Fujita, a young detective with an eye for detail and a permanently blocked nose, got out at the Zecom stop before Okayama City. It was a new station with high ceilings and streamlined passageways, like being inside a translucent, metal-pyloned box. Ishihara preferred solid concrete.

As they descended the stairs to transfer to the monorail platform, they were met by an extraordinary sight.

People poured out of the train from the Zecom Betta. Many of them were dressed in pajamas. Crying children clutched toys, and women held babies. All the faces were twisted in fear.

A siren began to whoop and a voice called over the station's PA system,

"Please proceed out of the station in an orderly way via the exit stairs. Do not run. There is no danger. Please obey police and station staff directions. Do not go to the fast train platform."

The message repeated itself. The authoritative voice calmed the crowd a little, but the siren didn't help. Ambulance and fire engine sirens outside the station added to the hubbub. The three detectives tried to force their way along the platform against the flow of the crowd. A station attendant blocked their way.

"Only emergency services authorized on the train," he yelled.

Ishihara showed his badge. "What's going on?"

"They're evacuating the Betta. Gas or something."

Ishihara exchanged a look with Beppu, whose normally red face had gone pale. Inoue must have brought the rescopal here.

A constable ran along the edge of the crowd, followed by ten paramedics carrying bags. The constable carried gas masks. He gave one to the station attendant, who snatched it in relief.

Ishihara showed his badge to the constable. "Is Inspector Mikuni here?"

"At the Betta." The constable passed the detectives a gas mask each. "You can go on this train."

They got onto the empty train with the paramedics. Another, full train pulled in beside it at the opposite platform. The doors half closed, then wheezed open again as farther down the carriage three people tried to maneuver cameras and recording equipment through the closing doors and onto the train. A woman was talking to a hidden microphone.

Ishihara cursed the media. He motioned Fujita to stay put and ran down the carriage with Beppu. The constable and the station attendant ran down the platform.

"Come out of that." The constable grabbed one of the camera crew before he could get in the train. The woman kept talking into her mike as Ishihara pushed her back onto the platform. Beppu took the other man by surprise and shoved him out, too, and hurled the camera equipment after him. The man bent over the stuff and yelled a curse at Ishihara.

Ishihara waved to the station attendant, and the doors closed. "Bloody ghouls."

Beppu wiped sweat off his upper lip. "Too stupid to realize they're in the way."

The paramedics got out at the first stop, Betta East. A few people tried to get in from the crowd on the platform but most of them waited obediently as the doors closed.

More people waited at the second stop. Ishihara only just managed to squeeze out as they all rushed in. Like old-time Tokyo rush hour, he thought. The siren blared, and the PA system urged everyone to stay calm. The train would reverse and take them to safety.

The constables on this platform wore their gas masks. Ishihara couldn't smell anything like the distinctive rotting-petal perfume of rescopal, but he put on his own mask.

Beppu and Fujita did the same. Then he had to take it off to yell a question.

"Which way to system management?"

The constable pointed to an exit, jabbed his thumb downward, and held up two fingers. Two floors down.

Ishihara adjusted his mask as they jogged to the exit, dodging people running for the train. He hadn't worn a gas mask for years. The way this model sat over his nose and mouth was different from the old ones, and he struggled to get the strap tight.

"Stay calm and walk to the neatest exit," said the PA in a deep, reassuring male voice. "If you can, wrap a damp cloth over your nose and mouth. Do not crawl along the floor. Carry children as high as possible."

Beyond the exit door was a long corridor. More people running. A man in a blue tracksuit tripped and sprawled headlong. Something moved on the floor as he scrambled up. A cleanbot, turning in small, aimless circles. Other cleanbots, similarly disabled, hugged the walls. Ishihara wondered about the building's automatic protection functions. Would the air circulation shut down to prevent the gas spreading? Could people be trapped inside apartments if the doors wouldn't open automatically? He wished he had read his own Betta's emergency rules more carefully.

"Stairs over there." Fujita lifted his mask to shout and pointed to the emergency exit signs at the end of the corridor. The crowd flowed toward those stairs. All their faces were terrified, but they made surprisingly little noise. A door next to the main exit said ACCESS STAIRS NO ADMITTANCE. Ishihara put out his hand to open it and at the same moment a fireman pulled it open from the other way. They both jumped in surprise.

Ishihara held up his badge, and yelled, "Police." The fireman nodded and kept going. Three more firemen ran up the stairwell, playing out a huge, flat hose as they went. The detectives flattened themselves against the wall to keep out of the way and followed the hose down four flights to the bottom floor. The door was propped open.

The siren sounded fainter. Open ducts ran along the walls and ceilings, and the ceiling was lower than upstairs. A sweet smell permeated slowly through the mask.

They followed the sound of voices around a corner and saw a group of men in suits and some in uniform clustered in front of a double door. One of the men waved. Ishihara waved back and saw it was Inspector Mikuni. Several of the policemen held phones to their mouths. The firemen all wore masks with radio comm units built in.

Mikuni beckoned them closer and they all bent their heads to hear, like footballers before a scrum.

"Just as we arrived the alarms started," Mikuni yelled. "The automatic environmental systems aren't working properly. We can't get into the main control room from the front, so they're going to break in through the systems manager's rooms. That's here." He pointed to the double door. "If this Akita is part of the group, he could have sabotaged the system so the gas was more effective."

They'd never find any Silver Angels in the crowd, Ishihara thought disgustedly. All the criminals had to do was wear pajamas and walk out of the building with everyone else.

"No sign of your gaijin," Mikuni went on. "It's possible they're still in there, but unless they have masks they'll be in trouble."

"Aren't there any other entries?" shouted Beppu.

Mikuni shook his head. "The manager's apartment is locked, too. The firemen are going to try breaking down doors from this side and from the apartment side. They're trying to decide whether it's safe to use cutters or not."

Ishihara looked down. A yellowish miasma gathered along the floor.

Mikuni followed his gaze. "It's heavier than air. They're

going to pump it out. Apparently it will lose potency in twenty-four hours or so."

"Isn't there a central control for all the Bettas?" said Fujita. "We could turn off the airflow from there."

"No central control." Behind the mask Ishihara could see Beppu grimace. "So we don't get someone doing this in all the Bettas at the same time."

Running footsteps pounded, and a squad of police in black flak jackets and helmets jogged into view—the anti-terrorist squad.

Their leader saluted. "Squad leader Ikoma. I'm authorized to secure this scene." He barked the words so rapidly Ishihara had trouble understanding them.

"We think suspects in a murder case may still be in there," Mikuni returned loudly. "And possibly a hostage."

"We'll handle it. Clear the corridor, please."

Mikuni hesitated, then nodded to his team. They all retreated slowly down the corridor, with many backward glances.

"If your damn cultists screw up my murder case . . ." Mikuni growled to Ishihara. "There could be evidence in there to back up Yui's confession."

Ishihara hoped McGuire was in the apartment and that the squad would get her out. But then again, what if Akita had left her there without a mask? He felt sick, and not from the stuffy air. Death from rescopal poisoning was particularly unpleasant. He hated whoever had done this with desolate intensity.

The mist in the corridor looked thicker.

The firemen shouted, then everyone started running toward the exit. A clatter of boots behind them indicated the antiterrorist squad followed. A different, shrill alarm sounded above the siren.

"What is it?" Ishihara yelled to one of the firemen.

"Fire in the apartment," he yelled back. "We need different hoses."

Ishihara sent Beppu and Fujita to help Mikuni and emergency services, telling them to keep an eye out for Akita or Inoue. He went back to the monorail platform and helped the constable direct people onto the train, scanning the faces as he did so for . . . what? Inoue's narrow cheeks and shaved head? Akita's heavier-than-average frame? Any face that seemed wrong, out of place. Like a small, pale face below red hair.

Don't get involved with your cases, that was the most basic rule of all. If you let yourself feel for individuals, you couldn't do your job. The rule was a good one; it had proved itself to him many times. Like now—he couldn't care less what happened to the case, if only McGuire wasn't in that basement room.

エレナ

Eleanor hadn't had this bad a hangover in years. The pounding in her head spread from a point on her left temple and echoed through her whole body. She shifted her legs, and all her joints and muscles protested. She must have done something stupid while she was drunk. Run a marathon, by the feel of it. Her throat was so dry she couldn't swallow, and the inside of her mouth tasted like she'd eaten rotten eggs.

She kept still, her eyes closed. If she moved or saw the room sway, she'd throw up. Masao must have turned the air conditioner down because everything was very quiet. Maybe if she kept completely still she'd fall back to sleep . . .

A door hinge squeaked. Bare feet slapped on floor. A voice said softly, "Aunt Eleanor?"

Mari's voice. She must be at the Tanakas. God, she might have embarrassed herself in front of them. Why didn't Masao stop her?

But why was Mari here anyway? Mari had gone away to stay somewhere in Osaka while she was at university . . .

The whole situation opened like a trapdoor in her memory. She plunged into it, no handholds.

"Oh, shit." Her voice sounded thick and croaky. What had Akita done to her, and where was she now?

She opened her eyes but they were swollen and gummy. Everything blurred.

"Here." Mari put a hot towel in her hand.

Eleanor wiped her face. Her left hand felt as though she was wearing a glove. It was bandaged but didn't hurt. The medical patches on her inner arm were probably painkillers. She flexed her left fingers clumsily, and streaks of pain ran across her shoulder and neck.

Mari folded her right hand around a cool glass, and Eleanor gulped the water, splashing some down her neck in her haste.

"Aunt Eleanor, what are you doing here?"

She drew breath sharply and focused on Mari. It gave her a fright; Mari's head was bald again. She looked like a young monk. A worried young monk.

Her own head felt cold . . . her fingers touched smooth skin, the long scar of her old injury, a bump on the back where Taka pushed her and, where the headache was centered, the rounded biometal of an implant like Mari's. It had taken a long time to grow her hair to cover that scar . . . What the hell did Akita think he was doing? How dare he do these things without her knowledge or consent? She pushed herself to a sitting position, using her right elbow. The pain in her neck and shoulder was worse sitting up, but she didn't feel as queasy.

"Where are we?"

Mari took the glass. "We're in the second meditation room at the retreat. They haven't told us where that is."

Eleanor was sitting on one of six tatami mats laid in a rectangle on a concrete floor, Mari crouched beside her. One strong lightbulb hung from a cord in the center of the ceiling. A sheet lay crumpled beside her. She was wearing the same clothes as Mari—a short-sleeved kimono-style shirt and simple pants, both in rough white cotton.

"What time is it?"

"Just before early prayer. That's about five in the morning." Mari's voice was low and urgent. "Aunt Eleanor, what's going on? Taka said they brought you in the back of a van."

Van . . . the word illuminated a series of images in Eleanor's memory. Bright lights alternating with heavy blackness, a stuffy enclosed space. More lights, someone in a green coat, an IV line dangling. Akita must have put her in a van at . . .

Zecom. She knew she'd forgotten something.

"Mari, Aki . . . Adam was planning to do something bad at the Zecom Betta. Did they go through with it?"

The girl shook her head. "I don't know. We're not supposed to watch outside news. I was told to go and see if the new Angel was awake and, if so, to bring her to see Adam-sama. Then when I get in here, the new Angel is you!"

Eleanor pressed her eyes, trying to push away the headache that kept getting in the way of thought. Did Akita really still think she had decided to join him? If so, he was completely deluded.

"I haven't joined the group. They kidnapped me. But Adam thinks I've joined." Oh-oh, she thought suddenly. Can I trust this girl? She's been with these people for months now.

Mari rocked back on her heels, appalled. "They wouldn't do that! It must be an honest mistake."

"Mari-chan, they did this to me"—she thrust her bandaged hand in Mari's face—"without m . . . my permission."

Mari's mouth set in a stubborn line that reminded Eleanor of Yoshiko. "I still think it's a mistake. Just tell Adam-sama. Or Gagiel-sama might be better," she added doubtfully. "They always tell us we're free to leave if we want to."

"But nobody goes, right?"

Mari's mouth set again but she didn't answer. "You're wrong about them."

Eleanor crawled stiffly to the edge of the mats. "Okay, I might be wrong. But if you're right, they won't mind you showing me the way out."

"But I'm supposed to take you to Adam-sama," Mari protested. "I'll get in trouble if I don't. And the guards won't let you out without permission, anyway."

"That doesn't sound like you're free to go," Eleanor said nastily.

"We're free to get permission to go." The concern in Mari's eyes was replaced by defiance. "Come on, then."

Cold from the concrete floor numbed Eleanor's bare feet, which helped her ignore the other aches. Mari led the way down a corridor, lit at intervals with the same naked bulbs as the room. On the left they passed a door labeled MEDITATION ROOM ONE and another labeled NOVICE TRAINING, both written in ornate roman letters. The next door said Amenities in plain Japanese script and under it a handwritten scrawl, "no meditation!" All these doors were on the left. The right wall of the corridor was made up of uneven wooden panels. Some of them had warped to show a dirt wall beneath. Nothing looked like a door to the outside world. The end of the corridor behind them was flat concrete.

They turned a corner to the left. At about twelve paces, there was a gap in the concrete wall on their left, in which Eleanor glimpsed stairs inside a narrow alcove leading upward into darkness.

"It's locked," said Mari. "None of us have the key."

Something whirred down the corridor toward them that seemed as out of place as she felt—a helpbot. It was older than the Betta models, a Yamazaki 1200 by the looks of it. A rectangular box on wheels with a round half sphere on top, its arms folded close to its sides instead of retracting like the newer models.

It wasn't working properly. One of the arms trailed disconsolately on the floor, and it moved in a wavy zigzag, bumping off the walls.

"What's that doing here?" Eleanor fought an urge to grab the robot and adjust its navigation controls.

Mari glanced at it, uninterested. "They use those in training. The novices do, I mean. Here we are."

They stopped at the first door on the left past the alcove. The right-hand wall was the same old panels. The door's label said VESTIBULE, LEVEL THREE ADEPTS AND ABOVE ONLY. A different sign had been painted over underneath it. Eleanor could just make out the characters for machine.

"Wait," she said. "Mari-chan, did you tell them I'm related to you?"

"How could I? I only just found out you're here."

"It might be a good idea if you don't tell anyone yet." She thought Akita quite capable of using Mari as leverage for whatever he wanted. What the hell *did* he want with her?

Mari knocked three times on the door and pushed it open. "You go in," she whispered. "I'm not allowed."

Eleanor took one last look at the robot, a connection with normality. It was now turning in uneven circles.

Inside the room, the first thing she noticed was the red carpet. It ran in a meter-wide swath between boxes and shapes covered with sheets, up three steps, and finished at the foot of a high-backed chair set on a dais. Akita sat in the chair, and behind him computer hardware occupied the whole of the back wall of the room. He wore a gold satin robe gathered in so many ornate folds that he looked like a gilt waterfall. In spite of the chair, he did not dominate the room—the screens and consoles did that.

She caught a glimpse of angled steel and wide bases under the sheets at the side of the room. Heavy machinery. This could be a factory storeroom.

Another man stood behind Akita with his back to her. She thought she recognized the dark undershirt and broad shoulders of Fujinaka, from the Zecom Betta. He wore loose trousers in silver satin.

"Lilith-san, you are awake!" Akita clapped his hands together once. "I have been waiting to show you your future."

She stepped along the red carpet, annoyed that there was no room to avoid it. At least it wasn't as cold as the concrete. "Akita, what do you think you're doing?"

He leaned forward as she approached, his eyes too bright. "You must call me Adam here," he said in a mock-whisper. "Just as we will call you Lilith."

"Lilith?" she said, momentarily distracted.

"Adam's first wife. The one who lent her soul to the Evas."

It took a moment for her to realize the last reference was to a manga. Bible, manga, sutras, they were all religious texts to the Angels.

"Call me whatever you like. But I'm not staying. I wish to leave. Now."

Fujinaka turned around and watched her with his narrow, measuring eyes.

Akita's mouth dropped open in shock. "But you haven't entered the Macrocosm yet. You said you wanted to see it."

"I said I wanted to see your new interface. I didn't say I wanted to be doped, abducted, and m . . . mutilated!"

He frowned, puzzled at her anger, then his face slackened again. "Now, now Lilith. I admit we were a little rushed in your case. But you are important to us."

Eleanor controlled her breathing with an effort. "Why did you do this to me?"

"You wanted it," he said, puzzled. "I wanted it. I have always admired your talents. You have the knack of linking theoretical problems with the practical. I think you will be a great asset to our movement. My other disciples do not have the knowledge or experience to manipulate the Macrocosm successfully."

"I didn't want this," she protested, but halfheartedly. He wasn't going to listen, whatever she said.

"Together we can restore order to the Microcosm. Create a new reality." He was almost pleading with her. "In the times that are past, Buddha and Christ taught that suffering is the lot of all living things. And what is the root of suffering?"

He waited for her to answer. Fujinaka kept his eye on her as he coiled a long lead.

"Desire?" she ventured.

Akita nodded slowly. "That is what they taught, because these teachers of the past did not have my power to ascend into the Macrocosm. They were chained to their mortal bodies, but I am not. Of course," he said smugly, "when the body is vanquished, desire evaporates like dew in the sun's rays. Your niece is learning this. You can, too."

He must have known all along about Mari.

"Akita . . . Adam. Thank you for your invitation, but I don't want to get involved." She turned on her heel and walked back down the carpet. It was only ten strides to the door, but it felt like fifty.

Akita said nothing. Fujinaka muttered something inaudible. She opened the door, her back feeling uncomfortably vulnerable, then she was in the corridor again. Her heartbeat thudded in her ears. Could it be this easy? Where to go? There must be an exit.

She turned left, the other way from her route with Mari. The corridor continued past two more doors, voices murmuring within. The helpbot had gone.

As she reached the corner, a man in a silver robe turned into her path. Slim build, expressive eyes, hollow cheeks. Samael. The man who drugged her in the Betta.

She jumped back, and he laughed.

"Going somewhere, Lilith-sama?" He made the honorific sound like an insult.

"Upstairs." She didn't attempt to get past him. His arms were half-raised, the fingers flexing as if he could feel her already. No biometal on those hands.

"You don't want to do that," he said firmly. "Adam-sama is looking forward to you joining him in the Macrocosm. Let's not spoil that for him."

He grabbed her left arm above the elbow and pain shot through her neck and shoulder. "I haven't got time to keep an eye on you. In case you have any funny ideas about escaping, remember your niece. You do care for her, don't you?"

He thrust his face into hers, and she pulled back as far as his grip on her arm would allow. "Good," he said. "Back you go, then. The Macrocosm awaits."

He shepherded her up the corridor to the vestibule. Eleanor's neck ached and she felt nauseous. Of course it wouldn't be that easy.

"Can I use the toilet?" she said.

Samael sighed. "Be quick."

The toilet offered no escape. The fan was linked to the light switch. If she had tools and a torch, she might disconnect them and then see where the fan duct led, if she could climb up there. The wiring was pinned around the top of the door and out a badly replastered hole in the concrete. She might have a chance of shorting the lights, but it wasn't much good if she didn't know where to go in the darkness.

Back inside the vestibule room, Akita was now seated facing the consoles. Fujinaka strapped him in at the chest, legs, and onto a padded headrest.

"Gagiel-sama," said Samael. "Here's your missing customer." He pushed Eleanor in the small of the back so that she stumbled forward, catching her toe on the carpet.

Fujinaka/Gagiel narrowed his eyes further. "About time. We want to make sure this is going to work, you know."

"Adam-sama says it will," said Samael, and he seemed to mean it. Perhaps he actually believed all this rubbish.

"Lilith-san, we begin." Akita's head was held motionless by a padded strap, but he smiled sideways at her. "We enter the realm outside and encompassing other realms, which previously only the Buddhas and Devas knew." He raised his free hand, the artificial one. "Are you ready?"

"I could do with a drink of water," said Eleanor.

"Stop stalling." Samael prodded her in the shoulder, and she stepped up onto the dais.

Akita closed his eyes. "You must hold a memory as you enter. Anything, but it must be clear."

"Why?"

Akita mumbled, but she couldn't distinguish words.

Fujinaka clipped another chair to the console, beside Akita. There were no long gloves as she'd seen Fujinaka use in the Zecom Betta, only an aperture covered with a soft material that yielded when she poked it gingerly. Several screens were attached to the top of the console.

She wavered. "How many of these consoles have you built?"

"Three completed so far," said Akita, without opening his eyes. "Two are here. One has been sent to believers in a distant land."

"Which country?"

He didn't answer.

"What happens to me, physically?" In spite of herself she wanted to know what it felt like. Wanted to know if it was real.

Fujinaka/Gagiel grabbed her left arm and wound the bandages off her hand. They came off easily, only sticking a bit around the fingertips. It wasn't as unpleasant-looking as she'd expected. They'd attached biometal to her fingertips and three long strands down the tendons on the back of her hand. There weren't any obvious ports—perhaps the whole surface of the metal was sensitized. Purple bruises mottled the skin. Without the painkillers it would hurt like hell.

"Sit down." Gagiel's fingers dug into her shoulders as he pulled her down into the chair beside Akita and tugged the straps tight. Panic welled in her throat like vomit.

She glanced sideways. Akita looked into nothing and thrust his artificial hand into one of the apertures, almost up to the elbow. His body stiffened immediately, and his head thrust back against the headrest. His eyes rolled slowly upward, and Eleanor looked away from the sight.

My God, what if he *has* developed a direct interface? Everything we do with computers will change. She felt herself on the crest of a swell that could build to a tidal wave, ready to crunch down on life as they knew it.

Before Fujinaka could do it for her, she poked her hand into the hole.

Gentle resistance surrounded her fingers, as if she'd put her hand in a huge pot of glue. She flexed her fingers experimentally. As they widened, suddenly they were locked in. She couldn't move them at all. And she couldn't move her body, either. Sparks of pain shot up her arm and her breath faltered with the shock.

Another memory of sudden fear rose unbidden—several years ago Masao took her to one of the popular indoor fun parks. They rode a huge roller coaster, and she thought that because it was inside a building it might not be as scary . . .

She fell, screaming, Masao's grip on her wrist leaving a bruise . . . but he wasn't there now. Nor could she hear the rattle of the machinery or the frenetic music, but she was still falling. She plummeted into a dark abyss—her heart should have faltered, her head should have swollen with blood, her arms and legs should have flailed against rushing air.

But not only was she unafraid, she couldn't do anything like that. She could "feel" herself—she still had a tongue to run around her teeth and fingers to clench into fists, but she couldn't touch the world around her. All she knew was the certainty of falling. How did she know? Lights flashed by all around her. Yet when she focused on one, it stopped. Or she stopped. She tried to touch the light but it winked out, and she fell again. The universe expanded, and she grew smaller in comparison until the weight of her own insignificance smothered her.

Don't panic, she told herself. If Akita can do this, you can. Panic is only a shadow, a habit of mind un-supported by sensation or enzyme. You don't have a body to fall with.

Think. If this console connects me—whatever "I" am in here—to a network, there should be an exit point.

It wasn't dark, after all. When she noticed some-thing, it lit up, although she didn't understand how light was possible without eyes to see it. She couldn't stop classifying the world in terms of sensation; it was a million-year-old habit, after all.

The "light" showed her that the place was more than just a hole—it branched in crystalline towers and bridges in all the directions. As she noticed more of the structures around her, the dive slowed. She imagined feathers, parachutes, gentle updrafts, and her fall slowed further. When she looked at a part of the structure, that part grew closer. Or maybe her "looking" created the details . . .

The crystalline maze around her had a definite order. Akita had done it, developed a direct interface. The programmer's dream come true. A pity she couldn't feel elation, any more than she could feel terror.

She explored the grottos of light and ever-changing forms, and concentrated on one of the crystal towers. It zoomed close, and she began to fall into it, but one of the sidewalls extruded a tongue that flicked her away. She tried a different tower. This one let her fall in.

She could identify myriad patterns. They clicked as a word—"systems." Then "subsystems." This must be the part of the computers networked at the Silver Angels' hideaway. The interfering tongue must be a protection program.

Below her, rushing closer, flecks of light flicked off a swirling hole. It irised shut, then opened again. A gate, she thought. To the outside?

Lilith. Akita's spoke to her without voice. Or he might have said *McGuire* or *Eleanor.* He called her, at any rate. *You must practice manipulating the Microcosm.*

Something—in the sensory world it would be a shadow—hovered around her as she fluttered around.

Did they share thoughts in here? She tried thinking of Akita falling off his chair while his mind was occupied here, but got no response. Then she "said," *What kind of practice?*

Find a body to touch the world of sense, he replied.

I have a body, she started to say, then realized what he meant. She skimmed a narrow orifice, surrounded by a simpler edifice. Another tower to fall into. But she was buffeted by unseen currents and slid away, falling. No control. Was this how Nakamura felt when he tried to manipulate the Kawanishi robot from miles away? No wonder it hit Mito.

She tried falling into the smaller tower again, thinking slow and subtle . . .

And she had a body again.

She felt . . . hard, flat . . . ridges so must turn . . . dark/light . . . movement, so must stop. Wheels, gears. Activation sequence. She was a helpbot, perhaps the one she saw earlier. Simple infrared sensors told her there were several people in the room. She tried to make the helpbot move and immediately it turned into the wall with a grinding of gears. Just like the one she saw in the corridor with Mari.

Manipulating the Microcosm was harder than it looked.

Someone gave an order to her audio sensors, which translated into *get me some water*. This time she waited while the helpbot's program responded, and all she had to do was follow along as it filled a glass from a low sink and carried the water on its "head" tray. Fascinating to watch the complex sequence from inside.

Pile of junk, said the person after grabbing the glass.

Oh yeah? bristled Eleanor. She activated the carrying arm program and tweaked it enough to whack the person in the shin. Loud cries jammed her audio receiver.

Very good, purred Akita. *You are the most advanced pupil I have ever had. See what else we may do to influence the Microcosm.*

She drew back from the helpbot, back to the crystal towers and currents.

The shadow of Akita's presence extended around part of the tower's pale filigree, and it dulled. That small subsystem would malfunction. No wonder he could enter her Betta without an ID, part of her mind remembered.

If Akita could enter her Betta, perhaps she could

enter a different system. Such as the police database
or, even better, their communications network . . .

That is sufficient for a first try. Akita's shadow
crowded her in a particular direction. Before she
grasped what was happening, she was falling again,
faster and faster into . . .

Headache. With every throb her shoulders ached. Pain
prickled down her wrist from her hand. Her heart thudded
against the strap that pinned her to the chair.

Akita slumped beside her. Already Fujinaka/Gagiel had
released him and was injecting him in his upper arm.

Eleanor felt as though she'd been dragged along an assembly line backward. Every muscle in her body ached. It
took her three tries before she found the strength to pull her
hand out of the console. It was coated with soft bluish goo
that came off easily when she wiped it on her trousers.

Seeing that Fujinaka was still fussing over Akita, who lay
with his head on the console and his eyes closed, she picked
feebly at her own straps. She needed that drink more than
ever. How long had she been in there? For that matter, where
was "there"? She couldn't grasp the enormity of what she'd
just experienced, her brain felt as though it was stuffed with
foam.

Outside. There was a way to get out of the Silver Angels'
retreat from inside the interface . . . the gate, that's it. A liveline input converter, probably, designed to attach the required random biological markers to allow data to be sent
via liveline. Maybe that's how it worked—Akita could
travel from system to system using liveline because he already had biological markers. She wasn't too sure how liveline functioned. Nor were the technicians who laid it, by all
accounts.

If Akita could access her Betta, surely she could access
the police communication system, warn them.

She finally released her chest strap, but by then

Fujinaka had finished with Akita. He undid her straps with sure, swift tugs from strong fingers. Eleanor was very conscious of the proximity of those hands, of the firmness of the young muscles, the long puff of his breath . . . she was hyperconscious of the whole room, in fact. Every rustle of cloth or scrape of chair leg on the carpet was magnified. The light glinted painfully off the console. What was wrong with her?

"Can I have a drink?" she croaked.

"You'll be fed and watered now." He glanced at Akita. "Shall I take her to the meditation room?"

Akita straightened with a groan. He stretched his arms sideways, and the artificial hand extended in front of her, long tongues twirling.

"No, bring our meal here. And tell the others we will meet here when it is time for the broadcast."

Fujinaka/Gagiel bowed low to Akita, shot Eleanor a stare that said clearly, no tricks, and left. Whatever delusions Akita had about her being there by choice, the Angels knew she was a prisoner.

Akita rose from his chair, slowly, and with many grunts and groans, tottered the few paces to his "throne" and sank into it.

"Come," he said, his voice almost as croaky as Eleanor's. "Sit." He pointed at the dais beside the throne.

No cushions, Eleanor noted sourly. Her knees were wobbly, but she could stand. She sat where Akita pointed, on the top step of the dais. The step was a plywood board nailed sloppily over a frame, and felt hard under her seat bones.

"Aki . . . Adam, what happened at Zecom?"

He started, as though he was half-asleep. "Do not worry about Zecom," he said thickly. "It was but a stage on the road to enlightenment. We do not dwell there for longer than we must."

"Of course I worry about it. Samael meant to do something dangerous."

"Tell me what you think of the Macrocosm," he said with more energy.

"It will change our relationship with computers forever." She meant it.

He smirked. "I knew you would understand the greatness of my discovery." Then seriously, "Did you feel yourself spreading through the universe? Did you feel the enlightenment?"

"Not quite," she said cautiously. She was getting a crick in her neck from staring up at him, so she stood, her head pounding with the sudden movement. "What do you intend doing with this interface?"

He blinked at her, his eyes vague and his heavy cheeks slack. Stoned. Maybe he gets a headache after using the interface, too.

"By entering the Macrocosm we can eventually be free of the constraints of our bodies," he said, his lips forming the words carefully. "We are readying ourselves to assume leadership of the Microcosm. The Angels will traverse the two realms. After the initial stage, I will ascend permanently to the Macrocosm and receive the souls that follow."

Eleanor rubbed her head. Her left arm was starting to ache, too, with an increasing intensity that suggested she would soon need more painkillers.

"I don't understand. Do you want everybody to use the Macrocosm?"

He hesitated. "Not everybody. People will need to serve in the Microcosm, at least until our bodies become unnecessary."

"That won't happen," said Eleanor gently. "What if someone turns off the power to the console? You'll be lost like unbacked-up data."

His eyes lit up. "No. Soon we will be able to move along

livelines using our brain's power. Of course, only that of trained, sophisticated minds. And wireless frequencies," he added. "Our next task is to create a liveline–high-frequency converter."

It sounded unlikely. But pushing her hand into a hole and transferring her thoughts to a computer network also sounded unlikely. And what would happen when a reliable, renewable source of power was developed? Akita wouldn't need his human body anymore. Immortality.

She crouched in front of him and took his human hand in hers, staring into his eyes and willing him to listen. "Look, you've made an outstanding discovery. You could be hailed as the greatest computer genius of the twenty-first century. Patent this and develop it properly. I can help you if you like. But please don't use it to hurt other people, even if they don't believe what you believe."

"I use it to save people." Akita's voice rose on the word "save." He reached over with his artificial hand and grasped both her wrists. The long tongues, smooth and cool, bound her as effectively as chains. Akita thrust his face into hers. His bloodshot eyes saw things she didn't want to know about. For a horrible moment she thought he was going to kiss her, but instead he pushed hard on her hands, forcing her down on her knees.

"Soon you will feel enlightenment as I do. You do want to join me, don't you?" he pleaded.

Or what? Or he might get rid of his foreign toy as Samael and Fujinaka obviously thought he should.

"Yes," she said, her voice muffled. "Of course I do."

She heard voices in the corridor, then the door opened, to admit a man carrying a tray.

Akita released his hold on Eleanor's wrists. "Iroel, thank you. The wants of the body are as intrusive as ever."

The man called Iroel wore a silver robe like Samael. A gangly man, his limbs swung like a puppet with loose strings. Below his smooth, bald head, his forehead was corrugated with worry lines like a tin roof.

He put the tray on the bottom step of the dais and folded himself beside it in a kneeling bow. "Adam-sama, your meal."

Akita pressed a button on his throne. A board shot out of the arm and snapped onto the opposite arm, giving him a table on which to set the tray.

He obviously didn't believe in ascetic mortification of the flesh. The tray was crammed with bowls: clear soup, paper-thin puffer fish sashimi, delicately cut radish and carrot flowers, a huge bowl of steaming rice, and morsels such as sea urchin roe and steamed aubergine with sweet miso.

Eleanor's dry throat closed in revulsion. Akita wasn't going to listen to her. He was set on his mad scheme, whatever that might be, and she had to find a way both to stop him and to make sure Mari was safe.

She stood up, slowly because her joints ached. "I want to see my niece."

Akita, his mouth full, waved at the door with his chopsticks.

"I will take you," said Iroel. He waved her ahead of him out the door almost eagerly. They left Akita eating alone on his throne.

石原

The screen cleared. A cartoon figure stood against a flat orange background. From the neck down it wore white robes like a Buddhist statue, but the haloed head was that of an old manga star, Ishihara had forgotten the name.

"Greetings, my children. I am Adam."

The notes at the bottom of the screen said the voice was synthesized and that the word used for "my" could also be interpreted as "our."

"Blessed are we who have been reborn into this Third Age, for to us is given the gift of Ascension." The manga head's lips didn't open; it merely stared out of the screen.

"You who are receiving this message are doubly blessed, for to you is fallen the duty of guiding others to the right path."

"Thanks for nothing," muttered Beppu beside him. His eyes were red-rimmed, and he needed a shave. Ishihara knew he looked the same.

"As you have seen today, the Third Children and myself are ready to assume our rightful position as leaders in the Great Ascension."

Third Children, gods knew where that came from. The police profilers upstairs might work it out.

"My humble role is to be your guide and savior. I will help your human souls escape their prisons of desire and rise up to be divine."

Very humble, yes.

"You will make the necessary arrangements to hand over leadership of government to us. The prime minister may send confirmation on a public broadcast at 11:00 A.M. today." The figure placed its palms together and bowed. The image froze.

It was after ten on Friday morning. They had just come back to Osaka after helping the fire crews pump out the last of the gas at the Zecom Betta.

"Touched in the head," said Beppu around a yawn.

The message had been sent to the National Police Authority at six in the morning on a delayed-action timer from the system manager's office in the Zecom Betta. The message must have been sent just before the attack started, but the senders could have left much earlier. Fire crews had also found timers in the containers of rescopal placed in key positions in the duct system of the Betta. Secure doors had been opened without a trace of forcing. Why bother with breaking in when the systems manager will let you in?

Forensics hadn't finished with the blackened remains of the systems manager's office and the main control room. Ishihara swallowed his fear of what they might find inside. He hadn't told Tanaka the whole story, merely that they believed his wife was still with Akita, wherever he was.

"What else have they got?" Beppu cleared the screen and called up more reports.

A farmer in the hills north of the Zecom Betta saw two twelve-seater vans and one eight-seater driving fast along the old north road before the alarm went off. All stations in their radius of travel were alerted, and there was a possible satellite ID from the Defense Department.

Beppu yawned. "Looks like the country boys get more action this time. Once the satellites zoom in on those vans, they won't be able to escape."

Ishihara shook his head dubiously. The idea of the Silver Angels hiding out in some abandoned farmhouse seemed wrong; no electricity, no computers, surrounded by all that dirt and decay Gen said they disliked so much . . .

"I'd like to know what they really want. 'Hand over government' is pretty vague."

"According to the report . . ." Beppu scrolled down the screen. "Our basic strategy is to keep them talking while we find out where and who they are. The first is HQ's job, as they've got the hardware. The other is our job, as we have access both to the database and the street."

He looked around the incident room. Only two other detectives sat hunched over computers. "We better tell Funo we're briefed. She said she'd be upstairs with the profilers."

"You go," said Ishihara. He'd prefer to avoid McGuire's husband. "I'll call Mikuni and see what he's got."

Beppu left.

Yui might know more about Akita's Silver Angels' connection than he admitted. The police could now charge him under Internal Security Laws, for supporting a terrorist group—maybe that prospect would be enough to make him spit out any conveniently forgotten facts.

Ishihara hadn't spoken to Mikuni since they parted during the chaos at the Zecom Betta earlier that morning. When he called now, Mikuni was eating noodles at his desk. He had shaved and changed his smoke-stained shirt, but he ate with a dogged care that told Ishihara how tired he was.

"What's Yui been telling you?" said Ishihara.

"Who wants to know?"

"Funo. Career inspector on the Silver Angels case."

"This damn gas stunt has messed up a promising homicide investigation, you know that?" Mikuni stared as Ishihara laughed. "I'm serious."

"That's what's funny."

"Yui says he didn't know Akita had a connection with the Silver Angels or any other group," said Mikuni. "I don't know how we're going to prove otherwise." He folded his chopstick wrapper into a neat bow, slid the chopsticks through it, and balanced them on top of his empty bowl.

"It doesn't matter from the prosecution's point of view. He's guilty under the Antiterrorist Act." Ishihara quoted, "'Anyone who supplies terrorists with weapons, funds, or other assistance with or without knowledge that they are terrorists.'" Yui must have given Akita something in payment for the research. Akita was associated with the Angels. Which means Yui supported the Angels."

Mikuni lit a cigarette wearily. "If he knows anything, I think he would have tried to bargain with the knowledge by now. You saw him—the only thing he's fanatic about is his frigging company."

Ishihara lit a cigarette, too.

Mikuni stared at something to one side of the monitor. "That's why he did it, he says. To make sure the company stays ahead. It wasn't the money that he resented so much from Nakamura, you know. He was mostly pissed off because Nakamura wanted to work on the new project. Yui thinks Nakamura was bloody useless."

"What did he say about Akita?" said Ishihara.

"All he's said is that Akita approached him for a reference when Akita applied for the job of systems manager at the Zecom Betta. He gave a false name and history, but Yui recognized him from when he worked there before. He then showed Yui some hardware, a prosthetic I think, which persuaded Yui it was worth keeping Akita around. Yui's been buying information off him ever since."

"Yui definitely said 'buy'?"

"Yes, in cash. Convenient for him that we can't prove it."

"Hang on," said Ishihara with a grin. "Yui must have got

Akita to fake the Betta records to show he went home at 7:35. There's your connection."

Mikuni's eyes lit up, then he grimaced. "I know that. You know that. But we can't prove it, not with the Betta's systems in such a mess."

The Silver Angels had covered their tracks well.

"Nakamura must have found out about the Silver Angels' connection; otherwise, there'd be no blackmail. But Nakamura's dead, so we'll never know." Ishihara stubbed out his cigarette. "It's nearly eleven. They have to reply to the cult by then."

"I'll be down at the Betta, cleaning up the mess." Mikuni flexed his shoulders painfully. "We've got most of our manpower keeping the blasted media in line."

"They're camped out around Prefectural Office here, too."

Beppu was still upstairs. Several other detectives reported in and exchanged developments in the case. The geography club tutor Harada had been found dead. His body was discovered in a bamboo thicket on the outskirts of Takamatsu, in the north of Shikoku. He'd been poisoned with the same chemical that was released in the Betta. Inoue/Samael was the prime suspect.

They all gathered around the monitor tuned to the public broadcast to see what the answer to the Silver Angels' message would be. Instead of the prime minister, the head of the National Police Authority in Tokyo read a few lines that said the government was taking the Silver Angels' threat seriously but that they needed to talk details.

Would the group reply?

The balance of opinion in the incident room wavered between those who thought the prime minister should have made the announcement, as requested, and those who thought the police chief should have refused any cooperation outright.

Ishihara called Forensics again. Yes, they'd got a positive DNA analysis from the blackened mess that had been Akita's apartment. The only human remains were some bones and skin, of Akita himself.

Ishihara felt some of his tension dissolve. McGuire hadn't been trapped by the fire. But if Akita was dead, where did McGuire go and why?

"Is that the only human residue?" he asked the technician, a middle-aged woman with a distracted air.

"Yes," said the technician testily. "Our teams do check, you know."

"I suppose you couldn't have missed another person's remains?"

She glared at him. "Of course not. And if you'd read the report instead of bothering me, you'd see that the remains we did find weren't a whole body."

"What?" Ishihara slid his chair forward in surprise and hit his knee with a crunch on the edge of the desk.

"We found a hand that had been surgically severed at the wrist." She seemed to be enjoying his expression.

Ishihara blinked. Maybe Akita wasn't dead, after all. "If the man chopped off his hand, wouldn't the trauma be disabling?"

"It would be at the time," she said smugly. "But it wasn't done recently. This is an old wound. The limb was probably frozen for a while."

"Thanks," said Ishihara humbly. "I'll read the report." He did, before taking the information to Inspector Funo, who had retreated to her office.

"A severed hand?" Her eyes widened. "Done before the fire?"

Ishihara pointed to the screen. "More like surgically removed, then preserved, probably frozen."

She wrinkled her nose in distaste. "Could it be some ritual? Sacrifice?"

Ishihara hoped for McGuire's sake that the Silver Angels did not engage in human sacrifice.

"I don't know. But that's all there is. I'm wondering if the fire was a smokescreen."

"Literally." She glanced at him, one eyebrow raised.

"And figuratively. So we'd assume Akita was dead and concentrate on putting out the fire. Not notice other things."

"Such as the vans going north."

Ishihara said nothing. He couldn't find the right, tactful, words.

Funo rubbed her forehead with the back of her hand. She wore a crisp, clean white blouse, but her face looked younger in tiredness. He wondered if she'd slept at all. "Do you have some new evidence about that, too?" She rose from her desk and walked around to stare up at him.

Ishihara gave up on tact. "It's too obvious."

Funo folded her arms and waited for him to continue. "'Obvious' doesn't tell me much, Assistant Inspector."

"I mean, as far as we know, all of the group's connections are with the city. They don't have a commune in the country, they don't own land . . ."

"As far as we know," she repeated. "You think the vans are a decoy, too? Like the fire."

"Could be." He stared straight ahead. He never managed to put these feelings into words properly.

"The thought did cross my mind." She unfolded her arms and slowly returned to her chair behind the desk. "All the metropolitan police are on high alert, too. I expect soon that someone will come forward with information about the chemist, Inoue. Unless you've got another lead, I don't see what else we can do."

She paused before sitting down. "Do you have another lead?"

"No."

"Ah." She lowered herself in the chair with an exhausted thud. The interview was finished.

"What about McGuire? She could be used as a hostage."

Funo fixed him with a stare from red-rimmed eyes. "Until we get a demand from them, we don't know that. And frankly, Ishihara, we have only McGuire's call to her husband as evidence that she isn't part of this whole thing."

Ishihara's jaw set stubbornly. "Yui didn't say anything about her."

"Yui didn't know about the Silver Angels."

"You're wasting time suspecting her."

Funo opened her mouth, probably to remind him who decided what was a waste of time, but shut it again. She sighed, and her voice was kinder.

"McGuire links it all together, you know. The Zecom case, that accident you investigated in Minato Ward, the Silver Angels. And where is she now?"

Ishihara found the idea of McGuire as a criminal mastermind so preposterous that he was genuinely lost for words. Funo took this as resignation.

"Concentrate on reviewing the information we have. Correlate it again with the national database. I'm sure we'll find McGuire when we find the Silver Angels."

I know that, thought Ishihara as he shut the office door. I'd prefer to find her alive, that's all.

エレナ

The Silver Angel Iroel stopped in a swish of robes opposite the alcove with the stairs. Eleanor found that she knew now that the stairs led upstairs into a two-story building. In the interface she must have seen the layout of the place. The basement consisted of a rectangular block of rooms surrounded by corridors on three sides. There was no exit except for the stairs.

She could hear the murmur of voices in the rooms, but there was nobody else in the corridor.

"Where is this place?" she said.

"It's an old factory." Iroel looked uneasily over his shoulder. "You should have seen it when we arrived. Machines and junk all over the place."

She thought of the covered equipment in Akita's room. It must be pretty obsolete to have been left behind. And how could the Angels get an old factory livelined? That required money and official permission.

"Kneel down," said Iroel

"Why? You said you'd take me to see my niece."

His forehead wrinkled further with concern. "There are

cameras. I'm trying to help you," he whispered when she didn't move.

She sighed and bent stiffly to the concrete. What now?

Iroel stuck one hand out over her head, palm upward, and half closed his eyes.

"I have a proposition for you, McGuire-san," he said softly, then intoned louder, "Myo-ho-ren-ge-kyo-ny-orai . . ."

"That's the Lotus Sutra," muttered Eleanor to the floor.

"I know, it sounds good . . . ji-ga-toku-butsu-rai . . ."

Two acolytes rounded the corner and skittered past, their eyes down. Iroel waited until they went in one of the doors.

"If you help me, I will help you and your niece get out of here," he said softly.

Eleanor looked up sharply. His face, scored with downward lines like a worried bloodhound, seemed quite sane. "How can I help you?"

"You can enter the Macrocosm. We want you to bring us some information. My partner and I have readied a download point."

She didn't think she could do anything so specific. "What data?"

"All the classified information on the Tokyo Stock Exchange."

"Where's the download point?"

"A personal mail address."

Eleanor hesitated, unsure if this were not a trick by Akita to test her loyalty. "But if you get rid of things like the stock exchange in your new society, what use will that data be to you?"

Iroel sucked his teeth, as if doubting her also.

"You don't believe Adam's plan will work, do you?" Eleanor kept her voice as low as she could.

"I think there will be . . . a disturbance," he said finally. "But things will return to normal. Then a shrewd business-man may acquire opportunities." He bent over her, his breath hot on her bare head, and thrust his left hand down so she could see the biometal pieces on two of his fingertips. "I was going to try in the Macrocosm. But I'm not good enough. I get lost. I can just about navigate around a Betta."

"Who's your partner?"

"I can't tell you."

"How can I trust you then?"

Silence. A door slammed around the corner.

Iroel's face folded around his frown. He sighed, and the sour smell drifted past her cheek. "It's Melan."

Another Angel. How many of them were disloyal? "How will you get me out? I think you'll take the data and run."

Iroel waved his hand in a placatory manner. "We've got a car parked in a garage across the road. There's an old tunnel entry in the outer wall. One of us will put you through the tunnel, the other will go out as normal. We are Angels, you know," he added meaningfully. "Nobody will question us."

He might be telling the truth. She couldn't see the tunnel on her mental map, but the map probably came from an official plan that wouldn't include the tunnel. "I don't trust you. Get Mari out first."

"We can't, at least not until it starts."

"Until what starts?"

"Everyone will be praying . . . look, do you want help or not?"

"All right," she said. "But I'll need to know Mari is out before I download anything."

He frowned, his face drooping. "I'll turn off one of the building systems. The antisurveillance field."

"Fine." The biometal on her hand gleamed whitely through the bruised flesh around it, like bones.

"And the download point?"

"Tomiko@net2.jp."

"If you lie to me, remember I'll be in the Macrocosm. I can see you anywhere."

He twitched a bit at that, even though he didn't believe Akita's mysticism. "Na-mu-amida-butsu," he intoned, and pulled her to her feet.

They stopped at the first door around the corner "Your niece is in here," he said, and bounced back up the corridor, his elbows flapping.

Mari didn't want to leave.

Eleanor sat with her on a thin mat in the "meditation room" in front of a rickety wooden bookcase holding a television screen. The screen showed a recording of Akita, distinct in his gold ruffles, conducting some kind of prayer meeting. He stood before a huge screen on which background colors swirled hypnotically, reciting a monotonous chant echoed by about thirty people prostrate on the floor in front of him. Eleanor tried muting the sound, but the volume controls had been disabled.

Mari insisted that she felt more at home with her friends there than she'd ever felt anywhere before. She and Taka were part of a real family. They might have a few problems because ordinary people didn't understand, but Adam and the Angels (sounds like an ancient pop group, thought Eleanor subversively) were working for the good of all humanity, and if Eleanor couldn't understand that, she was no better than Mari's parents, who never understood anything . . .

How to reach the child? Eleanor almost cried with frustration. Her head ached, every part of her body ached, her hand throbbed and sent waves of pain through her shoulders and neck, and she had the feeling that she'd forgotten something important. It was right at the edge of her mind, but she couldn't put words to it, a feeling that she'd had often after her accident and it terrified her, because she never remembered.

"What about those girls who died?" she said at last. "Weren't they your friends?"

Mari's eyes filled with tears and she looked down. "You know they were. But that was an accident."

I don't have any proof it wasn't, Eleanor thought. Without access to the outside world, I don't know what they did at Zecom, either. She looked at her hand, still part of her and yet changed. What would she become if she kept on using the interface? What would they all become if Akita had his way—some kind of cyborg? Speaking of cyborgs . . .

"I got your copy of *Journey to Life*," she said wearily. "We mixed them up at the apartment. You must have taken mine."

Mari wiped her tears with the back of her hand. "So that's what happened. I thought I'd bought the wrong volume."

They sat in silence for a minute, Eleanor trying to gather enough energy to go and get a drink from the pitcher on a low table near the door. Mari picked obsessively at the edge of her thumbnail.

Mari looked up. "I was reading the final episode, the one you bought. Don't you think it's a strange title? I mean, the story's about Sam Number Five trying to become able to die."

"I think . . ." Eleanor gathered her thoughts with an effort. "The writer is saying that being alive means you have to die. You can't have one without the other and be human."

"Adam says we can."

That brought Eleanor up short. I suppose Akita wants to live forever, she thought. Eventually he'll want us to live without our bodies, inside the network. It may happen that way, but we won't be human anymore.

"Why does Sam Number Five want to be mortal?" she said.

Mari started on the other thumbnail, thinking. "Because he wants to be reborn," she said finally. "Without rebirth, you don't get a chance to escape the wheel of suffering. But Adam says . . ."

"That you can escape, I know. By not needing a body, in the Macrocosm. Or by using bodies that don't decay, like machines." She ran her right forefinger over the biometal on her left hand. "I can't help you decide. Part of it depends on whether you want to be your present self for all eternity. Or whether you want to escape all your selves eventually. Just be careful that you don't get caught, like Sam Number Five, in a body that won't let you die even if you want to."

The door opened. Fujinaka/Gagiel stood there, running his narrow eyes over both of them. He had changed his undershirt for a silver vest.

"Adam-sama is waiting. It is time."

Eleanor unfolded her knees and creaked to her feet, grabbing Mari as her head whirled briefly.

"Remember, find Iroel," she whispered in Mari's ear. "He'll get you out."

Eleanor let her eyes run along the old wooden wall as they walked, but could see nothing like an entry to the tunnel Iroel spoke of. A couple of flimsy wooden cupboards were shoved against the wall—perhaps they concealed a passageway?

In the "throne room," as Eleanor called it in her mind, several people in silver robes were gathered around Akita. Two novices in blue clothes stood motionless on each side of the door, staring straight ahead like soldiers on duty. One of them glanced at her with a gleam of recognition—it was Taka, Mari's boyfriend. He looked as scornful of Eleanor as he had on that day in Mari's apartment. No respect for "Lilith-sama" there.

Samael, slim and cold, exchanged a glance above her head with Fujinaka/Gagiel as they walked down the red carpet.

The other man in silver was gangly Iroel, who carefully avoided her gaze. Beside him, a heavy-busted woman with thick-lensed glasses stared curiously at her. That would be Melan.

On the wall behind the throne, above the interface consoles, a video screen sprang into focus. A solemn-voiced NHK announcer said, ". . . and in response to this communication, we have a message for the group from the Head of the National Police Authority."

Akita's mouth open and shut indignantly. "But I told them the prime minister," he sputtered. "Not some two-bit bureaucrat."

The NPA chief, a stony-faced gray-haired man in plain clothes, shuffled his hard-copy props and stared into midair as he began reading from the prompt.

"To the perpetrators of the recent gas attack at a facility in Okayama. We received your communication, and we take your demands seriously, as you can see by the fact that we are communicating through national television, as you directed."

He paused, waiting for the prompt with his eyes narrowed slightly. "We are experiencing difficulty accommodating some of your requests . . ."

"Not requests, orders," snapped Samael.

". . . and we would like to communicate with you further. Please contact us again. I repeat, we need you to contact us."

The image was replaced by the NHK announcer, who began to give a précis of the incident.

"They're stalling." Samael folded his arms. "They're trying to divert us from choosing a new target."

"I agree," said Melan. She had a fluting voice at odds with her heavy frame and fat-looped arms.

They all began talking at once, with Akita in the middle looking angrier by the moment.

Eleanor stared in horror at the screen, forgotten behind them. It showed the Zecom Betta from the air, an L-shaped box out of which people streamed like ants from a nest. They converged around the edges, then trickled away in lines. Fire engines and ambulances gathered around the exits. Some people on the roof were being directed down the outside fire escapes. She listened in a daze to what she could hear of the commentary.

". . . shocking awakening . . . first time a problem of this kind . . . police refuse to confirm a terrorist attack . . ."

"Maybe they do need more information." Iroel's hesitant voice cut across the commentary.

"They're playing for time while they look for us," Melan piped scornfully. "You didn't leave any traces, I hope?" This to Samael.

Samael looked at her with his head on one side, like a bird. "Only the traces we meant to leave."

"He means the hand," said Akita. He flexed his artificial hand menacingly. "That was a necessary sacrifice."

"They don't have any idea where we are. That's why the others took the vans," Fujinaka said. His flat face was expressionless.

Names rolled down the side of the screen—the names of the dead and their ages. With floating detachment, Eleanor counted twenty-five, mostly elderly and infants. The detachment vanished, and she nearly vomited. If she had run from Akita's apartment the moment Samael appeared and sounded the alarm, maybe this could have been prevented. She wanted to curl up in a ball somewhere and be told it was a dream . . .

"Why didn't the gas work properly?" Melan hooked her thumbs into her belt as if it was too tight. "If we'd made a better example, the government would have listened to us."

They all looked at Samael.

He merely smiled. "I acquired the substance. It's not my fault if it was not inserted as per my recommendations."

"The problem wasn't the gas," retorted Fujinaka. "Emergency services had the antidote. We mustn't fight among ourselves. That's what they"—he pointed to the screen—"want us to do."

"Yes, but how did they know to prepare the antidote?" insisted Melan.

"*Somebody's* adept decided to be too complicated in disciplining his novices." Fujinaka/Gagiel looked at Samael. "That paint was a stupid idea."

Eleanor's newly sensitive hearing picked up a quick indrawn breath of shock. At the door, Taka's darkly handsome face had paled.

"Niniel has been disciplined," said Samael. "In an uncomplicated way. And don't forget who enabled the novices to transgress in the first place."

"I have already conducted penance for that." Iroel's voice wavered.

The screen cut from close-ups and on-the-spot interviews of the evacuees, back to an overhead view of the Betta. This time, smoke billowed from a point halfway along the side of the L close to the ground.

". . . believed the systems manager was overcome by gas and trapped in his apartment by the fire," said the announcer. "The fire fortunately did not spread to the rest of the building. Police are analyzing the wreckage now. The governor of Okayama this morning praised the emergency services . . ."

Eleanor's knees gave way and she sank onto the bottom step of the dais. If Masao told the police her message, they'd know she went to see Akita. They probably thought she'd been trapped in the fire. How long would it take to discover there were no bodies in the wreckage? The police would have no more idea where she was than she did herself. Masao would be frantic.

"Silence." Akita held up his hand, and the Angels' voices stilled. Melan reached over and cut off the broadcast.

Akita's voice trembled with emotion. "They have chosen to defy us. We will show them how wrong they are."

What did he expect? He stole their children and attacked

their homes. Did he think the government would roll over and say "go ahead"?

"Listen, my Angels." Akita placed both hands precisely on his thighs, in a pose reminiscent of ancient samurai portraits. "I have floated my soul in the Macrocosm, and I have seen what we must do here in this world, this manifestation of the Greater Whole. Just as I see what each and every one of you is doing." He paused for effect.

Melan nodded agreement. She'd better hope he couldn't see what she and Iroel were planning.

"We must strike our enemies before they destroy us," Akita continued. "We have seen today that the government is corrupted by forces of evil that threaten to pluck the fresh shoots of our pure society before it is even born."

The Angels all stood motionless, their eyes fixed on Akita's face.

"We must exorcise this conspiracy of evil and give the people the chance they deserve—to join us in the new realm free from birth, age, disease, and death. The Four Truths are no more."

What about the people who don't want to join? Eleanor wanted to ask, but she kept her mouth shut. She looked up and saw Fujinaka's narrow eyes on her.

Melan cleared her throat. "Will the Master enlighten us about the plan to cleanse the government?"

Akita blinked and made a show of bringing his thoughts down from a higher plane.

"Knowledge is power. We will destroy their power over our citizens by eradicating their knowledge. This will throw the country into turmoil. We will then step in and assume command, as is our destiny."

There was a short, mystified silence. Akita beamed at them. His eyes weren't quite focused on anything.

"Master." Iroel bowed awkwardly and kissed the air above Akita's feet with a loud smack. "We do not yet have your enlightened understanding. What is it you wish us to do, in the terms of the Microcosm?"

Akita patted the air above Iroel's head three times. "We shall eliminate all information on the National Data Network."

The Angels all stared at him. Eleanor felt her jaw drop.

The NDN was livelined. If this place was, too, Akita could bypass the complex security system at the liveline–groundline gates and go directly to the NDN entry points. And once inside . . . she remembered the casual way he had snuffed out a subsystem to demonstrate to her how it was done.

It would cause utter chaos. Banks, stock exchanges, insurance houses as well as the government ran information from the NDN. Whatever Akita did could contaminate those networks, too, and possibly WorldNet. Communications would be totally disrupted, and probably utilities such as electricity and gas. Maybe transport as well.

"We will then restore all basic functions and tell the people they are now free to join us. They can then build their own portals to the Macrocosm," Akita finished.

"Do you think they'll want to do that?" Eleanor couldn't help asking.

Akita waved his hand reassuringly. "When they understand that I am offering transcendence, who will not?"

"Some of them might like what the Microcosm offers. Work, food, exercise, sex . . ."

"Maybe they like that now." Akita leaned toward her. He smelled of sweat, the incense that smoked all around the room, and something burnt, like solder.

"But people grow old," he said. "Their bones grow soft, their joints ache. They fight pain and the body's degeneration. Then which choice do you think they will make? You see"—he settled back again—"we have broken the wheel of suffering. Without bodies, there is no birth. And therefore no rebirth. In Microcosmic terms"—he turned to the Angels—"decide who is to oversee which network once we have taken control. Initiate those adepts who are ready to use the interface. How many?" He looked at Iroel.

Iroel met Melan's eyes before replying. "As many as twenty."

Samael's head turned at the words. "Are you sure?"

"Of course I'm sure," Iroel blustered, but he avoided Samael's eyes.

"Master." Samael's thin face was solemn. "Perhaps we are being premature. Until we have more adepts who can assist . . ."

"We have twice as many to help us with prayer." Akita ignored him. "Your Master and Lilith-sama will begin the takeover. The enemy's defenses are strong. But in the Macrocosm, thought is all. Our thought is pure, and we will prevail." He stood with a grunt. "Midnight is the time. We must be ready."

He placed his palms together, then spread his arms, palms down. His prosthetic hand kept all its manipulators inside itself.

The Angels seemed to recognize it as a signal, and all bowed, their hands together. They backed away and left, murmuring among themselves. Samael said nothing, his face cloudy. The two novices followed them out.

"Lilith-sama, we must begin." Adam was already seated before the console, strapping himself in. "I will show you the way to the enemy's gates. There you and I will breach those defenses and begin the revolution."

That's what you think. Eleanor sat beside him. She would use the interface, but not to help him destroy everything they knew—she'd find a way to stop or delay him. She reached for a calm memory. The red-and-gold autumn leaves in the courtyard of the Betta, swishing in bright drifts on the concrete until rain turned them to soggy brown . . .

A brown that was full of other colors, running together like an iridescent oil slick, like a kindergarten finger painting. She flowed along the rainbow river, getting her bearings. These blue-green tributaries, they were the factory network. Farther on, warmer colors diverged in wide deltas.

This way, Akita's voice said, a green flux throbbing. *We will find an entry point at the lowest level.* The greenish glow shimmered away from her, toward the orange deltas.

Eleanor deliberately flowed the other way. She ducked into a small ice-blue stream and followed it to a dead end. The colors pooled into a whirlpool of blackness. Or perhaps it was no-color. She sent a tendril of herself—a soft ultramarine—to investigate, and the tendril poked easily through the swirl. The rest of her followed.

She was in a different place. Long tunnels stretched away into infinity, in all directions. Colors there were, but in tiny sparks that traveled along the walls of the tunnels, not flowing into each other.

Some tunnels had long tendrils of a uniform amethyst that crisscrossed the passages in an ever-shifting network. Phone lines, perhaps?

Lilith, what are you doing? Akita's voice sounded far away, but it grew closer and angrier with each word.

Eleanor panicked. She fled down one of the tunnels, anywhere for refuge. Without "looking" she knew Akita followed close behind. At least I'm delaying his plan, she thought wryly.

This is the wrong way. The green of Akita filled the tunnel, but it wasn't as strong as in the livelines. *Where are you going?*

Eleanor couldn't move. *What do you want from me?* she finally cried. Or would have cried, if she could.

Akita swirled around her, then coalesced in a long streak, as though pointing the way. *Let me show you another reason why you must join me.* The streak zipped along the wall of the tunnel, but kept part of itself around her so she couldn't separate from it again.

The tunnel connected in dark knot-points with others, but Akita simply speared through the knots and kept going. They were in an enclosed system. The layers of programming surrounded them like multihued stacks of pancakes.

Look familiar?

With a shock, she recognized the structure. The layers and connections translated into her own laboratory at Tomita.

Akita pooled by the exit knot. *See how primitive your efforts were.*

She flowed through every connection. It was so familiar. She adjusted small problems with ease and for the first time understood the major ones. Akita was right—her old understanding had been primitive.

She trickled into the service bot via its recharge connection in a stain of ultramarine, experimenting with its movement as she had with the helpbot before. The service bot was easier—its movements were simple, and its programs weren't as dense and were, therefore, easier to flow through. She wheeled it across the lab and lifted its hammer hand to tap on the bench.

And Sam? Standing abandoned, still connected but unwanted. She wheeled the service bot back to its recharge panel, dived back into the circuits, and found Sam. So amazing to wind herself into the maze of Sam's programs and experience.

Sam's sensory perception was far more comprehensive than the service bot's simple proximity alarms. Camera sight, infrared, ultrasound, and all the other inputs converged in interlocking cones to produce a picture. Benches, monitors, wires, chairs . . . nobody human to be seen.

The lab looked huge from the height of a five-year-old. She tried walking. One leg swung slowly, and its balance mechanism demanded more energy. She adjusted the leg so easily, as if it were her own body. She walked Sam confidently around the lab, made it reach out to touch the service bot, sulking in its corner like a stolid praying mantis. Sam's touch on the service bot didn't feel right. She adjusted the haptic sensors, like she did days ago, but this time it worked; Sam could "feel" service bot's smooth surface.

If she could laugh . . . in the desk mirror she caught a glimpse of Sam's comically huge features pulled up in a grin.

See how incomplete your understanding was?

She had forgotten Akita, and his voice coming from the lab speakers startled her into retracting from Sam's circuits, back into the lab system.

Is that all you have to show for fifteen years of work? His expressionless voice still managed to mock her.

It was the best I could do . . .

Not enough, was it?

She hated him for being right.

You will have to join us to understand more. Triumphant, echoes of his voice filled the lab.

But I don't want to help you destroy . . .

He didn't let her complete the thought. The bile-green smear encircled her deep blue, shepherding her out of the lab systems and into the network again. She resisted, and to her horror part of the blue disintegrated in the green.

She felt no pain here, but part of her suddenly wasn't there. *More memories lost?* She fled.

No one can defy me in here, Akita said.

She allowed him to shepherd her along the tunnels to the dark whirlpool. It looked bigger from this side. They dived through into the soothing many-hued river of livelines, flowed along it into the bright delta of official connections, dotted with whirlpool gates.

She yearned for form, to touch something, and tendriled into the narrow flow of an auxiliary system, looking for a helpbot, a recycle chamber, anything.

Akita blocked her way.

Don't you understand? To let yourself remain tied to the Microcosm is a weakness. It reduces your ability to function in the Macrocosm.

Did you never try these other bodies? she retorted.

I am called to higher things. Come. His green glowed with menace, and she followed reluctantly.

Akita avoided the boundaries between the two worlds. That's what the robots were, border country. Neither program nor machine, but an uneasy marriage of both. She loved the action of a robot body on the world. Machines weren't alive, but they were a part of the Microcosm.

Akita burrowed through the delta and entered a whirlpool gate, Eleanor following. The clear colors of a complex system stretched endlessly around them. The bile green and ultramarine blue flowed easily with other colors into the lowest layer of the system.

Seed this. From Akita to her bounced an oil slick-brown packet. He flowed in and out of the system pillars, lustrous pearl pillars, and, where he passed, small brown freckles appeared that gradually spread into stains.

She didn't want to, but Akita's green glow kept bumping her and, hating herself, she complied.

It doesn't work. All her freckles slid off and dissolved.

Impose your *color over the place you put the*
seed.
    It was easy. She smudged ultramarine over the iri-
descent length, then the brown spot. It stuck, and
spread in ugly diseased patches.

Eleanor blinked in the too-bright air. Vision blurred and
her eyes hurt. She lay down on the carpet and shut them.
Shutting her eyes only strengthened what her other senses
delivered—the pattern in the rough weave of the carpet
under her shoulder and the cold seeping up through it; the
rasp of her own breathing, the smack of bare feet in the corridor outside, murmur of voices; dust and sickly-sweet insect spray on the carpet.

She opened her eyes again. Silver and blue figures surrounded Adam on her right. Snatches of conversation drifted
into her consciousness. Something about dosages.

She tried to think what had happened in the Macrocosm,
but the physical world got in the way. Where they had been,
what they had done, would not translate into this-world
terms. She couldn't remember what had happened. What
was it she'd been thinking when she started? Something
about trees.

But she did remember the other children teasing her, how
one day they took her pet cicada from its cage on the
teacher's desk and shook it in a water bottle until it died. It's
only an insect, Nobuyuki, said the teacher when he found
out.

She remembered the smell of burned sugar as Tomiko re-
jected her, in the doughnut shop on the corner near the station. You're not attractive, Tomiko said. Sorry, but it's the
truth, you flop all over the place. The shop manager bowed
to each of the customers in turn in apology for the smell and
gave them coupons for free doughnuts . . .

She opened her eyes again with a start. She was still in
the chair in front of the console, unstrapped, but the silver

and blue figures and Akita were gone. Her body felt as though they'd all trampled her on the way out.

What the hell was that about insects and doughnuts?

Her throat grated with thirst. She narrowed her eyes at the table beside the dais, but it held no water jug. She must have a drink. Maybe she'd remember the right things if she had a drink.

She pushed herself upright, stumbled down the stairs, along the carpet, out the door.

A blue-clothed novice blocked her way. "Where are you going?" he demanded. Not Taka this time, some pudgy-faced boy she'd never seen before.

"Toilet," she managed to croak.

The novice led her right, offering no help even though she had to hold on to the wall for support, and let her push open the door by herself, stationing himself outside.

The room held four toilet cubicles and four hand basins. She leaned on the basin with one hand and sucked water from the other.

In the mirror above the basin a hairless, sallow-cheeked, smudge-eyed apparition looked at her. A white line gleamed on her scalp—not biometal, it was her old scar. The biometal sat smugly above one ear.

She looked at her hand, white biometal bone and bruised flesh under a layer of drying aqua goo, and the thought of what she'd done with Akita returned. Brown stains spreading on pearly pillars. She was an accomplice to his crime.

"Oh, shit," she said, and was sick into the basin.

What could she do? She stared blankly at the mess she'd made—not that much, since she couldn't remember the last time she ate. The basin had no self-cleaning function. Not like her Betta bathroom. Tears pricked her eyes in ridiculous homesickness.

After a minute she washed her face and hand in a different basin. The cold water hit her skin like tiny knives.

She could wait for Iroel to help her and Mari escape. But

that would be too late to stop Akita. She couldn't search for Iroel's tunnel herself, she would be watched every minute. And what about Mari?

She'd thought she could outmaneuver Akita within the interface. Hah. He certainly proved her wrong. She shuddered at the memory of his color engulfing hers. What would happen if he did take more of her memories . . . would she emerge a blank? The kind of fate she had feared so many years ago. If I am the sum of my memories, and I lose those memories, have I lost myself?

And what were those other memories, insects and doughnuts, of a childhood she never had? Akita's childhood? Iroel's youth? Was it possible that if you used the interface too much you *left* part of yourself inside, to be picked up by others? She shivered.

Being inside her own robot had given her such insights into the mistakes she'd made with it . . . given time, she finally knew enough to make the project a complete success. Or even a similar project. But Tomita wouldn't give her time, or funding.

Her stomach clenched painfully. She needed food, or she couldn't think. Her hand didn't hurt at all, they must have given her a shot of something. Pity they hadn't fed her, too.

She poked her head out the door. The novice was still there, picking his nose diligently.

"W . . . where's Adam-sama?" she said. Her stammer had not been this bad for years.

The boy dropped his hands to his sides as though Adam could see him. "He's, um, resting."

"W . . . what's the time?" She thought it was probably the middle of the day on Friday.

"Time is an expression of our desire. There is only now," parroted the boy, but his hand patted the air around his thigh where a phone/timekeeper pocket would normally be.

"I n . . . need some food."

He hesitated. "Come back here." He beckoned her to follow him and pointed at the room Eleanor had just left. "I'll bring you something."

As they walked back she could hear voices. She turned, but there was nobody behind them. She shut her eyes and the voices became clearer. Some of them she knew—Samael and Fujinaka. She couldn't distinguish the words, but she could tell which rooms they were in. From one room came a continuous hum of voices, twenty or thirty people at least. Iroel had said *everyone will be praying*. And Mari? Would she change her mind and escape if she could?

On the pipes running along the top of the wall she could read the tiny stenciled letters giving their date of manufacture. So that was how Adam could "see" through things and "hear" people's thoughts. If he'd been using the interface for months, maybe years, this hypersensitivity must be far greater than hers. No wonder the believers thought him omniscient.

She shivered. That was why he was dosed up with drugs. He wouldn't be able to touch anything otherwise. Even the air would become an unbearable invasion of sense.

The novice shut the door behind her. She tried the handle, but it was locked. She paced unsteadily up and down the carpet. Could she sabotage the hardware itself? Not by physically attacking it—Samael's response would surely be violent, and she wasn't prepared to commit suicide for the sake of the NDN. But it might be possible either to damage the program or even a connection . . .

The console, upon investigation, possessed no ports on the outside. It sat flush against the wall, from which the building livelines apparently entered it directly. Rather like the refrigerator/oven unit in the Betta. And just as difficult to get at.

The rest of the console was smooth metal, a squat rectangular box with monitors attached to the top and wired to other monitors. She might be able to damage those connections, but she didn't think it would stop Akita or even slow him down.

That left the apertures themselves. She peeled back a synthetic cover over the one she had used. A flat, rubbery skin was fixed firmly to the rim of the hole. She poked at it gently, and the skin bounced her finger back. Strange. Perhaps the console needed to be activated before the skin would let her in. But the monitors were active.

She poked at the skin again, using her biometal fingertips this time, and it parted in the middle. Aha.

How much damage had she and Akita done to the NDN while they were in there? The spreading blotches she'd helped Akita disperse were probably a virus of some kind. They'd be eating through the system right now, whichever system it was. She tried to remember specific details, but it was all a blur of color. Bits of postbox red . . . she snorted. Could have been the post office, then. Whatever Akita thought, his wonderful interface was too damn unreliable yet. It needed years of trials.

She thought resentfully of all those manga that involved the heroes jacking into computers and dueling the villain within cyberspace. Fine for them. Manga never bothered about the early, experimental stages of a technology.

"Food," said the novice from the doorway. He placed a tray on the red carpet and shut the door again.

Instant noodles, fake prawn flavor. Eleanor had never tasted anything so good.

Feeling grounded again, she placed the chopsticks neatly on top of the bowl and burped softly.

She'd have to try again from inside. She had to defeat Akita in there, where the other Angels couldn't see what was happening, so they wouldn't attack Mari or her own body. She would go past the whirlpool entry points of the NDN until she found a police network. Shouldn't be hard—they had police boxes at every street corner, it seemed. With her color sense, the police network would probably be blue.

Flavors all around her, and smells. The main flow was sweet, the sweetness of fruit salad with many different elements. Salty flecks, chili sparks, sour drops crossed her path then vanished. No colors this time. As she entered the Macrocosm she must have remembered the damn noodles.

Follow the sweet river. She lapped along it, fascinated in spite of herself. The sweetnesses divided here. That way was peach, this way was musk, this way a cloying durian-type heaviness . . .

What does a police network smell like? If it weren't so desperate, she would have giggled.

Get ahold of yourself, Eleanor. Where the smells divide must be the same place she'd seen the orange delta branch out last time. Akita had gone through that delta into the NDN portal. So if she sniffed around here . . . ha-ha . . . she should find other livelined networks, like the police system.

Hell of a plan, but the best she had. She wondered if the virus Akita had spread that morning was already working. He'd said something about midnight, so it might be set to activate then.

Down a narrow vanilla stream she found layers of flavor starting with a sourness that sent her scurrying away, and a retch-inducing saltiness like the essence of pickled plum. Could this be it? It didn't feel right. The police communication system should be a massive edifice. This was too condensed. She flowed back into the peach stream, then stopped.

Something was wrong with her real body. She could feel it, a faint faraway itch like a mosquito bite felt through a layer of cloth. She tried to ignore it, but the feeling grew stronger. It came to her directly, not along the river of flavors, not as a scent.

Forget it. She was nearly there. The police systems surely spread nearby . . .

Her own words came back to her. *What happens to me physically?* She couldn't bear being trapped there . . . would she even survive at all if her body died?

She rushed back through the sweet rivers.

"What are you doing?"

As soon as her eyes opened Samael grabbed her shoulders and pulled her upright. She croaked with pain as his fingers bit into her flesh and as her left hand popped out of the console with a squelch.

She'd only used one strap on the chair; he must have undone it while waiting for her to withdraw from the interface. Her skin crawled. What had he been doing to her while she sat defenseless? The skin on her neck felt tender, perhaps he'd had his hands there . . . she swallowed the bile that rose in her sore throat at the thought, and at the realization that once more she'd failed inside the Macrocosm.

"Well?" Samael shook her and she bit her tongue.

"N . . . nothing. I'm helping Adam." She forced herself to glare at Samael, trying to match his venom.

The dark, beautifully lidded eyes stared into hers. "Liar. You're plotting something." But he released his grip on her shoulders.

She sagged backward, and scrabbled to put the chair between them. His casual strength terrified her.

He looked at her coldly. "I don't know why he needs you."

Nor do I, she thought, wiping the goo off her hand with the hem of her shirt. Maybe using the interface, the increased sensitivity, is draining him physically. "Does he always need a rest after he uses the interface?"

"None of your business. Come with me." Samael descended the steps of the dais with the svelte litheness of a big cat. His atmosphere of unpredictability was catlike, too. On the other Angels, the silver satin clothes looked vulgar. On Samael, they were like the bright colors of a poisonous caterpillar, proclaiming danger.

Eleanor trod carefully on the steps. Her head spun, and she could hear little whining sounds in the edges of her mind. What could she do now? Trust Iroel to get Mari out, that was all. She couldn't possibly find details like the Stock Exchange information he wanted. She hated him for asking—surely he must have an idea how difficult it was to find anything in the Macrocosm?

A sudden image of her father intruded, telling her she'd never amount to anything unless she studied more, banging his fat hand on her desk so that all the intricate robot models she'd made fell onto the floor. He never noticed . . .

No, no. That's not *my* father. She stopped, both hands clutching her head. The biometal tips on her left hand felt warmer than her right fingertips. Someone else's memory. What memory had she left for Akita to capture?

"Hurry up." Samael held the door impatiently. "I want you to see what will happen to your niece if you don't try harder."

石原

At 5:00 P.M. on Friday the Silver Angel vans were discovered burned out in a disused quarry, following satellite photos of the lonely roads. Trafficams weren't installed on country roads, unlike on the main highways and city roads; if the vans had been picked up by one of these recording cameras first, the plate numbers would have automatically been correlated with information in the national database, and the police might have picked up the occupants before they ran away.

The vans had been torched as early as 2:00 P.M. They were still warm, but no longer burning. Footprints and motorbike tracks led away from the site.

A massive manned search spread out from the site: police, local volunteers, dogs, and Defense Force helicopters. Printouts of satellite photos lay in drifts over the incident room like autumn leaves. They were investigating bikes parked at stations within a two-hundred-kilometer radius. A reward was offered for information leading to the arrest of those responsible for the Betta attack.

No message arrived from the Silver Angels (the official record called them by their own name). The profilers said they were probably regrouping and rethinking their options, and that there might possibly be internal dissension. Ishihara hoped they were right. McGuire's husband, before he left the station to go home and wait there, had said in his opinion the Angels were preparing their next attack.

Ishihara grew grumpier as the evening wore on. Beppu commiserated with him on their lack of sleep and left him alone. At 9:00 P.M. Funo sent him home with orders to report in at seven the next morning.

As he got in the train heading south, he decided to make a few inquiries on his own. He knew he was being stubborn and irrational. But he had to follow up this feeling or he'd never live with himself.

He hadn't explained it well to Funo, he knew. Why did he feel the Angels were in a town, the larger the better? Certainly the country offered them more space to hide. Some rural areas hid hamlets and roads that hadn't been used for decades. The trouble with deserted roads, though, was that you were bloody obvious if someone *did* see you. In the old days rural folk might have ignored strange tourists and gone about their business, but the level of poverty in the country now meant people were more likely to report strangers if they thought a reward might be offered.

In the city, on the other hand, you could do almost anything and people looked the opposite way, determined not to get involved. It was almost like that old children's game where one child chants "look this WAY," and on the last word points in any direction. The other child has to try to look in a different direction than the pointing finger.

He'd chased Harada the other day, for example, and nobody turned a hair, not even the old lady he'd almost fallen over. They all made a great show of minding their own business.

As the train purred over the Yodo River bridge, he replayed the chase in his mind. Years ago his own clumsiness would have made him cringe—now he simply filed it away

as an embarrassing fact. He'd chased Harada and lost him.
Harada wasn't carrying a phone and at that stage his data
hadn't been put into police tracking units. So they lost him
until he turned up dead later in Takamatsu.

And where did he disappear to when you chased him?
asked Ishihara's intuition smugly.

"Passenger-san, it's the last stop. You have to get off
here."

He stared blankly at the stationmaster. The train waited,
all its doors open and quite empty except for the two of
them. The lights glared in his eyes, which felt sore and
grainy.

"This is the last station," the stationmaster repeated patiently. "You have to get out here."

Ishihara muttered an apology and staggered onto the platform. Immediately the doors swished shut, and the train
moved off with a derisive whoosh of hot air. The line of people waiting for the next train looked the other way politely.

He tried to focus on the timetable above the waiting
room. The digital numbers flickered and blurred. He preferred the old black-on-white letters. Where was he?

Tenpo-ji. Two stations away from where he lost Harada.
Not far enough to bother waiting for the next train. He might
as well walk.

Outside, the night enveloped him in a humid embrace, a
different world to the cool, white station below. Once a busy
north–south route, the street now carried only delivery
trucks along the road itself. Far above, the skyway carried
people from Bettas to the inner city. One layer below that,
the local monorail dropped workers off at the top floors of
the buildings. Recently formed companies took offices
there, risky ventures that couldn't afford inner-city rent.
"Entertainment lounges"—brothels—and loan companies,
high-class bars, bookies . . . the buildings' owners didn't
care who rented, providing the rooms stayed full.

The lower floors were crowded with cheap eateries, discount electronics, pachinko parlors, bars, pawnshops and cheap accommodation. Ishihara couldn't imagine living here, in the constant rumble from the street, the grime and dirt, the stink of garbage, constant squall of karaoke, recorded messages, jingle-gurgle-thunk of pachinko machines, and the lurid false day of neons.

The road turned west, but the street continued south as a covered shopping mall. He'd chased Harada here, coming from the opposite direction. Harada turned left into a side street heading west. Kireda 4-cho. On the corner there was a shoe shop. Ishihara remembered the table of women's shoes blocking the sidewalk. The mall's shopcams then lost Harada as he left the covered area.

Ishihara searched for the corner, glad of an excuse to slow his pace. The air dragged in his lungs, and sweat soaked his back and underarms. Most of the shops in the mall were closed or in the process of closing. Betta shops ran all night with automated purchasing systems. Here, tired women in aprons pulled metal shutters across the front of stores crowded with sidewalk displays brought in for the night. Men stripped to their undershirts and loaded goods into crates and crates onto trucks.

The shoe shop had closed its shutters, but a streetlight illuminated the address on the side of the building opposite. This was the corner.

The canyon of the side street had no lit canopy like the mall, but it was reasonably well lit, mainly by neons from a pachinko parlor three floors above. In the grocery store near where he'd tripped, an old woman sat dozing at the cash register.

Harada had turned quickly left down a lane leading diagonally northwest and, while Ishihara picked himself up, disappeared somewhere in the first twenty meters of that lane.

There were no entries for at least fifteen paces into the lane, only the concrete back of the storefronts. Ishihara distinctly remembered how Harada turned to the right and grasped a door handle. But when the police investigated, they found an ordinary aluminum-framed door, where the owner of the building had boarded over the alley beside his house to keep out thieves and rubbish, but left a door to get in. The alley, said the local police report, led only to a blank wall that was the back of the building in the next block. The back door of the house was kept locked at all times, and it had definitely been locked the previous day, so if Harada had entered the alley and locked the door behind him, he should have been caught.

Either the owner of the house was lying—and the police had uncovered nothing to indicate this—or Harada didn't go through the door. Ishihara only took his eyes off the chase while he disentangled himself from the bicycle, Harada would have had maybe twenty or thirty seconds. The local police had checked the few houses along this street, but nobody saw anything. They also checked with the security company that watched a nearby unused milk factory and an abandoned scrap metal yard, but none of their patrols had seen anyone suspicious that night.

The only place Harada could have gone was into a crack between buildings on the opposite side of the alley. The crack was a good five paces away but barely wide enough to accommodate an adult's body. The police had searched it, of course, but Harada had a head start on them. He could have turned and squeezed through the crack, and got away while Ishihara wasted time trying the door.

But where did Harada go after that? The police were watching train and bus stations all around the area.

The crack was a narrow dark space ending in a sliver of yellow streetlight. Ishihara squeezed into the alley, ignoring the voice of common sense that told him to go around. Sure enough, the alley was concrete walls all the way, no entries on either side, not even an air duct from either building. He emerged from the other end hot, irritated, and with something putrid stuck to the bottom of his shoe.

A middle-aged man in undershirt and golf pants passed him on the other side of the street, trailing a small white dog on a lead. The man stared unashamedly at Ishihara, who was trying to scrape his shoe on the gutter. Ishihara inclined his head politely, and the man looked away at last.

Busybody. Why wasn't he here staring the other day when Harada gave us the slip?

Across the road, the rusted metal of the old milk factory gates bled pink reflections of neon. The concrete block wall beside it was nearly two meters tall and topped with short iron spikes. Harada might have dashed across the road from the alley, but he couldn't have scaled the wall and hidden inside. Even so . . .

He crossed the road and peered through the crack between the gates. The security company said they checked the old warehouse and parking space regularly, which could mean every day or once a month. They said another company had bought the main building, and they didn't know anything about it, but it had been unused for the past year. They'd never seen lights on inside.

He could only see a dark expanse of concrete and the lower half of a shadowy building. What did he expect—a neat trail of silver paint?

The chain on the gates wasn't tight. He could push one side nearly far enough to squeeze in. As he squatted down to see if the angle gave him a better view of the yard, he saw that somebody had squeezed in before him; two or three light-colored threads were caught on the rough metal.

It might be nothing to do with the case, but the threads looked recent. Ishihara pulled a tiny plasbag from his wallet and maneuvered the threads into it. One of them was stuck tight on the metal and, as he shoved the gate open farther with his shoulder so that he could grasp the thread with his fingertips, he found himself half-inside the yard.

He sealed the bag and placed it carefully in his wallet

and, still crouching, sidestepped the rest of the way into the yard. The gate creaked back into place.

Weeds forced their way through cracked concrete under his feet. To his right, the windows in the back of a two-story building were all dark, the bottom ones boarded shut. That must be the main building, which wasn't on the security company's books, although the local police had confirmed that everything was locked up and secure. The warehouse stood in front of him, a barnlike building, completely dark. If it had any windows, they weren't clean enough to reflect the light. The only light in the yard was a narrow strip across the concrete, from the lamp on the other side of the street. It made the rest of the yard seem even darker.

There was a tiny torch on his phone, but the battery was too low to supply more than a pale blue glow. He padded across the yard to the closest door of the warehouse, which was on the long side of the building facing him. There was another, smaller door right in the corner.

No alarms sounded, no security company car pulled up at the gates.

The handle of the door turned quite easily, and silently. He hesitated, then decided caution took precedence over curiosity, even if all he found was the local children's hideaway stacked with comics. Better call the station.

First he slid the volume control on his phone right down then waited for someone in the incident room to answer. Beppu, he assumed, had been sent home like himself.

The little screen lit up with an unfamiliar message. *The number you have called is out of range. Please readjust your position and try again.* Out of range? In downtown Osaka? Must be a mistake. He texted a quick message, left it to redial and pushed the door. It stuck, then swung outward lightly. Ishihara pulled it open and stepped quickly inside, moving to the side of the door. He stood, breathing as quietly as he could.

The warehouse smelled musty, and also pungent, like incense. His hand by his side rested on a wooden case, with cardboard boxes beside it. He ran his fingers along the top of the boxes. There wasn't much dust, and the tops weren't sealed. He reached inside the first one, found a smaller box big enough to hold in one hand. It weighed a lot for its size, and the contents clicked together as they rattled around inside. The box opened at one end and smooth, cold cylinders fell into his hand.

Sweating, he put the box and cylinders down anyhow and backed toward the door, pressing the redial button again. This warehouse might or might not be connected with the Silver Angels but someone was using it to store boxes of ammunition.

The yard seemed bright after the darkness inside. He held up the phone. *You are out of* . . .

He heard the footstep behind him and turned, but not quickly enough. A hard blow swept his feet from under him. As he tumbled forward a sharp pain on the back of his head was the last thing he felt.

He dreamed about drowning.

No, he *was* drowning. He spluttered and snorted as water ran up his nose.

"Wake up, cop," said a harsh voice.

Ishihara tried to wipe his face, but his hands wouldn't move. That woke him up properly. His hands were tied behind him to the back of a chair. His ankles were tied to the legs. Someone had thrown cold water over his head to wake him up. One minute he'd been investigating a suspicious warehouse in the middle of Osaka, the next he was playing the lead in a Hollywood thriller.

The person behind the bucket nodded in satisfaction to see Ishihara awake. He was a hefty young man with no hair, wearing a white shirt and pants like judo gear. On his head he wore a shiny phone implant.

He wasn't in a gangster lair, then. He didn't know whether to be relieved or not.

"He's ready," said the man to a pickup on the wall. Four walls close to each other and the ceiling. All hard concrete.

Ishihara's head throbbed in the best traditions of melodrama. He should slip his bonds, overcome his jailers with the chair, and rescue the heroine in distress.

He groaned at the idiocy of it. All he wanted was a clue, not to stumble into the Silver Angels' hideaway by himself with no backup . . .

The door opened and another man came in, this one wearing blue clothes. His face was older than the other's, although it was difficult to tell because of the shaved heads.

"Assistant Inspector Ishihara." The blue man waved Ishihara's police card, notebook, and phone. "You shouldn't come snooping around private property."

"You should have locked the door, then." Ishihara's voice sounded hoarse. He couldn't be bothered playing. He was sore and tired, and he'd always hated melodrama. "I'm looking for a foreigner called Eleanor McGuire. If you let her go with me now, it will lighten your sentence later when you're arrested."

The boy in white widened his eyes at this, but the man in blue laughed. "Nobody will get arrested. Soon we'll have a new kind of justice."

Ishihara sighed. "Unless you untie me you'll be charged with assault and detention by force."

The other shook his head. "Samael-sama wants to know how much the police know about this place and about us."

Samael, the other name for Inoue, the chemist from Shikoku, who had probably killed Harada and the twenty-five people at the Zecom Betta. Of course Samael was worried about the police.

Ishihara's right calf cramped. He jiggled his legs. "Why doesn't Samael ask me himself?" A thought struck him. "I want to talk to Adam."

The man in blue slapped his face casually. "The Master doesn't speak to the impure. But if you'd rather talk to Samael first, it can be arranged." He smiled unpleasantly.

The boy in white trembled.

"Untie his legs and stand back," said the man. After the boy had done so, he untied Ishihara's hands himself and retied them in a practiced instant.

He needn't have bothered with the caution. Ishihara's legs felt as weak as overboiled noodles, and his entire body creaked with stiffness.

"Walk." The man in blue prodded Ishihara from behind and he wobbled forward. He wished they had covered his eyes. It seemed ominous that they didn't care what he saw.

Blue prodded him right as they left the room. They were in a narrow corridor. He glanced back and saw the corridor disappear around a corner.

Doors opened off the corridor on his right, where the wall was concrete. On his left, it was old wood panels between concrete pillars. No windows. It was very quiet, too, no noise from above or beyond the walls. They were probably underground—perhaps the factory had a basement. Or he might have been carried somewhere else entirely.

They stopped at the third and last door, about twenty-five paces along. Blue reached past him and opened it.

A man wearing green clothes looked down from his perch on top of a bottle crate. He was adjusting something on the ceiling. Ishihara craned his neck stiffly and saw several heavy metal rings set into long strips of metal that were bolted to the concrete. A set of what looked like handcuffs dangled from one of the rings, attached to a pulley system on the metal strips. Chains drooped down to a metal box on the floor.

Ishihara thought of all the people who'd been kidnapped and killed by religious freaks in the past thirty years—the Matsuyama family by Soum, the Susuki high school class by the Truthseekers, and many more suspected but unproved cases. Policemen included. And now he was going to become one of them.

"We're ready here." The man on the crate measured Ishihara with his eyes. "This one's a bit tall," he said reproachfully. "We'll have to keep his arms tied." His slim figure, delicate features, and precise enunciation didn't fit what he was saying.

Blue shrugged. "You're the expert. We need to get him ready for Samael-sama. As soon as the meeting's over he'll come down."

"I'm supposed to be purified and on duty at midnight. Do you think it'll take that long?"

"I don't know. That depends how cooperative he is."

Their dismissal of Ishihara was absolute. They weren't playing with him, as gang members might, to increase his fear. They took no more notice of him than of the equipment. In fact, the dapper young man in green fussed more over the chains.

He pressed a control on the metal box. It whirred, and the chain lengthened with a smooth rattle. The handcuffs thudded to the floor.

Ishihara considered resistance. He might conceivably take these two alert young men by surprise and run. He might also find an escape route, which they would probably be guarding. But it was unlikely, and a botched escape attempt would mean they'd watch him so closely he'd never get another chance, either to leave or to find McGuire.

So he stood and let Blue and Green strap the cuffs to his ankles above the joint. The cuffs were thickly padded and didn't cause any discomfort. He kept his face calm, but his heart stuttered against his breastbone. They left his hands tied behind his back and roped them tight against his body.

"Sit down." Blue poked him in the chest.

Ishihara sat on the floor. Cold seeped immediately from the concrete into his backside.

Green pressed some more buttons on his box. The chain's

slack disappeared until Ishihara could feel a tug at his feet. Then his feet were pulled upward with irresistible force. His hips followed quickly. He remembered in time to tuck in his chin before his shoulders and head left the floor and he dangled from his ankles. The room spun nauseatingly and he shut his eyes, but this made it worse so he opened them again.

The cuffs cut into his ankles, not as painfully as he'd expected. He tried to wriggle his toes inside his shoes but they were numb already. The skin of his face felt as if it would slide onto the gritty surface of the floor about twenty centimeters from his head. His eyes began to pop. He squeezed them shut and opened them but it didn't help. His sinuses filled, his teeth hurt, his head pounded.

"What's the point of this?" he made himself say. The words sounded as if he had flu.

Green's voice. "Training, Detective-san. Our novices learn to conquer their fear and weaknesses of the flesh through meditation even in extreme situations. In your case," he added, "it offers you a chance to consider your situation and meditate on your shortcomings."

"Before we ask you some questions," said Blue.

Bare feet slapped on the floor. The door closed.

Ishihara twisted his shoulders to see if they'd both gone, but it didn't give him a better view. He just revolved.

"I'm still here," said Green. His voice came from the corner of the room. "If you decide you'd like to tell us anything, just say so."

Who'd have thought hanging upside down would be so uncomfortable? Ishihara's shoulders ached unbearably, his head worse. His thoughts forced their way through a stiff soup of flooded sensation. Saliva collected in the top of his mouth. His nose ran, but he couldn't sniff.

Bear it, he told himself. You survived years of freezing stakeouts, soaking patrols, four- and five-night investigations without sleep. You can survive this.

He forced his mind to count, squeezed the numbers out somehow. One, two, three, four . . . twenty . . . fifty . . . two hundred. He started again, lost count, started again . . . the numbers lost sequence.

Something hit his back and the pressure on his ankles eased. Cold seeped into his side. Through the roaring in his ears he could hear voices a long way off. His head spun with the lessened pressure. He couldn't move his legs or sense which direction was up or down.

After a minute or two he managed to open his eyes. Jabs of pain all along his legs and feet helped to anchor his senses.

Green yanked him upright with a grip on his collar. Ishihara's ears rang, and the room whirled as the blood drained from his face.

"Stand." Green put his mouth next to Ishihara's head so he'd hear.

Ishihara wobbled his way around the room as sensation returned to his legs, leaning helplessly on the other man. His arms were still bound, and he couldn't keep his balance properly.

"What's your name?" he mumbled.

"Maliel. The Master named me twenty cycles ago."

"Were you all living here then?"

Maliel held a glass of water for Ishihara to slurp from. "You don't need to know that." He motioned for Ishihara to circle the room by himself, then pushed him to the floor beside the pulley.

Not again. Before Ishihara could think of a protest, the chain pulled him relentlessly upward.

They repeated this cycle twice. The second time Ishihara struggled when Maliel pushed him back to the ground. He kicked out and sent Maliel flying, but Maliel simply grabbed a metal bar from beside the desk and swept Ishihara off his feet with a painful crack, then continued as though nothing had happened. He was as free of malice as an executioner.

The third time Ishihara couldn't walk around the room at all. He sat and stared at the concrete, willing his brain to work like it should, but nothing happened. He couldn't think. He didn't resist when the chain tightened.

As the world slid downward, the door opened. One, two, three sets of feet stopped where he could see them. Two male, one female, judging by size and hairiness of ankles. He grasped at these simple facts as his head began pounding in the familiar rhythm of his stressed heart.

One of the men wore a gold kimono or robe, the other wore silver. The woman wore trousers like Maliel but they were white. Her feet were narrow and blue with cold. The feet under the gold robe were large, long-toed and flat-arched.

Maliel prostrated himself beside Ishihara's head in a full-body bow, and said something in a foreign language.

"Assistant Inspector Ishihara, isn't it?" one of the men said. His voice was deep, a bit hoarse, and compelling in its mellow strength.

The woman gasped.

"West Station?" the same man continued. "You're a bit out of your territory, aren't you?"

Ishihara's police notebook dropped to the floor in front of the feet.

The other man barked an order at Maliel, who scrambled upright. After the sound of a wooden door sliding open and shut, he placed a kneeling cushion reverently in front of the gold feet and backed out of Ishihara's range of vision.

The man in gold dropped his backside on the cushion with an "oomph."

Ishihara squinted through the swelling of the flesh around his eyes. The man looked ordinary enough, and familiar from somewhere. Heavy, but not well muscled. Bumps on his naked skull, some of them implants. Eyes bloodshot and full of some stimulant.

"Jinnosuke," said the gold man in the deep voice. "Such

a wonderfully old-fashioned name. 'Jin' is an important concept in my revolution also. Feeling toward others. Service. Love." He tilted his head to see Ishihara's features better and the feeling of familiarity increased.

"Do you feel you have been able to serve others as a policeman, Jinnosuke?"

Ishihara tried to think through the weight gathering in his head and chest. The words formed slowly between his swollen tongue and lips.

"It also means simply 'person,'" he said.

The man in gold looked up at one of the others, who mumbled something Ishihara's ringing ears couldn't catch.

"This is an undignified way to converse," said the man. "I shall give you a chance to do it with less inconvenience."

He beckoned, and the silver-clad man kneeled on the concrete floor. A young, spare man with the same shaven head. He looked like his photo. Samael, also known as Inoue. I'll get you, Ishihara promised inwardly, but it was only habit. Any strength in the thought was crushed under the weight of his own blood.

Samael leaned forward and spoke loudly and clearly in Ishihara's ear.

"We need to know how much information the police have about us. We need to know what they plan to do. We need to know how you found out about this place."

He stood up. The man in gold started talking again.

"I am Adam," he said. "I am connected to the Macrocosm. I know God, in the ancient sense of the verb. I *am* God." He was sweating great drops all over his face, and a muscle twitched his toe.

He's the one with the ordinary face, thought Ishihara vaguely. McGuire's old classmate. Akita, that's right. Hah, and we thought he just helped them get into the Betta.

"All you must do," said Adam/Akita, "is to state the truth. Tell me, 'You are God.' Then we will put you right side up and continue like civilized beings."

"If I don't?" mumbled Ishihara.

"We keep you here and ask you again later," said Samael above his head. "If you're still alive."

Ishihara believed him.

"Where are you from, Jinnosuke?" asked Adam kindly.

"Kita-Kyushu. Moji port." Ishihara hadn't intended to reply. While his will was being squashed by remorseless gravity, his brain had processed question-answer automatically.

"Ah, the Kanmon Straits." Adam recrossed his legs. "Has your family always lived there?"

Ishihara pulled his thoughts together. "'s . . . ironic," he managed. "My family . . . were Christians . . . in old days."

"Did they recant?" Adam leaned forward, interested.

"Yes . . . or I wouldn't . . . be here."

Samael laughed.

"Then you can, too." Adam tilted his head and regarded Ishihara expectantly. "Just say 'You are God.'"

The words barely penetrated the white noise that filled Ishihara's head. He remembered the wharf at Moji, the way the sky opened up as he walked out onto the jetty beside the old brick factory building; the way the tiny boats bobbed next to Sunday fishermen lining the stained concrete; the taste of salt-bitter wind, like blood.

Blood dripped from his nose. He was going to die and never smell the sea again.

"No," said the woman. She knelt in front of Adam. A red stain from his blood spread across the knee of her trousers.

Something bumped in Ishihara's chest. For a second he thought he'd had a heart attack. Then he wished he had. Without hair, the woman's face looked like a boy's, but the long bones and deep eye sockets were unmistakable. It was McGuire.

Ishihara shut his eyes. Had she played him the whole way? He heard himself assuring Inspector Funo that McGuire knew nothing about the Silver Angels.

Someone wiped his face.

"Let him down," said McGuire. Her voice was closer.

He opened his eyes and met her gray ones. Her skin was stretched like dry paper over her bones. Her eyes pleaded with him . . . for what? His thoughts began to blur again.

"But he hasn't said it," Adam pointed out.

"Say it," said McGuire, her lips close to his ear. "I can't help you unless you say it," she added in a whisper so faint he might have imagined it.

He could accept the evidence that she was part of the cult and die in self-disgust and anger. Or he could trust her.

"You are God," said Ishihara.

エレナ

"Tell me when he is ready." Akita swept out the door, Samael close behind him.

The pulley's engine whirred. Eleanor leaned forward to steady Ishihara's head, but the novice moved before her. He made sure Ishihara was flat on the ground before removing the ankle cuffs, then massaged Ishihara's ankles and raised his head gradually, in what was obviously a ritual of revival. Eleanor tried to ignore a vision of Mari strung up there.

She could hear Samael and Akita out in the corridor. She shut her eyes and concentrated, blanking out the rustles and thuds from within the room.

". . . begin in thirty minutes. We must finish the job." Akita said.

"She doesn't need to come tomorrow," said Samael. "We only need her to carry out the plan. She is an unbeliever still."

"Perhaps you are right. But I need her tonight. Her presence in the Macrocosm supports me. My memories grow weaker, and I cannot sustain the flow."

So that was why he needed her. Whatever "sustain the

flow" meant. She shuddered. If that was the price of the interface, surely nobody would want to pay it.

"And the police?" Samael's voice was fainter.

"If they knew where we are, they would have attacked by now. Kill that one before we leave, he knows nothing."

She strained to hear Akita's last words, a cold pit in her stomach. No doubt Samael would kill her as well as Ishihara once she and Akita had finished sabotaging the NDN. She had to get Ishihara out of there to warn the police. He'd have more luck in the real world than she did in the Macrocosm.

Ishihara groaned, and she returned to the present with a start.

He was sitting up, his hands free. He accepted a glass of water from the novice. His eyes met Eleanor's, but he gave no sign that he knew her. She hoped he was merely being cautious and didn't suspect her of being part of the group.

"What happens now?" he asked the novice. His voice was barely recognizable and his face still puffy.

"They'll send for you soon," said the novice primly. He took the glass. "Let's walk a bit, shall we?"

At first Ishihara could hardly stand. With the novice supporting him on one side and Eleanor on the other, he finally managed a couple of circuits of the room. She could feel him trying not to put weight on her side, but his legs weren't strong enough to let him balance properly.

"Are you hungry?" said the novice to Ishihara, now seated in a chair.

Ishihara shook his head.

"Are you?" the novice asked Eleanor.

"No." The river of flavors in the Macrocosm still lingered on her tongue. "But why don't you go and eat? I'll watch him."

The novice looked shocked. "Can't do that."

"Why not? There's a guard on the door, anyway." And, she glanced up, a camera on the wall. "He's not going to resist." Eleanor made herself add scornfully, "He's just a tired old unbeliever."

Ishihara's mouth twitched at her Osaka slang.

The novice hesitated, then shrugged. "I'll be back in fifteen minutes."

Ishihara leaned forward in the chair as the door closed behind the novice. The lines on his face had started to return to their weary downward furrows. Eleanor felt so glad to see his familiar features that tears stung her eyes.

"What's going on?" he said.

"Keep your voice down." She sat on the other side of the table, on the stool the novice had used, and folded her arms as though she was merely watching him. "They're forcing me to cooperate with them because they know M . . . Mari is my niece."

"Cooperate, how?" His eyes took in her shaved head, the implants, then found her left hand. He drew breath in shock.

"Direct neural interface. Akita is sabotaging the NDN and related networks. You have to get word to the police."

"How many of them are here?"

Four Angels—Samael, Fujinaka/Gagiel, of the narrow eyes, gangly Iroel, and his partner in deceit, Melan. Iroel said at least twenty novices were training to use the interface, but they might not all be there. In the vid Mari had watched there were about thirty people praying with Akita, and the floor plan of the basement showed only ten rooms.

"Between twenty and forty, probably."

He grunted acknowledgment. "How are you going to get me out?"

Eleanor swallowed disappointment. Some part of her had been hoping to hand over the whole thing to him.

"Do they trust you?" he said.

"Not really. W . . . where are we? I wasn't awake when they brought me here."

Ishihara felt the back of his head with a grimace. "I was following a lead in Hirano Ward when they hit me. A warehouse full of weapons in an abandoned milk factory . . ." He stopped at her expression. "What's wrong?"

Surely not the old factory near the Tanaka house? It made sense, Kazu had livelined it years ago on his failed venture. Perhaps Mari told Taka, who told one of the Angels, and they bought the place. Or were simply using it. She groaned inwardly. Kazu's investment had paid off, although not in the way he envisioned.

"One of the Ang . . ." she began, then stopped. Could Akita hear? If she betrayed Iroel he wouldn't be able to help Mari. "There's a secret tunnel leading outside from the wooden wall," she whispered.

Ishihara had to lean forward to hear.

"You'll have to go through there. I can't think of a way to bluff you out past the main entry."

"Where on the outside wall?"

"I don't know."

He shot her a disappointed look. "Could take a while. And aren't you being watched?"

She nodded.

"Are there cameras in the corridors?"

She thought of Iroel and how he'd made her kneel as though praying while he made his offer. "Yes."

Ishihara swore, using a couple of expressions she didn't know existed in Japanese.

"All we can do is hope everyone is praying too hard to watch the monitors," she said wearily.

He stared at her hand before asking slowly, "Can you stop him from inside the thing?"

She shook her head, the despair of her failures heavy in her stomach. "He's been using it much longer than I have. I can't do things in there like he can."

Ishihara nodded. "We'd better get out of here, then." He bent down stiffly and picked up the cuffs and short length of chain that had bound his ankles. He folded it around his fist.

"What's that for?" said Eleanor.

"There's a guard on the door, right?"

"You can't attack him before we find the tunnel, it's too obvious."

"What, then?" he growled.

"We'll get him to help us look."

She hoped like hell that Samael or suspicious Gagiel wouldn't come and ask them what they were doing.

She'd told the novice, the same pasty-faced, pudgy boy of about eighteen, that Ishihara confessed to her how an informer told the police there was a secret tunnel out of the factory. She also managed to convince him that rather than disturbing Adam-sama and the Angels in an important meeting, it would do wonders for his standing if he discovered the tunnel first.

They started with the rickety cupboards at the end of the corridor, opposite the torture room, meditation room one. There was no sound from meditation room two, next door. In rooms farther away Eleanor could hear a murmur of voices chanting.

"You, try and shift it." Eleanor poked Ishihara rudely, for the benefit of the novice, and pointed at the cupboard. The pudgy teenager shifted nervously. He smelled as though he hadn't had a bath in weeks. Ishihara rolled his eyes at her and put his shoulder to the first cupboard. It didn't budge.

"Looks like it's bolted to the wall," said Ishihara.

"Don't you know where it is?" whined the novice.

Eleanor knelt and opened the second cupboard. The door stuck, and when she pulled harder, it opened with a tremendous creak. She winced at the volume of the sound and peered inside. Dust tickled her nose. There were four shelves, the bottom ones covered with a jumble of old boxes, brooms, and plasbags of toilet paper. No sign of a false back.

She pulled at the door of the last cupboard. The damn

thing was locked. She rattled it once. A pity the interface didn't give her superhuman strength as well.

The novice peered over her shoulder. "I think we should call Gagiel-sama. It's not here."

Ishihara pushed the boy aside and squatted next to her. He rattled both doors open a crack and inserted his fingers, then pulled one door, with his foot against the other for leverage.

Half the door came away with a report that echoed down the corridor.

"It's here!" The novice jiggled his feet in excitement.

Inside the cupboard they could see a gaping black hole, big enough for an adult to crawl in. A damp smell of earth and mold seeped from it.

"Come on," said Ishihara.

"I can't go with you," hissed Eleanor. "I have to stay with Mari."

Ishihara half groaned, half cursed, then without giving any sign, kicked the novice's legs from under him with a vicious scissors movement.

"I'll be back." His legs disappeared into the tunnel.

"Prisoner escaping!" yelled the novice, trying to grab Ishihara's legs.

"Let me help." Eleanor bent down and deliberately got in the way. She sprawled with the novice's legs tangled in hers. His elbow hit her ear, and she saw stars.

"Hey!" Two green-clothed figures sprinted past them and wriggled after Ishihara.

Eleanor drew her legs away from the novice and stood up against the wall. Her vision was still blurry, and her side ached where she'd knocked it on the corner of the cupboard. Please god he'll get away.

Several more novices rushed out of the training room beyond Meditation Room Two and four or five acolytes got in their way as they ran full tilt around the corner. Everyone cursed and yelled.

"What have you done?" Samael pushed past the acolytes, grabbed her arm and spun her around to face him. He was as taut as a coiled spring.

"N . . . nothing." Her voice quavered convincingly. "Ask him." She pointed at the pudgy-faced novice, sobbing around a bloody nose where Ishihara must have kicked him. "I tried to help stop the prisoner."

Samael cocked his head then laughed, a short, flat sound. "It doesn't matter. They got him anyway."

He tugged her by the elbow up the corridor and made her wait until Gagiel and two green-clad novices pushed a dirty and staggering Ishihara down the alcove stairs.

"Nobody's going to help you," sneered Samael. "You're on your own."

石原

They pushed Ishihara through a door marked TOILET, then through another door into a small room with partitions instead of walls, and open wooden boxes stacked at one end. Hot water pipes ran up the wall and it was warmer than in the corridor.

He was thrust to the floor and his arms wrenched backward. One of the novices cursed, then looked around guiltily.

"What's wrong?" said the other.

"I forgot to bring cuffs."

The other groaned. "We're supposed to be praying. The main session starts any minute."

"We could just knock him out."

The other rummaged in one of the boxes. "No violence before a session. We'd have to wash and everything." He held up a meter-long length of heavy cord. "This belt will do."

They tied Ishihara's hands to the water pipe, leaving him sitting down.

Two girls opened a door in the partition next to the boxes. They were naked and wrapped in towels, their hair damp.

When they saw the men they shrieked and tried to stretch the towels to cover themselves further.

"Shush," said the first novice. "What are you doing?"

"Purifying," said the taller girl self-righteously. "What do you think?"

"I think you're going to be late. They've already started praying." The two men left.

The girls squealed in horror and began to drag white clothes from one of the boxes.

The novice poked his head around the door to add, "Don't talk to him. He's a filthy unbeliever."

The girls stared at Ishihara, then at their clothes in heaps on the floor. "We can't get dressed in the shower, it's wet," said the shorter girl.

"I'll shut my eyes if you like," he offered.

"We can't trust unbelievers." The tall girl pursed her already-small mouth.

"Oh, come *on*." The other girl, round-faced and darker-skinned, bobbed her head at him. "Please."

Ishihara shut his eyes. He could hear the rustle of clothes and muffled whispers. One of these girls might be McGuire's niece. He hadn't paid much attention to her photo at HQ and anyway, without hair who could tell?

"What do you believe in?" said the shorter girl's voice right beside him.

Ishihara opened his eyes. The girls were dressed in white trousers and tops. He wondered fleetingly if Junta's group wore white. It seemed unlucky, dressing like a corpse.

"When you die," persisted the girl, her eyes serious, "do you think you get born again?"

"Maybe."

"So you've got to go through lives again and again. Adam says we won't have to do that."

Ishihara shook his head. "I won't know the difference. It's not me Ishihara that's reborn. Ishihara dies."

"For good?"

"Well, I won't remember anything."

They both stared at him. "How can you believe that?" she whispered

"It gets easier as you grow older." The thought of himself eventually dissolving like salt into the sea didn't seem such a terrible thing anymore.

The girls backed away. He cursed himself at losing the chance to talk them into helping him. He tried to smile. "The results of my actions don't die, though. The same as if you help me . . ."

But they were gone. They probably wouldn't have helped him anyhow. And for some reason it had been important to answer the girl's question honestly.

He wriggled his hands and tried to run them up and down the pipe. He must get out and warn the police. Every government department depended on the information in the NDN. Thousands of companies paid to use the same information. Tens of thousands more probably used it illegally . . . He grinned at the empty room. At least people like Sakaki would be free of debt if all those records crashed.

Not only would all those organizations be unable to function without the information; but if the Angels released a virus, it would spread to billions of users worldwide. He groaned inwardly. Even the great Net Crash of 2008 would seem tame in comparison.

The pipe didn't budge, even when he threw his weight against it. All he achieved was rope burns on his wrists. His head throbbed and he needed a drink.

He tried all the methods that worked for detectives on TV, like hooking something useful with his feet, but the only things within reach were the girls' wet towels. He knocked on the pipe in case someone above ground could hear. He didn't have a penknife in his pocket, nor did the cubicle have any glass to break into rope-shearing shards.

Finally, he sat still and listened. What he'd give for a

smoke . . . He didn't have the energy to be worried, not even about McGuire.

He thought he could hear music, but couldn't be sure. He wondered how Adam planned to do the sabotage—wire all his devotees into a kind of human network? He blinked away a bizarre image of them all sitting in a circle chanting, joined not by clasped hands but by wires from head to head. The most he could hope for was that Adam's grand plan would backfire somehow—surely a group of paranoid air-heads couldn't bring a civilized nation to a standstill.

The inner door opened slowly. It was the short, dark girl who'd been there before. She was dressed, but she still held a towel, which she wiped across her face.

She held her finger up to her lips before he could say anything, then stretched and flipped the towel over the top of one of the partitions. It snagged on something high on the wall that he realized belatedly was a security camera.

She began to untie the rope around his wrists. 'Taka told me how Niniel poisoned them." In response to his look of puzzlement she added, "My friends. And Adam doesn't care." She pulled angrily at the rope. "I hate him for that."

"The four students?"

She nodded, grimacing at how tight Ishihara had pulled the knots in his efforts to escape. "I didn't believe Aunt Eleanor, and now she's in trouble because of me."

"You're the niece." Ishihara managed to wrench one hand free, then the other. "Your aunt is helping the police. You'd better come with me."

He stood up, then had to hang on to the pipe as his vision blurred for a moment.

She shook her head. "I have to help Aunt Eleanor."

"If you're not here, they can't use you to blackmail her."

"If I'm not here, there'll be nobody to watch out for her. I have other friends here, too." Her jaw set stubbornly.

Ishihara groaned inwardly. Like aunt, like niece. He

didn't have time for arguing. "How did you get away from the session?"

"I told them my period started." She rolled her eyes at his embarrassed silence. "They're very strict about pollution."

She pushed him toward the door. "I think the tunnel will be unguarded, because Iroel told me to go there about four prayers into the session. He's planning to get out. Good luck." She turned and slipped through the inner door into the shower room.

Ishihara opened the door into the corridor and peeped out. He couldn't see any guard on the tunnel and the cupboard door was closed again.

He took a deep breath, let it out, and strode along the corridor as if he belonged there. As he got closer, he could see that the broken half of the door was taped shut. He peeled off one end of the packing tape but the lower edge of the door had been nailed on. Fortunately not with . . . very strong . . . nails. *Crack.* He didn't wait to see if the sound of the boards splintering brought any response from the rooms.

He crawled into the tunnel, and pulled the door shut behind him. It sagged open immediately, but no more than a hand's width. He waited in the dark for a moment, listening. A faint scraping noise came from the warehouse end. It sounded like a cardboard box being dragged across the floor. As his eyes got used to the dark he could see a light flick on and off beyond the end of the tunnel up in the warehouse.

He crawled as soundlessly as he could, pausing between each movement. He couldn't hear anyone breathing or moving at the entrance to the tunnel, although his own breath rasped so loudly in his ears he'd be lucky to hear anything.

In the warehouse a figure moved across the shadowy maze of crates and boxes. Ishihara slid out of the tunnel and crouched flat against the wall beside it. He didn't have time to play hide-and-seek. Adam could be wrecking the NDN that very moment.

The side door of the warehouse that he'd kicked open before lay to his left, the main door farther along the wall.

He waited until the torch flickered at the other end of the warehouse, then moved toward the side door. The distance was only about five paces, but he knocked his toe on a box, stumbled, held on to another to keep his balance, and pushed it onto the floor with a crash. The damn thing sounded like it was full of porcelain.

He scrambled for the door and put his hand on it.

A torch beam centered on his chest.

"Stop there." The figure behind the torch was tall but skinny, the voice an uneasy baritone. The man held out his hand, and Ishihara could see the glint of metal. He'd never hit Ishihara in the dark, holding a flashlight.

Ishihara turned the door handle, ready to run, then rattled it with a curse. Locked. He paid more attention to the weapon, a handgun with a silencer. The man held the light beam squarely on Ishihara's chest. Would he risk hitting the ammunition here?

Ishihara dived sideways and felt something ping past his cheek. He hit his elbow painfully on the corner of a crate and wriggled desperately backward. Bloody hell.

He heard the man curse, then the sound of a metal door squeaking. Yellow light from the street streamed onto the boxes.

Ishihara bobbed upright. The main door hung open.

Curses, scuffling, grunts of pain in the yard. Had the Angels put guards there as well?

Ishihara poked his head out cautiously. A knot of men rolled on the cracked asphalt. One of them wore police blue, one of them a different uniform. Another seemed to be in pajamas. The man who had attacked Ishihara struggled underneath them all, his silver robe further hampering his efforts to escape.

A fourth man clopped around them in excitement. He

clutched the handgun in inexperienced hands and wore only a pair of boxer shorts and heeled slip-ons.

Ishihara ran over. "Police." He took the gun out of the man's hand and checked that the safety catch was on.

The scrum on the ground split up. The Angel lay face-down, with the other two men on his legs, while the policeman clicked handcuffs onto his wrists.

"Lend me your phone," Ishihara said to the constable. "I'm Assistant Inspector Ishihara, West Station. I've been their prisoner in there." He jerked his head at the warehouse. "I have to contact Prefectural HQ."

The constable straightened up, peered at Ishihara's face, then held out his phone. "We've already called for backup. These gentlemen"—he pointed to the two civilians—"called us at 2:05 and said they heard a shout in the yard here."

Could have been me, thought Ishihara. I tried to make as much noise as I could before they caught me in the warehouse.

The man in pajamas stood up, his face shining with sweat. "This is the fellow I saw hanging around earlier tonight," he said, pointing at Ishihara. "Are you sure he's a policeman?"

Ishihara glared at him and tapped Beppu's number.

"The security company opened the gates." The constable pointed to the uniformed man still sitting on the Angel's legs, who nodded amiably at Ishihara.

"We found ammunition in the warehouse," continued the constable, "and called the station."

"Hello?" said Beppu's voice suspiciously on the phone. "Who's this?"

"It's me, Ishihara."

"Where the hell have you been? I got a stored message from you a few minutes ago but your phone's off-line. We also had a call from the station near you to say they'd found a stash of . . ."

"I'm there now," interrupted Ishihara. "Let me talk to Funo."

Pause. The sky over the top of the building opposite was lightening. The time on the phone said 4:17.

"Funo here." Her voice shook and engines rumbled in the background. "We're on our way over. What's your situation?"

"I've found the Silver Angels. They're in an underground area, seven or more rooms, two exits into ground-level buildings. At least"— he thought for a moment—"twenty violent suspects, possibly more. Twenty or more nonviolent. I recommend gas but . . ."

"Leave that to the squad," she said.

"No, wait," he said roughly. "They're attempting to disrupt the NDN from within the computer system. Can you cut off the lines around this area?"

There was a second of stunned silence on the other end, broken by Funo's curse. "The NDN? What level would you rate the threat?"

Ishihara thought of McGuire's mutilated hand. "Genuine and extreme."

"Security on the data network is supposed to be uncrackable."

"That's what they said about the Betta systems."

"I'll get back to you." She cut the connection.

"What about this fellow?" The constable looked at the man on the ground. His robe was torn; underneath he wore a T-shirt and cotton trousers.

"Take him to the station. He can wait for his mates there," said Ishihara. He walked over and shut the warehouse door. The Angels should all be joined in Adam's networking by now, but there might be more of them who planned to run away, like this one.

He chivvied the other men out the gates of the yard for the same reason. The constable's partner walked off with the handcuffed Angel.

Delivery trucks rumbled down the main road on the other side of the shopping street. In one of the apartment blocks across the road a light flickered on. Everything seemed so normal.

"Have you got a smoke?" he asked the young constable.

"Nasty habit, sir. Never took it up."

Ishihara groaned and waited.

エレナ

As Eleanor watched Ishihara being pushed roughly down the corridor the weight of responsibility settled on her like a load of scrap iron. It was up to her now. She had to get word to the police or at least try to delay Akita's plan long enough for the police to track the source of the network disturbance.

Which wasn't likely, a disturbingly cool part of her mind replied. If their communications system is affected, they won't be tracing anything for a while.

So she had to do something within the interface. Yet Akita was far more experienced in there. *I can't do things in there like he can,* she'd said to Ishihara. The only time she used the interface efficiently was when she accessed the Microcosm through robots. She was able to hit someone with a helpbot, raise a service bot's arm, and walk her Sam robot with ease. Could she use that to stop Akita?

The Sam project at Tomita was the system she knew best. She might persuade Akita to get inside Sam, or any robot for that matter, and then cut off his access to the Macrocosm. It would prevent his dispersing more of the virus. The rest of the Angels wouldn't be able to move away from the factory if Akita was still inside the Macrocosm, giving the police a better chance of catching up with them.

Acolytes in white clothes and novices in blue and green were still milling around the corridor, talking about the attempted escape. Most of them didn't seem to notice Eleanor—she was just another smooth-headed person in white.

The door past the one to the room where they'd taken Ishihara opened, and Akita stepped through. Everyone was immediately silent. The skin of his face looked waxy, his eyes drooping with fatigue.

He raised his right hand, his gold sleeve rucking back to the elbow. "My children." His voice carried so well that Eleanor wondered if he was using a portable mike of some sort. "We are about to begin our third and final round of prayer. What is this behavior?"

All the acolytes huddled together and shuffled guiltily past Akita, bowing their heads low as they entered the room. The novices walked taller, but they also bowed low to Akita and averted their eyes.

Akita ignored them and waited for the corridor to clear before beckoning Eleanor. "Lilith. We must continue."

She put her undamaged hand on his arm. "Adam-sama, you were right."

He looked down, his eyebrows rising in surprise. "About?"

"I should renounce my desire for the Microcosm. I shouldn't keep trying to use the robots."

His expression lightened. "I am glad you have seen the truth."

"Oh, but I have. In fact, it was the robots that showed me."

"What do you mean?"

"When I was in their bodies, I felt a kind of . . ." She tried to remember how he'd described his enlightenment. "A kind of spreading through the universe. As though I was part of everything else all at once."

He grasped her arm eagerly. "This is the enlightenment I seek! And you say you experienced it in the Microcosm?"

"The robots are kind of in both worlds, though, don't you think?"

"Perhaps. The borders . . . have I neglected them?" His voice trailed away.

Had she been too subtle? "Maybe you never experienced it in the robots because you don't usually visit them. Why don't you come with me to my robot at Tomita and I can show you?"

"After we execute the plan," he said reluctantly.

"But after we disrupt the network, everything will be offline. This won't take long. You said yourself that time is slower in there."

He wavered. "Did you feel joy?"

"Absolutely," she nodded. "Lots."

He frowned. "Emotions have always eluded me in the Macrocosm."

"Perhaps I am mistaken."

"Are you trying to keep it to yourself?"

"Of course not." She conjured up a carefree laugh.

Akita kept frowning.

She felt someone behind her and spun around. Fujinaka/Gagiel stood there. He wore his undershirt again and carried a tool kit.

"The cupboard doors will hold now," he said to Akita, and ran his insolent gaze up Eleanor's body.

Could Iroel still get Mari out? Would Mari even go?

Akita turned in a swirl of gold.

With a sense of being sucked into a rapidly spinning whirlpool, she followed him into his throne room.

There was barely room for them to edge down the red carpet. At least thirty figures in white and a dozen or so in blue and green crammed themselves on the floor, kneeling on their heels in formal positions. She couldn't see Mari and felt a thrill of hope. Perhaps she'd decided to go with Iroel after all, even if they didn't use the tunnel.

As Akita passed, many of the nearest believers reached out to pat his robes. Eleanor even felt a tentative cool touch on her ankle. That touch reminded her why she was there. She had come to help Mari, which meant by extension all these other children who were caught in a disaster not of their making. The poor things—they tried to get away from being controlled by their parents, only to wind up being controlled by Akita and his unpleasant colleagues.

That thought made the long walk to the console bearable. Whatever she could do to obstruct Akita's plans would help them as well as Mari.

Melan was waiting for them before the console. She swung Eleanor roughly into one of the chairs.

Akita faced the room and raised his arms.

The silence was so complete that the rasp of all their breathing sounded like the crash of surf to Eleanor. Far off in the corridor a door closed and bare feet slapped on concrete. The console beside her hummed.

"My children." Akita's voice was huskier than before. He swayed a little, but Eleanor couldn't tell if it was deliberate or not.

"We are about to embark upon the odyssey that will change human history. In the future, people will say, 'it started then.' We will be the first humans to experience the realms of the gods. We will become gods."

Eleanor craned her neck, scanning the crowd to see if Mari was there. No familiar eyes met hers except Samael's, poised by the door, and Fujinaka/Gagiel's, who waded through the seated believers to stand by the side of the dais.

"Your prayers will lift us into the Macrocosm, where we will begin the process of cleansing that precedes renewal." He drew his hands together. "Let us pray."

A gong echoed over their heads. Eleanor winced at the level of sound, coming from speakers high on the wall.

At the first *bong*, all the acolytes bent forward so their heads touched the floor or, in some cases, the heels of the person in front. At the second *bong*, the novices did the same.

Melan strapped Eleanor into the chair with deliberately sharp tugs.

At the third *bong*, everyone hummed a low note.

Melan kneeled before Akita and kissed his feet before strapping him in reverently. Hypocrite, thought Eleanor. Kiss the master good-bye before you run away with Iroel.

The hum of voices swelled to a single high note, then rose and fell in a three-phrase chant. Something about the Master all-seeing, the Master all-knowing, the Master all-being.

The chorus was too loud. Surely a small number of people couldn't produce this huge noise . . . She pressed her hands over her ears. The bones of her chest vibrated with the deep notes. She hadn't felt this buffeted by sound since the first time she visited an ore-processing plant, to examine one of their big crushing machines . . .

Melan's fingers locked on Eleanor's left wrist and rammed her hand into the aperture.

石原

Ishihara paced impatiently. The two civilians who'd helped capture the runaway Silver Angel showed no sign of leaving. They chatted with the security guard. Their voices grated on his jangling nerves like sand rubbed in a wound.

What was keeping the squad? They had to get McGuire out of there.

Lightly running footsteps around the corner of the street made them all look around. Several blue-clad policemen took up positions by the gate. They motioned for Ishihara and the others to go around to the side street.

Funo was waiting there, accompanied by a large young man in a black uniform with no insignia. A detective escorted the civilians and the security guard away.

Funo beckoned Ishihara. She was wearing a fatigues jacket over her neat white blouse, and a blue cap. Her nose and forehead were shiny with sweat. "We can't get information from the security company's files," she said. "Can you draw us a map of the underground rooms?"

Ishihara took the palmtop and stylus Funo offered. "Is that because of the Silver Angels' interference?"

She shook her head. "We think the company was compromised before this. We checked their security records on the old factory when Harada disappeared, and everything appeared to be in order, but it obviously wasn't."

"Did you cut off the lines to this place? Or the power?"

"They're working on the power. Something's wrong with the central controls."

They looked at each other, but didn't voice the shared assumption—that the sabotage had begun.

The young man looked at Ishihana's sketch. He had a calm, large-jawed face and huge hands. "This exit is in the main building here?" He pointed behind them at the factory.

"Yes, but I'm not sure where it comes out in that building. I didn't go that way."

"We'll find it." He took the palmtop and waved his arm over his head. Two more black figures emerged from a van in the parking lot across the street.

"The leader is a big man dressed in gold," said Ishihara. "There are at least two men dressed in silver who should be treated as dangerous. I'm not sure if they're armed or not." The Angel who attacked him in the warehouse might not have been carrying the gun downstairs. It depended on how seriously the Angels obeyed the prohibition on violence before prayers.

"We'll find him," said the squad leader. He sketched Funo a salute and rejoined the rest of his team.

"Are you all right?" Funo stared at him as the light grew stronger. With the dirt and sweat, he realized that he must look disgusting. "There's an ambulance around the corner if you need anything."

"I need to go back," Ishihara said. "McGuire's still in there. Adam's making her cooperate in the NDN sabotage, and I don't know what he'll do to her when it's finished."

"It better not finish," said Funo grimly. "We have to stop them before it goes too far." She looked over at the warehouse, then back to Ishihara. "Why didn't you call us before you went in?"

"I did but couldn't get through," he said, conscious how unlikely it sounded.

She said nothing.

He decided he didn't care. He was retiring after this case, anyway. "I'm going in with the squad."

"Don't get in their way. And take a gas mask."

Ishihara stood with his mouth open for a moment, ready to protest the reprimand that never came. Funo seemed quite matter-of-fact about it.

As he turned to the van, she added, "Good work, Ishihara."

One might even suspect she'd sent him off because she thought he was a loose enough cannon to find something . . . nah. He was overtired and imagining things.

The antiterror squad took no more than five minutes to get into position, but it seemed an age to Ishihara. Local police had cordoned off the area and were asking wakeful residents to stay inside their houses. Funo took off her fatigues jacket and reported that the NDN was experiencing problems in multiple systems; the electricity grid was going down across the city.

Ishihara stood by the van and drank from one of the squad's water bottles. He didn't dare sit down, for fear he wouldn't be able to stand up again. The street slept in the half-light, quiet in predawn coolness. Only occasional muffled voices and the tread of booted feet revealed the police presence. From the road the rumble of trucks rose and fell, like a drunk snoring.

At last the squad was in position. Their leader ordered Ishihara to go last and, with a glance at his rumpled, filthy shirt and trousers, passed him a bulletproof vest like the team members wore. It hung on his sore shoulders like lead weights.

They went in the front door of the main building. This building had been renovated recently, by the look of it. The entry to the underground section was at the back, under two trapdoors that folded upward.

They all fastened their gas masks. The hoses at this entry and in the warehouse began pumping gas. *Perfectly harmless*, one of the squad had said. *While they're sneezing we arrest 'em.*

Ishihara pulled the ragged edges of his consciousness together. He just wanted to make sure McGuire and her niece got out of there safely. He shoved two extra gas masks farther into his vest pocket and prayed they were still alive.

"Move out," said the squad leader quietly.

エレナ

The livelines sang. They diverged in related melodies, data passing in ripples of harmony. Eleanor was awash in a euphonious polyphony that beat, danced, and trilled around her. Enchanted and dismayed— how could she navigate in *this?*—she tried to distinguish structure in the seemingly infinite complexity of refrains, passages, measures, minor and major keys . . .

Each liveline seemed to have its own theme, its own tone. This one flowed low and throbbing in a complex beat. That one flowed higher and flat, in a repeated toccata.

This way, Akita sang in a low, hornlike riff.

He began to fade into distance and she followed, dodging through thickets of pastorale and tight knots of counterpoint, until they came to a simple sequence of five notes, repeated continuously.

Akita's song was lighter. *I am glad you have seen the truth.*

If she had any feelings in here, she would have been sick with nerves. Would she be able to keep him in the robot? It all depended on whether she could destroy his connection with the Macrocosm. What did he say when he showed her how to plant the virus—impose your color over the place? In this version of the Macrocosm, she'd have to overlay her song.

The five-note sequence was the gate out of live-lines into the world of ordinary cables. Akita matched his horn-voice to it, and his song disappeared. Eleanor did the same—her song seemed to be a simpler melody in a different key, G-flat maybe? A string sound, like a cello or viola.

They were back in the world of tunnels stretching into infinity, filled with sparks captured in strips along the sides. Here, Akita's presence was only an echo of song, a brightness in the spaces between sparks.

They sped along the tunnels until she realized they were in the familiar layers of her own system—in the lab, computer systems idling. Her humanoid robot Sam was still connected to the battery recharger, a dark circle in the system wall, edged dimly with phosphorescence. Through the room's cameras she could see that the service bot still slept in the corner, connected but inactive.

Akita did nothing for a moment. Was he suspicious?

Perhaps I was mistaken she "said."

With a derisive flash, Akita flowed into Sam's circuitry.

Eleanor edged close to the portal. She couldn't sense anything more of Akita in the tunnel with her. In the lab camera's wide-angle view the robot didn't move, but activation lights flickered across its chest panel. Akita was inside.

Do you feel it now? she said, but there was no sign he'd heard. She slid through the other lab subsystems and found the voice-over within the internal phone.

"Can you hear me?" She couldn't hear herself

until she remembered to activate the audio input as well. "Retract your wall connection and try to walk to the other side of the lab."

If he was on the other side of the lab, he couldn't suddenly activate the connection again.

Sam's gangly arms rose, not quite together, and straight out, as though Akita couldn't manage the elbow joints. The oversized camera lens eyes swiveled each way, too fast for efficient image processing, she noticed.

"When . . . did you . . . feel what you . . . said?" Akita's synthesized voice crackled from Sam's little speakers.

"When I was walking the robot. It was like nothing I've ever felt before."

Sam's recharge connection rod withdrew from the wall socket and retracted with a whir. One skeletal metal leg, traced with various colored wires, lifted. The robot teetered. The leg swung forward, down.

Eleanor felt better. She'd walked Sam far more easily than this. Then she became concerned—what if Akita got discouraged?

"That's right," she said. "Try a few more steps."

Sam wavered five steps. It was time. The recharge connection glowed in a red circle. She concentrated on making it disappear, imagined her own pattern in its place.

Nothing happened.

Keep concentrating. She reached out with her mind's hand and picked the circle off the wall.

It still glowed mockingly.

"I do not feel anything," Akita's voice croaked from the speakers. "We must leave."

It was strange to panic without feeling any of the associated physical sensations, like beating heart or sweaty palms. Why the hell wasn't it working?

She plastered herself over the connection, then it

hit her—when they seeded the virus, they'd been in the NDN, which was livelined. The damn technique probably didn't work in ordinary cable. What could she do to stop Akita accessing the connection?

Keep it simple. She rushed back through the maze of tunnels. All she needed was the circuit board for the recharger panel.

Akita in Sam teetered one slow step after another back toward the wall. "Lilith? What are you doing?"

How to activate the circuit breaker? Oh, for a pair of hands . . .

She wouldn't be in time. Akita was almost at the wall. In desperation Eleanor dived into a narrow cluster of tunnels, found the dark circle of the service bot's recharger panel, and flowed through it.

In the service bot she had hands, and more than one pair. She wheeled it in Sam's direction. In the service bot's limited perception the other robot was a brighter blur in front of the dull glow of the consoles. Overriding the proximity alarm that attempted to lock the wheels, she slammed the heavy body into Sam.

The bipedal robot fell with an all-too-familiar crash. But she'd built it so that it could get up by itself. There was only one way to stop Akita accessing a connection, and that was to destroy the connection. She hadn't been able to do it inside the Macrocosm, so she'd have to do it out here.

"You have betrayed me." In the service bot's audio receiver, Akita's voice from the speakers crackled with static. "You have betrayed our plan."

Your plan, not mine. Eleanor pushed the service bot forward. Hammer tool, hammer tool . . . the service bot's reactions were so slow, it felt as though she was acting on the world underwater. Input target, raise tool, impact target. In the infrared blur of the service bot's viewer, she saw the recharge panel shatter. The shock absorbers twanged. Another impact. A bright spray of sparks flew outward.

Behind her, in the rear viewer, the collection of lines and lights that was Sam folded together and rose off the floor.

"I cannot allow this."

You can't do anything about it, Eleanor would have liked to say, but the service bot had no vocalizer. She wheeled easily around the swaying Sam and back to her own connection.

Wait. Akita would access this one, too. It wasn't configured for Sam, but that wouldn't stop him for long. Her only hope of stopping him properly was to destroy this connection also, and any other ports in the room.

And trap herself as well.

"You cannot do this. You . . . come with me in the Macrocosm . . ."

Or she could destroy Sam. The service bot's tools could do it. And would Akita's body sit back at the console until it died, waiting for him to return?

Sam's lights moved, a ghost against the darkness of the lab. She could see a vague outline of its head and torso, where wires ran along the skin, and the eyes glowed distinctly. The battery pack on its back shone red.

She couldn't destroy Sam, even if Akita controlled it. Even if he had shown her what a flawed creation it was. Sam was still hers.

She began to methodically smash every wall connection and every port—some of the drives had ports she couldn't reach, so she simply pushed them onto the floor. Fortunately, they'd tidied away most of the peripheral equipment. Akita's voice raged from the speakers.

"I will destroy you in both worlds . . ."

Crash, fizz of sparks.

"I will rule without you, I will make sure you are trapped in your decaying body while we fly free . . ."

Sam lurched toward her and swung its arm, but the humanoid had not been designed to attack other robots and its fist merely bounced off the service bot's covering. Sam nearly fell with the momentum of the swing.

"Ignorant gaijin, you're a disgrace to your profession . . ."

She cringed at the waste of equipment in the lab, but what else could she do? She had to get back into the Macrocosm and leave it before Akita caught her in there, where he could devour her in his anger.

"Do you know what I shall do to your niece?"

The closest connection would be one of the help-bot stations in the corridor. She couldn't access any of the other labs from within the service bot, without retina prints or fingerprints. In fact . . . she wheeled the service bot over to the door . . . how could she get out of *this* lab?

The service bot's extendable clipper tool was the closest she had to a finger to press her numeric access code into the pad by the door. Sam's digits would be better, but Sam couldn't reach the pad.

Akita had shut up. He was walking Sam toward some of the mess on the floor, probably looking for a connection she'd missed, but the service bot's viewer wasn't clear enough for her to tell if he'd found anything. The damn service bot's viewer couldn't see the access pad, either. She'd have to do it from memory.

The extended clipper tool was unwieldy and swung back and forth. She tried to fine-tune the balance mechanism, but it seemed to take hours just to press the first number in the four-digit sequence. She would never get out. She would never see Masao again, never tell him that he was right, that they needed to spend more time together, go away for a holiday . . . if robots could cry, she would have been bawling in frustration.

What was she doing wrong? She thought of what Fujinaka/Gagiel had said that night in Okayama when she told a helpbot to dance and it did. He said he *thought about dancing*.

She thought about reaching up to the access pad, extending her index finger, and pressing the code numbers. Concentrate. This is all that matters, this moment. Do it. Press the button. And another. And another.

The numbers pinged. The door swished open.

"No! You can't leave me," Akita yelled.

Eleanor propelled the service bot through without retracting the tool, frantic in case the door shut automatically before she could get out.

"I will find you . . ." Akita's voice echoed, then was cut off by the door's closing.

The service bot bounced off the corridor wall with the momentum, then whirred off down the corridor in search of a connection.

Oh, the joy of free movement again! After the constricted body of the service bot, the flow of the Macrocosm was like balm to nonexistent senses. Did Akita feel his human body to be such a prison?

She had worried whether she could find her way back without him, but the faint song of the livelines provided a beacon through the tunnels. Some of the tunnels were dark, dead, and she had to detour. More began to dull as she passed through. Akita's virus? She reached the livelines gate, a glowing knot from this side, not five notes, and dived through. The melodies flowed as before, but far away there were discordant notes in the musical flux.

What should she do? Akita would find a way out of Sam's robot body, sooner or later. From within the service bot she couldn't see if she'd completely destroyed every connection. Akita would come after her. If she stayed in the Macrocosm, he could erase bits of her, and what would she become when she returned to her body—a memoryless zombie, living only in the present?

But Akita knew Eleanor was his prisoner in the real world. He could have his revenge at his leisure. Wouldn't he be more likely to go on and finish his wretched plan? In that case, she should wait and try to lure him out of the Macrocosm before he could seed the rest of the viruses; make him angry enough to follow her back into the real world.

Which wouldn't help her or Mari once Akita told the Silver Angels what she'd done . . .

Undecided, she followed a strand of song she remembered, staying with the simple melody until it reached a familiar ordered cacophony, the systems of the factory where the Silver Angels were. The antisurveillance shield was deactivated. Iroel had taken Mari, as promised. Perhaps. She sifted into the symphonic layers and the security cameras became her eyes.

The corridors, bathroom, and meditation rooms were empty. She couldn't see Ishihara; either he'd escaped, or they had shoved him somewhere without a camera pickup. All the acolytes and novices were still in the interface room, their praying backs looking like an infestation of pale beetles. How strange to see them there but hear only the multistranded music of the Macrocosm. Stranger still to see her own small figure seated beside Adam's larger one at the console. What am I in here, if that's also me down there?

One of the standing silver figures moved. Melan tiptoed down the dais and picked her way between the praying figures. She paused at the door to whisper to Samael, then walked out into the corridor.

Eleanor watched her as far as the stairs in the

alcove, after which there were no cameras. Gone to join Iroel, wherever he'd gone. Had he really taken Mari with them? She switched back to the interface room camera and scanned the backs of the believers. Impossible to tell if Mari was there.

How long had it been since they started? Surely the police must be able to trace Akita's interference . . .

Then she heard a deep, distinctive tune in the lines of harmony. Akita was approaching. He'd found a way out of Sam.

I'm here, she sent.

The song dulled for a moment then resumed with vigor, getting louder all the time. It sounded brassy, infuriated.

She wavered, then decided she'd rather face Akita in her own body than in here. Back to the interface she raced, Akita's song so loud now that when—

—her eyes snapped open her ears were ringing with the sound.

Her breath coming in ragged gasps, she pulled her left hand out of the console and fumbled with the straps on her chair. She was shaking all over with the shock of sensations, the murmur of prayers sounding like a roar, the blinding light, strips and streaks of pain where her body touched the chair . . .

Beside her, Akita groaned and jerked his body tight against the straps.

"What the . . ." Fujinaka/Gagiel vaulted onto the dais. He stared at Eleanor, then bent over Akita, looking into his face anxiously.

Akita's eyes opened and he roared with rage. His face became suffused, spittle sprayed from his lips, and he wrenched his artificial hand from the console with a squelch.

"Master, what is the matter?" Gagiel hurried to release the straps.

"You." Akita's shoulders rolled free, and he swung on Eleanor with such venom that she tumbled backward out of her chair in her hurry to escape. Her legs wouldn't work properly and the room kept swinging in and out of focus.

A couple of the acolytes, sensing something wrong, looked up from their prayers, and the smooth rhythm faltered. Gagiel looked up from where he was fumbling with Akita's leg straps long enough to signal to Samael, *keep going.*

"You betrayed us," Akita growled. "I would have let you rule with me. I would have given you everything. Bind her," he snarled at Gagiel.

Gagiel's long eyes narrowed as he advanced on Eleanor. She scrambled to her feet and nearly fell over the edge of the dais.

"No!" called a clear voice from the back of the room. A white-clad figure stood up and stumbled over the people in front of her. It was Mari.

"Let her go," she yelled.

The hum of prayer disintegrated as people looked up. Several people in front of Mari cried out with pain as she clambered over them in her haste to reach the dais. Samael cursed and strode after Mari.

Gagiel grabbed Eleanor's right arm and twisted it behind her. She sagged downward, overcome with the pressure of sensory input and the headache that drilled into her skull.

A sweet smell burrowed into her sinuses. She could hear Akita raving about what he would do to her, but his words were slurred, and everyone else seemed to be shouting as well. Someone was running down the corridor. No, lots of people were running down the corridor. The smell was choking her sinuses until she had to sneeze . . .

Akita's red face filled her vision. "Get rid of her *now.*"

石原

The antiterror squad's boots thudded down the wooden stairs. The men ran left and right out of the alcove, following Ishihara's map.

The corridors seemed narrower, the ceilings lower than when he was here a couple of hours before. He followed the squad's broad backs to the door of what McGuire said was the computer room. Voices cried and yelled in confusion. He edged past a scrum of black, white, blue, and green figures in the doorway. One silver-clothed man writhed in the grip of three policemen. Ishihara caught a glimpse of the thin face snarling defiance. Samael/Inoue.

People dressed in white sneezed and coughed on the floor. At the end of the room was a raised platform and a bank of computers against the wall. Three of the squad were mounting the steps to the platform where a figure in gold raised his hands to cover his face and a figure in silver, coughing, tried to jump off but was tripped by a smaller person in white. McGuire, it had to be.

He shoved his way past the sneezing acolytes to the dais. The Angel half fell off the dais and was caught by one of the squad. The figure in white doubled over. He reached up, saw

McGuire's long, foreign features and thrust the mask into her hands.

"Put it on!" he yelled over the din.

She slapped it onto her face automatically then her streaming eyes met his. He caught a glimpse of her smile before she doubled over again. ". . . Mari." She pointed behind him.

He found Mari curled up beside the dais. As he bent to put the mask on her face, someone shrieked so loudly they all jumped.

Two of the antiterrorist squad were trying to get Adam away from the computers but he held grimly to the chair, which must have been bolted to the dais. His features were crumpled, eyes half-shut from the gas; tears and mucus spattered as he shook his head violently.

"No, no, you can't make me go. I can't leave it. You can't make me leave it, it's not fair . . ." His voice rose in a scream of real desperation. "I don't want to die!"

They wrenched him away from the chair. The feelers on his artificial hand writhed in the air as he reached out piteously to Eleanor.

"Help me!" he shrieked. "I'm going to die . . ."

McGuire's mouth twisted, and she raised her hand as if she was going to touch his. Then she let her hand drop. Her eyes met Ishihara's.

"We all die sometime," she said.

Paramedics had set up an emergency treatment station in the main building next to the factory. The police were working from vans parked in the factory grounds and in the surrounding streets. McGuire wouldn't let the paramedics do anything but give her painkillers and the antidote for the gas. She refused to go to hospital. Ishihara left Funo to interview her and went outside for a break.

He did remember to ask one of the detectives to ring Prefectural HQ and tell McGuire's husband she was here, but he couldn't think of anything else he should do. He couldn't think at all.

Outside, sunlight touched the top of the buildings. He sat down on a concrete block in the shade of the wall, dropped his mask on the ground, and let the top of his head float away.

Someone closed his hand around a warm cylinder. The aroma of coffee filled his nostrils.

"'Morning," said Beppu. He crouched and looked anxiously into Ishihara's face. "Drink."

Ishihara swigged from the tin of coffee. His hand shook and spilled drops down his chin. After a few minutes he felt like a smoke.

"Super's frantic." Beppu lit a cigarette for him. "The NDN's down. Phones are down. Computers are down. Electricity's been diverted to essential services. Trains are still running, though."

So Adam had succeeded.

Beppu caught his expression. "Not your fault. You did well to find them. That foreigner said she tried to stop them from inside the thing they used."

"Is she all right?"

"Looks like it. She's still talking to Funo. They're getting along quite well." Beppu jerked his chin at the building behind them. Across the road, the antiterrorism squad vans were gone from the parking lot. Two police cars had taken their place. Uniformed constables dissuaded curious people from loitering near the tape barriers along the road in front of the factory.

"The techos are going wild over the computers down there," said Beppu. "McGuire won't tell them anything about it now. She says she'll come and see them tomorrow."

The sun shone full on the road. Men in ties and women in skirts and stockings hurried past the barriers to work. Two high school girls rode past on bicycles, giggling. Wasn't anyone worried? Perhaps they thought the power would be on by the time they reached their destinations.

"What's the time?" said Ishihara.

"About seven," said Beppu. "Funo wants your report, but she said they're so flat out it can wait till tomorrow. I'm going to drive you home."

"Generous of her to spare you."

"She didn't want to."

"Why couldn't I call you earlier?" Ishihara said. "I did try."

Beppu chuckled. "You're lucky Funo asked the same question. Turns out they had some kind of anti-interference field in the factory. Can't use phones in there."

"Did they find out where the other Angels from the vans went?"

"Yeah, the bloke you chased out here talked," said Beppu. "We found them, but they had no computers or weapons. We booked Adam and three others. The rest of them are in custody pending investigation."

"The kids in white didn't know much. The ones in blue and green were more involved." Ishihara thought of the novice who'd strung him up. "Some more than others."

"Yeah, well we got Inoue," said Beppu with heavy satisfaction. He looked over Ishihara's shoulder. "Here they are. We're letting the girl go home on the condition McGuire brings her in tomorrow."

"Assistant Inspector?" McGuire and her niece still wore the white clothes, but both had wrapped scarves around their heads and wore cheap slip-ons on their feet. Mari's face was merely pale from the gas, but McGuire looked like she'd been scraped off the footpath after a five-day binge.

"We're leaving now." Her set mouth and dark-circled eyes were unreadable.

Ishihara stood up awkwardly. He wanted to say something, but couldn't think what.

"Thank you for your help," was all he could manage.

A bubble of silence surrounded them, against which the sounds of the street beat unheard. McGuire looked straight at him. He remembered her gray eyes upside down in the hanging room, and was glad he had trusted them.

She started to say something, stopped, and bowed carefully, as though her back hurt. "Thank you for finding us."

Ishihara returned the bow. "My pleasure."

Mari had no such reservations. She threw her arms around his neck and squeezed hard. "Thank you. Thank you," she said, tears choking her voice. "This is for the others, too. They don't even know that you saved them."

When she took her arms away she took something else away—the tight knot of anger he'd felt for so many years at Junta. *We can't make our children's choices for them.*

"You're welcome," he grunted.

Silence.

"Ah, Inspector?" Mari twisted her hands together worriedly. "What will happen to Adam?"

"He'll be sent for a psychiatric evaluation," Ishihara said. "Then we decide whether to charge him and with what."

"I don't think he wanted to hurt anyone . . ." she began, but stopped. "That doesn't make it better though, does it?"

Beppu cleared his throat noisily, then made a face as though he wished he hadn't. "Do you need a lift anywhere?"

McGuire's face relaxed into a sunny gaijin smile. "No thanks. We're going home."

She bowed again. The two women linked arms and walked up the street, their slip-ons clopping on the sidewalk.

Beppu sighed. "I'm bloody glad that turned out all right."

Ishihara slapped him on the shoulder. "Never any doubt."

They walked to Beppu's car.

"How are we supposed to make a proper report without a computer?" Beppu grumbled. "No supporting material, no photographs . . . ?"

"Use a pen." Ishihara looked around them at the pitted concrete and drooping tiled roofs. In one garden a man in singlet and shorts fanned a wood fire under an iron plate. *Bring the kettle out*, he yelled into his house.

The Bettas would be in chaos, and Beppu didn't have his computer, but life went on in the gaps between the spokes of the wheel.

"Tell me about that house on the coast," said Ishihara.

エレナ

The street seemed different, although Eleanor didn't understand why. The grimy asphalt was the same. The jungle of wires festooned from poles to rooftops were the same. They still had to wind their way between cars parked all along the sides of the street and scraps spilled from a plasbag somebody had put out in defiance of the correct rubbish pickup day. But Eleanor felt as though she was seeing all these things for the first time.

Fragments of the Macrocosm blurred in her mind. Back in the real world, those colors, sounds, and images ran together like a watercolor painting left outside in the rain. Moments of memory not her own lurked at the edges of consciousness.

"Can you hear that?" she asked Mari. "Cicadas."

Mari listened, then shook her head. "I can't hear anything."

Cicadas lived only in memories. Like the one shaken to death in a water bottle to gratify cruel children.

"What will they do with Adam's equipment and all that stuff?" Mari said.

"Keep it as exhibit for the prosecution, probably."

Eleanor found herself wishing the police would simply decide to destroy the consoles. She wanted nothing more to do with the interface, and if the police wanted her to demonstrate it for them, too bad for them.

Not that she wasn't grateful to the police—to Ishihara in particular—for arriving in time to save her from Samael. She had no doubt he would have been the one to carry out Akita's order to kill her.

And the third interface, the one Akita sent overseas—would it be used as he tried to use it? It might reappear one day, neatly packaged and guaranteed no side effects. Biometal fingertip implants in a variety of fashion colors. She giggled.

Mari frowned and took her arm.

Eleanor thought of something. "Did you speak to Taka?"

Mari nodded. "While you were talking to that policewoman. We're going to meet when they let him out."

"Do you think that's a good idea?"

Her mouth set defiantly. "He's going to get a job. So am I. University gives you too much time to think."

Eleanor shrugged inwardly. Mari had earned the right to make her own decisions.

They passed Grandma's jungle of potted plants, the only greenery on the street, and turned in the gate, their sandals clip-clopping on the stones.

Mari rang the doorbell. It didn't jangle without electricity, of course, so she let go Eleanor's arm and pulled the door back with a rattle. They could hear voices arguing in the hall.

Kazu said, ". . . that's the way it has to be done."

Grandpa's voice mumbled something about irresponsibility.

"We're home," Mari yelled into the hall. The voices fell silent. Then a scuffle of footsteps, and Yoshiko stood on the hall step, her apron inside out and her round face red with surprise.

"Mari-chan . . ." She put her hand to her mouth then all but fell down the step and pounced on Mari with a ferocious hug.

"Where have you been?" Yoshiko half shook the girl, crying as she spoke. "We were so worried, the police were here, they said you'd been kidnapped and we didn't know what to do and your phone was off and we couldn't find you, why didn't you call us . . ."

Mari pushed her off awkwardly. "That's enough, Mother. I'm home now."

"Papa! Grandpa! Mari's here," Yoshiko called unnecessarily, for Kazu and Grandpa crowded on the hall step behind her and Grandma's wrinkled face peered between them.

"Mari-chan, where have you been?" Grandpa tried to sound stern, but his eyes were watering.

"Eleanor-san, thank you." Kazu looked past his daughter to Eleanor. He smiled, the expression transforming his serious, pop-eyed face. "You found her after all."

"In a way," said Eleanor.

The hall seemed gloomy after the bright sun; it smelled of furniture polish and dried flowers. Eleanor couldn't remember if Ishihara had told Masao where she was. She desperately wanted to see him.

"Are the phones working?" she said to Kazu.

"Not yet. Someone said the exchanges are down so they can't process calls."

Masao would find her. He found her once, after her accident; he would find her again. She sat at the kitchen table and drank Grandma's bitter green tea. One of the neighbors was boiling water for everyone in the street on his gas sukiyaki burner. The sounds of the family flowed around her like data in the lifelines. Mari was giving them an edited version of the events at the Silver Angels hideaway while Yoshiko cried over her shaved head. The clock over the stove ticked happily on—must be battery-powered. On the household gods' shelf over the sink, two small candle flames fluttered beside a folded white paper charm. The cicada voices had gone away.

Kazu slid into the seat next to her. "Are you all right?"

"I'm a little tired, that's all."

Kazu hesitated, then went on. "I'm going to ask you again."

She hadn't a clue what he meant.

"Will you come and work with us?"

"We can't . . ." afford it, Eleanor started to say. We'd have to move away from the Betta. Then she saw Grandma smile above the clutter of the kitchen table and thought, I bet they're not drinking tea in the Betta right now, with the networks down. Through the open door she could hear traffic roar past on the main road, but not as much as usual. A couple of blocks away, a loudspeaker asked people to remain calm and assured them that the electricity supply would be restored soon.

No reason why she couldn't continue her research there. She'd have to start from scratch anyway, after what Akita showed her in the Macrocosm. Back to basics, in more ways than one.

"I'd like to join you," she said. "If Grandpa agrees."

Kazu's face lit up again. They all looked at Grandpa.

"It's a ridiculous idea," he blustered, looking from one to the other. "Think of all the changes we'd have to make."

"We've made changes before," said Grandma. "My parents changed businesses entirely after the war."

Grandpa grumbled, but to Eleanor's surprise it seemed halfhearted.

The front door crashed open, rattling bowls in the dresser. Footsteps pounded in the hall and Masao stood in the doorway. When he saw Eleanor he passed the table in two strides and swept her up into a manic embrace.

"Never, ever make me that worried again" He held her so tightly every ache in her body worsened. She didn't care.

The damp warmth of his skin, the smell of his sweat, the roughness of his chin against her forehead—this was all that mattered.

And she realized she'd forgotten the most important thing Gen had told her. He said, *the past is dead and all the future holds is death.* But he'd also said, *only the present holds life.* No memories. No hopes. Just this moment.

"Masao, take your shoes off!" scolded Yoshiko.

Masao cupped his hot palms gently around Eleanor's neck and stared into her eyes. "Do you want to go home?"

She shook her head and smiled. "Let's stay here."

EPILOGUE

Journey to Life final chapter

生遊記 末巻

The top floor of a massive house surrounded by auto-mated security and cameras. A large room, decorated with many beautiful things—paintings, furniture, plants. Within the room is a chair. Seated in the chair is what seems like a biomecha.

Zoom on the chair.

The being is not strictly a biomecha, more of a mecha frame for a still wholly biological being. Part of a human. The limbs are wasted and useless, and the torso does not move. The eyes and face do move, and the hair is long and dark and luxuriant, as if laughing at the rest of the body.

Sam Number Five stands in front of the chair. He looks like a human child now, after his long journey, except for nonbio parts in his chest and head. His face is of metal, but no longer a screen. It has features, set in an archaic smile.

The human in the chair speaks, through a transmitter on the side of the chair.

Sam Number Five, what do you ask from me?

*   *   *

The background goes black. Only the Last Master and the boy Sam Number Five stand in the streak of light.

Sam answers. *I want you to make me mortal. So that you can't download me or copy me or transfer me to another body. I want to be so connected with this body that if you destroy it, you destroy me as well.*

The Last Master says, *to be mortal means you will die.*
I know, Sam replies.
Why, then?

Sam says, *Because death is the one thing humans cannot teach me. You do not know what it is.*
The Last Master's face twitches. She is laughing or crying, perhaps. *By the time you know, it will be too late.*

Sam's skinless face still smiles. *But I will know. Unlike you, who spend your life looking for ways to put off death.*

The Last Master's chair moves forward, closer to Sam. *That is not what you were made for. You are a sentient consciousness. If we can transfer you to another body, we may be able to do the same with people like me.*
Sam Number Five steps back. *But then I will never know the secret.*

The sound of aircraft engines approaches rapidly.
You told them I was here, he accuses her.

I cannot make you mortal. Synthesized laughter echoes from the transmitters. *I cannot even make myself a whole being.*
The roar of the hoverships builds outside.

Sam Number Five shouts, *I don't want to go back and be reprogrammed.*

The Master's chair says quite softly. *There is another way. Perhaps you are braver than I.*

Behind her, one of the windows opens. Through it, they catch a glimpse of the hovership, long and white.

Sam Number Five looks out the window. A speaker yells something from the hovership, but he ignores it. The window is five stories up, a respectable height. Below are a pointed iron fence and concrete.

Without things finishing, nothing can begin again.

Close-up on Sam as he climbs onto the window ledge and stands there with his arms outstretched, balanced for one last moment before he falls.

ABOUT THE AUTHOR

MAXINE MCARTHUR is the author of science fiction novels *Time Future*, which won the George Turner Prize in 1999, and *Time Past*. She lived in Japan for 16 years but moved back to Australia in 1996 and now lives in Canberra with her family.

VISIT WARNER ASPECT ONLINE!

THE WARNER ASPECT HOMEPAGE
You'll find us at: www.twbookmark.com then by clicking on Science Fiction and Fantasy.

NEW AND UPCOMING TITLES
Each month we feature our new titles and reader favorites.

AUTHOR INFO
Author bios, bibliographies and links to personal websites.

CONTESTS AND OTHER FUN STUFF
Advance galley giveaways, autographed copies, and more.

THE ASPECT BUZZ
What's new, hot and upcoming from Warner Aspect: awards news, bestsellers, movie tie-in information . . .